MAJOR GENERAL SPURGEON NEEL, M.D., M.P.H.
U.S. Army, Retired. Former Deputy Surgeon General:

". . . a fascinating account of small unit actions and their medical and human consequences"

". . . a vivid description of the desert battlefield and those who live and die there"

". . . a blend of combat, airborne and special operations, tank battles and medical scenarios"

". . . humanizes the events of the conflict . . . from the desert to the White House"

"This book should be read and studied by all those charged with the responsibility of developing tactics, technique training, and materiel for medical support of future military operations, world-wide."

". . . makes me feel like I was there."

". . . one helluva good story!"

MAJOR GENERAL JOE S. LAWRIE, U.S. Army retired,
Former Commander of the 82nd Airborne Division:

". . . proof that concerns about duty, honor, and country still live."

". . . highly graphic, highly detailed, including thoughts of romance, family and problems of living in a charged atomosphere."

". . . gutsy, exciting and useful in showing how dedicated individuals come through in times of crisis."

". . . about men who knew the value of self-reliance, integrity, and discipline."

". . . a small slice of the superb medical facilities provided for our soldiers at the front."

". . . a fantastic, yet authentic, tale of real individuals under pressure to save those damaged by battle"

"All ranks will relish this book and all will be proud of our medics."

"The authenticity and realism will keep you reading well into the night."

"There will be a teary eye, too."

THE RISING STORM

A Novel

About the Persian Gulf War

Richard Holt

Senior Editor - Mary Margaret Williamson
Book Design - Charlotte St. John
Cover Art and Design - Costner Graphics
Graphic Production - Image Masters, Inc.
Typography - Paula Metheny

Library of Congress Cataloging in Publication Data

Holt, G. Richard
The rising storm: a military novel about the Persian Gulf War / Richard Holt.
p. cm.
ISBN 0-89896-272-2 s.14.95
1. Persian Gulf War, 1991--Fiction. I.Title
PS3558.0396R57 1993
813' .54--dc20 93-651
CIP

LARKSDALE

Manufactured in the United States of America

The Rising Storm

is dedicated to

- My wife, Jean, who provided the total support and nurturing for our family while I was in the Gulf War, and who encouraged me to write this book and supported it all the way;

- Our children, Allyson, Andrea, and Adam, who kept my heart alive during the War with memories of them;

- My parents in Missouri, who gave me my sense of duty and responsibility, especially my father, the greatest American Patriot I know;

- All my other family members who kept me in their thoughts; and our friends, who helped my family and took care of my patients while I was gone;

- My colleagues in the 13th Evacuation Hospital (now 13th Combat Support Hospital), Wisconsin National Guard, who shared the isolation and challenges of wartime medicine;

- Sergeant Randy Vail, for whom the Lord guided my hand to save his life, and who has now dedicated his life to the ministry;

- And to those we could not save.

DRAWN FROM DIFFERENT BACKGROUNDS
THEIR LIVES INTERLOCKED DURING BATTLE
. . . in the desert and skies of the Persian Gulf

Major (Doctor) Thomas Mortimer Neel - Young trauma surgeon Army Reservist who was fresh out of training and beginning a new surgical practice in Kansas City when recalled to active duty. A former flight surgeon and Green Beret, he was sent to the Gulf with his combat support hospital.

Sergeant First Class Trinidad Gonzales - Tank platoon leader with the 3rd Armored Division. Catholic, Hispanic, and the father of three daughters, he continues the fight he started years ago in Vietnam.

First Lieutenant Winfield Scott Porter - A West Point graduate, he comes from a prominent military family. A veteran of Honduras and Panama, this Special Forces A Team leader must lead his team into Southern Iraq on a vitally important, but dangerous, mission.

Captain Jonathan "Tex" Weatherby - Commissioned into Army aviation as a member of the Texas A & M Corps of Cadets, he gained combat experience in Panama. His arrogance and unorthodox flying during missions for the 2nd Armored Cavalry Regiment threaten his career and his life.

Specialist Allen Jay Anders - A Blackhawk air evacuation medic with the Wisconsin National Guard, Anders is at a critical crossroads in his life. A senior in college, he is pulled from his premedical studies to risk his life to save the sick and wounded in the Gulf War.

Staff Sergeant Lucius Tatum - A giant of a Black man from Washington, D.C., his volunteering for airborne duty gave him a ticket out of the slums and respect from his peers. Deeply religious, and with a strong love for his family, he sets aside his personal fears to lead a squad of young and inexperienced paratroopers on a night combat jump into Iraq to battle the Republican Guard.

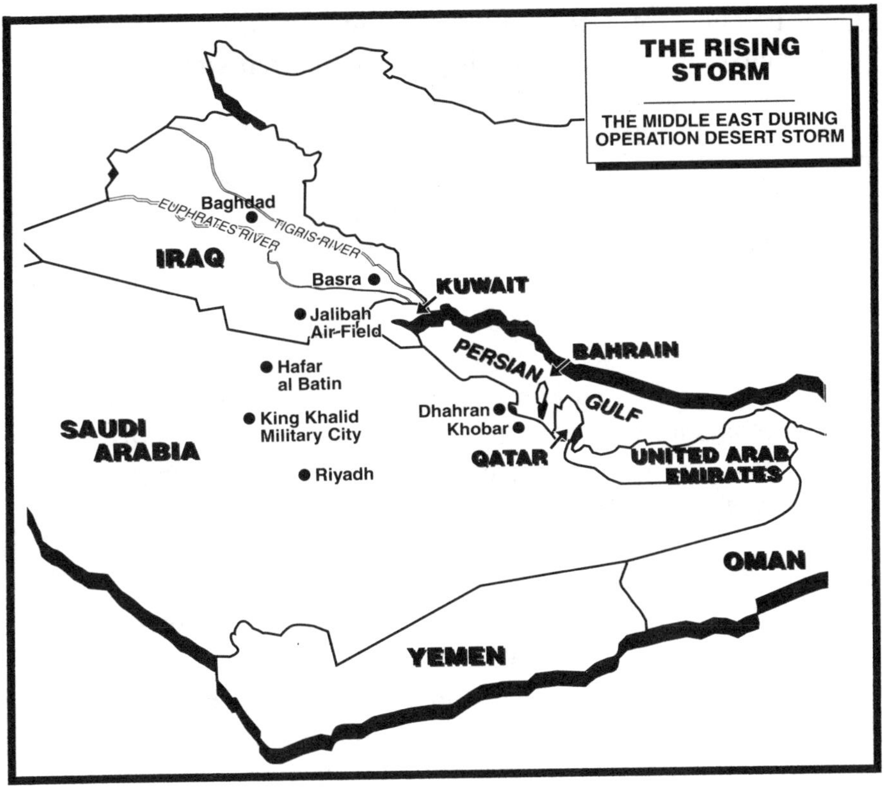

Prologue

Beneath the dark, cloud-filled night sky, the roads were treacherous. The rain of the previous day had begun to cool on the ancient pavement. Patches of ice mingled invisibly with damp flatstones, making driving on this barren stretch of land a calculated risk.

The truck lumbered along under these conditions, the driver oblivious to their existence. Lost in the appeal of reaching his destination, where a hot meal and dry clothes awaited, he was understandably in a hurry. The truck's interior was only marginally warm, and his coffee container had long since been drained. This long trip from picking up supplies had taken its toll, and occasionally the man's head would nod to his chest, only to jerk up again when the truck's wheels began to leave the pavement.

As exciting as the events taking place in the Middle East were, the radio had long since lost its appeal, and was now softly trumpeting muted stains of some pre-World War II love song. He wished he had listened to the man in charge of the depot and stayed the night there, arising early in the morning for a safer trek to his destination. His uniform was crumpled and odiferous and he disliked not being clean. The greasy food and acidic coffee had soured his stomach and he just wanted to lie down and sleep.

He began to think of his wife back home, probably having finished her ritual night-time bath and preparing now to retire for the evening. He had been away from her too long, and could almost smell her freshly washed hair in the foul truck cabin. Closing his eyes, he could visualize her smile, her dancing eyes and the crinkles of lines around their corners. How he missed her, so far away from home . . .

Suddenly, the truck lurched and veered to the right, as if on a course of its own. He quickly opened his eyes, and saw, to his horror, an explosion of light just to the side of him. Then the truck dropped off a rocky escarpment, descending into a black abyss.

PART ONE

DESERT SHIELD

CHAPTER ONE

The patient was clearly having difficulty breathing!

THE EMERGENCY ROOM at St. Mary's Hospital in Kansas City seemed unusually busy for a Friday morning in November. There were the usual colds and sore throats, coughs that might prove to be mild cases of pneumonia, as well as the minor aches and sprains that came with trying to handle slick porch steps during the first slick freeze of winter.

In Trauma Room Two, the scene was nearly frantic. John Doe, identity unknown, had just been delivered in a city-owned ambulance by the emergency medical technicians after his truck apparently veered off the highway and tumbled down a steep embankment into a culvert. The truck's sole occupant, the driver, was discovered by rescuers pinned between the seat and steering wheel, semi-conscious. Kansas City was celebrated for rapid ambulance response, and the time between accident and presentation at the emergency room was a scant 17 minutes.

The ferocious activity with which the emergency room personnel attended John Doe was similar to that caused by dipping your hand into an ant mound, except the trauma team's intent was to help. As the nurses stripped off the victim's clothing and began to measure vital signs and insert IVs, Dr. Thomas Mortimer Neel entered the treatment room. Neel's features suggested he was younger than his thirty-five years, a situation he had once sheepishly admitted was embarrassing. Now, he realized his youthful looks and tall, slender physique would serve him well when he entered middle age. Sandy hair and horn-rimmed glasses framed a moustached, middle-American face of English-Irish ancestry. The eyes were blue, keen and intelligent.

Those shrewd eyes speedily took in the scene. Four years of medical school, five years of general surgery residency and a final year of trauma fellowship had provided Neel with the knowledge and experience to handle just about any medical emergency.

The naked patient on the stretcher appeared to be about fifty. He was clearly having a hard time breathing. A large bruise was beginning to form on the front of the man's chest just to the left of the sternum, but there were no other apparent injuries except for a bruised, lacerated lower lip. His eyes were closed and he looked unconscious.

As Neel strode to the patient's side, he pulled his stethoscope from his coat pocket.

''Vital signs?' he asked the male nurse next to him.

''Hey, Doc Neel, how's it going? I'm sure glad to see you here—this guy's going downhill fast.''

''Vital signs?,'' Neel repeated, without taking his eyes off the patient's chest.

''Heart rate's about 120 and respirations are labored at 48 per minute. The worst problem is his blood pressure, which keeps reading out at 130 over 110.'' Sensing Neel's seriousness, the nurse was now all business.

Neel ordered a complete chemistry and hematology survey, and enzymes for liver, cardiac and muscle. He issued his orders to no one in particular, confident someone would immediately take the responsibility and get those tasks accomplished, the usual procedure in a Level One trauma room.

Neel finished listening to the heart and lungs and examined the patient from head to toe, his fingers moving as surely as a concert pianist's. His rapid survey revealed no other obvious damage.

''Vital signs?'' Neel asked again.

''Same, Doc. No change.'' That information confirmed Neel's clinical impression.

''Get me a chest tube tray and a pericardiocentesis tray right now,'' he ordered.

In less than a minute, someone rolled the trays on two metal stands next to Neel. ''You wear 7 1/2 gloves, don't you, Doctor?'' Neel peered down at the petite nurse who had asked that question. Momentarily, his thoughts were yanked away from the patient. *Man,* he thought, *they do get younger and prettier every year. Or maybe I'm just getting older and my standards are slipping.*

''Yes, Sherri, and get me a 32 French chest tube. Get the

closed suction drainage ready, too.'' As Sherri moved off to do those jobs, Neel again turned his full attention to the patient.

All right, let's see what we've got here, he said to himself as he began methodically to characterize the victim's injuries. *The patient is moving all extremities, as well as his head, his reflexes are okay, so he appears to be neurologically intact. His lips and nailbeds are slightly cyanotic so he's probably not ventilating satisfactorily. Better get some arterial blood gases once I get the heart and lungs taken care of.*

Neel opened the chest tube tray, put on his sterile gloves and readied the instruments while Sherri painted the left chest with a swab of Betadine. A few sterile towels were placed over the site and Neel quickly injected a local anesthetic into the region of the 6th intercostal space in the anterior axillary line. *That ought to get both air and blood out,* he mused, *if there's any there.*

He made a quick incision in the skin between the 6th and 7th ribs, separating the soft tissues and muscles with a large hemostat. Neel was left-handed, so inserting a left chest tube was always easier than a right, where the arm and shoulder tended to get in his way.

Probing an index finger into the incision, Neel bluntly dissected the remaining soft tissues until he could feel the pleural covering over the victim's lung. With his finger still in place, he inserted the hemostat alongside it and punctured the pleura. An audible 'hiss' of released air erupted from the hole, confirming Neel's suspicions of a tension pneumothorax from air trapped in the chest cavity.

''That's it,'' Sherri said, opening the sterile package as Neel picked up the chest tube inside. ''I've got the suction set up when you're ready to hook up.''

Neel thrust and pushed his finger deeply into the patient's chest, widening the break in the pleura. The chest tube was quickly inserted, directed up toward the left shoulder and sutured into place. The nurse connected the tube held by the doctor to the closed suction water drainage device, which allowed the air leaking from the damaged left lung to exit from the tube when the patient exhaled, bubbling into the floor-level container. Sterile water in the container prevented any air from reentering the patient's chest when he inhaled. With time, the lung would self-seal.

Neel listened to the patient's lungs with his stethoscope and nodded with satisfaction. "We'll get a portable chest film in just a few minutes to check on tube position and the possibility of blood lower in the chest, but first I've got to needle the heart."

The beating heart is surrounded by a tissue sac called the pericardium, which serves to protect and lubricate the heart during its 100,000 or more daily beats. Normally, the amount of lubricating fluid in the sac is slight and does not interfere with the heart's contractions. However, when a blunt or penetrating injury to the chest is present, blood sometimes forms in the sac, restricting full expansion and contraction of the heart, thus decreasing its output of fresh blood. When blood accumulates in the sac, blood pressure measurement is affected, narrowing the ratio between the systolic and diastolic pressures, a condition known as pericardial tamponade. It is always life-threatening.

Dr. Neel believed this patient had sustained a powerful blow to the chest during the accident, which had ruptured the lung tissue, producing an air leak into the chest, as well as a possible rupture of a blood vessel in the heart muscle or the pericardial sac.

In accord with American College of Surgeons' trauma protocol, Neel had first improved the patient's ventilation by inserting the chest tube. Now it was time to deal with the possibility of blood in the heart's protective sac.

After changing sterile gloves, Neel placed a long, thin cardiac needle on a 10-cc syringe. By inserting the needle into the pericardial sac, trying not to damage further the heart muscle that was beating constantly, Neel would withdraw the blood restricting the heart's pumping action. The trauma doctor smiled to himself as he recalled a cartoon he had once seen posted on the thoracic surgery resident's call room door. A heart surgeon was looking over his auto repair bill while the mechanic was ragging him about how high surgeon's bills were. The surgeon then replied that the mechanic ought to try working on an engine's interior while it was running like heart surgeons have to.

Neel felt for the xiphoid process just below the sternum and inserted the long needle just under the skin. He injected 1-cc of local anesthetic as he slowly inserted the needle through the tissue of the triangular region, easing the patient's possible discomfort. When Neel had first learned this technique, he had hooked up the needle to an electrocardiograph and used it as a probe, finding the heart by the electrical signal on the machine. After over a hundred of the procedures, he was positive he could find the sac with his eyes closed.

Envisioning the three-dimensional anatomy of the chest, Neel angled the needle approximately 45º to the sternum and pressed on. Holding a slight suction in the syringe, he would know when he entered the pericardial sac.

The trauma room intercom suddenly came alive. "Doctor Neel, can you take a phone call?" The switchboard operator's nasal midwestern 'twang' reminded Neel of his mother's voice. "Not now, Mrs. Blackburn, I'm really busy."

"Well, Dr. Neel, all's I know is this man says he's captain somebody and needs to talk to you real bad."

"Just get his name and number and I'll call him back as soon as I can." He added "please" as an afterthought. Usually, Neel was polite to a fault, which he realized made him unique among his colleagues. *Some time,* he thought, *someone's going to startle me when I'm doing this and I'm going to ram this needle right through the patient's heart.*

He settled down, concentrating. After advancing the needle nearly three inches, and checking the angle of insertion several times, he was rewarded by the sudden sight of blood seeping into the syringe. "Bingo," he declared, "the sac's full of blood."

Sherri handed him another sterile syringe after the first filled. Neel withdrew about 15 cc before no more appeared. Removing the needle, he announced to no one in particular, "If blood reaccumulates, we may have to take him to surgery and cut out a pericardial window so it can drain. Then we'll try to find the bleeding point." He was always the consummate teacher.

"How are the vital signs now?" he asked the male nurse.

"Heart rate's down to 85 and respirations are 24. BP's better at 124/90."

Neel nodded at the good news and grinned boyishly, finding it hard to believe he had actually acquired the skills to save lives and that he had done so on countless occasions. For a small-town boy from south Missouri, he had come a long way. But never too far to forget his roots.

Neel moved to the head of the stretcher and stared at the patient's feature's. Lips pink and relaxed, no longer pursed from labored breathing. Eyes open and alert.

"Hi, how are you feeling now, sir?" The man turned his head, looked at Neel, managed a feeble smile and nodded his head.

"What's your name?" Neel asked, as much to see if the man could vocalize well, as for the information.

"Robbins. Tom Robbins." The reply was weak and soft, but clear.

Good, his vocal cords are fine and his diaphragm is probably okay, too. "I'm sorry if I hurt you with those sticks on your chest, Mr. Robbins, but you had some pretty serious problems that needed prompt attention. Do you hurt anywhere else?"

The patient thought for a second, mentally assessing his body. "All over!"

Neel laughed and smiled. *He's going to be all right. I can feel it.* "Well, I'm going to just check you out all over again from top to bottom, then we'll admit you to the intensive care unit." Neel completed his secondary survey of Robbins, issuing appropriate orders as he did. Finally, he turned away from the patient to wash his hands, almost knocking over Sherri, who had been waiting quietly behind him.

Shaking her head ruefully at their near collision, Sherri smiled and handed him a slip of paper. "Here are the blood gases—they look pretty good."

Neel digested the information, agreed, and handed the slip back. *Boy, I'd better watch out, this nurse is a bit much.* Then he thought of his wife, Marty, at home, and instantly felt guilty. Strengthening his professional resolve, he turned back toward the patient.

"Where do you live, Mr. Robbins?"

"Shawnee Mission." Robbins' voice was more tired than it had been a few minutes before.

"Kansas, eh? Well, you'll be happy to know we even treat 'Jayhawkers' at St. Mary's," Neel said with a laugh. His jest was answered by a smile from Robbins.

"As soon as we contact your family, I'll let them know you're going to be fine. We'll keep the chest tube in for several days until a leak in your lung heals, then we'll take it out. We'll be watching your heart, too, for any recurrence of blood in the sac around it. I doubt if that will happen but we'll check it out anyway."

Neel rested his hand on Robbins' shoulder and squeezed it

gently. *This is what medicine is all about,* he thought. *Getting these hurt folks back home to their families and to all the things that go on in their lives. I'm really glad I decided to practice in Kansas City. Nice place to work, good midwestern patients who usually do what you ask them to without complaint. And a great place to raise a family. Plenty of hunting and fishing and great colleges and professional sports. I'm looking forward to a nice, quiet life here with Marty and the kids.*

He thought 'kids' even though there was only the one on the way. Marty was three months along, conceiving just after they moved to Kansas City from Baltimore, where Neel had completed his trauma fellowship. They had postponed children until he finished his fellowship training. Now, they should be able to settle down and enjoy raising some. Marty had a job teaching mathematics at Rockhurst College and could probably continue there indefinitely. She liked her career and was good at it.

Neel left Robbins in the trauma room as he was being prepared for transfer to the trauma ICU. St. Mary's was unique in the midwest because of its new, state-of-the-art trauma center, including an ICU. Neel had trained at Maryland's innovative state trauma center and felt he could accept no less than the best in his new practice. A doctor simply could not practice excellent trauma care without MRI and CAT scans, dedicated trauma operating rooms with the latest in equipment, and the specialized trauma beds produced by Kinetic Concepts. He felt anything less limited his ability to effectively apply his sophisticated training. *No, I just couldn't practice without all of this.*

As he sat down at the physician's desk in the ER trauma center to write admission orders for Robbins, Neel made a mental note to call up old Cleo Wolf in northern Missouri near the Iowa line to check how the pheasant and quail were this year. *I missed opening day, but maybe I can get up there to hunt next weekend. I don't have Army Reserve drill and I'm not on call. Maybe Marty would go up with me and visit her friend Mary in St. Joe. I sure hope I can get in some good hunting this winter I love that hunting. I'll also call Joe Edwards and see if his dogs are ready to go this year.*

He noticed the telephone message Mrs. Blackburn had taken, taped to the light over his E.R. desk. During the excitement of the emergency, he had forgotten all about the call. He pulled the

"Post-It" loose and checked the caller's name: Captain Carlos Flores. Flores was the personnel officer for his army reserve unit—the 252nd Combat Support Hospital. Neel knew there was no drill that weekend, but just then, he glanced at the TV in the physician's lounge. Only the picture was on, without sound. A CNN reporter was interviewing some marines in the Saudi Arabian desert.

Oh no, he thought, as the shocking reality sank in. With measured calm he picked up the phone and dialed Flores.

* * *

A cold wind chilled Jay Anders' neck, prompting him to raise the collar on his forest green Eddie Bauer windbreaker. The walk from his small apartment to the arts and sciences campus of the University of Wisconsin at Madison was only about 15 minutes, but the brisk morning encouraged a quicker pace, reducing his transit by several minutes. Anders decided he had time to stop by the student union for a quick cup of coffee before continuing to class.

The union was so warm he debated whether to remove his jacket. Realizing he'd have to first take off his backpack, then his jacket and then reverse the process in only a few minutes, Anders shook his head wryly and moved quickly toward the coffee counter. An efficient young man, he never wasted time or effort unless there were tangible results. He poured in as much sugar as he could easily dissolve in his styrofoam coffee cup. As a pre-medical/bioengineering student, Anders knew his brain needed glucose to function at its best and he wanted as much out of his brain as he could muster. He was holding on to a 3.93 grade point average as a first semester senior and had posted straight-A's at mid-term for his 18 credits. Final examinations in less than three weeks would demand plenty of study to keep up that high average, but Anders had always loved learning and he seemed to thrive on the challenges of a dual major.

The son of dairy farming parents from Cataract, Wisconsin, Jay had known since childhood that farming was not for him. At first, his parents had been concerned, in their typical upper midwest fashion, that the integrity of the farming lineage would be broken if Jay pursued his interest in medicine. Later, though, they realized his true talent when a calf suffered a broken leg and Jay set it and splinted it better than old Doc Leeuven, the town veterinarian. Jay's touch with injured animals was shadowed, however, by his sincere and deep interest in people, their thoughts, concerns, hurts, inadequacies, and troubles. Neighbors and friends were always talking to Jay about their troubles and he had a reputation as the best listener in the county. He had a genuine compassion for people and when his parents finally realized that, they accepted his desire to become a doctor.

To the casual observer, Jay Anders as good as had that medical diploma in his hand, what with high grades in a tough collegiate program, fine interpersonal skills, excellent recommendations from the pre-medical advisory committee and a very high M-CAT score. But no one except Jay Anders knew the depth of his own insecurity and sense of inadequacy. He had only really known his own small-town family physician, and although Jay had extensively read lots of medical novels, he still could not convince himself that he, Allen Jay Anders, smalltown boy from Cataract, Wisconsin, possessed those really special, God-given skills he'd need to become a physician. Nevertheless, he went along with the plan to apply to medical schools the fall of his senior year, this year, with one exception he had not sent any of the applications on to the medical schools. He sent in his transcripts from Wisconsin, had his M-CAT scores and letters of recommendation forwarded but not his signed, formal application.

As things stood, he really didn't know what to do. He guessed he'd finish out the semester, then enroll for his final semester in order to graduate. But what would he tell his parents and friends when he received no letters from medical schools requesting interviews? Pushing with effort the troublesome, recurring dilemma from his mind, Jay walked over to the newspaper rack outside the bookstore and glanced at the headlines while he sipped his coffee. "13th Evacuation Hospital From Madison Called Up For Mobilization." *The 13th Evac. I know some guys from that unit, some in school right now. Also, that cute Susie what's-her-name who's in law school here is in that unit. Boy, would I like to be mobilized with her.* He immediately cringed—*my folks wouldn't like to hear me talk about that,* he reflected.

They hope I'll marry some farm girl from around La Crosse, settle down back home and raise half a dozen kids while taking care of the whole county. And come out to their farm every Sunday for pot roast and stewed tomatoes. They couldn't see me marrying a woman lawyer; Dad would swell out of his bib overalls. Well, maybe not, he countered, *maybe they're more flexible and sensible than I give them credit for. Anyway, nothing's about to happen, so I don't need to worry for a long time.*

He scanned as much of the story about the Wisconsin National Guard hospital being mobilized as he could see, but since the paper was enclosed in a metal dispenser, he couldn't turn to page 12A to finish it. Jay knew he'd find out more on the weekend from the scuttlebutt in his own Guard unit, the 428th Air Ambulance Company. He had joined the Guard to help pay his college expenses and had quickly become fond of the pilots and crew chiefs. The Guard had sent him to the 91A medic course at Fort Sam Houston, Texas, two summers ago and he had since risen to the rank of Specialist Four.

Being a medic (even in the Guard) gave him the "sense" of being a physician without the awesome responsibility that went with that role. Any injury or illness he had treated in the past, had been done with the knowledge that a physician would soon take over the care and set things right if he had messed up. He was terrified of the responsibility. The fear was irrational, he knew, because he could handle animal problems; it was just that he was afraid of making a mistake and hurting a human being.

Ah, I've got to get this out of my mind and focus on my classes today and tomorrow before the weekend. I've got the paper in thermodynamics to finish and the homework in physiological chemistry. Then, on Sunday night, I've got to read that long article for the bioethics class and write a commentary.

Jay zipped his windbreaker, took a last sip of coffee, tossing the cup into a trash can as he left the union.

Professor Danemark was in rare form. A physicist by education, his doctoral dissertation had addressed energy loss in the form of heat dissipation in microprocessors. The work concluded that 'fast' computers required some sort of cooling system during prolonged use to prevent heat buildup within the console and resultant microchip damage. That research had led to an invention, a patent and huge royalties for the University of Wisconsin. Only five percent of the profits generated from licensing the patent actually found their way to Dr. Danemark, and it was obvious he didn't spend his profits on frivolities such as haircuts, clothing or shoes. His lapels were at least six inches wide on heavy wool suits that appeared to predate Woodrow Wilson. However, when someone in the country had a thermal problem in any kind of a computer system, they called the professor.

Professor Danemark was delivering a diatribe on the trade agreements that gave the Japanese an advantage in exporting microchips to the United States. He was such a devout Japan basher that rumors had sprung up that he had been a prisoner of the Japanese during WW II. No one knew for sure, and no one had the nerve to ask.

Jay settled into his seat, took out his lecture notebook, and arranged the standard engineering student note-taking instruments before him on the tabletop: fine-line black roller ballpoint, 0.5-mm lead pencil, red ink rollerball, pen eraser, yellow highlighter and a small clear plastic ruler. Anders was more meticulous than most about his tools and always arranged them in a certain order on the desk. To others he was a bit obsessive-compulsive, but Jay had not yet realized that those niggly traits, when applied properly, could produce a successful and competent physician.

Jay noticed a newcomer to the class, a tall distinguished-looking man, about fifty, seated at Dr. Danemark's right. The visitor's suit was expensive, his hair neat and well-groomed and his features intelligent behind wire-rim glasses. His hands were his most distinguishing features. Seated not six feet from the stranger, Jay noticed the long fingers with their immaculately cared-for nails; masculine hands to be sure, but also quite delicate. The man's hands slowly intertwined and opened, each move graceful and precise. These must be the hands of a concert pianist, Anders thought, or maybe a professional safecracker who is here to tell about his wayward career. He smiled to himself at that unlikely possibility, because somehow it seemed perfectly feasible that Professor Danemark could have such a miscreant for an acquaintance.

Suddenly, Danemark turned toward the class and held up his hands for attention. The class was already staring at the professor and his guest, so there wasn't much change. "Young people, we are fortunate today to have a guest speaker who will present some real-life applications of several of the principles of thermodynamics we have been trying so hard to learn." He paused so the effect of his last several words would be clear.

"It is my pleasure to present Dr. William Fletcher, chairman of the department of cardiothoracic surgery at the University of Minnesota. Dr. Fletcher is well known for his pioneering work in developing thermal transducers for studying cardiovascular function. His curriculum vitae is thicker than the Madison phone book, so I won't even try to condense it. Without further ado, I present Dr. William Fletcher, M.D."

He emphasized the 'M.D.' so the students would distinguish Dr. Fletcher's title from that of doctor of philosophy, the usual professional credential of the undergraduate and graduate faculty.

Dr. Fletcher rose rather elegantly and walked to the podium with such fluidity Anders would not have been surprised if he had once been an Olympic medalist in the pole vault. When the man spoke, his voice was clear and commanding, with just a hint of crisp Canadian accent. *Now here's a man,* Anders concluded, *who could be a real role model for a guy like me.*

"First of all," Fletcher began, "I'd like to extend my appreciation to Professor Danemark for the invitation to speak to you this morning. He and I have collaborated on a number of projects and I, like you, have learned a great deal from him." The doctor paused to smile and sweep the room's occupants with his gaze.

Fletcher continued. "Much of our current work on thermoelectric devices are based upon significant studies by Geddes at Purdue University and Baker at the University of Texas at Austin. "Don't ever forget," he admonished with a flick of his finger toward them, "to give credit where it is due in any of your work. Not only is it the honest thing to do, but it lends credibility to your character."

Fletcher began his lecture on the basic electrochemistry of two metals in contact, then progressed to describe the unique properties of a thermocouple. He talked about his search for a noninvasive means of identifying very early rejection reactions in organ transplants and how he and Dr. Danemark had applied bioengineering principles to do so. He began to show slides of his experimental thermocouple implants.

The surgical slides of the harvesting of the organs from the donor and their implantation into the recipient patient's chest were simply fascinating to Anders.

While other classmates were obviously less enthralled with

them, Anders was completely absorbed. He debated about asking a question for several minutes, then timidly raised his hand, half hoping Dr. Fletcher would not acknowledge him.

"Yes, do you have a question?" Dr. Fletcher asked.

"Sir," began Anders, "after the surgery, how do you keep open the small air sacs in the transplanted lung? I understand the lung produces a surface active agent that keeps them from collapsing, and I wondered if the transplanted lung can begin to produce this substance in a new body?" Anders was afraid he had asked a foolish question, but he really wanted an answer.

Fletcher considered the question a moment, then smiled disarmingly at this precocious student. This was why he spoke occasionally at universities, to stimulate and uncover the special mind. "Your name, please?"

"Anders, Jay Anders, sir," he stammered.

"Well, Mr. Anders, you have asked a very astute question. The answer has three parts. First, immediately postoperative, we place an air tube which has a forked end into the trachea, each end in one of the two primary bronchial branches of the trachea. Through this tube we are able to force air down each primary bronchus to ensure symmetrical ventilation and inflation. We are able to keep the pulmonary alveoli inflated with a positive end-expiratory pressure ventilation we call 'PEEP.'

"Second, we instill a synthetically produced surface active agent, or surfactant, down the tube to keep the alveoli open temporarily. Third, after several weeks, the newly transplanted lung begins to manufacture and secrete its own surfactant, which carries on the work of the artificial agent. When given an opportunity, the body actually tries to help us with our healing efforts."

Dr. Fletcher met Anders' gaze with a strong one of his own, almost creating a visual bond. Anders finally broke the spell by nodding a "thank you," and looking down at his notebook to make note of the answer.

The rest of the hour, Fletcher further described this research and the clinical application of a selenium-platinum thermocouple, complete with a miniaturized radio frequency output device that was implanted in the chest of a heart-lung recipient.

The principle was that when areas of the heart or lung became nonviable, either because of a graft rejection phenomenon or from obliteration of the vascular supply, the thermocouple would sense a small incremental decrease in organ temperature, which could then be identified by remote sensing and recording of the output, utilizing an RF sensor placed on the patient's chest in the exam or ICU room. The device could also sense an increase in organ temperature that might be associated with infection. Anders was fascinated by the device and decided to talk to Dr. Fletcher after class.

When the lecture ended, and after all the trivial questions had been asked by those students who wanted Professor Danemark to see them at the podium, Anders walked up to Dr. Fletcher.

"Sir, I really enjoyed seeing and hearing about your work today," Anders said politely. "It must really be satisfying to be able to help people like you do."

"It is, indeed, Mr. Anders, and I suspect you have some interest in medicine yourself. Am I correct?" Anders nodded. "Your question was obviously not just to impress your professor, but indicated to me that you have a real grasp of medical problems. Are you applying for medical school, Mr. Anders?"

Anders dropped his gaze and stared at Fletcher's polished cordovan shoes. "Yes sir, but I don't have all my application material ready yet."

Fletcher sensed the indecision in this young man's voice and made a quick decision to intervene. "Look, son, here's my card with my academic office address at Minnesota. I've got funding for a student investigator in my project for next summer. If you think you might be interested, give me a call after final exams and come up to visit the facility over Christmas break. If you're impressed, we can talk then about your working with me next summer. What do you say?"

Anders accepted the card and looked directly at Dr. Fletcher. "Thank you sir. That's very generous. I was fascinated by your surgery and research and it would be a great honor for me to visit you. I'll definitely call you." They shook hands for a long second, Anders feeling the strength in Fletcher's hand. Then, Professor Danemark rushed up and reminded Fletcher that they must hurry to the luncheon at the university president's home.

Almost mechanically, Anders made his way back to his apartment, hardly aware of the temperature, the wind, the traffic, or any of his usual distractions. He picked up the small stack of mail for him the landlady had slipped through the mail drop in his apartment door. His place was neat and he liked to keep it that way. He could no more have just stepped over his mail and left it lying there than he could have failed to pick up a piece of trash in the grass in front of the president's home. He was just that type of person.

His excited mind was considering the opportunity Dr. Fletcher had presented and he was already figuring when and how he would get to Minneapolis after finals. He placed Dr. Fletcher's card on his desk top next to the phone and began to absent-mindedly leaf through his mail. He saw the envelope from his Guard unit and wondered why it had been sent via 'certified mail.' *Probably a small check for some new allowances for having completed a recent qualification course. They said it would be figured into a bonus for me.* His curiosity increased as he opened the letter and realized there was no check inside. Instead, it appeared to be a set of military orders from 4th Army Headquarters. As he read on, he felt his heart sinking and his stomach coming up to meet it. 'You are hereby ordered to proceed immediately to the nearest U.S. Army mobilization station with your assigned unit for the purpose of entering active duty.' His mind could not fathom what that would mean to his college career and his plans, but his gut was already relaying the bad news.

* * *

Sergeant First Class Trinidad Gonzales climbed into the M-1 Abrams tank designated for him as platoon sergeant. Short and compact, Gonzales was all gristle and sinew. But his rock hard exterior covered a sentimental interior, obvious whenever he was with his wife, America, and his three daughters, Rachel, Maria, and Sara. With them, Gonzales was a big teddy bear who could be persuaded to do just about anything with a smile, giggle or hug. After living through hell in Vietnam, he had vowed on his return to devote his time to his church and his family, and to providing adequate sustenance for both.

A straight, rule-obeying soldier, the only nonconventional act Gonzales allowed himself was to wear a gold cross around his neck next to his dog-tags. The crucifix had been given to him by his mother (God rest her soul) before he went to Vietnam and he vowed never to take it off. Family and church were important to him and he created a small niche in his professional military life to allow them to be with him at all times.

Trinidad thought of his family as he stood in the turret hatch, his shoulders touching the .50-cal machine gun mounted next to the hatch opening. A dichotomy in personality, Gonzales was both warrior and religious; a killing machine when necessary, and a loving husband, father and parishioner at other times. Because these conflicting and opposing roles had caused him considerable anguish in the past, he had come to compartmentalize the different roles and emotions and to let them overlap only enough to keep him human.

He placed the headset and microphone on his head and plugged them into the platoon communication net. After bringing up all of the tank commanders on the net and verifying their readiness for mobilization, he called the platoon commander, First Lieutenant Rick Hanes, a squared-away officer from Keokuk, Iowa, who had the respect of Sergeant Gonzales and the other men in his command. Although he could see the lieutenant's tank 50 meters directly ahead, because of the roar of a dozen main battle tanks, Gonzales was obliged to use the radio.

''Green Three, Green Three, this is Green Two, over.''

''Green Three here, Green Two, give your status, over.''

''Green Three, we have all vehicles in the black and ready to go on your command.''

''All right, Green Two. Let's head 'em out in column formation on the road until departure point alpha, then move into echelon formation after the turn north. We'll proceed in echelon to the point of departure where we will fire smoke and move toward the objective in line. Do you copy?''

The maneuver had been planned last night in the command tent at the temporary bivouac site, but Gonzales went through the formalities as they always did, by the book.

''Roger, Green Three. Column will begin moving in one minute. Green Two out.''

Gonzales keyed into the entire platoon-wide net, accessing each tank commander. ''Green Two to Green Flock. Commence movement in one minute. I repeat, commence movement in one minute. Green Two out.''

Having taken care of getting the platoon started on this morning's exercises, Gonzales leaned back against the metal of the turret hatch hinge. Hard and cold, it reflected the terrain and the weather of this central valley of West Germany. The exercise had brought their company-sized task force to the Vogelsberg-Hassberge mountain region for an exercise to "defend" the Fulda gap against imaginary Communist invaders from the East. Nearly the entire defense of western Europe in the scenario of a Soviet invasion focused on the relatively easily traversed valley extending from Czechoslovakia into Hof, West Germany, then through Neustad and on to Fulda. From there, Frankfurt would be accessible and consequently all of western Europe. Because of the perceived importance of the region, most of the Allied military contingency plans and exercises focused on defending the Fulda gap from invasion.

They had made camp, erected their tents and begun the process of temporary living in a wooded area about 25 kilometers southeast of Bad Hersfeld. Their brigade was permanently barracked at Kassel, a beautiful village within easy movement to the Fulda area for an armored force.

Gonzales and his men were used to these winter exercises in the mountains and plains of Germany. They had accustomed themselves to the freezing temperatures and they wore excellent cold weather gear. The hulls of their tanks were quite cold, so cold in fact, no one dared touch them with bare hands in the dead of winter, but once the big engines fired up, the interiors were at least cozy, if not warm.

The column formed after pulling onto the road from a clearing in the adjacent woods consisted of staggering or alternating tanks with approximately 50-100 meters between the tank in front and the one to the side. The platoon leader assumed the second position in the column behind the lead tank, with the platoon sergeant behind and to the left flank of the lieutenant. This formation was used most frequently by the platoon for road travel, movement in limited visibility, or when passing through woods and defiles. It also allowed the platoon to deploy quickly into other formations and was the easiest formation to control.

The gravel-based road had been widened sufficiently for the column to travel with ease and the lead tank reached Point Alpha about 30 minutes after moving out. The lead tank commander used his green flag, held out in his left hand, to signify the turnoff point, and each tank followed.

Although the M1A1 tanks were easier to handle than earlier

versions, it still required a certain precise timing and position awareness on the part of the drivers, and they conducted the formation changes with the same attentiveness as a drill team on a parade ground.

As each tank turned and came into echelon formation, Gonzales felt a sense of pride in the men's skills. As a unit, they had yet to see combat—in fact, he was the only combat veteran in the platoon—but he felt confident that if they were ever called upon, they would come through fine.

In the echelon formation, the platoon could approach the line of attack with protection for the right flank, which was exposed to a tree line. Any attack from the front or sides would allow the tanks to fire in that direction without hitting the tank adjacent to it.

The ground they were traversing was a broad field, perhaps a kilometer wide. They crossed a small creek without difficulty and approached the ridge that would become their line of attack. The lead tank commander extended his arms directly outward, the left holding a green flag, the right a yellow, indicating the platoon would assume a line formation in defilade just below the crest of the ridge. The unit had been on strict radio silence, except for individual intercoms, since the point of departure. Lieutenant Hanes and Sergeant Gonzales dismounted their tanks and walked slowly toward the top of the ridge, armored binoculars in hand. As they low-crawled up to the crest of the ridge, they could hear the deep-throated rumble of the Abrams gas turbine engines behind them, surprisingly quiet in their idle. They both put their field glasses to their eyes and observed the scene before them.

A special Soviet-style training unit of West German tanks was lying in ambush just inside the tree line of a thick wooded area. The high ground leading down to their position was marked with isolated trees and rock formations. Snow had not yet fallen here, but the trees were bare and offered little protection from view. The ambush was well planned by the "Warsaw Pact Aggressors" and would be difficult to outsmart, but Hanes and Gonzales were masters of this immense chess game with its giant pawns and they enjoyed the challenge. Quietly, they discussed the options and agreed on a plan. Lt. Hanes slapped Gonzales on the shoulder. "You sneaky Mexican greaseball, I'm damn glad you're on my side."

Gonzales grinned, taking no offense at the insult. He had called the lieutenant 'red-necked, dirt-stomping poor white trash' before, which had sent the easy going, former farm boy into a fit of laughter. But if anyone besides the two had hurled those words, sorry would have been that individual. As they walked back toward their tanks, Lt. Hanes told Gonzales to make the necessary arrangements by radio. Each platoon leader and platoon sergeant carried a separate, personal radio transceiver allowing him to contact other ground troops or air cover in the area. Since Lt. Hanes always wanted to go into an exercise holding the winning cards, he made sure of all his options before the game began.

One of those options was an acquaintanceship with a Second Armored Cavalry helicopter pilot named Jonathan "Tex" Weatherby. Captain Weatherby commanded a troop of Apache attack helicopters staged out of the Bad Hersfeld Army Airfield and he was flying a 'training mission' of his own somewhere in the Fulda gap. The captain always loved a fair fight, or for that matter, an unfair fight, and was always more than eager to reap humiliation upon the West German units simulating Soviet forces.

The two officers had discussed contingency plans in a clandestine, disguised conversation several nights ago, over beers in Hanes' tent. Although Weatherby was arrogant and brash, in other words, typically Texan, he was also a superb Apache attack pilot. Gonzales had not been privy to the clandestine conversation the two officers had had in the privacy of the tent. Indeed, he had never met nor heard of Captain Weatherby, and only knew that there was a "phantom" aviator who would be responding to a special call upon Lt. Hanes' request with a real surprise for the OPFORCE tanks.

Gonzales picked up his special transceiver after remounting his tank and punched in the prearranged call frequency, one not currently in use by the participants in the exercise. "Geronimo One, Geronimo One, this is Santa Ana, over." He repeated the call twice until he heard the crackling of a transmitter come on line and the deep voice of the pilot in command.

"Santa Ana, this is Geronimo One, over."

"Geronimo One, Farmer James needs some eggs delivered as soon as possible. Coordinates are 624321, do you copy?"

"Roger that, Santa Ana, coordinates 624321. What is your position relative to the farm? Over."

"Geronimo One, we're approximately 1000 meters due south just behind the prominent ridge feature. And we've already had breakfast. Over."

"Okay, little buddy, we're going to drop some CARE packages for the farm animals to chew on. On our way. ETA five. Out."

Gonzales switched off the transceiver and laughed silently to himself. *Those "Soviet" Krauts are going to be in for one big surprise in about five minutes.* With hand signals, he communicated the plan for an all-out assault of the position in six minutes, on the lieutenant's command. *The men know what to do after that. Man, I wish I had a camera for this one.*

In exactly five minutes, four slim-profiled Apache helicopters slipped into position some 500 meters behind the line of ambush tanks in the treeline. Although the pilots could not see the ambushing tanks, the lead weapons officer had an excellent fix on their positions with his infrared heat-sensing system. Once all the gunships were on line, Captain Weatherby initiated the action by firing his 2.75-inch rockets, which held a combination of dense smoke-producing canisters and sound grenades, which could rupture the eardrums of anyone not wearing hearing protectors or a radio headset.

Almost simultaneously, the other three gunships fired their smoke and sound rockets, all impacting in an area 100 meters deep around the tanks. The tanks never knew where the rockets came from or who had fired them.

As soon as he heard the sound detonations, Lieutenant Hanes turned to the line of tanks and gave the arm signal to charge. The twelve tanks leaped forward, almost as one, cresting the ridge and reaching top speed as they roared down the slope toward the woods below.

As the dense smoke began to wear off, and the temporary deafening effects of the sound detonators diminished, the "Soviet" aggressor tankers began lifting their turret hatches, coming up for a look. Barrel-to-barrel with their tanks, they found the American tanks nosed up and ready to fire. Atop the second and third tanks were Lieutenant Hanes and Sergeant Gonzales, both with wide grins.

"Gentlemen," Lieutenant Hanes said in stilted German, "do you wish to surrender?"

Now this, Gonzales thought to himself, *is what we used to call a 'Mexican Standoff,'* and he began to laugh aloud.

That evening, Lieutenant Hanes was radioed a terse message to return to Kassel with his men and tanks, posthaste! He and Gonzales were sure their gooses were cooked and that the brigade commander had found out about their "trick" The C.O. was not a humorous man.

After an all-night road march, they returned their tanks to the motor pool near company headquarters, had a quick shave and combed their hair. Still in their tanker's coveralls, helmets in hand, they presented themselves to the brigade commander's briefing room. It was warm inside and they helped themselves to the always present hot coffee and donuts, supplied courtesy of the sergeant-major.

Soon, other commanders and senior NCO's in the brigade command structure began arriving, adding further to their confusion about the reason for their recall. Unless the meeting was being held to hold them up as a bad example to the rest of the brigade, Hanes and Gonzales felt it was unlikely they were present for a reprimand. Rumors abounded, but the senior commanders in the room refused to confirm or deny any.

"Attention, commander in the room." All the men quickly rose to their fee at attention as Colonel Larry Burgess strode forcefully into the room. A soldier's soldier, Burgess was tall, handsome and competent, and he wore his West Point ring like a bride wears her new wedding ring, for all to see. The other side of his personality was that he was a man on his way up the ladder to general, and he was going to make it. Woe to anyone who stood in his way.

I wonder if his wife ever tells him to take out the garbage, Gonzales mused. *I'll bet not.*

"At ease, men, and take your seats," Burgess began. He stood before them, hands clasped behind his back, looking as if he were about to deliver the Sermon on the Mount.

"Men, we belong to the best brigade in the 3rd Armored Division, which is the best division in the U.S. Army. I have always felt, since I became your commander, that we have a destiny, a rendezvous with history that will soon become a reality. Because of our excellent record, because of our high success in exercises against the enemy aggressor forces (it seemed to

Gonzales that he purposefully directed a stern glance toward them), and because of the faith our president and commander-in-chief has in our abilities, we have been selected to lead the forces against evil and malice in the world.'' He paused to take a deep breath and to swallow, possibly for effect, or possibly because he really was overcome by what he was saying.

''Gentlemen, we will soon be heading for the Persian Gulf where we will point our tanks toward Iraq and Saddam Hussein and kick his butt out of Kuwait and back to Baghdad where it belongs.'' When Burgess ended his statement, his voice was almost shouting and everyone could see a large blood vessel in his neck pumping.

As the news sank into the awareness of the assembled men, there was a wide array of opinions and comments.

''All right. Let's go cream the S.O.B.!''

''Mess with the Best, die like the Rest.''

''Oh, no, I'm getting married next month.''

''My enlistment's up in three weeks; I'll bet the Army screws me!''

''I'm ready! I was born ready!''

The colonel surveyed the room. Satisfied he had sufficiently aroused their interest and enthusiasm, he turned the briefing over to Major Jesse Moore, the operations officer, who described the deployment plans.

As the major talked on, Gonzales slowly lost contact with the room and his surroundings. He had not been prone to flashbacks about his Vietnam experience for many years, actually since he married America. He had superficially discussed it with troopers who asked about armored ops there, and at social occasions with other Vietnam veterans, but something about this sudden deliverance of the news that he would be going back into combat against an enemy, to kill or be killed, had unleashed the dogs he had held at bay for so long. He could feel himself drawn into a whirlpool of memories—he could almost smell the thick jungle stench, hear the sounds of war, the screams, the burning flesh, the fear. He felt himself becoming cold and he almost shivered.

But the worst memory of all, even more seared on his brain than the firefights and the killing and dying, was the memory of his return from Vietnam. He had flown home almost directly from the jungle, still wearing his jungle cammies and web gear. As he walked into the airport at San Francisco, there was a large group of antiwar demonstrators, probably from Berkeley, who had accosted the returning soldiers. They had hollered revolting names, accused them of killing civilians and babies. The last straw had been when one of the dirty, wimpy-looking men dressed in jeans and a flower shirt had spit directly into his face and called Gonzales a 'dumb wetback killer.' He could still feel the repulsive spittle on his face and the cold rage that welled up inside him. He would literally have torn that demonstrator apart had not some of his comrades pulled him away. Even now he could feel the strength of that emotion, some 25 years later. *After all, he had risked his life for his country and what did he do to deserve such treatment? Forget about what it had done to his 'macho' image of himself—it was what it had done to the very heart and soul of his being that worried him now. I couldn't take another rejection by our country again. I just couldn't take it,* he moaned to himself, as he lowered his head and pressed his palms against his eyeballs, trying to block out the distressing events he was trying hard not to relive.

* * *

Tex Weatherby brought his AH-64 Apache attack helicopter in for a perfect landing at Bad Hersfeld Army Air Field. He loved the feeling of landing and always envisioned himself as a great bald eagle, coming down from a high hover to land in a nest perched on the bluffs overlooking the Missouri River. Of all of the helicopters he had flown, the Apache was the most responsive and the most like his 'vision.' He had once flown a sailplane from an airfield near Waco, Texas, and that thrill was perhaps the greatest of his life—he had wanted never to return to the ground.

As a child, growing up on a ranch in central Texas, Tex had experienced dreams (at least he believed they were dreams, but was never 100 percent sure) that he was able to fly through the house and out into the yard after everyone was asleep. The reason he could still not bring himself to believe completely it was a dream, was that the experience had been so real, so authentic—he had felt the wind on his face and the effects of centrifugal force in a sharp banking turn. He had once seen 'Peter Pan' on television quite by accident and recounted that his childhood dreams had been just like that. Wisely, he never told anyone of his dreams, figuring they would only laugh at him.

Weatherby taxied his chopper to the edge of the flight line and systematically shut it down. The weapons officer, chief warrant officer Phil Romano, completed his post-flight checklist about the same time as Tex, and together they stepped down from the aircraft.

Tex turned back toward the helo to gaze at it from about 50 meters away, the same way one might turn back to look at his favorite car to see if it still excited him to look at it. From a purely aesthetic point of view, the aircraft was ugly and ungainly.

It looked like a killer bee that really had his hormones in gear. The armored crew compartment was wider and more comfortable than its predecessor, the AH-1 Cobra. It would withstand hits from weapons up to and including a 23-mm cannon. It had a nose-mounted sighting system and multioptical sensing devices and carried as its usual armament, a 30-mm chain gun containing 1200 rounds, located in a chin turrent under the weapons officer, as well as four Hellfire missiles and under each wing a pod of nineteen 2.75-inch rockets of varying munition. The Hellfires were laser-guided antitank missiles and could be used to "ride" laser beams from another spotter helicopter or from a soldier on the ground. All-in-all, the Apache was one hell of a fighting ship.

Weatherby turned around and walked with his characteristic bow-legged swagger toward the munitions shed. Staff Sergeant Lloyd Starr came out to meet him, wiping his dirty hands on an even dirtier rag, raising the question in the captain's mind as to which was cleaning which.

"Hey, Captain, how's it hanging out there today?" Starr was from Tennesse and moonshine vapors still seemed to emanate from his mouth when he talked.

"Sergeant, I think you and I had better finish our little transaction from this morning." In a lower voice, Weatherby admitted that "those damn concussion and smoke rockets were the best ever, Lloyd, and I might just give you two quarts of that bourbon instead of one. I wish I could have seen the looks on those bugger's faces when the smoke cleared and they saw those tanks staring them in the face." Weatherby guffawed and slapped Starr on the back, nearly knocking him over.

Starr recovered quickly. "Cap'n, the word is out all over the base about that deal, but no one can figure out where all that shit from the sky came from. You better lay low for a while and keep quiet.''

''Hell, fire, man, I can't stage a finale like that without taking a curtain call. If you've got it, flaunt it, and I've sure damn well got it.''

With that, Weatherby shot the sergeant an exaggerated, flamboyant salute and turned quickly on his heels toward the operations hut, not waiting for a return salute. Starr just stood there looking at him for a while, shaking his head. *He's a damn hot chopper pilot,* Starr had to admit, *but I wouldn't give a wooden nickel for his personality and I damn well wouldn't fly with him.* The armorer wiped his forehead with the dirty rag, applying unconscious black camouflage to his forehead, and went back to his work.

Weatherby threw open the door to the operations shed and entered with a grin on his face to match the Cheshire cat's. The squadron exec, Captain Everett Hill, was standing at the weather map getting an update on the Area of Operations, something he always did before posting the next day's training schedule.

Weatherby walked up to him and stood, expecting to hear some questions about today's unorthodox fire and maneuvers, but was greeted only by a concerned look on Hill's face. *Whatever is going on,* Weatherby thought, *is definitely not good. Hill never worries about things unless they're big time.*

''All right, little buddy, let's hear it—what catastrophe has got your bowels in an uproar this time?'' Weatherby asked.

''You haven't heard yet?'' Hill replied. Answering his own question, he said, ''No, of course not, you were out having fun, while I, the planning officer, was stuck with drawing up the orders.''

''What orders, Ev, and start cutting through the bullshit, like now,'' Tex fired back.

''Well, I figure since you never learned how to read, you don't know about a certain Saddam Hussein in Iraq who thought he'd just add a little country, namely Kuwait, to his nest. Seems as how the whole damn world, especially the United States, is going to rack his billiard balls for it and guess who gets to help do it? Us!'' Hill changed his expression from concern to outright eagerness. After all, this would be his first real war.

Tex, on the other hand, had been initiated during Operation

Just Cause in Panama. He had loved the action and this news was about the best he could possibly have, with the exception of his wife and two sons visiting from Fort Rucker, Alabama. He was on an unaccompanied tour in Germany and spent most of his free time drinking and playing sports, not reading the newspaper. But, he was definitely aware of the events in the Persian Gulf and had been hoping that the 2nd ACR would be called into the fray.

"Hot damn, Ev, that's the best news I've heard in a long time. What say you and me blow this place and go back to the BOQ for a drink? I've got to do some serious work with my sand wedge if I'm going to play in the Iraqi Open."

They both left the hut laughing, two friends and warriors headed for they knew not what. But whatever was waiting for them, they'd face it head-on.

* * *

Staff Sergeant Lucius Tatum was already tired of the sand, and he'd only been in the desert for three months. His 2nd battalion of the 82nd Airborne Division had been sent to Saudi Arabia in the early phase of the rapid deployment of troops, to block a possible Iraqi invasion. At first, it was exciting, what with the possibility of repelling an invasion, and with the knowledge that the whole world was looking to this small, elite force to stop the aggression of Saddam Hussein. However, the immediate threat of invasion had passed and boredom had replaced it.

Tatum's company was camped near the junction of the Iraq-Saudi Arabia-Kuwait border, about 50 km northeast of Hafir al Batin and 20 km south of the Kuwaiti town of Al Salmy. It really didn't matter to the paratroopers how close they were to a city or town—they never got to see it anyway. In fact, their entire exposure to Saudi Arabia had been in the form of desert, desert and more desert. It was hard keeping one's emotions under control in such prolonged isolated conditions and it was straining Sergeant Tatum to keep his men occupied and not depressed or fighting with one another.

At first it hadn't been too bad—setting up the general purpose tents for living, admin, supply and mess, as well as sand bag duty, guard duty and bunker detail, had kept them busy. Now, all of that was routine, and routine in this God-forsaken desert boiled right down to boredom.

I guess it really isn't 'God-forsaken' if you think about it,

Tatum considered, as he stood next to the elevated bunker in the northeast corner of their camp. *In fact, so many religious events occurred here in this Arabian Desert that it is almost humbling to be here.* Tatum had always considered himself a religious man, as far as that went in today's world. He certainly had grown up in the knowledge of the Bible in the small A.M.E. Black church at the corner of 'N' Street and Maryland Avenue in Washington, D.C. In fact, he used to feel that the church was the only safe haven for him in the crazy streets of the nation's capital.

His mother had taken him to church with her so often it seemed it was his second home. He could recall sitting on the front row of the small church listening to his mother lead the even smaller, but no less vocal choir in some really rousing gospel songs. His mother, trying to raise five children by herself (his daddy had been killed by a hit and run driver when Lucius was ten), had made sure they had plenty of food, plenty of love, and plenty of Scripture to help them grow up to be 'good people.'

Tatum had become somewhat lax over the last few years in his involvement with the church, but had recently taken up systematic reading of the Bible whenever he could after the division chaplain had brought over some Old and New Testaments with new desert camouflage covers. Tatum thought the camo cover was a bit too much, but he was receiving great solace and strength from his readings—in fact, he had just read some psalms in the relative privacy of the bunker before he stood to stretch his legs.

Yeah, life in the camp had become pretty routine. Up about 0600, hit the latrine, start water boiling on the small diesel/kerosene fuel stove for coffee or cocoa, then over to the mess tent to pick up some random variety MRE's for breakfast. MRE stood for 'Meals, ready-to-eat'—the joke was that it was a triple lie, for they were not meals, they weren't ready, and they weren't edible. However, it was the only show in town, and except for the occasional fresh bread and fruit that showed up mysteriously in the mess tent, there really wasn't any choice. The men had learned which of the dozen or so entrees they found most palatable and traded them like baseball cards until everyone was as satisfied with their meal as they could be under the circumstances.

Tatum tried to get the ham omelette for breakfast, frankfurters for lunch and chicken-ala-king or chicken and rice for supper. Peanut butter, jelly and crackers were a delicacy. The revered fruit cocktail of the old C-rations of the Vietnam era had been replaced by the dehydrated fruit that looked like styrofoam and tasted almost as bad. By far the best part of the MRE was the cocoa in some packages. Tatum had been eating MRE's for over three months and still hadn't figured out a pattern to which packages contained the cocoa. *Perhaps the Army did that to keep us wondering,* he thought—I wouldn't put it past them.

He gazed out over the desert beyond the sand berm that kept stray vehicles from wreaking havoc in their camp after dark, and thought about what the future might hold for him and his men. The deployment from Fort Bragg, North Carolina, had been swift—they had departed from adjacent Pope Air Force Base a scant 24 hours after receiving the call. He had barely had time to have supper with the family, tuck Lucius Junior, Samantha and Jessica into bed with plenty of hugs, kisses and promises, and then spend a few hours of private time with Mary before he left.

His Army career, because he chose to be airborne, was full of deployments and exercises away from home, and while the family was getting more accustomed to it, it seemed to be getting progressively harder on him.

The mail was so blasted bad over here, especially to this desert outpost, that he had received only a handful of letters. They had been his sustenance and salvation, and he had reread them at least a hundred times. He always pulled out a snapshot of his family to look at whenever he read the letters. *God, he missed them—but there was no earthly way to know when he might see them again. The buildup of troops in the Persian Gulf was just starting and there was a long way to go until they could take on the formidable Iraqi army.*

He looked down at the sand and kicked a stray sandbag hard several times with the tip of his Corcoran jump boots. *Well, I'd best be about my business; I can't hide out here all day.* Waving a hand in farewell to the half-asleep bunker guard, he walked back toward the admin tent, picking up his pace as he did.

The admin tent also served as the command and control center for the company. A GP large tent, it was surrounded by a double wall of concertina wire buttressed by sandbags around its four walls. There was a protective trench next to its entrance, which could hold 20 soldiers in the event of a mortar or rocket attack.

The tent flaps were raised at each end in an attempt to siphon in whatever small semblance of a breeze might come along. The day promised to be warm and still there seemed to be little intermediate air flow between a complete calm and a 'Shamal' sandstorm in the desert. The unfailingly hot August and September weather had been replaced by humid, calm and warm air that was just as hard to get accustomed to.

The first person Tatum spotted in the tent was First Sergeant Leroy Washington, a pugnacious veteran who could have played on the Redskins front line if he hadn't had such a benign personality.

''Hey, Brother, what's happening?'' Washington's asked as he looked up from some list he was reading. First sergeants' lives revolved around lists and Washington's was no exception.

''Leroy, I was just thinking about—''

''Lucius, now that's a potentially dangerous situation, you thinkin','' Washington interrupted.

''—Thinking about how we need to plan some sort of training exercise to get these men back on their toes again,'' Tatum continued. ''You know we can only do limited P.T. in the morning and late night, and we haven't had any really good training missions for over a month now. I think we're gonna get soft, and if that happens, we're gonna get into trouble if the shit hits the fan.''

The first sergeant leaned back in a camp chair much too small for his frame and kicked his boots up on the desk with some effort, oblivious to the sand he had scattered on the papers there. ''Now just what you got in mind, sergeant, to keep our men in prime, A-number one fighting condition?''

''Well, I think we need to establish some small observation posts about two klicks north, spread 'em out so they're not on top of each other, then send out recon patrols from those posts toward the Iraqis, to see what they're doing. We know next to nothing about what we're facing up there.'' *Army intelligence! Ha,* Tatum thought to himself, *now there's a real contradiction.*

Tatum continued. ''We could rotate two squads to a post, with the third squad back here in garrison. We stagger the replacement schedule so that everyone gets out there for two weeks a month. We practice the whole shooting match; patrols, communications, close air support, artillery targeting just like we was planning for the real thing. It's bound to happen soon, whether we get into a shooting match in this part of the desert or another, it's bound to happen.''

Tatum stood silently while Washington considered the idea. Not one given to snap decisions, but still a good thinker, the first sergeant was a man who looked after the men under him, including Lucius Tatum, whom he respected considerably. Washington looked back at the man who had proposed the plan. *Someday Tatum would be at least first sergeant, if not sergeant-major. Hell, the man is smart, capable, experienced, and well-liked. If he didn't do something foolish and get himself shot, the sky could be the limit for him.*

Finally, Washington decided. ''All right, Lucius, you start drawin' up some plans for this idea of yours. I'll run it by the captain, but I can't see any reason why he'd axe the idea. He'll want to pass his magic wand over the final plan, but it's a good idea so let's go with it.''

Tatum was pleased with the reaction and had turned to go back to his squad area to draft an outline plan when Washington called out to him.

''Just one more thing, Lucius, before you go'', the first sergeant said.

''Yeah, Leroy, what's that?''

''You got any extra peanut butter and jelly?''

They both started laughing for the first time in days.

* * *

The night air was cold and damp. There appeared to be no one visible on the beach along the section of coast along the southern edge of Oman, near Salalah. The only sound was the monotonous crunch of waves onto the sand, the same sound that had been recurring for thousands of years.

Then, almost in the blink of an eye, there was a slight change to the pattern of the incoming waves. A small black form, no, actually two, appeared at the breakwaters in the dim moonlight. The objects seemed to be flat but with rounded edges and with small, irregular shapes at the periphery. As a particularly large wave brought the objects closer to shore, it could be seen that they were inflatable rafts, occupied by men dressed in black, with darkened hands and faces.

Upon reaching the sandy shore, the men quickly swung their inboard legs out of the raft and silently ran with it to the nearest small brush-covered bluff, about 100 meters inland. They accomplished this easily enough and set about deflating the raft and burying their paddles. With weapons ready, a small overwatch force had deployed forward of the working crew. One tall, slender figure departed from the overwatch party and quickly and efficiently made his way forward to the top of the largest dune.

He extracted a pair of night vision goggles from a waterproof case and began to survey the terrain to the north. He observed in this manner for about 15 minutes, then replaced the goggles in his case and retraced his steps to the overwatch party, which had been joined by the rest of the men.

First Lieutenant Winfield Scott Porter put his mouth to the ear of the executive officer, CWO2 Billy Nichols, of the Special Forces 'A' team now positioned on the beach. He whispered, "The coast looks clear ahead, but I want to send Davis and Purcell out about 2 klicks each to scout. Have them break squelch on their transceivers to clear our moving up to join them otherwise, have them hightail it right back. Under no circumstances do they reveal their positions."

Nichols moved over to the team sergeant and operations NCO, Master Sergeant Hector Lopez, and motioned for Sergeants Willie Davis and John Purcell to join them. Through a series of hand motions and signals they were all familiar with, the exec got the plan across to them. Lopez would monitor their frequency and let the lieutenant know how the men responded. Davis and Purcell slipped off into the night and were lost from sight at once.

A U.S. Army Special Forces 'A' team is composed of 12 men and is usually commanded by a captain. However, 1Lt. Winfield Porter was not just any lieutenant, and as his actions had shown in Honduras and Panama, he was more than capable of commanding his own team. Besides the commander, the exec and team sergeant, the 'A' team also had two each weapons, medical, communications, and engineer NCO's, as well as an intelligence sergeant. All were E-5 or above and had been in the army for at least 4-5 years before being considered for special forces.

The qualification school was intense, six months long, and covered airborne, water, land infiltration and exfiltration skills as well as political and socioeconomic training to help prepare the team for working with indigenous personnel. All troopers are required to possess skills in a foreign language pertinent to their battalion's area of operations. It is conceded that the Army Special Forces represent the elite of the non-conventional forces of the free world, although the Navy Seals might not concede that point readily. Each Special Forces 'A' team member was cross-trained in at least one specialty of warfare skills, giving the team its special depth of capabilities, allowing it to stand alone in the field on missions of extended duration.

The men on this beach tonight had been together as a team for over two years, and worked with real harmony and efficiency. As Porter sat back on his haunches, his 5.56-mm CAR-15 autorifle at the ready, he reflected on how much the members of his team meant to him. Not a man much given to sentimentality (that had been bred out of him by three generations of military leaders before him), he nevertheless felt a sense of team spirit and loyalty that he knew was special between men with highly developed skills. He had felt the same way about his high school basketball team when they had won the state AAA crown. Porter had left his hometown of Augusta, Georgia, after graduation, to attend West Point and hadn't returned for years. The last time he had visited Augusta was when he had finished airborne training at Fort Benning, Georgia, and was driving to Fort Bragg to join the 82nd Airborne. The high school at Augusta had seemed smaller than he had recalled, but when he entered the gym and had stood at the free-throw line of the basketball court, it had all come back to him. *Oh, those were the easy days,* he now knew. *No command responsibilities, no worry about the lives of your men, no . . . .*

His thoughts were interrupted by a hand flash from Sergeant Lopez. The scouts had found no problems and had given them the go ahead to advance. Lt. Porter nodded his head and the men began walking toward a dark mainland ahead of them single file in a half-crouch to minimize their horizon exposure.

This silent file of highly trained men had a mission to accomplish—locate and plant destructive charges on a coastal radar station that received signals from the entire Arabian Sea. Although the mission was only an exercise, the radar station was manned by Omani troops who had no prior knowledge of the team's goal this dark night. With tensions high in the Persian Gulf states, it was possible that, if detected, the team could be fired upon by friendly Coalition troops. However, it had been decided that the most realistic training could best be obtained by a clandestine mission with a small number of allied personnel in the 'need-to-know' chain. Thus this training carried high stakes and made the men more wary than their training back in Germany out of their base at Bad Tolz near the Austrian border.

Sergeant Lopez walked directly behind Porter, with perhaps five meters between them. Even in the dark, Lopez could imagine the form of the lieutenant—his slow, languid gait that ate up the distance because of his long legs, the broad shoulders that never seemed to tire when humping an 80-pound rucksack, and the large, strong hands that could break a man's arm with one twist. *Like a big panther, or cougar,* Lopez thought.

The incongruous part of Porter's body was his face; sandy hair always flopping down over his eye like JFK's used to, and the boyish features that tried to be serious, but always seemed to be friendly no matter how stressful or dangerous the situation.

The lieutenant's eyes were blue and warm most of the time, but the sergeant had seen them turn the color of cold steel on several occasions, once when a Carolina redneck had made a rude remark to the lieutenant's date. The lieutenant had a strong sense of right and wrong instilled in him from an early age, and in a flash the redneck was bent backwards over the bar with the lieutenant's big hand ready to crush the inconsiderate slob's larynx. No one in that bar had ever said a word out of line again, and the lieutenant transformed quickly back into his usual pleasant self. *I'd hate to make him mad myself,* thought Lopez, *but then I know better than to step out of line with him.*

Just then the lieutenant held up his hand to halt the column and rolled his finger in a circle, indicating that they should all gather around him. Porter had seen the outline of the radar dish in the near distance and was correlating the visual image before him with what was in his mind from the satellite photos he had seen several days before. It was claimed he possessed that rare gift of a photographic memory and no one on the team had seen evidence to dispute that claim.

Porter took out a small penlight with a red lens, and, forming a shelter with his body, began drawing on a special 5 x 7 inch tablet that amplified the red light wavelength. The drawing was crude, but accurate, and depicted the important locations of the installations previously identified on the recon photos. In turn, Porter pointed to each man, and then to a position on the map, confirming their task in the mission. With hand signals nearly as complex as those of a third base coach to his players, Porter completed the tasking and cupped his ear as a symbol for questions. He then looked each man in the eye, sending them off to their jobs with a nod. He and Sergeant Lopez moved forward silently to provide cover for the men as they approached the installation.

The plan called for the mission to be accomplished without their detection by the Omanis. Sergeant Santori, the demolitions expert, a fitting job for a Brooklynite, would place the modified charges against the proper support beams of the radar tower structure as well as the incendiary device that would burn the radar receiver after it toppled to the ground. The charges had been modified for this mission, however, by replacing the explosives with a high-pitched alarm device that would be triggered by a long-distance transmitter. Timing devices were not used much any more because they did not allow for enough flexibility in exfiltrating the team to safety.

Sergeant Miller was in charge of joining the installation's communications input/output through the judicious placement of one of his 'black boxes,' which no one else understood, really, and which he never cared to explain. On command, the device emitted a powerful jamming signal that covered a wide-spectrum frequency range and debilitated all but the most powerful handheld transceivers, which were usually used for local air traffic. To interrupt local FM transmission, Miller used an explosive device that released a 'smoke' of metallic chaff, interfering with and deflecting FM signals. Miller had finished two years of college in electrical engineering before he decided to "have some fun and games." He planned on returning to finish his degree on the Montgomery G.I. Bill. Practical experience like he was gaining would not be found in E.E. labs at any university.

The men were traveling relatively light for this mission—they each carried their choice of personal weapons, usually the CAR-15, the shortened version of the M-16, and a 9-mm Beretta or a Colt .45 automatic. The older men tended to prefer the .45 with its superior stopping power, but the younger men had been trained more recently on the Beretta, which had a distinct advantage with its 15-shot magazine. All carried a KaBar knife attached to their web gear with the handle downward, so it would drop into their hands for quick and silent desheathing. Since most special forces personnel had a strong fascination with weapons, each carried a variety of stilettos, throwing knives and shiriken stars, as well as a demolitions knives. There would be a boot knife as well as a thin stiletto strapped to the forearm. Each man had a theory about how these weapons could get him out of a troublesome situation and they carried them like rabbits' feet.

In the dim moonlight the men went about their tasks, setting charges and electrical devices, helping each other when necessary. Doc Warner, the medic, had the keenest sense of hearing on the team, so he positioned himself close to the personnel barracks to listen for any impromptu visits by Omanis answering the call of nature.

However, this time all went well, and the silent figures withdrew into the shadows of the night as they slipped away from the installation and returned to the beachhead using a reverse- or back-azimuth for direction. When they all arrived at the rubber rafts, Lt. Porter pointed to each member in turn, who gave a 'thumbs-up' signal to certify his task had gone according to plan.

While the men uncovered the rafts and reinflated them, Porter turned seaward and pointed his unidirectional laser beam directly outward, flashing a predetermined signal of laser bursts. He repeated the signal at five-minute intervals until he saw the answering flashes at least five kilometers out at sea. *Looks like the submarine's ready and waiting for us,* he thought. Then, he quickly shot a compass heading on the light at sea and ran to join his teammates in the second raft. As the men dipped their urethane foam-silenced paddles into the water, the lieutenant turned back toward the mainland. He reached out to accept the remote control detonator from Sergeant Santori. He nodded to Miller, who fired the remote control for the electronic jamming equipment back at the installation and then, after taking a deep breath, fired his own detonator. The men stopped paddling and swiveled on the sides of the raft to watch the remarkable display of 'military fireworks' rigged up by Santori as well as to hear the penetrating and raucous sounds from the noise charges.

Porter turned to the men in his boat, and announced in a clear voice heard for the first time that night, "Men, it don't get any better than this!" His grin stretched from ear to ear and back again.

CHAPTER TWO

FORT McCOY WAS just north of Interstate 90, a 45-minute drive from La Crosse, Wisconsin. From April to October, the vast military reservation was a beautiful composite of firs, pines, wildflowers and green grass. The climate then is temperate and refreshing and the Wisconsin National Guard outfits that do their two-week annual stints at Ft. McCoy enjoy the training and the setting.

Enjoyment was no part of that pastoral scene in December, Neel grumbled, as he drove from the airport at La Crosse toward Ft. McCoy. Thick snow had enveloped the region and the temperature had plunged to well below zero. Fortunately, the highways were cleared so Neel could relax during the drive. For some obscure reason, Fort McCoy had been chosen by the Department of the Army to be a mobilization site for Army Guard and Reserve units being prepared for deployment to the Persian Gulf. A large enough post, it still wasn't totally prepared for numbers of troops that were there or scheduled to be.

Neel decided that the rolling hills and farmlands of southern Wisconsin were little different from those of Missouri. In fact, there were a lot of similarities between Kansas City and La Crosse, except for size, probably because both were located in the Great Plains, both adjacent to a large river. Similar to an art enthusiast who enjoys visiting the art museums in the cities in which he is traveling, Neel always tried to visit health care facilities. He hoped to have a chance to visit the famous Gunderson Clinic in La Crosse and to learn more about the phenomenon of large physician clinics that seemed unique to Minnesota and Wisconsin. *Maybe the weather is so cold,* he thought to himself, *that they save on heating bills with everyone in one big building.*

After a short time, he could not prevent his thoughts from returning to the subject that had distressed him since he received word of his recall to active duty. He had gone home as soon as his patients had been taken care of on rounds, and found Marty just having returned from teaching her afternoon classes at the college. She had seemed in an unusually good mood and he sensed she was really happy about her pregnancy and the forthcoming birth of their first child. *She'll make a great mother,* Neel concluded, *probably a lot better parent than I could ever hope to be.*

Marty was the most attractive woman he had ever seen that first day of their meeting in Baltimore. He was attending a research consortium meeting at the University of Maryland with the director of the trauma unit, and Marty was there as a representative from the University's robotics center. Although the topic of discussion was interesting - to respond to an NIH call for proposals to develop a remote diagnostic module for victims of nuclear reactor accidents - he was totally involved with taking in this intelligent and competent young female assistant professor. That day she had worn a black business suit with a white collar with her hair done up in a bun. With only a faint hint of lipstick and makeup, her auburn hair was accentuated. The soft skin of her neck flowed into an athletic figure that was terrific. He was smitten at first sight.

Throughout most if not all of his medical career, he had subconsciously thought of women as somewhat subservient to men - the nurses, technicians, therapists, all those females tended to subjugate themselves to the doctors. And some females who had been gutsy enough to go on to medical school and become physicians themselves were often on the other end of the curve and pretty much did nothing to attract him to them. But this woman was another matter entirely. As the discussion progressed and he watched her and listened to her contributions to the discussion, he knew she was 'the one.' However he almost totally torpedoed any chance with her, when, after she had obviously noticed his staring at her for the better part of an hour, she looked directly at him. "And you, Doctor, what do you think of that conclusion?"

He had nearly dropped his teeth. All he could manage in response was a stammering, "Well, uh, I, uh, really couldn't follow that last point very well."

She held his gaze for a minute, then smiled that terribly disarming smile. "That's what I thought you'd say." Turning to the others, she continued the discussion on the analog to digital conversion of radioactivity input data for computer analysis.

After the meeting, he had maneuvered his way to her chair, and held out his hand, having regained his composure and sense of direction. "Hi, I'm Tom Neel from the Trauma Center."

"Hello, Tom. Marty Schaefer. I didn't mean to put you on the spot this morning, but you were making me uncomfortable staring at me like that." She smiled to show him that she took no offense from his attention.

"Yeah, well, I guess I need to get away from the hospital more and learn how to behave in public," he replied with a laugh. *Wow! She's even more attractive up close.* "I'd really like to learn more about your work, Marty. Do you have time some evening to have supper with me?"

She gathered her papers on the table, organized them in her soft leather briefcase, stood, and leaned toward him. A full minute seemed to pass. "I'd like that, Dr. Thomas Neel. Maybe I need to get out and see what the world looks like myself. When do we go?"

From then on, there was no question in his mind that she was the woman for him. She had awakened feelings in him repressed for so many years by his studies and long working hours. They went motor-sailing on the Potomac, horseback riding in western Maryland, skiing at Lake Placid and to cultural events in an attempt to improve his 'one-sided personality.' Marty did change his life and he welcomed her zeal. When his fellowship at the Trauma Center was drawing to a close, he proposed and they were married in April at a beautiful Methodist church in Baltimore. All of his family came from Missouri, and hers from Virginia and it was a grand affair. A marriage made in heaven.

She wasn't particularly thrilled with leaving the East Coast though, but certainly preferred Kansas City over his other prospect, Louisville. She made plans to teach mathematics at Rockhurst College while she worked on her doctorate in robotics and artificial intelligence at the University of Kansas in Lawrence, only an hour's drive from their home. In fact, all was rosy and settled and planned and stable, until he had come home that fateful afternoon.

She had looked simply radiant that day, her long hair flowing down over her shoulders, wearing the stylish maternity dress in which she still looked sexy at four months of pregnancy. He hugged and kissed her and she could read immediately the trouble in his eyes. When he told her, she glared at him for a minute, then slowly turned and locked herself in the bathroom.

What a thing for a doctorate-level mathematician to do, he thought, as he knocked on the door. *I guess she's just still kind of a little girl underneath all that knowledge and confidence.*

"Go away," she sobbed from inside the bathroom, her voice muffled by her face in her hands. "You don't care about me, or this child we're going to have. All you care about is being a hero like your father - a dead hero!"

That hurt. A lot. Neel's father was an Army medic who was killed in Vietnam when Neel was ten. His death had been a tremendous shock - he and his dad had been great buddies. His father had been on patrol in the jungle with his platoon when the unit was ambushed. The elder Neel had set up a small aid station for the wounded men beneath a large tree and was tending to the 8-10 men who were wounded. A Viet Cong grenade had come flying over the tree and landed right in the middle of the wounded men. Without hesitation, Neel's father had thrown his body on top of the grenade and absorbed the blast, killing himself, but protecting the wounded. Tom's father had planned to return to college in Springfield, Missouri, after that Vietnam tour and eventually to become a physician. All those plans vaporized in a second. The President had presented Sergeant Mortimer Neel's Congressional Medal of Honor, awarded posthumously to the family, and Tom Neel could recall the ceremony at the White House as if it were a color video that could be replayed over and over again in his mind. Tom had missed his father fiercely and no doubt his dad's influence had played a role in the younger Neel's decision to become a physician.

In part, Marty was right. Neel was haunted by the knowledge that his father had displayed tremendous courage when he covered that grenade with his body. He must have known, even for an instant, that he would never see his family again, never become a physician, never be a grandfather. Tom Neel just wasn't certain if he would have had the same courage as his father had to do something that heroic and had often hoped, in an admittedly perverse sort of a way, that he would someday have the opportunity to see if he was as brave as his father. The real problem was, he finally came to realize, that he wasn't certain he was really that brave, and he was afraid he would fail and have to live in shame before his father for all of eternity. It was a heavy burden.

So Tom Neel had set out to prove his courage to himself in any way he could find - mountain climbing, snake hunting, sky diving, barefoot water skiing, anything that had any element of danger. During ROTC at the University of Missouri, he had gone to airborne school and air assault school, both requiring a fair amount of courage to jump from an airplane at night or to rappel from a helicopter 100 feet above the ground. Later, after college, he had fulfilled his military obligations for the ROTC scholarship by serving as a team leader with the Army's special forces, completing that rigorous training with flying colors, even becoming a diving officer. Before he met Marty, if something was dangerous, Tom would try it.

At the end of medical school, he knew he had to become a surgeon - the 'fighter pilot' of the medical profession. Not just any kind of surgeon, but a trauma surgeon, who dealt with the most challenge to the skills of a physician - literally life or death hanging in the balance of a few minutes' time. Again, a challenge to his courage and skills.

So, yes, I guess Marty is right when she says I'm driven by my dead father's legacy, he thought as he stood outside the bathroom door. *But, I'm not in control of it any more; it's bigger than me, bigger than my marriage and my career. It has a life of its own and it's going to play out the way it wants to.*

He was finally able to cajole her out of the bathroom to sit on the sofa while he fixed her a cup of herb tea. Marty was being very careful in her nutritional intake for this baby - she really wanted it to be as 'pure' as possible.

He had brought her the tea and sat beside her. "Marty, we have to get this worked out so it won't affect us the rest of our lives. Millions of men have been called up to war and left their families and come back to start right back up where they left off. Why can't that work for us, too?"

She looked up at him with a look that was combination fury and plea. "Tom Neel, I know you and you're going to go over there and do something stupid and then you won't come back to us and I'll have a child who never knew his father." She started crying again and he felt really helpless.

He held her hand. "Now look at me. I will be very careful and not take any chances and I'll be safe the whole time. No one has anything better to come back to than I have, and I'm sure going to do just that.''

''Damnit, Tom, why can't you just call up the army and tell them you can't go, that your wife is pregnant and you need some sort of exemption. Tell them you're too valuable to the community or something and they need you here. There *must* be a way to get out of it!''

How could he tell her that he didn't want to? That it was one of the most important things in his life that he must go there and find out what war is like and what his father must have felt. Perhaps only then could he put his father to rest. No, he couldn't tell her that, she wouldn't understand. Maybe she'd go for a patriotism angle.

''Honey, we live in the best country in the world - a free country. We all have an obligation to protect America's ideals and freedom in the world. I have a responsibility to do my part as a patriotic American.''

''Forget it,'' she hollered. ''Let someone else go.''

Well, that didn't work.

''Why would you put me and the baby at this risk?'' she continued. ''You paid your obligation to the army with four years of active duty. You didn't owe them anything. Why did you have to join the reserves so they could break up our family?'' She really resented him right now and nothing he could do or say would help. He'd best just leave it alone and let her get over this in her own way. Although he didn't tell her, he suspected he'd joined the reserves to keep open the possibility that something like this would happen. Well, now it has, and he had an unhappy wife who might be gone with his unborn child when he got back. *Man, am I stupid, or what?*

Marty had finally calmed down and hours later they had made love in the king-sized bed in the bedroom overlooking the park. They had talked a lot more over the next several days, but he knew she still harbored some very hard feelings toward him and the air was decidedly strained. He cradled her in his arms and tried repeatedly to reassure her.

It had also not been easy to make arrangements at the trauma center for someone to take his place, especially since he had been there only five months. He finally convinced John Shell at the trauma center in Baltimore to take a six-month sabbatical and replace him while he was gone. John was single and had run through most of the women in the greater Baltimore area, so he was eager to check out a new female hunting lease. If Neel was gone for longer than six months . . . well, he'd just cross that bridge later.

Their last evening at home had been really uncomfortable. Tom had already packed his field gear, sewn all of his patches and tabs on the newly-issued desert fatigues (BDU's—'battle dress uniform') from the unit and packed the necessities he thought he might need. He always prided himself on having thought of all contingencies and prepared himself for them.

Marty drove him to the K.C. International Airport where he was to catch the plane to La Crosse. Just before he boarded, he kissed and hugged her and told her he loved her. She looked at him sadly and said "Goodbye, Thomas Mortimer Neel. We'll miss you." And then turned and left, obviously crying.

Now what did she mean by that? he puzzled, as he settled into his seat.

* * *

Neel met up with the rest of his unit at the processing center at Ft. McCoy. They had traveled earlier to set things up. Although he had dressed in his cold weather clothes, the cold at McCoy seemed to permeate into his bones - as if he were trapped in a frozen meat locker.

The officers were assigned to an old WW II-era barracks that was heated (when it worked) by a coal furnace. This particular building was nicknamed "The Swamp" by its occupants and it became their center of social and emotional support. They processed through the Soldier Readiness Center (SRC) where other reservists like themselves had been called up to man the garrison at McCoy to perform the enormous administrative tasks of processing thousands of men and women to go overseas to the Persian Gulf or related destinations. The process was tedious, and the soldiers were stuck in long lines for each processing station.

Specialist Four Jay Anders was in Building 9105, waiting to go through the fifth of what seemed like a hundred processing stations. His aviation unit had not been issued desert fatigues yet, so he was wearing his olive drab zippered flight suit and boots. It was comfortable and he could easily unzip it to expose whatever part of his anatomy was needed for exam, blood sample, or inoculation.

He had talked to all of his instructors and secured a promise to give him an incomplete grade in his classes this semester. That would allow him to take the final exams upon his return (whenever that might be) and complete the courses. He had gotten his friend, Jeff, to move into the apartment and watch his belongings, and had taken care of the many little items of business that don't receive much attention until you have to leave the country for an extended period. Like stopping your mail. And keeping your college loans from coming due while you are temporarily out of school. But he had gotten all that done, and now he was in the hands of the U.S. Army - *I wonder why that worries me?*

Most of the personnel being processed through the SRC were reserve components - Army National Guardsmen and Army Reservists. Most wore uniforms devoid of any special insignia or awards, because they had been in non-active duty units and had little opportunity to attend special schools or to attain special qualifications. A few soldiers with prior active duty boasted badges or awards on their BDU's but they were rarely seen.

However, as Anders was sitting in the waiting area patiently awaiting for his immunization record to be reviewed and updated with the necessary shots, a tall, lean officer approached and took a seat at the end of the line. While most units started the in-processing together each morning, it usually ended with some individuals being detained at one station, while others proceeded in sequence faster than the rest. This caused the unit processing to break up and be handled essentially as individual soldiers. The waiting was quite frustrating to some individuals. As the major took his seat, a nurse captain came over to him, offering to allow him as a field-grade officer to be taken care of preferentially and not have to wait like the others. Without hesitation, the major smiled, shook his head and declined.

Now that reaction really intrigued Anders, because all the other officers that he had worked with, particularly in aviation, would have expected to be treated preferentially, and likely would have created a disturbance had they not been. *Now there's an interesting officer,* Anders thought, as he shifted in his seat to get a better look.

In contrast to most of the older reserve officers he had seen here, the major appeared trim and fit, and he wore his camouflage fatigues as if they were specially fitted. His face looked intelligent and was framed by a close-cropped haircut, unusually close in this Reserve processing center. The major had no combat patches on his right arm, but had a chest full of badges - expert field medical badge, senior flight wings of some sort, senior parachutist's badge and air assault badge. His name tag on the right breast read ''NEEL''. *Just what branch of the army is he in?* wondered Anders. *I can't see his left collar.*

Anders stood up and stretched, dropped his manila folder of papers along with his garrison cap on the chair to reserve his seat and walked past the major to get a drink from a nearby water fountain. As he passed the major from the left on returning to his seat, he recognized the caduceus of the medical corps. There was also a 'SPECIAL FORCES' tab on his left shoulder and a unit patch he didn't recognize.

Well, I'll be darned, Anders thought, *this doctor has really been around. I wonder if he's a reservist or one of the active duty people they've yanked from some post to augment a reserve unit going to the Gulf? If he's not active duty now he sure was sometime in the past.*

Then it was Anders' time to move to the head of the line to be immunized by several young female NCO's who enjoyed seeing him unzip his flight suit and expose a muscular arm. Major Neel played the 'musical chairs' game and moved to the next seat in line. He watched the young aviation medic zip his flight suit back up and wondered what aviation unit he was with. There were no identifying insignia on a flight suit save for the velcro badge over the left breast that told your name, rank, branch of service and depicted your aviation qualification - pilot, crew member, flight surgeon, or so forth. This young man's badge carried the wings of a crew member and the rank of specialist four. That probably makes him an assistant crew chief or a medic, Neel surmised, depending on whether he crewed in a Chinook or a Blackhawk.

Neel was an inveterate people watcher who enjoyed figuring out jobs and personalities from appearance, demeanor and actions. He liked to think of himself as a modern-day Sherlock Holmes (small-time, of course), and he practiced this skill constantly. Although most of his talent came from his medical training of close observation, he was also born with an inquisitive nature, something that must have exasperated his parents at times.

The young man at the immunization station was polite and

deferential to the female personnel, but he also seemed somewhat shy. Neel had noticed that he had not participated in the almost obligatory griping and moaning by the other enlisted men in the waiting line, and had somehow seemed bored by it all. His blond hair and light complexion probably placed him as a Scandinavian, so I'll bet he lives in the Great Lakes area somewhere, probably Minnesota or Wisconsin. That could have been me fifteen years ago, he thought, when I finished college and entered active duty to repay my military obligation.

As a sole male survivor of a military person killed in combat, especially one who was awarded the Medal of Honor, Neel could have attended one of the military service academies if he had chosen. However, he had decided to accept the full ROTC scholarship to Missouri U., to be closer to his mother and two younger sisters in their hometown of Joplin.

He still felt that he was the head of their family and tried to help them whenever he could. His mother had worked as a receptionist for an ear, nose and throat physician in Joplin and his sisters were in high school while he was in college. He had tried to go home from school whenever he had a free weekend, foregoing a social life for his perceived obligations to provide support for his family. Once he was graduated, his sisters were either working or had gotten married, so he felt he could loosen his grip a bit and have a few adventures of his own.

He had volunteered for the airborne assignment and, since he was already jump-qualified, he was assigned to the 82nd Airborne Division at Fort Bragg as a platoon leader. Neel found he had a natural talent for leading men and he relished the excitement and danger (yes!) of an airborne assignment. After a year in the 82nd, he had volunteered for special forces training, completed the qualification, and was assigned to the 7th Special Forces group at Fort Bragg as an executive officer.

Still single, he had thrived on the long deployments to exotic areas, the training exercises, and the camaraderie of the men. But, he had known since his father had died that he wanted to become a physician, and he had finally settled down in the fourth year of his military obligation and applied to medical school. Of course, his first choice was back home at Missouri, and fortunately the dean of admissions was a former military man and Vietnam veteran, so Neel was accepted almost immediately after the interviews, the acceptance sealed with a strong handshake.

During medical school and general surgery residency (the toughest residency except for neurosurgery), he had maintained his military standing with an assignment to a large Army Reserve aviation battalion in St. Louis. He had taken his entire vacation one year (plus one week of administrative leave, allowed because the chairman of surgery liked him) to attend flight surgeon's school at Fort Rucker, Alabama. That part of his life - the army affiliation - was as important to him as anything, and he would not, no, could not give it up. Now it had gotten him into a real quandary, with his wife more upset with him than she had ever been, his home mortgage just barely going to be covered by his wife's teaching salary, a new baby on the way and maybe to be born without a father in attendance, and his future generally quite uncertain.

The members of his unit had received new orders yesterday at the barracks, informing them their recall to active duty could extend up to a year, "at the discretion of the Commander-in-Chief." He had called home last night, worried that she had received a copy of the orders at home. She had not yet, but she was still very upset over his absence. The phone call had made him so tense he had gone to sleep (finally) with a headache and had also awakened with one. *How could anything good come of what was happening?* He shook his head in consternation and frustration and sighed. *What in the hell am I going to do,* he wondered? *Right now,* he guessed, *just 'go with the flow.'*

The rest of the mobilization time was spent in unit training - primarily to learn the customs of an Arabic world, to practice chemical and biological personal protection, and to issue gear. A considerable amount of time was spent on learning how to don the MOPP suit against what was generally considered to be a virtually certain use of chemical and biological agents by the 'forces of evil' if war broke out in the Persian Gulf. Nothing much was said about a nuclear attack because everyone knew you'd be a 'crispy critter' no matter how you tried to protect yourself. Neel and Anders both realized independently that it would be next to impossible to care for casualties in the MOPP suit, but put that idea into the back of their minds in hopes that the conflict would be settled peacefully.

Briefings about the desert heat and sun in the Middle East began to seem almost attractive to Neel as he suffered through the minus 20º weather and constant snow. An avid runner for fitness, he was forced to take a bus to the Fort McCoy gymnasium where he ran around the inside of the basketball court for exercise—12 laps equaled one-mile and watch out for the layups when you pass under the goals. Exercise had become very important to him as a form of mental therapy against the boredom and the uncertainty of his future (and would become even more important, as he would find out, in the desert). The daily life of a surgeon is filled with nonstop activities from sunup to sunrise and then some, so this interminable waiting with too much time on his hands was getting to him. It didn't help when he called home and found Marty had become cold and impersonal toward him in their conversations. He felt he was losing the special bond that connected them, and he hadn't even left the country yet! *God, I need your help,* he prayed at night, lying on a soft bed with a plastic pillow - *help me get my life back in order. Everything was going so great for us. Now it's falling apart and there doesn't seem to be anything I can do about it.*

He was becoming depressed. He knew all of the clinical signs and symptoms, recognized them in himself. He thought about seeing his combat support hospital chaplain, but realized he'd see the man back in Kansas City after they returned and didn't want that hanging over his head. He could see the post chaplain at McCoy, but he was busy with really serious separation problems in anguished soldiers. So, he'd have to deal with it himself and keep it to himself, although he knew professionally that was not the best way to handle it. *I think I'll feel better when we get to the Gulf and I can be a physician again,* he concluded. *At least that's something I can do and do well - I hope we go soon if we're going.*

His wishes were fulfilled two days later when the unit was told to pack all their gear into two duffel bags (labeled A and B with their name and last four digits of their SSN stenciled on the bottom) and be prepared to leave at a moment's notice. True to military form, the moment's notice was just that - they had to quickly load their gear on any available bus and were driven to Volk Field to board their aircraft. At first glance, there was no telling Volk Airfield was actually an air field, because it had as much snow on the runway as there was on the surrounding countryside. Hoping someone knew what they were doing, Neel deposited his duffel bags on the growing pile and waited to board the plane. Because the huge deployment force had quickly outstripped the capabilities of the military air transport system, civilian aircraft like this Northwest 747 had been contracted to airlift troops to their destinations in Europe or the Middle East.

Having spent a lot of his military time flying in helicopters, C-130's, C-141's and C-5A's, the thought of a luxury liner air flight to Saudi Arabia brought a smile to Neel for the first time in weeks. *Maybe things will start going better now,* he thought, as he strapped himself into the seat.

Specialist Anders looked across the aisle and saw the same major seated there that he had seen at the examination and immunization station. He appeared to be relaxed. *How could he be so relaxed?* Anders thought, *when he knows where we're going and what we might do - I am so nervous that I'll do something wrong and hurt somebody. Please, dear God, don't let me screw up,* Anders prayed, as he closed his eyes for the takeoff.

* * *

Sergeant Tatum's plan to conduct training patrols in the desert had been approved by the chain of command all the way up to CENTCOM. It was highly doubtful, however, that Tatum's name had been associated with the plan once it had risen past battalion level. Certain types of individuals had a penchant for taking a subordinate's good idea and somehow transforming it into theirs. They also had a knack for recognizing a bad idea and avoiding it. This same 'alteration of attributable origin' is known to also occur in other situations in our society such as the corporate business world and academia. It can be the fate of a junior member of a team to have his best ideas pirated (except by the few honest intermediate level managers) and not receive credit for them.

However, that sort of problem never bothered Sergeant Tatum - he figured the Army owned him, lock, stock, barrel and ideas. He didn't need any personal credit for doing his job well, but he didn't mind an occasional acknowledgment of that fact. He was still on a low enough level of the command structure that he usually related only to the senior NCO ranks above him, rather than to officers. As he progressed in the ranks in the future, however, he knew he would have to develop the 'political' skills so important to the NCO leaders that allowed them to walk that thin line between obeying orders from the officer in charge and actually doing what needed to be done in the best way.

Tatum had never thought of himself as a 'racist' in the

counter-definition of the word, but he knew he had a personal problem with white men in general who had been born with proverbial 'silver spoons' in their mouths. *Why was it that they were chosen to be the 'haves' while I was chosen to be a 'have-not'?* he would wonder, when the topic had somehow come to his mind. There were plenty of military officers in Washington, D.C., and, in order to earn extra money for their family, his mother had worked as a part-time maid for a number of them. As a child, Lucius Tatum would sometimes accompany his mother to their homes by public transportation, always admonished by her to stay out of the 'white folks' way, look invisible and don't talk in their presence. He had seen how condescending many of them had been toward his mother and her black son, as well as how some of them had ignored the Tatums, as if they truly didn't exist. Tatum had tried hard not to let these memories and feelings affect his military career, but he knew they were just held at bay beneath the surface and he feared they might cause him a problem in the future. But recognizing and understanding his feelings was a strong step toward overcoming and dealing with them, and he hoped the Lord would give him the strength to be fair.

Sergeant Tatum had become only a minor player in his own training plan, but he didn't mind. He needed to 'do something' as much as his men, and he was hoping this desert training would give them a better chance of survival if and when the war began. He was pleased to take out his squad to patrol and he helped pick the site for their remote outpost. Tatum and Corporal Sammy Billings, assistant squad leader, had decided to lead a patrol each to man the two remote outposts in their platoon's assigned sector. The base camp had been set up about five kilometers north of the Division and was formed from two-man camouflage tents and recessed bunkers for protection from fire. Latrines were temporary catholes that were covered over when full, then redug elsewhere. Every effort was made to keep the base camp as unobtrusive and low profile as possible.

Camouflage netting in desert colors had been suspended over each tent and over the supply area, only partly to protect men and equipment from the bright sun. Although overflight and reconnaissance by enemy aircraft had been almost nonexistent to now, the platoon was still concerned that enemy patrols or a recon-in-force would expose their position.

For several reasons, the company commander had decided to send out the squad patrols to their observation posts in daylight. First, it was possible to travel too far in the desert at night, because distance was so hard to gauge, unless you counted paces. Second, if the Iraqis practiced effective darkness light and noise security, the patrol could literally stumble into a whole nest of enemy troops, risking American lives, as well as causing an international incident during this period of uneasy standoff. All these possibilities kept the American troops on edge.

At 0600, Tatum was ready. He was up an hour earlier, had heated water for coffee over his sterno stove, then eaten some crackers and grape jelly for breakfast. There wasn't really any MRE for breakfast (not even the highly salted 'omelet with ham'), and Tatum was never much for a big breakfast anyway, unless he had done enough P.T. to work up an appetite. His men had awakened silently and dressed, not so much out of concern for sound security as simply a desire not to awaken their non-patrol friends unnecessarily. They wore desert camouflage BDU's over long underwear to protect against the chill morning. Later in the day, they'd likely remove the undergarments as the heat increased. They had laid out their gear last evening, but would check it all again before departing.

Tatum was sitting on a wooden litter container that served as both a seat for eating chow and as an all-purpose table. Later on, if they stayed at the outpost long enough, one of the division chaplains or his assistant might find his way out, then the box could be used as an alter.

"You know, Sly, I don't think I ever appreciated a great cup of coffee before I came over here. You know, *really* appreciated it." He sipped his coffee from the canteen cup and made a wry face. "This stuff tastes like a pair of two-week-old socks."

Corporal Sly Rodriguez, always optimistic, smiled. "Sarge, look at it this way. If you had grown up in New Mexico like I did, and drunk that coffee on the reservation, the kind so strong it ate a hole right out your stomach and through your belt buckle, you'd learn to love *this* stuff." Sly's smile was lop-sided. No one had ever seen or heard him laugh, but that smile was a real demonstration of feelings in the normally taciturn non-com.

"Well, man, I hope this stuff keeps you awake enough this morning so you can get us to where we're going without them

A-Rabs spotting us.'' Tatum was an excellent field soldier and he had a keen sense of direction, but those abilities paled next to those of Sly, a 'Mestizo,' a combination of Mexican and Indian, who had grown up on the border. The desert land of Sly's home was similar to the Arabian desert and Sly could use the desert to his advantage, and not be overwhelmed or frustrated by it. Tatum had picked Sly to come with him and Private First Class Jesse Jones, another black man, on this first patrol. At some time in the future, he knew he'd be happy with his decision.

The men rechecked their weapons, packed their rucksacks with three days' provisions and slung their extra two-quart canteens around their chests. Although they would travel light by a combat infantryman's standards, they still needed radio transceivers, long-distance telescopes and extra ammunition for this reconnaissance mission. In three days, they would vector in a replacement crew.

The basic concept of the observation posts was simple enough - locate and watch the enemy front lines along the critical 10-kilometer front by using six 3-man outposts. They would practice camouflage techniques, living under harsh conditions, observing and reporting. It was a good training mission, but it could also provide valuable intelligence about the disposition and activity of the Iraqi front lines, then that information would be correlated with satellite recon photos. Because low-level aircraft over flights were still considered too inflammatory, the presence of American troops with direct visual access to the enemy was strategically valuable.

Tatum walked over to where Rodriguez and Jones were preparing to don their gear. ''All right, let me look you over now,'' he said to the two men.

Jones, used to Tatum's constant concern, said, ''Okay, mom, wanna check my school bag, too?'' He opened his rucksack and showed Tatum the contents as he inventoried them: ''Two pair extra socks, one pair skivvies, two t-shirts, extra 'drive-on' rag, six MRE's, rope, camo net, sunscreen, Tylenol, chewing gum.'' Then Jones pointed to the rest of the gear - ''entrenching tool, two flashlights on LBE, two compasses, knife, two two-quart canteens, two one-quart canteens, two hundred rounds of ammo, knife, sniperscope, helmet, M-16 with 200 rounds, .45 with 30 rounds, gas mask, MOPP suit, poncho, and shelter half.'' They would have to sleep in the desert wrapped in the shelter halves because sleeping bags were too bulky.

Tatum nodded and grunted. *Looks okay,* he thought, *but what are we missing? Anything?* He knew they could get emergency supplies from a supply team, or even call in a helicopter pick up for evacuation if necessary, but that would mean compromising the mission and he wouldn't do that except in dire emergencies.

He turned to Rodriguez who had displayed all of his gear like some vendor in the roadside market at the entrance to his Indian reservation. Sly had vowed he would not stoop to peddling wares for a meager living in his life, so he had joined the army the day he graduated from the government high school on the Mescalero Apache Indian Reservation. He hitched a ride to the Alamogordo recruiting station and was promptly put on the next bus to Albuquerque for processing, his sole belongings wrapped in a small blanket and tied with a rope. Sly had found his niche as an army pathfinder and Tatum trusted Sly's instincts as much as his training.

''All right, Sly, I know you don't need much water, but carry as much as you can to help out us guys who sweat a lot, okay?'' There was a fine line between carrying the water you needed and the physical chore of actually carrying the weight of it. But, for three days, they would do fine.

''Sly, I also want you to pack this new scope the lieutenant gave me.'' He slipped the cover off a compact periscope that expanded from one foot to three, with lenses at right angles to the shaft at each end. ''This baby may keep us from getting our heads shot off.'' Sly examined it, resheathed it, and tied it to his rucksack. He shrugged on the ruck with ease. He was a man of ordinary size, but extraordinary strength.

Tatum located the platoon sergeant and told him they were heading out. There was no fanfare and no bugles as in the old calvary days when a patrol left or entered the fort, just a few waves and comments hurled their way as they passed. All three men wore sunglasses and Kevlar helmets, but planned to switch to tying 'drive-on' rags to their heads as soon as they left the sight of camp. The helmets were just too heavy and uncomfortable for a stroll through the desert.

Sly took a compass reading, squinted at the horizon and put

the compass away for the trek. Each man shifted his load until it was as comfortable as it was going to get and they moved out.

"Okay, let's do it to it," Tatum said as they crested the small sand berm around the outpost and began walking north toward Kuwait.

They quietly talked about the many things military men chat about, when together—women, food, sports, music, past experiences. Sly was not much for prolonged conversation, but he did inject comments when he was asked his opinion or when he had something special to contribute. He had become more talkative since he joined Tatum's squad last year, likely because he felt comfortable with the men and knew Tatum would not compromise his 'personal space.'

Sly's eyes appeared glued to the horizon as he led them along an imaginary straight line over the desert terrain. *I'd be lost in an hour here,* Tatum decided, comforted by having the division's best pathfinder leading this mission.

"Hey, Sly, when you gonna find you an Indian squaw and settle down and have some little braves?" Jones was always needling Sly in a way that would have turned Sly cold if Jones had been a white man. "If you don't get a woman soon, my man, you gonna flat out explode. What you doin', tryin' to be some Indian priest or something?"

Tatum always looked at Sly during these exchanges to see if he could detect any emotion from him, but still found none.

"Jesse," Sly began, "what you don't understand is that Indians are above all those physical needs that drive you mere humans to do what you do. We Indians are like the great eagle, soaring in the sky, watching you do your foolish things."

Jones was never really sure whether Sly was serious or just putting him on, so he pressed a bit.

"You know, man, I've never seen or heard tell of your going out with a woman since you've been with us. Now that ain't healthy, and, it'll screw up your mind not to have a woman every now and then. Everyone needs that, unless you are one of those guys who likes other 'braves' better."

Jones barely had time to start a chuckle and break a smile at his own words, before Sly spun around and in one quick, almost invisible motion, had the sharp tip of his slim commando knife stuck up Jones' large right nostril. Jones stopped dead in his tracks.

Before Tatum could respond, Sly removed the knife, smiled at Jones and said, "I like you, Jesse, but don't talk like that again." He resheathed the knife and picked up his exacting walk as if nothing had happened. Tatum and Jones looked at each other, startled at the quickness of Sly's move and Jones made a mental note not to bring up that subject again. Tatum wondered why the remark had set off Sly so uncharacteristically, suspecting there was something in Sly's past that might have sparked the reaction.

They continued on for another half hour, mostly in relative silence, until Sly stopped short. He asked for Tatum's powerful daytime 50-power binoculars and then surveyed the horizon carefully. Neither of the other two could see a thing.

"We're here," Sly said quietly. They had walked north about five kilometers, and, according to the map, were about two kilometers inside Kuwait. Sly had seen the sun reflect off a moving Iraqi vehicle about a half kilometer away and the binoculars had confirmed a fairly large enemy encampment.

"Let's find the highest sand dune around that gets us closest to them but still has some camouflage possibilities," Tatum ordered. They surveyed the terrain in front of them and picked out several possible sites. They duck walked to each of them, inspected them, looked at the Iraqi camp from each position and chose one. Although not ideal, the small sand rise they had chosen was about six feet high, broad, and L-shaped, giving them protected observation from two sides.

They set about digging a network of four trenches, each about six by three feet long and connected in the middle, so the resultant design resembled an 'X'. The slits were dug about three feet deep and the sand removed formed a third side to the 'L', on the west. All the work was done on the south side of the rise, away from the Iraqis, so they were in defilade and thus not exposed to the enemy.

The men lined their trenches with shelter halves and suspended the sand-colored camouflage netting over the trenches to decrease their chances of detection and to provide some protection from the sun. They stowed their gear in the fourth trench after each had selected one for sleeping and concealment. Rain wasn't too likely this time of the year in the desert so they did not bother with drainage holes. They dug their latrine catholes behind a smaller rise about 50 meters south of the OP.

Tatum scooped out a small trench in the crest of the rise and lined it with a nylon cloth, then set up the high-power observation scope so it did not offer a visible profile. The lenses on all their scopes were non-reflective, an absolutely crucial feature for reconnaissance in the desert sun. Through the scope Tatum could easily inspect the Iraqi camp, noting its size, arrangement and complement. Fortunately, the terrain sloped down toward the Iraqis, leaving the American observers on higher ground.

Tatum took out his squad leader's notebook and painstakingly drew diagrams of the enemy position, marking placement of tanks, fixed artillery pieces, bunkers, and other details. He would brief the company commander in two days and wanted his report to be complete and accurate.

Jones and Rodriguez were resting in their trenches, cleaning their weapons. Sand was a real problem for the M-16's operating mechanism and the weapons had to be cleaned at least once a day. A condom on the end of the muzzle kept sand out of the barrel and they wrapped their rifles in clean t-shirts for additional protection. The .45 pistol was not as easily jammed by sand and a holster was adequate protection.

The men agreed to two-hour watches—the tiresome task of observing through the scope made longer stints counterproductive.

When Tatum's shift was over, he was relieved by Sly, and Tatum backcrawled to his trench. It was time to report to platoon headquarters to detail their position. He took the transceiver from its protective case and extended the flat black antenna to its fullest then laid back in the trench to keep the antenna below the crest.

Turning to the preset frequency, Tatum whispered, "Shepherd One, Shepherd One, this is Sheep One, come in."

Radio transmission was excellent in the desert and the base answered quickly and clearly: "Sheep One, this Shepherd One, we read you five by five, over."

"Shepherd One, we are in position. Prepare to receive coordinates, grid 5 AH37788556. Repeat, grid 5, coordinates AH37788556. Do you copy, over?"

There was a slight pause while the radioman copied down the coordinates on the map and the lieutenant identified the position. "Roger, Sheep One, we have your position. Where is the Wolf, over?"

Tatum had to smile at the Army's not-so-subtle attempts to

conceal the identities of the friendly personnel and the enemy on these missions. *Who thought up the call signs for these transmissions,* he wondered? *Probably the 10-year-old son of some colonel back in the States. They probably paid him a consultant's fee, too.*

"Shepherd One, the Wolf is 500 meters due north. Appears to be all or part of an AD, over." AD meant armored division, full of tanks and mobile artillery.

"Roger, Sheep One. Stay alert for the Wolf. Can fetch you if need be. Any further intel? Over."

"Negative, Shepherd One. Will recontact at next call time. All A-OK. Out here."

Tatum replaced the radio in the cover and stowed it in a large zip-lock plastic bag. *Can't be too careful with this apron string back to momma,* he concluded. *No fun if it gets suddenly hot here, and the damn radio won't work.*

He laid back and tried to get comfortable enough to take a nap, but he was too high from the excitement of setting up this post so close to the enemy. He knew that if they were discovered, they would be shot or taken prisoner. He had heard the Iraqis were experts at terror and torture and he wasn't sure which was worse, to be captured or killed. *The trouble with a mission like this was you had too much time to think about the danger you were in and that began to act on your mind.* His thoughts turned to his family and he decided to write a letter.

Tatum opened his ruck and retrieved another zip-lock - he'd never again take the bags for granted at the grocery store - and took out a writing tablet and pen. Over the next hour, he studiously wrote his wife, carefully working out his thoughts before committing them to paper. Finally, after finishing, he settled back to reread the letter, as he always did, to see if it sounded right.

> *Dear Honey:*
>
> *Nothing much going on here with me. We're just doing some training work to keep busy and keep everyone on their toes. The officers continue to give us plenty of stuff to gripe about, but I guess it could be worse.*
>
> *I really enjoyed getting your last letter - but it took*

almost 4 weeks to get to me. It means a lot to me to hear about what the kids are doing, or saying. I miss you all so much. We're not keeping our minds busy enough, so mine just keeps on thinking about you.

The food is still the same, no change. I think I'm putting on some pounds, but its hard to tell with these loose fitting BDU's. We try to run and do P.T., but it gets so hot during the day we can only do them early in the morning. And these MRE's are just all fat and salt, so I pick out the fruit and crackers and (yes) the fruitcakes and eat them. But I'll keep watching because I know you don't want your baby coming back to you fat!

I've been working recently with Indian Sly and I think he needs to find a woman. Why don't you ask Maria G. if she knows any nice Mex-Amer. girls at Ft. Bragg we could fix him up with. Ok? He's getting too weird by himself.

How are the kids doing in school? You tell them to study hard and learn a lot. I didn't get a chance to go to college but I sure want them to go. I don't care what they make of themselves, but if they go to college, they at least will have a chance. After I retire, I'll get me a job with the post office and we can afford to send them to a good state school like Virginia or N.C. I'll be the proudest father alive if I could see them graduate. Just keep telling them that.

Honey, I know it won't, but if something was to happen to me over here, you've got to help the kids get scholarships or go to West Point or something. We don't have enough insurance to pay their way right now. Don't worry about it, but just think about it. Tell Lucius Jr. to keep practicing his basketball. He's gonna grow up to be a great player someday, I know - maybe even get a college scholarship. Tell Samantha and Jessica to keep looking pretty and to learn how to make my favorite fried chicken and grits for when I come home. And also how to make that sweet potato pie, with whipped cream on top. Man, what I wouldn't give right now to be able to eat a whole pie!!!

Well, hon, I've got to go now. Remember, things are quiet and I'm safe so don't worry about me. I love you and the kids so much.

Love,

Lucius XXOO

He was satisfied with the letter, and had just finished inserting it into the envelope when Sly whispered to him. ''Sarge, come here a minute.'' He put away the baggie and slipped up the rise to where Sly was using the scope. ''I think they're saddling up a patrol of some kind. Look, see here.''

Tatum stretched out on his stomach in the warm sand and looked through the monocular eyepiece. There indeed was activity at the western end of the trench and he could see armored vehicles being lined up and loaded. As he watched, the Iraqi column started moving, and exited the encampment heading southwest. He counted four tanks, eight armored personnel carriers and three trucks.

He pulled his face away from the scope and looked at Sly. The man's face gave no hint of his emotions at all. Tatum wiped the sweat out of his eyes and looked at Sly again.

''Damn, they're headed toward the platoon outpost. We'd better get on the horn!''

* * *

Tex Weatherby was sitting in the operations tent on an old truck seat appropriated from some derelict vehicle earlier in the week. Tex was contemplating the shape of a clear plastic water bottle. *I wonder if they have a machine that blows the shape of the bottle or whether they stretch the plastic over a hot mold? I'll bet they stretch it over the mold like a condom and heat it up 'til it takes the right shape.* He tossed the bottle into an open container. *Man, I've got to do something interesting or I'll go out of my gourd. I'm already thinking about bottle-forming condom machines!*

The squadron had been at the newly created combat (forward) heliport for just one week. The base was about 20 kilometers northeast of Hafar al Batin, in the northern Saudi desert. The field wasn't much to look at - a long helicopter landing strip with a logistics camp next to it, but separated from the field by a sand berm. The camp was guarded by a platoon of MPs and security was tight, so close to the Kuwaiti border. The only redeeming feature of the place was a tent with two refrigerators stocked with cold Cokes! There was also a volleyball net in the sand which helped the aviators work off some restlessness.

Weatherby's main problem was boredom. Since arriving after a short flight from King Kahlid Military City International Airport, his choppers had been undergoing desert conversion, designed to decrease wear and tear from sand and wind. The pilots had not flown in a week, and had not had an exciting flight in a month. All that forbidding, challenging desert was out there, including the potential for a firefight, and here they were, sitting on their butts. He never had liked paperwork, feeling a flight commander should lead by example, not memo.

Weatherby was considering going down to the tent for a cold one when the radio receiver suddenly came alive. The communications specialist on duty quickly put the earphones on and answered the call. He sat up quickly and motioned for the captain to take the headphones.

''Captain Weatherby here, sir,'' Tex said, using the standard address in case a superior officer was calling.

''Captain Weatherby, this is Colonel Smitts.'' Smitts was the lieutenant-colonel who commanded the second battalion of the 2nd Armored Cavalry Regiment.

''Yes, sir, colonel, what can I do for you?'' Weatherby was commander of I Troop and subordinate to Colonel Smitts.

''Tex, we've got a problem to head off. An 82nd Airborne observation post just beyond the Kuwaiti border has reported a small Iraqi armored column moving out and heading south. I don't know whether the Iraqis realize it, but there's a company-sized unit of the 82nd directly in their path. The unit is bivouacked and has no indigenous armored protection nor any transportation capable of evacuating them in time. Division doesn't want to commit artillery and start the war, so they want us to go out and scare them off.

Specifically, I want you to turn them around. Understand so far?''

''Yes sir, I got it,'' replied Tex.

''All right, son, now here are the coordinates.'' He gave the last known position of the column of enemy armor plus the positions of the basecamp and the observation post where Tatum was located. ''Take a small flight of Apaches and -58's and turn 'em around. Do not, I repeat, do not fire upon the Iraqis unless you have to in order to protect the American ground troops. Do not fire on the enemy if they fire on you, just back off and call in. Do you understand?''

''Yes, sir, colonel, I will not fire on the column unless the ground troops are in danger,'' Tex repeated.

''Now, Tex, you're real good, but I don't want any of your tricks that could start this war before we're ready. You got that, captain?'' Smitts was almost shouting now.

''Yes, sir, I'm on my way. I'll call you when we've spotted the column.''

''Good luck, Tex, we're counting on you.'' The colonel hung up. Tex just looked at the phone and then at the radioman. ''Red, get me Jones and Bell and Foxie and Roger, now!'' As the specialist used the compound loud speaker to alert the others, Tex had already left the tent on the run to fetch his flight gear. Enroute to the flight line he met the others and filled them in.

He and Roger would be in one Apache AH-64, while Foxie and his weapons officer would be in the other. Bell and Jones were warrant officer pilots of OH-58 Kiowas, observation helicopters specially fitted with laser range finders and optical target acquisitors. They could lock the laser in on any tanks for the Apache's Hellfire missiles in case a firefight developed.

Tex's adrenaline level was rising exponentially and he had never felt more alive. It took only ten minutes to get the helicopters fired up and cleared for takeoff. Fortunately, the Apaches were already loaded with munitions, because the armorers had had nothing better to do.

The flight took off in formations of two, the Kiowas in the lead; their target acquisition system was more sensitive than the Apaches'. Tex keyed into the flight's assigned frequency for a radio check: ''Red River flight, this is Red River One. Proceed with radio check, over.''

''Red River Two, check.''

"Red River Three, check."

"Red River Four, check, boss, all in."

They flew for just over five minutes when Bell cut in and said, with obvious excitement, "Red River One, have sighted enemy column four klicks ahead." They were just passing over the basecamp coordinates and Tex saw the airborne company formed into a hasty defense around the perimeter of the camp.

Damn, Tex thought to himself, *those boys are done for unless we can turn the injuns around and head 'em back home.* He radioed to the observation helicopter to advance within one kilometer of the enemy column, observe and report.

A minute later, Bell was back on the line. "I count four T-55 tanks, eight BMP's, and one ZSU-23, all on line."

Tex thought quickly. The improved T-55 had a turret-mounted machine gun that could be a problem. The big threat of the BMP infantry vehicle was that it carried the AT-3 Sagger anti-tank missile which could easily take out a helicopter if the gunner was any good at all. But his main concern was the ZSU-23 mobile antiaircraft artillery, which fired a 23mm explosive round. The guns used the principle of scattering many burst of charges at the target to effectively blanket the zone of contact. It was very fast and very deadly. *Well,* Tex thought, *this is just like the setup at the Alamo, except the defenders of the Alamo didn't have Captain Tex Weatherby to come to the rescue. Well, let's do it, no sense waiting.*

Tex radioed Foxie and told him the plan. He could tell Foxie was concerned, but what the hell, something out of the ordinary had to be done.

All those lectures in Soviet tactics might prove useful now, Tex thought. They had been taught that the Iraqis followed Soviet style in placing the commander of a tank column or task force in the lead tank, to demonstrate his courage and leadership. Tex would have crossed his fingers for luck except both hands were busy handling the cyclic and collective, the Apache flight controls.

The Iraqis had approached within a kilometer of the Americans' ground position, making the confrontation between Iraqis and helicopters a giant closeup screen for the paratroopers. All Tex was thinking about was the possibility his plan might fail. If so, his flight was as vulnerable as the American ground troops. Besides, if the ground war started before the Coalition was ready, many servicemen and women would be killed before the tide could be turned.

"All right, Foxie, you take the right, I'll take the left. Let's go. Now!"

The two Apaches swooped in on the enemy column, making a tight turn to approach the lead tank from either side. Before the Iraqis could turn, the two American helicopters had nosed up to each side of the commander's tank, hovering a scant 20 feet from the turret. There were sixteen Hellfire missiles and seventy-six 2.75-inch rockets aimed and locked onto the lead Iraqi tank turret, enough to vaporize the tank and the ground it stood on. Tex flipped on his laser target finder and zeroed in the laser range finder onto the T-55, warning the Iraqi commander he was a dead man if he didn't change his mind.

It was a strange sight for the American paratroopers as they watched the two Apaches sticking their weapons right in the Iraqis' open mouths. Several of the GIs pulled out their cameras and began taking pictures, certain they had Pulitzer Prize material this time.

The second thought in Tex's mind was what the hell was this SOB in the tank going to do? Seconds became minutes. The gunships swayed slightly to stay within 'ground effect' and maintain lift. Sweat dripped from beneath Tex's helmet and behind his aviator sunglasses, stinging his eyes. Regardless, he would not release his gaze from the tank turret.

Very slowly, the turret hatch began to lift. A leather-helmeted head appeared and soon the Iraqi tank commander stood erect in the hatch. He swiveled his head from one helicopter cockpit to the other, then settled on Tex's. He shielded his eyes from the sun better to visualize this crazy American pilot of the daredevil helicopter. He leaned slightly to the right to read the printing on the side of the helicopter 'The Eyes of Texas.' The Iraqi smiled slightly. He himself had a degree in civil engineering from Rice University and had lived in Houston, Texas, for five years.

He knew the Texas college students made some funny motions with their fingers, but couldn't recall them. He had made the decision to halt the column and turn around and now he wished somehow to signal this to the crazy pilot. Then he held up his right hand, made a fist and stuck out the index and little finger, waggling them a bit. Then he touched his helmet in a short salute and disappeared into the tank, closing the hatch behind him.

Almost immediately, the tank began moving in reverse and made a 180º turn, moving back alongside the column, which slowly turned and followed him.

Damn, thought Tex, *that cameljock just insulted me. He gave a University of Texas 'Hook 'em Horns' sign, and me an Aggie. Maybe I'll blast him for good measure.*

After Tex watched the Iraqi column move far to the north, back toward their lines, his helicopters flew slowly back over the paratroopers' camp. Below them, the men were waving their hands in the air, shouting and jumping up and down. *I'll bet those boys want to buy me a beer,* he thought, *if only there was any in this dry hole of a place. Well, there's always Fort Bragg, home of the 82nd. He'd never have to buy his own drinks anywhere on that post again.*

Tex realized he'd better contact the battalion commander before the old man found out about the confrontation from someone in the 82nd.

"Red River One to Red River Leader, Red River One to Red River Leader, over."

The transmission was scratchy and then Tex saw the black clouds coming toward them from the south. *Better get home quick,* he thought, *before the storm arrives first.*

"Red River One, this is Red River Leader, how do you copy?" Colonel Smitts must have been sitting by the radio with the headphones already on.

"Red River Leader, copy fine. The Indians have run back over the river and are headed toward their reservation. No arrows fired. I repeat, no arrows fired. Over."

"Nice job, Tex. Just hurry on back. Weather's getting bad here. Report when you land. Acknowledge. Over."

"Yes, sir. Request cold Cokes be waiting for the red hot cavalry. ETA five. Red River One out."

After a last low level flyby, Tex and his flight left the camp and flew southwest toward their base.

Tex smiled and sighed. The only other time he had felt this good was with some girl named Rosita down in Nuevo Laredo when he was 16. That was his first time, and afterwards he had driven back to Waco with much the same feeling of male power he had at this very moment.

Tatum had received no further radio messages since he had informed the company about the Iraqi column. He didn't know what had happened and was feeling very uncomfortable about the whole situation. Tatum was considering breaking radio silence and calling in to find out what was going on. He had picked up the transceiver and turned it on when Jesse tugged at his boot. Tatum scrambled up the rise and scanned the horizon behind and to the west of them where the column had headed.

Sure enough, it was the Iraqi column! They were back. But what had happened? They had heard no sounds indicating a firefight and they were sure close enough to have heard them. Whatever had happened, the Iraqis were back and headed into their camp.

Damn, I'd give my last grape jelly packet to know what went down.

* * *

The activity in the port of Ad-Damman was as frantic as it was frustrating. Sergeant Gonzales was standing on a pier with several dozen men from his platoon, waiting for any sign of the tanks that had left Germany for this bustling Saudi Arabian port over a month ago. It was damn near January 1991, and still no sign of 3rd Armored's vehicles. Each day for two weeks they had gone out to the dock designated to berth their ship, waited, then gone back to the huge warehouse that was their living quarters. There were over 500 soldiers in the building, all with their cots jammed against one another, so there was no privacy at all.

The latrines were overflowing most of the time and there were warnings about cholera or some other disease caused by poor sanitation. They could only shower quickly in a small amount of cold water once a week, so the men on the dock were all in serious need of a wash. But with all of them stinking, none of them noticed.

Down the dock about 100 yards, Gonzales could see the U.S. Army harbormaster conferring with a small group of Arabs and Americans. There was considerable paper waving, shouting, gesticulating, and a general impression of total frustration. So many ships were being off-loaded in this usually quiet port that the task was barely manageable. General Pagonis, chief logistician for the U.S. Central Command, was doing an amazing job of bringing personnel and materiel to the Persian Gulf, but much of the delay was right in this port. Most of the heavy equipment that couldn't be airlifted had to come by ship and many of those ships were stacked up offshore like dominoes, waiting their turn to off-load.

One of the men with the harbormaster detached himself from the group and walked toward the tankers. They saw he was their battalion supply officer, Major O'Connell. He approached the troopers and Gonzales could see the major's face was red from the constant heat and pouring with sweat. They were all overheated.

"All right, Sergeant, we're finally going to get some tanks today." Major O'Connell took off his helmet and wiped his face with a dirty rag, then wiped his glasses with it. *I don't know how he can see through those glasses,* Gonzales thought, *but then maybe he really doesn't want to see things clearly. Might make him more upset.*

He pointed to the aft hold of the large cargo ship at the pier. "The first platoon's tanks will be off-loaded from there, about one every two hours. That way, you and your men can get 'em running and move 'em over to the secure area I showed you last week. They'll work continuously until this ship's empty, so I suggest you work out a shift schedule for your drivers and maintenance troops. Unless something happens, I figure we'll have all our tanks off in about four days. Lieutenant Barnes will be my man covering your paperwork, so you have to get with him before you can receive the tanks. Any questions?"

"Sir, have these guys on this ship ever off-loaded tanks? What I mean is, do they know how to sling and suspend them, let alone lower them on to the deck?" Gonzales was concerned about the safety of his men, since he had noticed some of most disreputable-looking crewmen on that ship's deck. "I don't know where those guys up there are from, but they don't look any too smart to me."

"Don't worry, Gonzales, they got the tanks onto the ship in Hamburg, so I guess they can get them off again here." But the major looked concerned, too, only he knew they had no other options.

"All right, sir, we're ready. Let's just get this show on the road. I never liked the smell of a harbor, so I wanna get outa here as soon as we can." After the major left, Gonzales gathered his men around him and divided up the work parties. They'd recruit others from the warehouse later.

Soon, several workers with hard hats appeared on the starboard stern of the ship. It was hard to figure their nationality, but Gonzales guessed maybe the Pacific Islands. They gestured to him and then to the operator of the huge crane amidships.

A 20 x 20-foot space had been outlined in yellow tape on the dock, the receiving area for the tanks. The plan was simple as explained by Major O'Connell—the crane operator would lift a tank from the hold of the ship, swing it slowly over the side and lower it, according to hand signals from Gonzales, onto the designated spot. The men would stand outside the area, and wait until the tank was safely on the dock before moving in, disconnecting the lifting chains and readying the vehicle for movement to the 3rd AD motor pool. While they were finishing, the ship workers would sling another tank down in the hold.

Each tank had built in hooking points on the hull so it was a fairly straightforward job to pick it up and haul it out of the hold. The real skill was in swinging the behemoth over the ship's side and on to the dock without losing control of it. That task demanded an experienced crane operator and Gonzales hoped they had one today.

The Abrams M1A1 main battle tank is the most advanced tank in U.S. service, possibly in the world. With a mesh of ultra-hard depleted uranium in its armor, the M1A1 weighs 65 tons, about the same as a small house. Its weight gives the tank a tremendous inertia that must be overcome when passively moving the tank, and once in motion, the momentum generated can be significant.

Gonzales had served with the 1st Cavalry in Vietnam, commanding an M-551 Sheridan. He had personally supervised his tank's movement by cranes and helicopters in the past and knew well the universal language of hand signals, which he felt every crane operator would know, too. Gonzales hadn't spent much time around the ocean growing up in El Paso, and he didn't like it. Even the big ship at the dock had a constant motion that made the sergeant feel a little queasy. Looking up at the crane, Gonzales could sense distinctly the relative motion between the ship and the dock.

Almost without warning, the first of the huge tanks appeared, rising quickly out of the ship's hold. *It's coming up pretty fast. I'll bet those bastards are under orders to unload this ship as soon as possible, and get it out of the harbor. Only you can't rush a good meal, a good woman, or unloading a tank. I'd better not get to thinking about the first two or I won't be able to concentrate on number three.*

As the tank moved laterally over the side of the ship, it was still traveling fairly fast, but not dangerously. Gonzales raised his hands over his head and began signaling the operator to move the tank toward him and his men. He had stationed them in a perimeter around the landing spot, but well back from it. They had all the tools, fuel, and the equipment needed to get the big tank fired up and moving.

When the tank was about 50 feet above the dock and moving toward its resting space, Gonzales signaled the operator to move the tank forward more slowly, but there was no change in its speed. Just as the tank was about five feet from the dock, the operator seemed to become aware the tank was moving too fast to land on the drop zone, so he stopped the crane's motion abruptly.

What happened next seemed to Gonzales to take place in ultra slow motion, although it was only a few too-brief seconds. The heavy tank's momentum carried it in an arc across the far end of the drop zone on the dock where it slammed into two of Gonzales' men who were not paying attention as they should. Instead, they were yakking about a female sailor they'd spotted further down on the dock. The bottom of the treads on the left side of the tank whammed both men across the back, hurling them across the concrete dock like bowling pins. Almost at once, the pendulum effect of the long crane line began to move the tank back toward the opposite side of the drop area, where two of Gonzales' men stood frozen by panic. Their mouths were wide open either in a scream after seeing their friends hit, or in utter incomprehension at what was about to happen.

Gonzales saw the whole incident unfolding before his eyes. Faster and faster, the M1 was arcing toward the other two men, chest high, and they could not move. Without hesitating, Gonzales galloped toward the men, placing himself directly in the path of the tank as it swung toward the ship. The rest of his men, not in the direct path of the tank, were scattering, looking back to see what would happen to the three in harm's way.

Gonzales tackled both men high and from behind. His old

football coach at St. Pius Catholic in El Paso, where he was linebacker on the Texas 5-A championship team, would have been proud of him. He knocked both men on to the dock face down, and dropped on top of them. With his eyes closed, and saying a quick prayer to himself, he drew the men closer under him. Suddenly he felt the tank pass over them, only inches away. Then he felt the thunderous earthquake vibration as the tank dropped onto the dock.

After a few moments of total silence, while Gonzales was certain his heart had stopped, pandemonium erupted. The team rushed to pick up Gonzales and the men he had just saved. His knees felt like putty, but, after shaking his head a few times, and taking a few breaths, Gonzales felt he was coming back to his senses. He was standing, facing the tank that had landed less than three feet from him and his two men.

Suddenly, remembering the first two men who had been hit, Gonzales turned and ran back to where a crowd had gathered. Several medics had already shown up from somewhere probably from the adjacent warehouse barracks. The medics had knelt beside the men, who were not moving. Gonzales pushed through the crowd to the fallen men. One was Thomas, a new kid from somewhere in Jersey, the other was Cortez, the loud-mouth from Spanish Harlem. The sergeant sank to his knees next to Cortez's body and glanced over at the medic, who was tucking his stethoscope back into a nylon field medical kit.

The medic just shook his head. "Sorry Sarge, they're both dead. Either the tank broke their necks or gave 'em some sort of closed head injury. Whatever, they're gone."

The medic looked genuinely sorry and Gonzales started to feel a lump rise in his throat. *How many times did I see friends and acquaintances lying on the ground somewhere in Vietnam and have a medic shake his head and start to repack his gear? These two kids had their whole lives ahead of them, for Christ's sake! They didn't deserve to die like this. And the damn war ain't even started yet.*

A flood of feelings jarred Gonzales - anger, sorrow, guilt. Vaguely, he heard an army ambulance siren and watched dejectedly while the attendants loaded the bodies on litters and moved them into the vehicle. Slowly, Gonzales turned and began to walk away when he became aware of two men striding next to him. They were Donnell and Smith, the two whose lives he had saved with his quick action. Both were married and had families. Gonzales had seen their children at platoon picnics and get-togethers and he remembered what good fathers they were. *The Lord works in mysterious ways.* He slung an arm over the shoulders of each and looked them in the eyes. Neither had ever seen Sergeant Gonzales cry.

CHAPTER THREE

ORDERS HAD BEEN issued to insert Lieutenant Porter's Special Forces A team into southern Iraq as close to its final destination as possible to minimize travel time across the desert. The Iraqi resistance movement was supposed to set up a clandestine drop zone 10 kilometers southeast of Jalibah, near the Euphrates River. By late December, the Iraqis had positioned a Republican Guard corps near Az Zubayr, just north of Kuwait. This Republican Guard unit had been targeted for intelligence gathering and target preparation by Porter's team. His would not be the only Special Forces team in the area, but if all went well, Porter's outfit could provide adequate reconnaissance for the Coalition forces without having to contact any other teams.

There was no moon at 0300, when the team exited the special C-130 Hercules in a HAHO (high altitude, high opening) jump. The air was bitter cold over the desert at 25,000 feet and Porter was thankful for the Gore-Tex insulated underwear beneath his desert fatigues and mostly for his multilayered, woven polypropylene jump suit. The team exited in a tight group, sticking close together after their chutes opened. The parachutes were special black nylon rectangular models that were highly maneuverable, using the same design for maximum lift as the wings of a hang glider.

The Green Berets were drifting through the air in a staggered sequence, with each jumper about 50 meters above and behind the one in front, so they could maintain contact without encroaching on each other's thermals. The first man in the long, stair-stepping line was Porter, who had a special HUD (heads-up display) inside his helmet visor, reporting various factors in the descent - altitude, forward air speed, air temperature. Porter's oxygen mask was connected behind his reserve chute to a small bottle with enough oxygen for a 15 minute drop. No more was needed because the critical oxygen area was only between 10- and 25,000-feet, where oxygen is insufficient. Each man had strapped on as much gear as he could, although an aircraft had also dropped a load of supplies close to the drop zone the previous night. If the Iraqi resistance had vehicles, the supplies could be found by homing on a radio beacon in the supplies.

Porter was navigating toward his drop zone using the latest model airborne laptop terrain and guidance computer, a Pathfinder III. The unit was attached with special velcro tabs to the top of Porter's reserve chute. The Pathfinder displayed a map of southern Iraq, specifically the 50-kilometer area surrounding their jump pattern. Iraqi resistance agents had been provided with a special radio-frequency transmitter whose signal was received by the Pathfinder and displayed on the computer's map as the target area. The jumpers' precise position was programmed at the time of the jump and Porter could see their flight path toward the target area displayed on the screen. Porter always thought the little computer resembled a flight simulator in some video arcade, but was grateful for the technology that let them exit the C-130 25-30 kilometers from their target and glide undetected onto the DZ.

Porter made a minor adjustment to their descent path as the computer suggested they had drifted to one side of the prescribed course. Their descent would take about 10 minutes, but it always seemed shorter when you were enjoying the ride.

The men above and behind Lt. Porter kept the pattern tight by following fluorescent tabs on the back of the jump helmet in front of him. The tabs were too faint to be seen from the ground. Quickly, Porter checked to make sure the column was intact and in place. It was. Each jumper had a short wave intercom in his helmet and mask that could be used to cover changes in plans, orders or just to keep track of each member.

The radio signal from the Iraqi resistance agents at the drop site had a preset frequency coded into the Pathfinder, which would not display the flight path if the transmitter had not been genuine. That factor gave Porter some comfort, although he was aware the transmitter could have fallen into the wrong hands, or the resistance agents might have been compromised. There was a chance his Special Forces team would be greeted by elements of the Republican Guard. If that happened, they would be defenseless, arriving in a drop zone with enemy soldiers already in place. There could be a slaughter, Porter realized, but he pushed the thought from his mind. There was nothing more he could do now.

Viewed from low altitude, the desert resembled an ocean. There were no significant features and the terrain was generally level. The Iraqi military seemed to be practicing good light discipline, because Porter could not detect any lights disclosing enemy positions. In fact, the only lights were from the city of Jalibah, to their left. Some road traffic could be seen near that city, but it was impossible to tell whether it was military or civilian. Both probably, Porter decided, since men and supplies were likely still being moved into position.

The air had an almost eerie quality to it. There was almost no noise save for the faint swish of the parachutes passing through the still night sky. The men knew better than to cough or clear a throat; they could be passing over an enemy troop position.

They had glided about 20 miles horizontally when the Pathfinder indicated with a silent display that they were within range of the visual strobe at the landing site. The strobe had a faint pulsing red light that would not adversely affect their night vision, but needed a specially adapted night-vision goggle to spot it. Porter moved his right hand from the parachute's toggle line and pulled down the goggles from their position against the top of his jump helmet. He flicked the power switch from 'Standby' to 'On' and watched surreal images of the desert begin to appear. Suddenly, as if a curtain had been drawn, the desert became clearly recognizable, with dunes and rises, rock formations and small shrubs. Roads, both formal and random, were visible on the sand.

Porter scanned the desert five miles ahead along the heading the Pathfinder indicated was correct, and thought he saw a faint pulsing light. As they glided closer, he could distinguish a flat area next to a gentle slope and a rock outcropping. The strobe was within the rocks to shield it from the north and east in case an Iraqi patrol was driving across the desert. Parked close in against the slope was a vehicle of some sort and Porter could make out several armed men in Arab robes standing between the truck and the strobe.

Not intending to glide directly into the drop zone from their flight path, he keyed his mask intercom and whispered, "three men and truck at drop zone, two klicks ahead. Let's do a 360º right wheelie and check it out. Stagger the drop toward the south. I'll come in first at the truck."

Porter pulled on the right-hand toggle on his parachute and

spilled some air creating a descending turn to the right. His plan was to circle slowly around the drop zone, still undetected by the men below, and recon for any trouble surprises. He could still see the men near the truck, and noted with satisfaction that none was smoking. The flare of a match can be seen for miles at night and it quickly reduces the smoker's night vision for several minutes. *Besides, it's not good for your health.*

Porter smiled at the thought of the current female Surgeon General trying to convince soldiers in a war-time setting not to smoke so they wouldn't get lung cancer or emphysema. *A bullet in the lung will do you in a lot faster*, Porter thought, scanning the terrain near the drop zone for threats.

As the drop passed east of the welcoming committee, Porter pulled a slow curve to the south, behind the dune. If he had noticed any abnormality at the DZ, the men would have landed to the north and slipped quietly off in the dark, leaving the waiting party to figure they simply had not jumped at all. Then Porter would have radioed his concerns to CENTCOM, who would have reevaluated the Iraqi resistance movement for reliability—at least Porter hoped it would work that way. You never knew when someone in a higher headquarters would simply turn off their brains and let vital information wither on the vine.

Porter began to complete his full circle turn to land in the cleared area just south of the strobe. The other team members would land in a staggered line to the southwest to provide fire cover and support in case of an ambush. He pulled the cord of his attached rucksack and felt the tug as it dropped on the line below him.

In a virtually silent landing, Porter pulled his toggle cords completely down to his thighs and made a soft jogging landing. *Not a bit like the parachute landing fall of earlier days, where all of this expensive and vital equipment I've got strapped to my body could have been damaged. And me, with it.*

Still loping easily, Porter popped the quick-release buckle on his harness and shrugged out of it. Quickly, he gathered the parachute in his arms and laid it on the ground with the harness on top to keep the nylon from billowing. He unslung the CAR-15 from his back and dropped to one knee. Porter looked around, noting their landings and the silent deployment of his men into a defensive line. They all remained still, trying to get a sense of the situation, yet ready to respond to any threat.

There was a light wind from the north and Porter could detect a faint odor of Arab body sweat. He had always had a keen sense of smell, better than normal eyesight and hearing, and he often used one sense to supplement the others. When quail hunting in Georgia as a youth, he would often go out by himself, with no dog, finding he could actually follow his sense of smell to the quail, just like a hound. He never told anyone about that skill, figuring no one would believe him, but the keen sense had helped him in enough other situations he had come to rely upon it as another edge in his reconnaissance bag of tricks.

From their "aroma," Porter could tell the men by the vehicle were Arabs and he sensed no fear in their body smell. He knew there were recognizable body scents for each ethnic group, probably related to their diets and the biochemical composition of their sweat. Porter often thought his primitive skill had been regressed in most individuals while humans developed in sophistication from caveman days. Maybe because he came from a long line of 'warriors,' the primitive skills had remained. Silently, he vowed to ask his father, Major General Nathan Hale Porter (Retired), if he also possessed special senses and if they had helped him during combat. *If I'm wrong, all he can do is give me one of these famous Porter 'frowns' and wonder where and when I lost a couple of my marbles.*

The lieutenant shook his head imagining such an interchange, then brought his full attention back to the moment. *Well, nothing here gives me a bad gut feeling.* He had taken off his jump helmet and mask and dumped his ruck. He could just make out the team sergeant approaching in a low crawl, and when he arrived, they knelt close together. With hand signals, Porter instructed the team sergeant to send out two men on each flank to make a wide sweep of the entire area, about 200 meters out from the vehicle and the Arabs. Master Sergeant Lopez scurried off to pass the order and they waited another 10 minutes until the four men returned. When the intelligence NCO indicated 'all clear,' the men waited for the lieutenant's next order.

Porter chose a horseshoe-shaped advance, so each man could cover 180º with overlapping fire. Once his troops were in position, Porter and the intelligence NCO, Sergeant John Purcell, advanced slowly toward the rear of the truck, checking behind the tarp over the cargo bed. Satisfied there was no threat, the team moved toward the three Arabs from behind.

The Arabs were crouched on their haunches in the sand, waiting quietly for the team to land. Porter and the sergeant drew their Beretta 9 mm automatics and unsheathed their KaBars.

Silently, they crept toward the Arabs until each was able to place the barrel of his handgun at the back of the neck of the two closest men. To their credit, the Iraqis neither started nor spoke. The third Arab, turning his head, saw the Americans for the first time, and, understanding what had occurred, smiled broadly.

''Ah, welcome, Lieutenant Porter,'' he said in perfect British English. ''We thought you had decided not to arrive at our party.'' His smiling white teeth looked like the white keys on a piano.

Porter spoke the password, ''Miami.''

''Hurricanes,'' the Arab countered correctly, most likely not understanding his response represented one of America's top college football teams in 1990. Probably one of the CENTCOM intelligence staff's alma mater, thus securing for the university a wee niche in the history of the Persian Gulf War.

Porter relaxed, taking his gun away from the back of the second Arab's head, but not yet holstering it. The combat knife was out of sight, but not out of action.

''Please allow me to introduce myself. I am Hussein, one of the few chosen to help you on your dangerous journey in this perilous time.''

Give me a break, Porter thought. *Is everyone in this frigging country named Hussein? Aren't there any guys named Abdul?*

''And these are my men, Abdul and Hussein.''

Well, what do you know, two Husseins and an Abdul, Porter mused. *This might make a great story someday back at Bragg.*

''They are my cousins and can be trusted completely.''

''I'm sorry, Hussein, old buddy, but I don't trust anyone but my own men. You have to prove to me first that you are trustworthy,'' Porter declared. ''Now, tell me what you are planning to do next so I can think about it.''

''Lieutenant, my orders are specific. I am to drive you to the sector assigned to you for your surveillance of the Republican Guard and to provide you with the supplies previously dropped by your aircraft. After I have deposited you safely in your area of operations, I will leave you alone and we will not be in contact again. Is that not how you also understand my role?''

Porter thought for a moment. This Arab was obviously the man he was expecting to meet and the plan was consistent with his briefing by the S-2 of the U.S. Special Operations Command last week. *Is there a flaw, a weakness, a threat here with this man? If there is, I sure don't see it or sense it.* Having made up his mind, Porter extended his right hand and shook the Arab's, which reminded Porter that, being left-handed, he would have to be careful what he did with his left hand around the Arabs. They consider the left hand 'unclean' because of its use in cleansing after bodily functions. Porter had pondered amusedly for several months whether there were any left-handed Arabs or if they were all terminated when their disgusting tendencies became apparent. He doubted he could ask any Arab for the answer to that one.

He turned to Purcell. ''Sergeant, bring the men in and check out that truck real well. If we ride in it, I don't want it blowing up on us.'' Purcell disappeared into the night, quickly returning with the rest of the team. While his team was preparing for the ride across the desert and stowing their parachutes and jump gear, Porter walked to the top of the sand rise and removed a black case from his ruck.

About the size of a portable phone, the Magellan NAV 100 MGPS receiver was a reconnaissance officer's dream. The hand-held device provided navigation and positioning capabilities using satellites to fix the user's position and could give one-second updates on the user's continuous position, navigation and velocity. Using its unit-to-unit downlink, the device had been programmed before the jump insertion with the data critical to his team's mission. Porter was fully synchronized with the Air Force and Navy in time and space and could radio intelligence data with calculations of target positions. The Magellan would provide targets of opportunity for bombs and missiles as close as 15 meters of averaged position accuracy. The unit was shockproof and waterproof (not usually much of a problem in the desert) and operated on special ni-cad batteries.

All special operations teams currently or soon to be operating out of Iraq were under operational control of the 18th Airborne Corps, whose area of operation (AO) was southern Iraq. To generate the data they needed to undertake insertion of these teams near the designated enemy targets, the corps utilized the

LANDSAT and SPOT multi-spectral imagery (MSI) integrated from these satellites to provide intelligence. Updates on targets for Lt. Porter's team would be relayed by satellite to his small, lightweight ground receiver (SLGR) or directly by Porter's team using the WRAASE weather receiver—a small, portable one-meter dish that picked up data from US, European and Japanese geostationary orbit satellites, the U.S. TIROS, and the Soviet METEOR satellites. The WRAASE image resolution was excellent within to 2 to 5 kilometers.

A terrain analysis had been conducted on the desert regions near the targets of Porter's reconnaissance and a base-camp area was selected. The area had an unusually large outcropping of boulders surrounding a central excavated area. The military geophysicists had surmised that it was the site of an ancient meteorite impact, but it all looked fairly innocuous from ground level. However, the site would provide cover, shelter and a unidirectional saucer-like platform for reporting, with rapid-signal burst transmissions. If enemy patrols should stumble onto the camp, its built-up walls would offer an effective defense, at least temporarily

Porter stood on the crest of the dune, flipped up the short, rectangular antenna and powered up the Magellan. In less than five seconds, the coordinates of their present location were displayed in the MGRS, followed by the heading and distance to the base camp. As they moved in on the site, the unit would recompute and display the heading and distance every second.

Geez, I feel like a kid in a video arcade, Porter grinned. *This technology is fine, but I'm glad I still know how to use the old iron compass, in case this thing goes dead or develops a glitch.* He walked back down the dune toward the truck, viewing with admiration the changing display on the Magellan. Both Husseins were already in the front seat and Porter crowded his lanky frame in with them. The aroma in the cab was pungent. Porter figured it was a combination of sweat, the heat, not having bathed very often, bad breath, and curdled goat's milk.

Porter pointed due east. ''Drive that way for about a kilometer until we can sort out the heading from this device.'' He held up the Magellan for Hussein number one to see, but not to touch. He admired the instrument and flashed his keyboard smile. On closer observation, Porter noted Hussein was a man of some bearing, with distinguished features and intelligent, penetrating eyes.

"I was a professor of economics at the university in Baghdad," Hussein explained, perhaps sensing Porter's curiosity. "My family was prominent and wealthy, so I was educated at Cambridge in England. A teaching post awaited me at the university here and I became dedicated to my students. However, my theories on economic stability for Iraq were threatening to President Saddam, so I was told to keep silent. I could not, and in retaliation, they came one night and killed my father and my two brothers, all successful businessmen."

Hussein looked at Porter with a cold, deadly passion. "I moved my family to a desert community not far from here and dedicated my life to ridding our country and the world of that piece of camel dung." He spit on the floor of the truck at these last words, narrowly missing the lieutenant's special reverse-skin cowhide desert jump boots.

"My people in this effort are very dedicated and are also willing to give their lives for the cause. Until our country is free, we will never rest. While you are out here in the desert, spying upon Saddam's Republican Guard, we will be watching over you. You will not always see us, but we will be there. Perhaps someday we may repay your helping us."

Porter nodded and looked out toward the desert. *How could he possibly understand what this man had been through?* His own father had lived a distinguished military career, as had his father and grandfather before him. All had been flag rank (one admiral and two generals) and all had distinguished themselves on the battlefield yes, even the Civil War counted. Major General Nathan Porter (Ret.) was now commandant of the Georgia Military Institute at Milledgeville, having retired from active duty as commander of the First Infantry Division (The Big Red One) at Fort Riley, Kansas. Porter had been a cadet at West Point at the time, and was allowed to attend the retirement ceremony in Kansas by the commandant of the military academy, Major General Thomas Swafford, an old buddy of this father's. As the young cadet had stood on the platform with his father and mother, he shared their remorse that his only brother, John Pershing Porter, was missing from the party. He had been killed in action in 1969 while leading a patrol of 101st Airborne (Air Assault) troopers in

Vietnam.

General Porter had always assumed John would be the outstanding military officer of his generation and was devastated when John was killed. The general had never really paid much attention to Scott, probably thinking of him as subordinate to John. But, with his brother's death, suddenly Scott was thrust into his brother's footsteps and success was expected. No, not expected—demanded.

Ever since he was a kid, Scott had tried to make his father proud of him. He excelled at sports and academics in high school and won an appointment to West Point on his own, without his father's influence. At West Point he had been on the track team and played baseball (his favorite sport), graduating 15th in his class of over 500 with a degree in mechanical engineering. Lieutenant Porter had gone on to jump school and Ranger School at Ft. Benning and was assigned as a platoon leader in the 504th of the 82nd Airborne. Three years later, he volunteered for Special Forces and lived through its grueling six-month course.

Assigned to the 7th Special Forces Group as an assistant team leader, he had participated in combat operations along the Honduras-Nicaragua border with the Contras, and in Operation Just Cause in Panama. After Panama, Porter got his own A team, was reassigned to the 10th Special Forces Group, and sent to Germany. The area of operations for the 1st Battalion of the 10th SF was the Middle East, and that duty led Porter to the Persian Gulf and this chunk of desert where he found himself sharing the front seat of a beat up truck with two Iraqi resistance agents.

Just how much more do I have to prove to my father? Porter wondered, *to make him see I am not my brother, but am equally as good a soldier and a man as John was. How much more?*

Porter turned his thoughts back to the Magellan and he gave Hussein number two, the driver, a new heading. Hussein seemed to have no fear of the desert terrain, even though he was traveling across darkened ground without lights. Porter expected them to crash off a dune at any time, ending their mission right then and there. These Arabs did all kinds of crazy things in the name of Allah—'*In Shallah* - as Allah wills it,' which must be similar to the American phrase "whatever happens, happens." Porter never believed that, though. *The poor guys in back,* Porter realized, *must be getting shook up pretty badly. But they won't complain. They'd rather suck raw eggs than tell me they were uncomfortable.*

After more than two hours, the truck was approaching the site proposed for their base camp. It was still quite dark, because the moon was new and sunrise was a few hours off. Porter told Hussein to stop the truck within 100 meters of the site indicated by the Magellan, then he stepped onto the sand. He pulled his night-vision goggles out of his rucksack and strapped them on. As he approached the depression, it began to take on the characteristics he recognized from the satellite photos.

The depression was large, about 50 meters across, with a natural perimeter of boulders nearly five feet high. On the south side, a narrow cut provided an entrance through the boulders into the central crater. There was a gentle downslope to the west, which could be excavated further to provide for drainage during frequent winter thunderstorms. The sand was soft near the perimeter, and observation posts as well as personal sleeping holes could be dug with plenty of concealment and protection from the elements. The only problem Porter could think of was how and where to build a latrine, but he'd figure that out later. Meanwhile, they could dig catholes away from camp.

Satisfied, Porter returned to the truck and told the men to unload the equipment and supplies and to set up camp inside the crater. Tonight, they would get some rest in their sleeping bags, and then begin in the morning to make this crater a habitable, if not exactly comfortable, base camp for their reconnaissance missions.

Porter went over to where Hussein was boiling water in a makeshift stove he retrieved from inside the truck. He knew Arabs loved their coffee and would go to great lengths to make it fresh, no matter where they found themselves.

''Hussein, thank you for bringing us here safely,'' Porter said, shaking the man's hand one last time. ''This is a fine place for us and we can do some good intelligence work out of here. We'll have supplies randomly air-dropped from different directions so as not to arouse suspicion about this area. If something important comes up, you know where to find us, but I'd just as soon you did not lead the whole Iraqi army to where we are, if you do not mind.'' Porter smiled at Hussein after the last sentence, to indicate his remark should be taken somewhat in jest - but not totally.

''Lieutenant Porter, you surely will see us again, but I know not when. You see, we are your guardians and we have a responsibility to look after you.'' Hussein bowed slightly.

''We can look after ourselves all right, thank you,'' Porter replied somewhat curtly. *I sure don't need some economics prof to watch my ass,* he grumbled.

When Hussein merely smiled, Porter walked back in to the crater to join his men as they settled in. *Would he ever need Hussein's help?* Porter shook his head. *No way, man.*

* * *

Neel was in a snoringly deep sleep in the aircraft over the Mediterranean when he was jostled awake by his seatmate leaning over to look out the window.

''Look at that, would ya?'' said the beefy captain with the beady eyes and bulbous nose who had insisted on either talking or eating during the entire flight.

Neel shook his head and blinked his eyes several times to clear the fog from his head. He put on his glasses and moved his face flush with the plane window. To the port side of the aircraft were two fighters, obviously escorting. Neel had always loved military planes, occasionally even wishing he had been born with better eyesight so he could have flown. For entertainment he often read *Janes' Fighting Aircraft of the World.* It was a far cry from his medical books, but it also was a wonderful diversion. He recognized the jets as U.S. Navy F-14 Tomcat interceptors, probably off an aircraft carrier somewhere in the Med.

''Why do ya suppose they're here?'' the fat captain asked, munching what must have been his five hundredth M&M.

''Well, we're probably getting close to the Arabian peninsula,'' Neel said, ''and I guess they're playing it safe. Wouldn't look too good for the U.S. to lose an aircraft full of military personnel, especially reservists, to the Iraqis so easily. I don't think the Iraqis would fly this far out, but they might. Also, I'll bet they want to make sure no friendly unit gets nervous and nails us with a missile, thinking we're the enemy. They do some pretty crazy things over here without thinking, then worry about it later.''

The pudgy captain nodded, apparently satisfied by Neel's reply. He took one last look at the jets, then settled back to give his undivided attention to his chocolate.

Neel was fascinated by the fighters. He could almost make out the two crew members in the cockpit of the nearer Tomcat. He figured their combat ops radius was about 500 nautical miles, so their aircraft carrier was probably somewhere between Cyprus and Israel.

Back in his pre-medicine days, Neel had been given a TOP SECRET security clearance to participate in some clandestine missions with a Navy SEAL unit. One of the missions was staged off the U.S.S. Theodore Roosevelt in the Pacific. He recalled his amazement and awe as he had watched the Tomcats catapult off the deck of the nuclear carrier. The F-14 had become operational in 1974, and Neel was on the Roosevelt in 1978, but the memory came back as if it were yesterday. He could remember the anticipation of the catapult crew as the aircraft was readied, and the almost orgasmic release as the fighter was suddenly hurled along the deck of the ship in the blink of an eye. He had wondered if sex was ever a come-down for the carrier-based jet-jockey.

Suddenly, for the first time, as Neel watched the escort aircraft maintain their precision formation with the jetliner, he realized he was actually entering a war zone. All the way through mobilization, training and deployment, he understood in his brain what was happening without truly believing it. But here, with these heavily armed war planes underscoring the situation, his gut began to twist with the stark revelation that he was going to war, as millions of American men had before him, and perhaps not coming back.

Sure, he had been on dangerous missions before, but then he was single, without a real care except for his mother and sisters back in Missouri. Now, he was a responsible physician, with critical skills that could save lives, married to a wonderful woman who was about to make him a father for the first time. He had a job, a mortgage, a retirement plan, and a future. And he might be killed over here. *There have been physicians killed in every war we've fought,* be said to himself, *and they weren't even fighting the enemy. They were only trying to be doctors.*

Neel loved the U.S. and had enthusiastically taken his oath many years ago when he was first commissioned to defend and protect her. After graduation from college, he had been a dedicated officer, but now, he was a reserve officer, and somewhere along the line, he had lost the expectation that he might just have to give his life for his country. Neel knew he had been softened somewhat during medical school and residency and had lost (or nearly so) his warrior instinct. *My father must have had it, hadn't he? At least before he was killed. Will I leave my not-yet-born child fatherless, as my father did to me? God, I don't want that to happen.*

Neel was deep in introspection and beginning to feel depressed when the plane began its descent to the Saudi airport. When they landed and as they taxied across the field, Neel saw an amazing number of military aircraft all types fighters, bombers, attack helicopters, Blackhawks, Hueys, Chinooks. They seemed to go on as far as he could see. Never had he seen such a vast collection of air power. *We're really serious about this,* he thought, gathering his gear.

Neel's first impression of Saudi Arabia was heat and wind. There must have been some rain, too, because there were puddles on the runway and the adjacent tarmac. *Funny, I always thought it never rained in the desert. Guess I've got a lot to learn.*

The men and women of the units that arrived in the jetliner were marched unceremoniously across muddy ground to a large tent for in-processing. After the continuous meals that had been served since leaving Wisconsin, most of the passengers weren't particularly hungry. However, it became obvious that with the heat of the region, they'd all have to increase their water intake. Few of them had bothered to fill a canteen on the aircraft, or even in Germany where bottled water was available, so there was some relief when a truckload of quart-sized bottled water appeared.

Neel was pouring a bottle into the canteen on his LBE (load-bearing equipment-harness) when he noticed a commotion at the far end of the tent. Curious, he wandered over and stood to the side, observing. A woman soldier who was having difficulty breathing was being examined by a young medic listening to her chest that was covered by a brown, GI-issue T-shirt.

When the medic looked up concerned, he spotted Neel, recognizing him as the physician he had seen at Fort McCoy. Quickly, Anders left the soldier's side and moved the few feet to Neel.

''Sir, could you take a look at this private, please?''

''Tell me what's happening with her, uh, Specialist Anders,'' Neel said as he tilted his head to the left so he could read Anders' name tag.

''Well, sir, she has a history of allergies and asthma, but was cleared to deploy from Fort McCoy. She started noticing some mild coughing and shortness of breath when she was on the airplane, but slept off and on and really did all right. It was when we marched into the tent here and everyone started walking around kicking up the dust that she started a coughing fit and now she just can't stop.''

Neel looked over Anders' shoulder. The soldier was sitting on a pile of duffel bags, leaning forward, with her mouth pursed into an 'O,' taking long, deep breaths. At the end of each inspiration she would start a spell of coughing until finally she had to take another long, slow breath. She appeared restless and anxious, and her friends were solicitous and sympathetic.

''Does she have any known drug allergies, Anders?''

''No, sir, none. She did come down with a URI when she was at McCoy just before we deployed.'' URI meant 'upper respiratory infection' and was common in the drafty damp barracks, barely heated by the ancient coal furnaces.

''All right, Anders let's both have a look at her.'' Neel moved to the young woman's side.

''What's your first name, Private McCaffrey?'' Neel asked.

McCaffrey looked at Neel, then at his rank and medical corps insignia. ''Char-,'' she struggled, ''Charlene,'' the last syllable drawn out into a wheeze, followed by another fit of coughing.

''Okay, Charlene, I'm Doctor Neel. I think I know what's happening with you and I'll take care of it as soon as I can listen to your chest and look you over.'' Neel smiled his boyish smile, quickly transforming him from 'Major' Neel to 'Doctor' Neel.

He picked up the sick woman's hand and counted her pulse for 15 seconds, then multiplied by four to determine her heart rate. *One fifty-six per minute. Definitely tachycardiac.* He observed her for a long moment, noticing her slightly cyanotic lips and nail-beds, her warm, clammy, almost sweaty skin, and her restlessness. He counted her respirations at ten a minute—definitely not an easy task for her, because of the coughing spells. There was an audible wheeze as she exhaled.

Neel picked up Anders' stethoscope (his was still in his kit bag) and listened to Charlene's back, first to the lower lung fields, then to the upper ones, going from left to right to compare the sounds. *End-expiratory wheezes on both sides, and definitely* worse *at the bases.* Then he listened to the woman's heart, found it still beating rapidly, but not irregularly and there were no abnormal sounds. He rose from his kneeling position and handed Anders the stethoscope.

Holding on to Anders' shoulder, Neel gently guided him to one side so they could discuss the situation quietly, where the woman couldn't overhear them.

''Okay, hotshot, what's wrong with her.''

Startled by Neel's tone, Anders looked up at him aghast. ''You, you want me to tell you what's wrong with her? But you're the d-doctor,'' Anders stuttered uncertainly.

''I know I'm the doctor, Anders. I don't close my eyes when I pin this brass onto my uniform.'' Neel touched the caduceus on his collar, insignia of the Army's medical corps. ''I know what her problem is, but I'm trying to find out if you know." Neel gently nudged his finger against Anders' chest as a gentle reminder of who the questioner was.

''Well, sir, you understand, well, I mean I really don't know for sure what it is ''

''Spit it out, son,'' Neel interrupted. ''That young lady needs some help and you've got to tell me how to treat her.''

Anders looked even more stricken. ''Me, tell you, sir?''

''Get on with it, Anders. What do you think she has?''

''I think it's an asthma attack,'' Anders replied with only a faint hint of confidence.

''That's better. Now what do you call it when a patient has a bad asthma attack that just won't go away?''

''Status asthmaticus, sir.''

''Very good, very good. Now, what's the basic problem in an asthma attack?''

''Well, the alveoli and small bronchioles become constricted and plugged with mucus, so the air gets trapped and can't get out.''

''Anders, you must make your parents very happy,'' Neel said. ''Now how can we open up those bronchioles and get rid of the mucus plugs?''

''Let's see, sir. We'd need a bronchodilator to open up the tubes and then something to thin out the mucus plugs so she could cough them up,'' Anders replied, feeling more comfortable with his lesson.

''Right. Now go get your magic bag of tricks and let's see what we can find to help her.''

Anders hurried over to his field medical kit and brought it back to Neel. It was a rather complete kit, issued to medics in an air ambulance company, and Anders had 'souped' it up with as many additional drugs and medications as he could obtain and stuff into the kit.

''All right, Anders, what's the best and fastest bronchodilator you can give me?'' Neel asked.

Anders thought for a second, then dug into a compartment of his kit, producing a small glass vial.

''Epinephrine,'' he said, smiling with his success.

''Excellent. Now draw me 0.1 cc of the 1:1000 solution in a tuberculin syringe.''

Anders did as he was directed, tipping the needle end of the syringe up and tapping it to get rid of any bubbles in the chamber. He handed it to Neel.

''Okay, now how do I give it?''

''Subcutaneously, sir.''

''Well, I'll inject it just into the very superficial subcutaneous tissues, just below the dermis, where the vascular arcade is dense and will pick up the drug and quickly circulate it to the heart and lungs.''

Neel explained to Charlene what he was going to do and why and, after she nodded, cleaned her forearm with alcohol and slowly injected the drug. He found her wrist pulse and monitored it while the drug was circulating. Normal circulation time from the skin to the lungs was less than a minute, so he expected to see a speedy improvement.

And, indeed, Charlene began to have less labored breathing and her lips relaxed. Her heart rate rose slightly due to the effects of the drug, which was also a heart stimulant. Then her pulse began to drop as blood oxygenation improved. When Neel was satisfied with her progress, he turned to Anders.

''Now do we have anything else we can use to dilate her bronchioles?''

Anders thought a moment, then raised his finger in anticipation. ''An inhaler, sir?''

''Right again, Anders. Have you ever been on 'Wheel of

Fortune'? Now get me what I need.''

The medic rummaged again in his bag and produced a small box containing an inhaler. ''Albuteral, Sir.''

''Fine. Now let's get her to inhale about three puffs and see if that helps.''

When Anders showed Charlene the inhaler she said she had used one before. She placed her mouth around the opening and inhaled as deeply as she could while depressing the plunger. She had a coughing fit after each breath, but managed to get three effective squirts.

''Okay, Anders, now listen to her lungs again.''

After Neel listened again to Charlene's chest, he asked the medic what he had heard.

''Much better, sir. Not as much wheezing on both sides, and the right seems to be better than the left.''

''That's right, Anders, that's just right,'' Neel replied, smiling. ''That's because the left mainstem bronchus departs from the trachea at a more acute angle, so it's a little harder to clean her secretions out of there. There's probably a big mucus plug sitting on the left side that needs to be coughed out. Now what can we do to help that?''

Without hesitation, Anders raised a bottle he had been holding in his right hand. ''Right here, sir, the magic potion. Guainefesin and dextromethorphan. To thin out the mucus and to let her get some rest from the coughing.''

''Bingo, Anders. Now give her about 15 cc and let her wash it down with a lot of bottled water.'' Soon, they noted Charlene was resting more comfortably and coughing less.

''OK, have some of her friends to carry her out of this tent into a shady spot outside and make her drink plenty of water.'' Charlene's friends helped her to her feet, and gathering up a couple of water bottles, led her outside. The curious crowd had thinned when it became obvious the soldier was not going to die in front of their vicarious eyes. Several of the hornier observers had cheerfully volunteered to give Charlene mouth-to-mouth resuscitation. She was a striking natural redhead.

As Anders packed up his medical kit, Neel plunked down on the duffel bags. ''All right, hot shot, tell me why she got into trouble.''

Anders found he couldn't think and pack at the same time so

he sat back on his haunches and stared absently at a personal bag with a 'SKI VAIL' message. *How incongruous here in the desert,* Anders thought.

''Well, sir,'' he began, ''we know she has a history of asthma, although she hasn't had any attacks for several years.''

''Fine, Anders. But what usually prompts an asthmatic attack in susceptible individuals?''

Anders tried to think back to all those lectures at the Aeromedical Center at Fort Rucker on pulmonary pathophysiology. Come on, brain, don't fail me now.

''Um, dryness of airway is one, sir.''

''That's right, Anders, now where could her airway have dried out?''

''How about back at Ft. McCoy, Sir, with the coal furnaces?''

''Right. Anywhere else?''

''Now I remember, sir. We learned at Rucker that the air in airplane cabins or cockpits is very low in humidity. And we've been on that airplane for over 20 hours.''

''You must be a boy genius, Anders. Now tell me what else can cause airway dryness and thickening of secretions?'' Neel looked up from the sand and gave Anders his best professional stare.

''Well, let's see, sir. Uh - well - gosh, I just can't think.''

''What about oral fluid intake?''

''Right.'' Anders brightened as he grasped what Neel meant. ''She must not have drunk very much water on the long flight, and it was pretty hot on the plane, so I guess she got dehydrated, too. I suppose that's why you wanted her to drink plenty of fluids, sir.''

''Right again, Anders. And the final precipitating factor was her sudden exposure to all the dust and sand in the tent here as we all kicked it up. Particulate matter, especially dust, can really bother some people with reactive airway disease and can be the final straw that causes the attack. We'll have to make sure she stays hydrated and keeps on taking her Robitussin. Also, don't forget that viral or bacterial upper respiratory infections can also thicken the mucus secretions and cause bronchoconstriction. If she has any purulence to her nasal secretions or sputum, then we ought to treat her with a broad-spectrum antibiotic.''

''Like ampicillin, sir?''

''Ampicillin would be fine or erythromycin if it's mainly a cough, rather than a nasal infection,'' Neel said. ''I don't have the foggiest idea why they let someone with asthma as reactive as hers deploy to the desert in the first place.''

''You know the Army, sir. They don't need a good reason.''

Neel laughed, got to his feet, and thumped Anders lightly on the back. ''How well I know, son, how well I know. Let's go see how our patient is doing, okay?''

Anders walked out of the tent with Neel. *'Our patient' he had said. I really like the sound of that. I also like Dr. Neel - he's a good guy. I hope I meet up with him again.*

Shortly after their encounter, though, both men were loaded on similar, but separate buses, headed for different destinations. Anders went with his air ambulance company to the other side of the airfield to board a CH-47 Chinook helicopter for transport to what would be his new home in the desert. Neel, his patient Charlene, and the rest of the newly arrived troops were taken to housing at a location called Kobar Towers, near the outskirts of Dhahran.

* * *

Without further mishaps, Sergeant Gonzales had finally finished the unloading detail and all the tanks and Bradleys had been secured to trailers for transport into the desert. Now it was up to the conglomeration of Reserve and National Guard transportation outfits to deliver them. Gonzales had personally taken aside a Guard corporal named Curtis from Illinois, driver of the 18-wheeler transporting Gonzales' own tank, and told him what would happen to him if he damaged or failed to deliver it. The M-1 was like his own personal '57 Chevy. Curtis, rather shy and quiet, had stared at Gonzalez and visualized a stiletto turning him into an instant soprano.

He swore to the crazy sergeant he would not let anything happen to his precious tank. Satisfied by his intimidation, Gonzalez went back to the warehouse barracks to prepare for his next move.

Later that day, he found himself in Saudi government housing, at Khobar Towers, which had been built by the Saudi king as a home for his Bedouins. His royal gesture was truly noble, but since Bedouins never lived in houses, let alone concrete apartments, a futile one. However, the apartments, garages and adjacent storage buildings served nicely as transient housing for up to 15,000 American men and women on their way to field deployment. Unfortunately, the concentration of troops made the complex a prime target for terrorists.

The area consisted of an L-shaped arrangement of buildings with only a single point of access into the entire complex: an entry gate heavily guarded by U.S. Army MPs well-protected by two sandbagged bunkers and by the concrete barriers designed to prevent an explosives-laden truck from reaching the GIs as had occurred to the marines in Beirut. The perimeter was enclosed by a six-foot chain link fence, supplemented by multiple rows of vicious concertina ribbon wire. Light infantry tanks (M551 Sheridans) were assigned to the MP companies and its 152-mm low-velocity gun or Shillelagh missiles could repel a light armor attack, or more likely, destroy any civilian vehicle bent on a terrorist attack.

The Sheridans were placed strategically at weak areas along the perimeter or where visibility was good and there was a reasonable field of fire. Their presence was augmented by several Bradley M2 infantry fighting vehicles with 25-mm chainguns and TOW II anti-tank launchers. The Bradleys were rapid-response units that could speed seven troopers to the scene of a firefight.

But the main MP patrol vehicle in this sprawling housing complex was the 'Hummer' - officially termed HMMWV, the high-mobility, multi-purpose wheeled vehicle designed to replace the Jeep, the Mule, and the Gamma Goat. Only the beloved M151 Jeep would be missed by the soldiers - they thought the Mule and Gamma Goat should have more appropriately been termed 'pink elephants.'

The Hummer was a squat, four-wheeled 1 1/2 ton vehicle with 15 possible configurations, including patrol vehicle, cargo/ troop carrier, armament carrier, ambulance and command (communications vehicle). Its 6.2-liter V-8 diesel could carry it at 65 mph for 250 miles without refueling.

The MP Hummer at Khobar was a patrol vehicle with a center hole cut out of its roof to mount a .50-cal. machine gun on a swivel platform. The patrols were constantly on the move up and down the streets, providing traffic control as well as surveillance and security.

Other MP's armed with M60 machine guns (7.62 mm) and M16A2 assault rifles (5.56 mm) manned stationary positions in small bunkers. A few MPs carried Ithaca model 37 Stakeout shotguns - a 12-gauge, pistol-grip gun favored by SWAT teams and military police units for close-in urban fighting and terrorist situations. Because the main threat to the temporary residents of Khobar seemed to be from terrorist-planted bombs or sabotage, the MPs were intent on controlling access as well as maintaining the security of each housing unit.

It was building security that elements of the 3rd Armored Division were assigned to handle during their stay at Khobar Towers. SFC Gonzales and six of his troopers were in charge of security for the 'VIP Building,' where field-grade officers were housed in a three-story, concrete structure with a single entrance. Two troopers were stationed just outside the door with one at a desk in the lobby. Gonzales' men had just relieved elements of the 1st Armored, which had the duty before being shipped into the desert a few days earlier. The officers of the 1st AD (including the assistant division commander, Brigadier General Alonso) had vacated the unit and it was currently empty, awaiting the arrival of new officers who had just landed.

Sergeant Gonzales and his men entered the building carrying all their gear. "All right, here's what we do," Gonzales announced in his vibrant bass voice, with its Hispanic cadence. "We're going to live on the ground floor, on both sides of the entryway here, so I want four of you to take the apartment to the left and three of us will take the right."

"Why do we get the ground floor, Sarge, and them officers the top floor?" whined PFC Willie Johns from Chicago. "I like the view better from up top."

"Shut up, Johns. You complain about everything. How would you like to sleep next door with 35 guys to an apartment and no working toilet? You got it nice here, so stuff it. Besides, if this building is ever attacked, we have the privilege of defending it from the ground floor to protect the officers upstairs."

A few of the men snickered, but stopped when Gonzales shot a stern glance their way.

"If we have the job to protect these officers, then that's what we'll do." Gonzales said firmly. "They got important decisions to make and we don't. So I don't want to hear any more crap. You got that?"

"Yeah, Sarge," most of the men muttered. They realized

this was a good assignment during their time at Khobar. They could just as easily have drawn duty in the chow line or picking up trash around the compound. As it was, they would spend 12 hours on duty and 12 hours off. However, it was a God-given right (or so enlisted men had thought for 200 years of service in the American military) to bitch and none of them would pass up any opportunity to do so. As any commander knew, if his men weren't complaining about something, he had a problem.

Sergeant Gonzales carried his own load of equipment and personal items into the apartment he had assigned himself and two others and dropped it all on the floor. He surveyed the room. *Not bad, not bad at all!* The apartment had a bathroom (yes, the water worked, as he discovered when he tried the spigots) and a nonfunctional kitchen without plumbing. *That's all right, I'm not going to drink this water anyway.*

Each bedroom in the apartment had two aluminum frame cots with a two inch foam pad on top, covered by gaily decorated Arabian fabric. He chose the 'hot pink' mattress and sat down to rest his feet. After testing the mattress by seeing how far his fingers would sink into it (something he always did first when he slept in a new bed) he unrolled his sleeping bag and laid it out. Next he unrolled a wool GI blanket, probably the same sort the U.S. Cavalry had carried in Custer's time and laid it over his sleeping bag. If the nights weren't too cold, he would sleep on top of the bag and under the blanket; otherwise, he'd crawl inside. There were two things he didn't like about the Army sleeping bag. First, it was too warm, and second, it narrowed at the ankles, making him feel trapped. He liked to sleep sprawled out on a bed and the bag cramped his style.

He unpacked his ruck and personal items and laid them out, deciding what should be repacked in case of sudden deployment or for a dash to a nearby bunker, and which were extraneous, for 'creature-comfort' only.

After repacking his combat gear, he set down the ruck and laid out the personal items he'd need in the apartment - shaving kit, hairbrush (his hair was still dark and thick, thank God), extra flashlight, mess kit with knife, fork and spoon, a zip-lock bag of clean underwear and socks, a spare set of BDU's, tanker gloves, and long underwear. He could repack these into a small desert camouflage bag for quick travel if he had to. He also placed a short stack of reading material next to his cot in case he had some free time during his off-shift.

At the PX in Germany several years ago he had come across W.E.B. Griffin's series, 'The Brotherhood of War' and had been hooked ever since. Gonzales was an avid reader and the series had captured his attention. He had since progressed into the final books of the series and had brought along the first two books, newly released, of Griffin's new series, 'The Corps.'

On the other side of the cot he placed his gas mask (an ever-present item that even went with him to the latrine and shower), his Kevlar tanker's helmet, LBE web gear with the attached flashlight on the right upper chest strap, compass on right lower, combat knife taped upside down on the left chest strap, a first-aid packet, and the waist unit with two one-quart canteens, four ammo pouches for his M-16, and a special case for his tanker goggles.

He unstrapped the .38 cal revolver in its shoulder holster and took it off, placing it next to the bed. As a tanker, he had found a .45 automatic too bulky. He had requisitioned and been issued the revolver and he felt comfortable with it. Tankers didn't usually carry M-16s, unless they were on duty outside their tanks, as they were now. They had not yet been issued ammunition, but he figured they would get it soon because of their guard assignment.

He set his one duffel bag against the far wall. Even though they had been allowed to travel with two (labeled 'A' and 'B'), he had elected to bring only one. Gonzales had been through enough deployments, and especially with his previous experience in Vietnam, to know you just couldn't carry two duffels, your rucksack, a personal bag, all your other gear and a sleeping bag from place to place in one move. He had learned his lesson and traveled as light as he could.

The duffel contained additional items that could be discarded if a fast move-out was required—extra BDU's and tanker coveralls, personal items, and an extra pair of boots. He would have left these items packed in the duffel except for one thing. He rummaged through the mid portion of the big bag until he found what he was looking for - his Sony Walkman and a bag of cassette tapes. Having grown up in El Paso, he loved country and western music, especially his favorite singer, Marty Robbins.

Gonzales inserted a tape, put on the earphones and lay back

in the bed. *Wait a minute,* he thought, as his head hit the cot, *there's something else I need.* He went back to the duffel and found his most prized possession—a soft, inflatable pillow. With a few deep puffs, he had a pillow that had traveled with him on many deployments and which helped make sleeping in a foxhole, on the ground or in the tank a lot more bearable. He laid back down on to the cot and listened to Marty wailing about 'El Paso City.'

Within an hour, Corporal Ben Thomas from Fayetteville, Arkansas, came in and shook him awake. Gonzales sprang to his feet, ready for action, and listened while Thomas told him of the call over the field phone wired into the entryway from headquarters.

"Sarge, we got a load of officers coming over in a bit. They just got off the buses over at the unit HQ and'll be here shortly."

"Okay, Thomas, get the men into the hall with full gear and let's get organized," Gonzales replied, as he began donning his web gear, helmet, and gas mask.

In a few minutes, all seven tankers had assembled in the entry hallway that would serve as the 'front desk' of the building. Someone had supplied a wooden desk and chair for the NCO in charge of the detail and a smaller desk and chair just inside the door where credentials and ID's could be checked.

"All right, listen up," Gonzales barked. "It's now 1000 hours, and the first shift will last 'til midnight. That's me, Johns, Thomas, and Rosales. The rest of you have the midnight 'til noon shift. That way everyone gets part of the night."

As he looked around the hall at the men, he thought how young they looked and how old he felt. *For chrissake, I'm 41 years old, old enough to be their father. Well, as long as that's true,* he conceded, *he might as damn well act like their father, too.*

"Now I'll tell you one more time and not again. These are officers coming here, field-grade officers, maybe even a general. I want you on such good behavior that you'd make your mothers cry with joy. Got it?"

They all bobbed their heads. For a squad of tankers, even coming in contact with a captain was a big deal, so being around field-grade officers (major to colonel) was almost intimidating.

"I want you to stand when they enter and exit the building and to show your best military courtesies. Right?"

Yes, they all said, looking a little nervous.

Gonzales looked out the door quickly and saw no one coming. He turned to the men and pointed to Johns. ''You, my man, will sit at that little desk just inside the door, rise to attention when an officer enters and say 'Sir, may I see your identification please.' You got that?'' Gonzales asked.

''Yeah, Sarge. I can handle it,'' Johns replied.

''No wisecracks, boy, or you'll be dog-meat,'' Gonzales warned. He turned to Thomas and Rosales: ''You two will take turns standing guard at the front door with your M-16s. When you're not on guard, you will be 'gofers' making sure we've all got plenty of water, MRE's and any other supplies Corps will decide to give us, okay? Anyone not on shift will bring back food from the mess for those who are. Siebert, you'll be in charge of the guard on the night shift. Make up a schedule of rotation for you and Burns and Miller and keep each other awake. I'll always be available if you're not sure about anything. No one gets into or even near this building without proper genuine US Army field-grade ID. Any problems, you detain the individual and call me right away. And, last, don't let any civilian Arab near this building. I don't care if he claims to be the king of Saudi Arabia, he's not getting in here, okay? I don't trust any of these guys wearing dresses and table cloths for hats. They all could be Iraqis for all we know.''

Gonzales searched their faces for questions and found none. He turned to Siebert. ''Your shift will hang around the front for a couple of hours to help the officers with their gear. Once they're moved in and squared away, you can hit the sack til supper.''

Just then, Thomas called out to Gonzales from outside the front door. ''Hey Sarge, looks like one of them coming now.''

Gonzales moved to the door and shielded his eyes to look to the east where a lone figure was walking toward them. The sergeant walked out of the building toward the approaching figure. As they neared each other, Gonzales could see this was a tall, athletic man, with a brown regulation moustache and horn-rimmed glasses. He moved with the ease of a long distance runner and was carrying his gear without any sign of fatigue. *Well, I'll be damned,* Gonzales thought, *he's only got one duffel bag, like me. We're the only two I've seen who didn't overpack.*

''Good morning, sir,'' Gonzales said as he saluted. ''May I

help you with your gear?''

''No thanks, Sergeant, that won't be necessary. But, some of my fellow officers are struggling with their bags and they might need some assistance from your men.''

Gonzales looked over the major's shoulder at a small band of men walking slowly, carrying or dragging their duffels along the walk. He turned, and with a hand motion, indicated to his men that they should go and help the struggling officers. As he turned back to the major, he noticed for the first time the badges on his BDUs - expert field medical badge, senior flight surgeon's wings, senior parachutist wings and air assault wings. And there on his left shoulder was the tab for Special Forces. *All right. Now here's an officer who's been around, and who knows his business, and a doctor to boot.*

Gonzales smiled. ''Welcome to Khobar Towers, Major Neel. I'm SFC Gonzales and I'm in charge of your security while we're here.''

Neel smiled at him, broadly and boyishly. ''I don't know that we're worth guarding, sergeant, but I'm happy to meet you.'' He stuck out his hand and exchanged strong grips with Gonzales.

As they turned toward the building and started walking, Neel looked at Gonzales. ''Just one important question, please, sergeant.''

''Yes sir, what would that be? Gonzales replied.

''Is there a real bathroom with real toilet paper in this building?''

They both laughed and Gonzales nodded. *This might not be so bad an assignment after all. Not all officers are pricks.*

* * *

A warm Coke is not a fitting drink for a hot-shot attack helicopter pilot, thought Captain 'Tex' Weatherby, as he set the drink next to his canvas cot. He had been sitting there, propped against his rolled-up sleeping bag and the goose-down pillow he had brought from Germany in an empty helmet bag. *In the Second World War, the pilots had nice billets in an apartment in England, a staff car to pick them up before they flew off on a dangerous mission to bomb Germany, and an English girl to provide proper leave taking. And, especially a cold Coca Cola to drink as one's last request. This really sucks. Eating MRE's like everyone else over here, and no separate officer's mess. Ain't that the berries.*

They ought to treat us special people special!

He got up, buckled his gas mask around his waist and his revolver over his shoulder, put on his soft cap (he refused to wear a Kevlar helmet when he wasn't going to fly, to hell with the 'standing orders') and walked out of the tent in search of his executive officer, Captain Everett Hill, his friend from Germany. He found Hill on the flight-line, next to an Apache helicopter, peering into the cockpit with SSG Tom Pingree. Pingree, a bright young man from Utah, was planning to attend college to get an aeronautical engineering degree once his enlistment was up. He was a competent, quiet individual, the antithesis of Weatherby. Whenever they were together, they made each other uncomfortable.

"Well, well, if it isn't God and his co-pilot," Tex yelled, referring to Pingree's deep religious convictions. Hill turned to Tex with a brow-tightening frown, while Pingree merely turned, saluted and went back to work.

"God-dammit, Skipper, you got no class, you know that?" Hill said as he dismounted the helicopter. "The sergeant here has found the air speed indicator is giving erroneous data and he thinks it's sand getting into the intake pitot. If that's the case, we've got a serious operational problem."

"Wait a minute," Weatherby said, "I haven't noticed any problems with the air speed indicator. What makes the kid think there's a problem?"

"He hooked the intake up to some sort of flowmeter he made back in Germany that creates a known velocity of air and compared it to the indicator on the instrument panel. That's how he found it out - why he suspected it, I don't know."

Damn. That's something that I, as squadron commander, should have come up with. And this tall, skinny Mormon outwitted me. I don't like it; I don't like it at all.

Tex climbed up to the cockpit and looked in at Pingree who was hanging almost upside down over the pilot's seat, working blindly with his hands behind the instrument panel. Tex waited a few minutes for Pingree to finish and when he didn't, pulled him (somewhat roughly) out of the cockpit.

"What are you doing in there, Sergeant?" He emphasized 'Sergeant'.

"Sir, I think we need to remove the air indicator lines in all of the aircraft and install a bypass filter to prevent blockage by sand. If we don't, it's possible the air speed indicator could either give inaccurate readings to the pilot or freeze on a fixed speed indication.''

If it gets up to regimental headquarters that I have to ground my aircraft to fix their air speed indicators, my ass will get chewed. Especially since no one else has reported a problem. And that major's promotion board is coming up in two months. I don't want anything to screw that up. Christ, I'm ahead of my classmates at A&M anyway, so I'd like to get picked up below the zone.

''Well, there hasn't been a question raised by any of the other squadrons so far. Why are you so certain, when no one else seems to be worried?''

Pingree's face slowly reddened, but he maintained his composure. ''Sir, I believe I have the only instrument in the theatre that can detect this subtle change. The others haven't any way to confirm the problem, even if they did suspect it. It's a weakness of the Apache, but it hasn't been a problem in other climates just in the desert with its high particulate content in the air.''

Weatherby looked at the young man for a while, mulling over the idea. *What Pingree was saying seemed reasonable, but how could he, the commander, explain it to higher headquarters?*

''What makes you think this is going to be a problem, Pingree?''

''Well, sir, I don't really know that it will be a problem. I just feel we ought to take the necessary steps to prevent a problem.''

''What kind of down time for these aircraft are you proposing?'' Weatherby asked, mopping the sweat off his brow with a white rag.

''I believe we could manage the change on all our aircraft within 72 hours, sir. That is, if Lieutenant Collier can get regiment to get the parts I'll need, sir.'' Collier was the squadron maintenance officer and an excellent man for obtaining needed parts - one way or another.

''And what do you think could happen to these aircraft if your change isn't made?'' Weatherby said this softly so Hill couldn't hear his question.

''It's possible, sir, that it could cause an error in distance navigation, so a pilot might not follow a given heading long enough and miss a landing site, or possibly overshoot his destination and get lost. If he doesn't have an accurate way to determine his air speed, especially in heavy winds - well, the desert looks the same from above, as you know, sir.''

The real problem was they had no air traffic control in the desert. Also, there were no set radio frequency emitters for the many Army and Marine helicopter bases. The larger Air Force installations were equipped with modern air traffic control facilities, but the desert pilots used dead reckoning for finding their way back—their hastily built bases were located by their coordinates on a map and with a radio transceiver to control lift-offs and landings.

''And, sir, we also need to build a maintenance hangar so we can keep the cockpit instrument panel clean while we're changing the lines,'' Pingree added.

Weatherby stared at the cockpit seat while he thought of the ramifications of such a change-out. *We've received no directions from regiment about any problem with the air speed indicator. And they've been very tuned-in to the problems of desert flying. Look at that fiasco in the Iranian desert when they couldn't get those big helicopters to fly in the sand. And all I've got to go on is the word of a kid who hasn't finished college yet, and who may just be trying to climb the ladder faster. If I request permission to put these birds down for three days, to fix something we don't know is even broken, headquarters is going to be on my ass so fast my head will spin.*

Tex decided. ''No, Sergeant, we don't have any evidence that this is an operational problem yet. When you can show me that, I'll reconsider.'' He started to climb down off the side of the helicopter when he hear Pingree mutter: ''But, sir, that may be too late for somebody.''

Tex chose to ignore both the comment and Pingree and jumped to the ground.

''Cool it on this thing, Hill. We don't need to fix what ain't broken.'' With that, he walked over to the mess tent in search of the mess sergeant, who had promised him today would be the day to drive over to the small Arab town just 15 miles away in search of fresh fruit and pita bread. *First things first, and I need an Arabic taco right now.*

As it does in military camps, word got around that Weatherby had nixed the idea of the air speed line switch-out and filter recommendation, and Tex's reputation, which was already marginal with respect to his consideration for anyone but himself, was further maligned. It suffered nearly irreparable damage though, when one of the Apaches carrying two new pilots was lost on a recon mission near the Kuwaiti border in a mild 'Shamal' sandstorm. Weatherby heard about it from Captain Hill when he entered the operations tent not three days after his conversation with Pingree.

Hill was sitting at the makeshift desk he used to fill out paperwork and make up schedules, talking on the field phone to regimental headquarters, about 30 miles south. Hill looked worried and was making notes on a yellow legal pad.

Weatherby took a paper cup from the large box next to Hill that served as Weatherby's command desk and poured himself some grape-flavored drink from an Igloo on the floor. It was warm and that didn't improve Weatherby's mood one bit.

Hill replaced hung up the phone and stared at his notes for a minute. ''Captain, Ingalls and Marshall are two hours late returning from their mission this morning. Regiment is sending up some OH-58 Scouts as well as asking a Marine unit east of here to get up a couple of SAR's to look in their sector. I tried to tell you as soon as I heard about it but I couldn't find you.''

That's because I was playing poker in the cook's tent, you prick. I didn't want anyone to find me. ''I was going over the dietary needs of the unit with the mess sergeant.''

Although Hill and Weatherby were both captains, Weatherby had over two years longer time-in-grade over Hill, so he was the commander. The regimental brass might have chosen Hill, if all things were equal, but it just wasn't possible to place a pilot in a command position with less flight time and lower date of rank over a more senior captain. The Army just didn't do that - never mind that the executive officer was more considerate of the men in the command or was less self-centered. That didn't figure into the equation, although it helped on the OER's (Officer Evaluation Record). Someday, Hill would be a commander, but until then he would be subordinate to Weatherby. It wouldn't have been so bad except Weatherby had a real dichotomy in his personality—he could be very friendly and fun in a social sense, yet he appeared to lack any introspection about his dealings with others.

Weatherby grimaced and sucked in his breath in a long sigh. "Show me their flight plan on the map."

They walked over to a large 3 x 5-foot plastic-covered grid map of their area of operations, which had been stapled to a piece of plywood and set on a makeshift easel. Hill looked at the clipboard in his hand, took up a black wax marking pencil and traced an elongated circle between their basecamp and the Kuwaiti border.

"Their mission was routine, just like always. Recon the border, looking for signs of movement in the Iraqi positions and report back. Our last report was at 0530 when they were on their return leg and had seen nothing. Both pilots were wearing night-vision goggles and had been wearing them for the entire mission."

"No reports of enemy fire?" asked Weatherby.

"*Nada* - perfectly quiet, routine mission." Hill rubbed the top of his prematurely balding head with his palm. It glistened with sweat, and the temperature of the room was not that hot.

"I recall that both Ingalls and Marshall had pretty low hours on the goggles. What kind of weather were they flying in up there?"

"Well, pretty typical for the nights we've been having - cool, windy and dry. No rainstorms in the area, according to our latest weather report. But the wind was picking up and Ingalls noted a headwind of about 20 knots and gusting on his last report."

Damn, these boys surely went down with that aircraft up there this morning. "No reports from another airfield that they might have set down somewhere else?"

"No, I've contacted all of them in our vicinity and they've heard or seen nothing."

Weatherby was pacing the floor now, thinking of all of the possible causes for the aircraft's disappearance. "Have you checked the maintenance records on that bird to see if there had been any problem with it?"

"Yes, I did." There was a long pause, as if Hill did not know how to phrase his reply. Weatherby turned to look at his exec, who finally met his gaze. "They had reported the air speed indicator had been causing them problems and the crew chief was going to check it out after this flight.''

Damn, damn, damn. I knew this thing with Pingree would come back to haunt me. But, hell, they could have just as easily have flown into a tower with their goggles on.

They looked at each other for a long moment until the field phone rang, startling them. It was regimental headquarters - a Marine SAR helicopter had found the smoking wreckage of an Apache 50 miles southwest of Tex's squadron's base. A preliminary report indicated no survivors.

Hill slowly replaced the phone, but would not look at Weatherby directly. ''Both men are probably dead, and the aircraft is burning. They were found 50 miles to our southwest and they shouldn't have been there. Regiment is sending out a crash investigation team, along with someone from the Fort Rucker Aviation Safety Board who is in-country. They probably won't know what happened for months, maybe not until this war is over.''

The phone call had confirmed Weatherby's worst suspicions. Rarely did good news come out of a missing aircraft report. Although there had been fewer aircraft accidents than predicted, they had still accounted for 15 lives lost so far in Army aviation alone. *Must have been those damn night vision goggles, right? Or could it have been . . . ?*

''I suggest we have an officer's call, Tex, and break the news. Those two guys were new, but they were good men and we need to let everyone know what's happened. And I'll need to revise the flight schedules with the loss of an aircraft and two pilots. The chaplain will also want to have a service for them here in the compound.''

Weatherby was starting to get one hell of a headache. *God, he wished he had a six-pack of beer he could turn himself loose on. It had always helped in the past when these things happened. Helped him forget and kept him from thinking he could be next. God, what I'd give for a drink.*

As they both prepared to leave the operations tent, Hill stopped short, turned, and looked directly into Weatherby's eyes. Hill's face was flushed and sweaty and he looked almost as if he was going to slug Weatherby. Unconsciously, Tex adopted a defensive posture because of the subtle threat.

''I don't suppose you'd care to reconsider your decision to

replace the air speed indicators on these aircraft, in light of what has just happened, would you?'' Hill demanded.

Weatherby thought about the two fliers who were now presumed dead. Both friendly, young, eager pilots. Athletic and competent, they could likely have been command pilots themselves someday. Both had families and he would have to deal with that issue sometime soon. He hated that the most, writing the letters to dead flyers' wives, thinking of what the children would miss in their future lives. *Damn, nothing is easy in this life. Sometimes I wish I could lay aside all this bravado and try to figure out how to be a nice guy - but maybe I can't and maybe I'm not. Damn me!*

Weatherby looked at Hill and nodded, his expression revealing resignation and concern. ''Yeah, Ev, we'd better do that. Work out a plan with Pingree and the maintenance officer to rotate our birds in for modification. Have them rig up a tent wide enough and high enough to get the birds in and out. And tell regiment what we're doing. If they get pissed, I'll talk to them.'' Tex shook his head and parted the tent flaps, then stopped short and turned back to Hill.

''If it was the indicator, and I'm not convinced it was, maybe we can keep some more bastards from not coming home from this God-forsaken desert.'' Tex left the tent.

Hill paused for a second, then followed him. *Maybe down deep inside that Texas redneck there might be a soul worth saving.*

CHAPTER FOUR

PATIENCE AND HUMILITY, thought Staff Sergeant Lucius Tatum, *were two of the most difficult traits to teach to his people.* And right now he was being tested on them to the maximum. *Granted that the traits were God-given, and aware that he could readily be a patient and humble father with his children, then why, couldn't he set a good example now?* He stood in the sand with his hands on his hips, squinting angrily at the two sources of his consternation--Privates Scarlotti and Joseph.

Tatum's company had been moved to a 'special' site in the desert where the 82nd Airborne was planning to train the paratroopers how to breach Iraqi defenses. Reconnaissance flights by Navy A-6 Intruders and Air Force AC-130s supplemented the information obtained from the extremely sharp resolution photographs taken by high-flying satellites. More information would be gathered by crucial on-site human intelligence.

By the time Tatum and his men reached the training area, its construction was nearly complete. Division engineers had reproduced the so-called 'Saddam Line' of barriers the division might have to breach to get at the Iraqis and their entrenched positions. The first barrier was an eight-to-ten-foot-high sand berm, the sand packed tight from weeks of construction. Behind it was a six-foot-wide trench supposedly filled with gasoline. To lessen the risks during training, the engineers had poured diesel fuel in the trench, because it was less flammable. Once the Allies had broken through the berm, it was presumed the Iraqis would set fire to their fuel trenches.

Beyond the trenches was a hundred yards of concertina wire followed by another hundred yards of a 'dummy' mine field. After the mine field was another smaller berm in front of the three-foot-wide and six-foot-deep trenches where the Iraqi soldiers would likely be dug in. Behind the infantry trenches, the engineers had constructed fixed artillery emplacements and partially buried tank positions to simulate the Iraqi order of defense.

Tatum's platoon was about to simulate the breaching exercise and his squad had the point. The plan developed by division staff called for an artillery assault supported by multiple rocket launches, combined with close air support from USAF A-10 Thunderbolt IIs, to soften the defenses and divert Iraqi attention from the forward breaching attack. The sand berm would be opened up by two Abrams M-1 main battle tanks equipped with huge bulldozer-like blades on their bows. Following the tanks Vulcan armored personnel carriers would fire into the wire and mine fields, opening a path for the division's ground troops to storm the Iraqi trenches and attack the enemy in hand-to-hand combat. Although the tanks would reach the trenches first and try to quell any Iraqi resistance, the division commanders believed fierce trench fighting might still take place.

The paratroopers' main problem came not from the breaching attack, but from their full chemical protective gear. The suits were oppressively hot and visibility through the goggles was terrible. The sensitivity of troopers' fingers encased in a thick pair of rubber gloves over an inner cotton pair was greatly diminished, too, making it difficult to insert a magazine into the M-16, charge it, flick off the safety and fire. Ever since basic training, the paratroopers had learned the feel of their weapons and it had become second nature for them to handle their weapons deftly and competently. It was upsetting to suddenly lose the 'feel' of their weapons in a potential life-or-death situation.

The unit had undergone frequent drills over the past several months in their chemical suits, but this was their first real exercise wearing them for an extended period. Tatum's consternation this early morning was caused by Privates Scarlotti and Joseph because they refused to keep on their gas masks for the very simple reason that they were both claustrophobic. Tatum understood their feelings completely—he, too, felt panicky when he stayed in the mask for long periods, but he had learned to keep his panic under control, most of it at least.

Because he could relate to their feelings, Tatum felt guilty coming down on them, but knew he had to. Division intelligence had declared they expected the Iraqis to hit Coalition assault forces with chemicals, both airborne gas and skin surface agents. Any soldier not fully protected could die during the breach. Although that prospect was sobering for all the men, it still didn't encourage

Scarlotti and Joseph to keep their masks on.

''I can't, man, I just can't,'' Scarlotti wailed in his nasal New York City accent. ''There's something wrong with my mask cause it just won't let me breathe.'' He was pulling apart the mask's filters in an attempt to locate some perceived abnormality. In fact, every mask had significant air flow resistance that caused most wearers to believe there was blockage in the filters.

Scarlotti was complaining to Corporal Tom Weiss, who had the dubious task of NBC (nuclear, biological and chemical) defense. Weiss's task was to conduct training in the chemical suits and to ensure each man was fully checked out in how to don and remove the gear and how to maintain his mask. A Montanan, Weiss was a slow-talking former cowboy, a sharp contrast in personalities with Scarlotti.

He was explaining to Scarlotti for the hundredth time about the dynamic flow characteristics of the mask. ''Look, knucklehead, there's nothing wrong with your mask. They're all like that—hard to suck air in and out. You just gotta get used to it or you're gonna die. You hear me, you're gonna die.''

Scarlotti glared at Weiss both in anger and fear. ''But, I'll go crazy and die inside this thing anyway. I just can't breathe.''

''Me, too, same with me,'' piped up Joseph, a skinny kid from Hoboken, New Jersey. It always amazed Tatum how such a skinny kid was strong enough to carry a combat load of equipment, a main and reserve chute, then jump out of an airplane without cracking every bone in his body like a dropped icicle.

Tatum felt he had to see these two men comfortable with the gas mask for two reasons: first, he really sympathized with them because he had experienced claustrophobic feelings himself; and second, the issue could be a matter of life and death for those men if the Iraqis actually did use gas. These were not men with an attitude problem—they were both good troopers who had never caused any trouble.

Tatum walked over to where the three men were arguing and held up his hand. ''All right. Tell me what the problem is here.''

Silence. Each man glared at the other, waiting for someone else to speak first. Finally because he was responsible for chemical suit compliance, Corporal Weiss spoke up. ''Sarge, Scarlotti and Joseph here,'' he nodded at them, as if they were in a large group and had to be pointed out, "say there's no way they can keep their masks on during this training exercise."

Tatum looked at both men, trying to appear understanding, yet firm at the same time. "You don't think you can breathe inside it, right, and you have this urge to rip it off?"

Both men stared wide-eyed at Tatum and nodded.

"And, Sarge, I get to having trouble breathing so fast that my face gets numb and my fingers tingle. I think I'm going to pass out," Joseph said.

When Weiss rolled his eyes in disgust, Tatum decided the training NCO had never experienced that feeling or wouldn't admit it. Probably the latter.

Tatum took off his Kevlar helmet and rubbed his closely cropped, curly hair. *It's been four days since I washed my hair. I hope we get a shot at the division showers tonight.*

Tatum made his decision. "Okay, I'll help you guys, but we'll do it my way. Don't forget that if a real chemical attack takes place, to hell with your trouble breathing, you got to keep it on. Verstehen?"

The men blinked. It was hard to think about dying when you were only nineteen.

"What we're going to do is this. Put on all of your MOPP gear, and keep your mask off until just before we hit the berm. Then put it on quickly, pull the cover down over your shoulder and leave it loose. Don't pull your straps tight so you'll have room to breathe around the mask. Every fifty yards or so reach up and tighten the straps a little bit so by the time we reach the final trench, you'll have it tight."

Scarlotti and Joseph looked at each other. They weren't too sure about this suggestion.

"That way," Tatum continued, "you'll get used to running in the mask and will gradually accept it tighter."

The two men were on the brink of indecision and could go either way. Tatum needed a clincher. "Just remember that when we hit the 'enemy' trench, I'll be popping tear gas and if your mask isn't tight it'll definitely ruin your whole day."

"Shit, Sarge, that ain't fair," Scarlotti said kicking up sand with the toe of his desert boot.

"Scarlotti, I'll teach you what's not fair. What's not fair is when the lieutenant has to write a letter telling your wife that you're one dead paratrooper because you didn't have enough sense to wear your gas mask properly when the Iraqis let fly with chemicals. She'll make sure her next husband is a lot smarter than you."

Scarlotti looked hurt. "There's no way I'm going to let my old lady marry someone else, Sarge."

"Then the best thing you can do, son, to keep that from happening is to listen to me and Weiss here." Tatum put a big hand on each of the men's shoulders. "Just try it this way for me, O.K.? I think you'll see it'll work for you."

Both men agreed and began putting on their MOPP suits. Tatum did the same, wondering to himself if he could follow his own advice as well as he could give it. He shook his head and vowed that he wasn't going to make his wife a widow if he had anything to say or do about it. He had too much to live for.

The predawn greyness had given way to the yellow-orange of dawn. The company was assembled in a large area flattened by the trucks and bulldozers the engineers had used to fabricate the barriers. As the word to prepare to assault reached the company commander, it was sent down to the platoons and then to the squads. Some semblance of order was beginning to appear as the men formed up into predesignated assault groups.

On foot, each platoon would follow a pair of plow-equipped M1 Abrams, 50 meters behind them. Once the sand berm had been breached by the tanks, they would move to the flanks in front of the diesel/gasoline-filled trench so the new M9 armored combat earthmovers and the M728 combat engineer vehicles could move through and attack the trench. The M728 had thicker armor as well as a lifting boom and a demolition gun, giving it greater capability in the face of enemy fire to plow sand into the trench and form a bridge, than could the more lightly armored M9. Coming behind the M728, the M9 could fill in craters and ditches and create antitank barriers if a counterattack by Iraqi armor occurred.

An M9 driver sits at the right rear of his vehicle, next to the engine and drive train. The dozer blade can be lifted and lowered by use of a ballast system, as well as canted from side to side. The driver is protected by Kevlar armor panels. The M9's cruising speed of 30 mph and water speed of 3 mph, propelled by tracks, gives it a greater capacity for mobility in the fast-moving environment of armor warfare in the desert than the older M728. It can also generate smoke from its two M257 66-mm four-barrel smoke-grenade launchers.

Tatum found out from a sergeant in the engineering company that the M9 could also launch teargas grenades and he planned to make use of their capability.

With his own chemical mask still in its carrying bag, Tatum walked slowly over to the nearest M9 ACE where he had seen the driver step down from the armored compartment. He raised his hand in recognition—he had played softball with the young man several days ago during a break.

The driver was black and they greeted each other with the typical modified handshake black soldiers had used since Vietnam.

''Hey, brother, you got some sweet little toy there,'' Tatum joked.

''Listen, man, that thing can flatten your house in about five minutes and you won't even feel a bump inside,'' replied the young black engineer, Corporal Sammie Greene.

''You gonna pop some smoke this morning for the troops?'' Tatum asked. '''Cause if you are, I need you to do something for me.''

''Yeah, I'm gonna do some smoke grenades right before we get to the Iraqi trenches, Sarge. Lay down some smoke afore your men gets in the trench and shoots them imaginary A-rabs.''

''Good, good. Here are two tear gas canisters.'' Tatum produced the small cylinders from inside his MOPP suit and handed them to Greene. ''Put 'em in your launcher in between the smoke canisters. I'll have my men move in front of your dozer right before the last trench and then when you see us there, just pop 'em, O.K.?''

Sammie grinned ear to ear. ''You got some honkie LT you want to cream, Sarge? Just show me who he is and I'll aim it his way.'' He laughed at the vision of a white officer hit by a tear gas grenade and not having his mask tight enough. Serve the muthuh right.

''No, not that, man,'' Tatum said quickly. ''None of that stuff, you hear? I just want some gas in the area to show the men how it would be if it was real gas. I want them scared shitless that their mask isn't tight enough and maybe they'd die next time. Maybe this'll keep 'em from getting killed when the shit really hits the fan.''

Greene nodded, but he also hoped the men Tatum was trying to teach a lesson weren't black. *Wasn't fair to pull a trick like that on a brother. Best to do it to a white man. Yeah, a white man.* He took the canisters over to the launcher and reloaded it, placing the tear gas in the number three and four positions in the four-barrelled device. That way, the smoke would already be forming before the tear gas hit. *Great, this will be the most fun I've had all week.*

Tatum returned to his squad. Briefly he went over the assault plan again. He had already explained it at least ten times that day. The troops all looked toward the company commander, who was standing next to his RTO, holding a transceiver handset, awaiting the assault command from the battalion commander. Finally, he shook his head, said something into the handset and turned to his platoon leaders, giving them the hand signal to move out!

Quickly, the word passed to the ranks and the men began to follow the giant behemoths as they moved toward the berm. With less effort than an elephant needed to push over a tree, the tank plows made a 20-foot-wide breach in the high sand wall. Some sand fell on top of the bow of the tank, but was quickly shaken off as the vehicle moved to widen the opening.

Once the tanks had opened the berm sufficiently, they moved rapidly through the breach and separated to the flanks, about 100 meters apart. The M9's and M728's followed, approaching the diesel-filled trenches on-line, shoving sand into the trench until a sand bridge was formed. The machines then crossed the bridge themselves, further packing down the sand, making its traverse by the troopers relatively easy.

By now, the men were double-timing, struggling to keep up in their ungainly MOPP gear. They had advanced only about 250 meters, but inside the suits each was already soaked with sweat. Their peripheral vision was reduced by the narrow-field eyepieces of the gas mask, requiring frequent head turning to see where they were as well as frequent nodding to check their path. In all, they resembled a group of bug-eyed aliens in bifocals for the first time.

Scarlotti and Joseph were breathing hard, despite their loosened masks. The going was rough and the exertion had most of the men short of breath in spite of their physical condition. Every hundred meters or so, the two men would stop quickly, shoulder-sling their rifles, and pull the straps tighter on their gas masks. They respected Sergeant Tatum and were willing to try his suggestion. But each man had decided they would definitely not have an airtight seal by the end of the assault. How could they, they rationalized, because they would be hot and out of breath and didn't think they could handle the total confinement of the mask.

The men ran heavily and clumsily across the roughly packed sand bridge. The engineers had already set fire to the diesel fuel in the trenches, although the combat bulldozers had pretty well pushed the liquid out of the foot soldiers' paths. There was a smell of diesel smoke, but it was noticeable only to those few who did not have a good seal on their masks.

The troops were finding it difficult to keep up with the engineer vehicles, which had moved ahead to tackle the concertina and antitank barriers. The tank-plows, M9's and M728's, worked together on this sequence of barriers, grinding up concrete posts and blocks with the broken and crushed concertina wire. However, because the vehicles were trying to keep up the momentum of the assault, they were not able to smooth out the debris from their destruction of the barriers. That caused the men to pay close attention to their footing, with everyone falling at least once while traversing the barrier strip. By now, the sweat inside their masks had condensed on the lenses and they could hardly see.

Tatum was struggling, too. He was a big man and made a fine target if he stood upright, so he was trying to advance in this assault in an infantryman's crouch, but was finding it difficult to still see where he was going. He thought he would prefer to crawl on his hands and knees, but realized that was theoretically dangerous for several reasons: he could tear his MOPP suit, and, if he came into contact with a persistent blistering agent, he would not be able even to see the enemy.

Tatum felt like a spaceman trying to flee a strange planet in a dream, to escape some hideous creature, but who couldn't manage to make his way through the weird craters and terrain of a strange planet. He looked around him and saw all the others also appeared to be having trouble. *Damn, this isn't anything like what the infantry assault on enemy territory looked like in the movie "The Longest Day." What has the 'Brotherhood of Arms' come to when we have to wear these weird suits in an American war.*

Finally, they were past the wire and barricade area and coming up on the mine field just in front of the simulated Iraqi trenches. According to the division breaching plan, now was time for Vulcan armored carriers to move forward and discharge special engineer teams with 'line charges.' These were 100-yard strings of tubing lined with explosives which, when detonated over mine fields, blasted a path for tanks and infantry. Tatum held up his men and signaled for them to assume a low profile while the charges were being deployed.

The engineer teams readied their devices and let them fly, six abreast, into the simulated mine field ahead of them. As the explosives fired, a terrific dust wall was formed and the tank-plows moved ahead two abreast with the M9's and M728's tucked in behind.

The men rose awkwardly to their feet and fell in line behind the slow-moving vehicles. Although they *knew* there were no 'real' mines in the field, the troopers seemed wary of walking outside the vehicle tracks. Maybe they were practicing for the real thing or maybe they didn't really *trust* the U.S. Army. After all, the Army once used live machinegun fire over barbed wire obstacle courses, didn't they?

As the armored vehicles approached the trenches, they spread out on-line, approaching six abreast. A network of interconnecting ditches, the trenches were marked occasionally by a fortified bunker, where a machine gun or rocket launcher would have been positioned.

The foot soldiers were to approach the trenches from behind the vehicles after they had formed a smoke screen in front of the trenches and then charge the trenches and fire into them after the tank-plows and combat bulldozers had buried as many Iraqis as possible. Essentially, the troops would kill or capture whatever Iraqis were still alive.

Inside his M9, Corporal Sammie Greene was having fun. He could almost visualize the enemy soldiers being buried under the blades of his machine. He could hardly wait for the real thing. Meanwhile, he was preparing to launch his smoke grenades when he noticed the two men Tatum had pointed out. *There are the two whities,* he thought, *who need a lesson about wearing their masks correctly.* He maneuvered his bulldozer to fix the men within the effective drop zone of his grenades, then launched all eight in their direction.

Sammie then moved slowly ahead, watching with glee

through his short window when the grenades impacted right next to the men. He saw them react to the tear gas, stopping to reach under their hoods to tighten their mask headstraps and stand still, obviously coughing in reaction to the gas trapped inside their masks. He saw one of them, the taller of the two, look up and identify his M9 as the one who had launched the grenades in their direction and saw him give a 'New York salute' with his fist raised against the other crossed-over arm.

Greene howled with laughter, rocking in his seat, as he moved the huge bulldozer forward to bury a section of the trench and collapse a sand-bagged bunker. He was thoroughly enjoying himself, seeing those airborne troopers, who thought so highly of themselves, losing their control on the entrenchment. *I love it, love it, love it,* he thought, happily as he hummed a rap song to himself about 'big white troopers coughin' in the sand.'

Tatum and his men jumped into the trenches and along the sides, swinging their M-16's from side to side as they moved their entire bodies around to look for Iraqi troops that weren't there. In a short while, the signal came to move through the entrenchments to an assembly area 100 meters ahead where they could remove their MOPP suits and drink some weak Kool-Aid. As the men slowly moved toward the assembly area and removed their masks, repacking them into the carrying bags after wiping the perspiration from the inside, Scarlotti and Joseph were both furious.

"Let's go find that SOB, man, and bust his teeth in," Scarlotti said. He had learned to fight in the streets of Brooklyn and was brought up never to let anyone do anything to him without retaliating. Normally, Joseph was not a belligerent man, but he was strongly influenced by Scarlotti and not smart enough to figure out when he was being used.

"Yeah, let's get him," Joseph agreed, looking hot and bedraggled, with reddened eyes and a runny nose from the slight tear gas exposure.

They looked around until they saw Corporal Greene dismounting from the M9, then walked quickly toward him.

"Hey, ape shit, what do you think you were doing out there with that tear gas crap?" Scarlotti hollered at Greene.

Greene jumped down from the track of the bulldozer directly in front of Scarlotti and tore off his helmet. "Who you calling 'ape shit,' you white pimple?"

Scarlotti grabbed Greene's tanker coveralls with his left hand and tried to pull him close to his face. The two men were of comparable height and weight, but Greene was more muscular.

"I'm talking to you, you African cretin," Scarlotti responded as he punched Greene low in the stomach with his right hand, which came around from behind his back in a lightning punch.

But Greene was tough and hardly fazed. He grunted heavily, then put his left arm in a head lock around Scarlotti and pulled him over his left hip onto the ground. He followed him down and tried to straddle his chest, but Joseph dove onto Green's shoulders, knocking him to one side. Soon all three were rolling in the sand, punching and kicking, while a crowd of troopers and engineers gathered around. The fight was quickly polarized. Not the two different units of men, but rather blacks against whites. If no one stepped in soon and defused the situation, a serious racial brawl could develop.

Tatum spotted the commotion and hurriedly finished removing his MOPP boots. He ran over to the fight, pushing aside soldiers who had jammed into a circle to watch. He knew the platoon lieutenant or first sergeant would be there soon unless he got things cooled down fast.

He reached down and grabbed Joseph by the back of his fatigue blouse and the seat of his pants, yanking him out of the fight and depositing him on the sand outside the circle.

"You," he pointed to a white private, "don't let him back in or I'll have your ass."

He turned back to Scarlotti and Greene, and grabbed each man by the ear, yanking them to their feet. *My mother used to do this to me and my brothers, and it used to work fine.* Each man grabbed at his ear, losing interest in the fight, trying to keep Tatum from pulling the ear totally off.

"All right, stop this shit," Tatum bellowed, in his deep bass voice. "Settle down or you'll each be missin' an ear. Got it?"

Each man tried to nod, but when that hurt too much, they spit out 'yeah' instead.

Tatum turned to the men surrounding him. "It's all over, so go get some water and get your gear cleaned up and packed." There was some muttering and a few glares, but the crowd slowly scattered and Tatum was left with the three culprits. He let go of their ears and stood between Scarlotti and Greene.

''What happened here, Scarlotti? And tell me the whole damned truth.''

Still visibly angry, Scarlotti knew he should not continue to be belligerent in front of Tatum. After all, even though Tatum was black, he was a good black man and Scarlotti actually liked him.

''Sarge, this ape-, I mean this SOB popped tear gas directly on us on purpose back there at the trench and liked to have killed us. He did it just 'cause he don't like whites, I think.''

Tatum was nearly at the end of his patience. He had been around men like Scarlotti all his life and detested their bigotry and their air of false superiority. On the other hand, he knew Greene had a kind of reverse discrimination problem and he had probably gone out of his way to aim the tear gas at these two men, which Tatum did not tell him to do.

''That right, Greene?'' Tatum asked, turning toward the sweating, dirt-covered tanker.

''Sure, bro, you told me to, right? And I was jist doin' what you wanted me to.'' Greene replied with a smug grin.

''You told him to do that?'' Scarlotti and Joseph echoed together, gaping in disbelief at Tatum.

Tatum held up his hand. ''Now wait a minute. I didn't tell him to bombard you with tear gas. You recall I told you that at the end of the exercise you needed to have your masks sealed tight? Right?'' The two troopers nodded. ''Well, did you?'' Tatum asked, pushing his face close to theirs.

Scarlotti and Joseph looked at each other and then at Tatum. No, they hadn't tightened their masks, they admitted.

''Remember that I wanted you to do that for a reason? Remember? But you did okay on the exercise, right, up until the very end?'' The men nodded again.

''If that had been real chemical gas the Iraqis had thrown at you, you'd be dead meat. And your poor wife and mother would be notified you're coming home in a flag-draped casket. You want that? You want your kid not to have a dad, Scarlotti, to grow up in New York without a father? And, you, Joseph, you wouldn't have any kids at all 'cause you wouldn't have any future. Now you two think about that and get your act together. And I don't want to hear any more of this racial name-calling you hear? You just might have had your life saved by this man across from you here. Listen, when the war starts, them bullets and grenades and gas don't care if you're red, white, or blue, they'll kill you just the same. You got that?''

The three men, sobered by Tatum's uncharacteristically long speech, hung their heads and scraped the sand with their feet, looking like three embarrassed baseball players gathered at the mound.

''All right, Scarlotti, and you, Joseph, get on back to the squad and get squared away. I'll be over there in a minute.'' Tatum stood and watched them drag over slowly toward the rest of the squad. Then he turned to Greene.

''You are too dumb for words, Greene. You act like this is some big game, don't you? Man, this is for real, and it won't get any easier. Sometime soon we're going to start fighting and men are gonna get killed -- black men and white men. And let me tell you, Greene, everyone's blood is red.''

The corporal started to say something, but thought better of it. He nodded slightly, turned and went quietly back to his bulldozer.

Tatum stared at his back. *Now there's one hard-ass black man. I wonder what happened in his life to make him so bitter? Well, I hope to God he gets over it, or it'll end up eating him up from the inside.* He shook his head, walked over and picked up his MOPP gear where he had thrown it hurriedly, and walked slowly back to his squad.

* * *

Neel was sitting on his cot in the apartment at Khobar Towers, staring at the letter. *How many times had he read it?* he wondered. *It was the last one he had received from Marty before they had left Fort McCoy, and the only link now between them, nearly half a world away. No one knew when any more mail would catch up to them or even if it would, because soon they would be going to their remote desert camp.*

As he looked at the letter, he could almost visualize Marty in the warm, long silk pajamas he had bought for her birthday at Victoria's Secret. She would have been sitting at the old walnut desk in their bedroom, maybe with the TV on—she loved to watch country and western performers, a strange interest for a woman from the eastern seaboard. He knew she had struggled with the letter, because she found it difficult to express her feelings satisfactorily on paper, and preferred to discuss them with him verbally. He began to read.

Dear Tom,

I'm sending this letter to Fort McCoy but I don't know if you'll get it in time. I just can't comprehend that you're going to be so far away and I'll be by myself here. I thought we got married so that we could be together all the time—??

Work is going well here, but I can't seem to keep my mind focused. I seem to lose concentration and all I can think about is this damn Persian Gulf thing. It's all over the TV news and the Kansas City Star is full of it every day. The students and faculty all talk about it—I just can't get away from it.

I'm feeling better now, not as much nausea. Dr. Williams said I was fine last week when she saw me, but told me not to worry so much. Ha! How can you not worry, when your husband is going to war? I know I'm a mathematician and supposed to think logically, but this is an entirely different matter. You're there and I'm here and I don't know when (or if) you're coming back. And, just to let you know what almost did me in, yesterday I got a letter addressed to you in the mail from the Army. I opened it up and it was a set of orders for you. What little I could figure out said that they had extended your recall to active duty for ONE WHOLE YEAR!!

Do you realize that if you don't come back for a whole year, your child will be over six months old and never will have seen his or her father? Tom, why did you allow this to happen to us? You could have quit the Army at any time—you put your time in and then some. Why did you put yourself in this position—a new house, a new practice and a new child!!

I alternate between getting so angry at you and missing you so much. I can't concentrate on my studies and think I might sit out next semester on my

Ph.D But, I'll keep working, both to keep me sane, and to help pay for this new house—someone has to.

Tom, just don't do anything crazy over there and get yourself killed or hurt. I don't know what I'd do without you. Maybe I'm just emotional because of my pregnancy, but it's not easy for me. Come back to us!!

Love,

Marty

Neel felt a lump in his throat every time he read her letter. *Damn, he missed her, but he was serving his country and doing what every good American should do in a time of need. So why was she on his case so strongly?* He tried to put himself in her place and realized she was lonely and hurt at the possibility of having the baby without him, and angry at having to take care of everything back home while he was in Saudi.

He folded the letter, put it back into the envelope, and packed it in the ziplock bag he kept his stationery in. He knew he should write her, but was so frustrated he was afraid that he might reply angrily. He definitely didn't want to worsen the situation.

Neel decided he'd turn to the best diversion he had found when he was frustrated and upset—exercise. Ever since high school, he had enjoyed and excelled in sports. It was a natural outlet and kept his body in better shape than almost all others his age. Trouble was, while at Fort McCoy he could go to the gym and fitness center each day, he hadn't had much exercise since arriving in Saudi Arabia. The weather had been rainy and cool—but today it looked halfway decent and he was determined to take advantage of it.

He took off his desert fatigues and laid them on the cot. He found his grey Army PT shorts, a pair of socks and his running shoes, and a grey sweat shirt with 'ARMY' on the front. He buckled his gas mask case around his shoulder and tightened the chest strap. He jogged a few steps in the room to see if it was comfortable and readjusted it until it was. The gas mask would be on his back and that would free up his arms for a natural swing. He found his aviator sunglasses and a sweatband, and left the apartment.

As he exited the stairwell and walked into the ground floor foyer that served as the security desk, he literally bumped into First Sergeant Trinidad Gonzales, who was talking to the enlisted guard. Gonzales was dressed like Neel, except his P.T. T-shirt said '1SGT GONZALES' on the back in stenciled letters.

"Excuse me, sir," Gonzales said, moving out of Neel's way.

"That's okay, sergeant, my fault. I was in a hurry to get outside and had my mind on other things."

"Yes, sir, I know how that is. You planning to run today, sir? Looks like the rain's holding off for now. Gives us a good chance to stretch out and get some exercise." Gonzales was fairly dark-skinned, powerfully built, but with little body hair except for his thick black moustache.

"Say, sergeant, why don't we run together, if that was what you were planning."

"Well, sir, I don't want to slow you up," Gonzales answered, more than a little uncomfortable at the thought of some friendly running with a field-grade officer. His world revolved around NCOs and junior officers and he was not much used to majors or above.

"No problem, sergeant. I think this weather and all will probably slow both of us down."

Gonzales glanced over at the enlisted man at the security desk who was drinking some bottled water. *Oh, well, what the hell. I'll never see this major again, probably. We'll both be shipped off to different parts of the country. He'll probably be in Riyadh in a nice apartment next to a fancy hospital and I'll be somewhere out in the desert, sleeping on my tank and showering every week or so. So why not?*

"All right, sir, I'm with you. Name's Gonzales, Trinidad Gonzales."

"Tom Neel, sergeant, glad to meet you." The two men shook hands and evaluated their respective grips. They did not try to 'outsqueeze' each other, but simply compared strength.

Each checked to be sure he had his active-duty military ID, which would be required for reentry into the building, then tucked the cards inside their socks so they wouldn't be lost. Gonzales let Neel exit first, then followed him out. He noted Neel was tall, lean and muscular, with a natural gait that hinted at long-distance endurance.

"How far do you want to run, sergeant?"

"Up to you, sir. I'll just try to keep up," Gonzales replied.

Like hell you will, Neel thought with a grin. *I'll bet you would try to run me into the ground. I've run against Hispanics like you before in college and they could run until they dropped.*

"Well, let's take an eight-minute pace and run for about an hour, how does that sound?"

Gonzales mentally calculated that at about 7 1/2 miles. *Might as well. I've been eating too many fatty MRE's and I need to get some of it out of my system.*

"Drive on, sir, I'm with you."

The two men went into the street that surrounded the compound and walked to the far side, just inside the tall wire fence concertina wire perimeter. There was still some concern about snipers in the land adjacent to the compound, and they could see men on top of the buildings in the compound surveying the distance through binoculars. There were also sand-bagged bunkers on the roofs, manned by machine gun crews.

The two men started running somewhat slowly, trying to gauge the other's pace and stride. They finally came into synchrony after about 100 meters into what Neel knew from years of competitive running was about the correct pace for an eight-minute mile.

"So where you from?" Neel asked. He liked this particular pace because it allowed physically fit runners to carry on a conversation for an extended time without getting short of breath.

"El Paso, sir. How about yourself?"

Well, I grew up in south Missouri, but I recently moved to Kansas City. I'm a reservist, by the way. And, while we run, you don't have to call me 'sir'," Neel said with his boyish grin.

"Yes, sir—I mean, okay, that's fine by me, if it's okay with you."

"So you're with the 3rd Armored?"

"Yeah, I'm first sergeant of a platoon of Abrams M1s. We're out of Germany and they hauled us down here so fast my head was spinning. Now, we gotta wait here guarding your building—no offense, you know—until we find some trucks to deliver our tanks to the desert."

"No offense taken, Gonzales. I'm damn glad you're there in

the building. I do sleep better at night knowing you all are downstairs.''

''What kind of doctor are you, major?''

''Surgeon. Actually, a trauma surgeon. I practice at a major trauma center in Kansas City. I guess that's why they shipped me here. They must be figuring on some kind of trauma here in the future.''

Gonzales turned and looked at Neel as they dodged around a Bradley fighting vehicle that partially blocked the road at an intersection. There was a soldier behind the machine gun who didn't look old enough to drive, let alone kill an enemy.

Gonzales wasn't sure if Neel was serious or just had a dry sense of humor. He'd reserve judgment on that.

''Well, Doc,'' Gonzales said, somewhat breathily, ''I sure hope I never have to see you professionally.''

''Same here, sergeant, same here.''

They ran in silence for a while, occasionally commenting on buildings that were heavily fortified and sandbagged. Probably housed intelligence units or communications equipment. Here and there were men playing football or catch with a softball, but all were wearing their gas mask carriers and their MOPP suits and helmets were 'grounded' close by.

There appeared to be a constant level of activity with units moving gear into a building or leaving and loading onto trucks and Saudi buses for transportation somewhere into the desert. Most were 3rd Armored, medical, or quartermaster.

They ran past a makeshift PX in an underground parking garage and noted the long line of men and women waiting to look over a paltry display. Still, it was something to do, and gave the GIs a sense of purpose they otherwise lacked.

The sun had broken through the clouds since they began the run and it was warming up. Both were sweating, but enjoying the exercise. For a short time, they were just two older athletes enjoying the company of the other—as if they had stepped out of the present state of affairs in the Persian Gulf and had engaged in a perfectly normal pastime.

''How long you been in the Army?'' Neel asked.

''All told, about 16 years. I was in during the late 60's and early 70's when I got drafted, then got out for about six years before I reupped.''

''Missed the Army, did you?''

''Actually, I did. I tried to open a Mexican restaurant in El Paso, and it did okay, not great, but I wasn't happy. I realized I had left the Army because I was bitter, but there were some things about active duty that I really loved. So, I came back in about '79 and here I am.''

''Were you in Vietnam?'' Neel inquired, studying Gonzales' reaction, already anticipating his answer.

''Yeah, I was there.'' Gonzales didn't say any more, just tucked his head down and picked up the pace a little.

There must be some real repressed anger there, Neel thought, reverting to his medical training. *Maybe he'll talk to me about it sometime, but I won't press it now.*

''You got any kids, sergeant?''

''Sure do, major. Three daughters back home in Germany with my wife. They're a Godsend.'' He smiled at the reminder of his three active chatterboxes. *Damn, how he missed his family.* ''How about you?''

''Well, I'm married and my wife teaches back home in Kansas City. She's pregnant with our first child and she's not at all happy that I'm here.''

''I know how that is, major. The wives really do need you there with them. You're like their—I don't know—their security blanket, I guess. Going it alone just isn't much good for them.''

Neel shook his head ruefully. ''I know that and it really makes me sick. But, what can I do about it? She just doesn't understand.''

Gonzales had never had an officer tell him his personal problems and he didn't know what to say. So he kept quiet.

''How do you figure a woman, sarge? You think you got 'em figured, and then they do a 180 and leave you with your mouth hanging.''

''That's women, major. You can't live with 'em and you can't live without 'em.''

They both chuckled at the old saying and settled back into their own thoughts. The run was nearly over and they would be back to the reality of where they were and what they were doing.

As they stopped running in front of their building and slow-walked to cool down, Neel said, ''I'd be happy to run with you again, sergeant, just come and get me. Not much going on here for me to do so whenever you're free, let me know."

"Great, major, I'd like that."

They shook hands again, walked up to the soldier standing security in front of their building, displayed their ID cards (although the guard knew darn well who they were—but after all, general orders were to be obeyed) and parted inside the building.

* * *

Specialist Anders was finishing up bandaging a crew chief's finger, which had been cut on a knife while he opened up a box of chaff for his aircraft. The metal strips were supposed to confuse a radar guided missile if one was shot toward the chopper.

The cut was clean and took only six sutures to close. Anders was very quick and deft with suturing, and had impressed several flight surgeons who were less proficient.

"All right, Sarge, it shouldn't fall off tonight, but if it does, just pack it in ice and bring it back." Anders grinned at the crew chief who was looking at him in horror. "Hey, don't be so serious," Anders laughed. "You know we don't have any ice here."

The crew chief relaxed and managed a weak smile. He could put an aircraft back together, but when it came to his own body, well, that was a very different matter.

"I want you to take these antibiotic pills three times a day, just before eating. Keep this finger dry and elevated as much as possible and don't pick your nose with it, okay?"

"Yeah, doc, I got it," the crew chief said, as he got up off the litter and tried to put his LBE gear on with one hand.

"Here, let me help you." Anders stood up and helped the sergeant with his web gear and buckled his gas mask carrier back on. The sergeant put on his helmet and slung his shoulder holster over his good arm. "What do I owe you, doc?"

"Just let someone else open the next box, okay, sarge? You're not cut out to be a swordsman." He put his hand on the crew chief's shoulder and helped him toward the tent flap just as two officers in aviator's suits brought another officer into the tent holding his lip.

"Have a seat right over here, sir, and I'll take a look at you." He motioned to another litter and Captain Tex Weatherby sat down, still holding a cool Coke can to his lip.

Where in the world did he get a cold Coke? Anders

wondered. *Maybe the rumor is true that chopper pilots have a real supermarket over there in the operations area. Boy, would I love a cold Coke.* He took the can from Weatherby's hand, feeling its coolness for a long second, then placed it on the Mayo stand next to the litter. He looked at it a second time, very longingly.

"Tell me what happened, sir," he said, as he began to inspect the cut on the captain's lower lip.

The captain tried to speak, but decided his lip was too painful and swollen, so he pointed to one of the other officers.

Captain Everett Hill cleared his throat and spoke seriously. "The captain here decided he was a one-man team in volleyball today and was all over the place. His mouth just seemed to have occupied the same place as another player's elbow, resulting in the humiliating injury you see before you." What Hill did not say was that it was Weatherby's unsportsmanlike behavior in hogging every play that had gotten a teammate, a fellow officer, upset enough to 'accidentally' do the damage.

"That's too bad, sir. Did it bleed very much?" Weatherby shook his head.

"Any loose teeth, sir?" No again. "Let me see for myself." Anders gently pulled the swollen, cut lip down to look at the anterior teeth and checked them for mobility. *Looks firm and there are no cracks. Good. However, the mucosa inside the lip is lacerated, so it has to be treated as a contaminated wound.*

"Well, sir, let me tell you—this laceration needs to be sutured. I'll be happy to have the ambulance take you over to the 13th Evacuation Hospital down the road where the facial surgeon could suture your lip. You probably want an M.D. to sew this up."

Weatherby thought for a second, looked at Anders, sizing him up and made his decision. "You do it," he said, through swollen lips, grimacing as he did.

That decision made Anders uncomfortable. He had never sutured an officer's wound, let alone an aviation commander. He had heard about Weatherby and the scuttlebutt had it that he was a pretty egotistical SOB, not too concerned about anyone but himself. What if Anders screwed up this suturing job and the captain got angry at him. *No, he didn't want to do it.*

"No, sir, I think you'd better go to the 13th. The doctor there will do a fine job for you." Anders nodded his head in emphasis.

Weatherby looked sternly at Anders and poked his right index finger into Ander's chest—you do it, he emphasized.

Obviously, Anders had no choice. So he nodded, and went about getting ready the sterile suture set. "Are you allergic to any local anesthetics, sir?"

Weatherby shook his head.

"All right, then, just lie back on the litter, sir. I'm going to inject a local to numb your lip before I clean it. That way it won't hurt to use the antiseptic scrub."

After Weatherby laid back, Anders drew up 5cc of 2% lidocaine with epinephrine into a syringe. Gently, he wiped the captain's chin and inserted the needle into the soft tissues below the lower jaw's canine tooth. He injected a steady stream of anesthetic as he advanced the needle toward bone. Once he contacted bone, he injected approximately 1/2 cc of the anesthetic in that area. He then withdrew and repeated the procedure on the opposite side of the jaw. Weatherby hadn't flinched.

"Sir, what I'm doing here is anesthetizing the mental nerves which exit their canals in your jaw to supply sensation to the lower lip. Once your lip is numb, I can inject directly into the cut, so it won't bleed very much while I suture it, and, being numb, I can scrub it without hurting you."

Weatherby looked at Anders and nodded both his consent and his understanding. Anders did what he had described to the captain, then gently washed the laceration with an antiseptic Betadine solution. He then put on sterile surgical gloves and tested the wound to see if it was completely anesthetized by pinching the skin with a toothed forceps. No reaction from Weatherby.

"Captain, I'm only going to lightly suture the inside layer of the lip, that is, the pink mucous membrane. If I suture it too tightly, saliva will get trapped inside and it will get infected. So I'll just pull it together through the wound with some absorbable stitches to hold it together."

Weatherby closed his eyes and tried to relax while the medic began the process of suturing his inner lip. He could feel Anders' hot breath as he worked with his face close to his. *Well, I don't feel a thing. This kid must know what he's doing. At least, I sure hope he does. Maybe I should have gone to the Evac Hospital. Nah, I just don't like being around doctors very much—seems like they can see right through you and figure out what you're thinking. Especially the 'shrinks.' They're the sneaky ones.*

"Okay, now, captain," Anders said, as he straightened up and wiped his brow with the back of his forearm. "I've got the inner layer closed and now I have to close the muscle. This is an important layer, but I have to make sure the pink part and the white match up perfectly. If it doesn't, other people would notice an irregularity, even a very small one."

Anders leaned down very close to the wound and with calm, steady hands, placed a nylon suture first in one side of the laceration, then the other, exactly at the junction. He did not tie the suture until he had pulled it up tightly to observe the alignment. "Um-huh, looks fine," he murmured to himself. Then he relaxed the suture so he could sew up the muscular middle layer of Weatherby's lip.

If that was not matched up correctly, Anders recalled from his basic medic training at Fort Sam Houston in San Antonio, the muscle could separate, and a trough would form on the lip, letting air and liquids pass through. *What did they call it,* he wondered to himself? *Oh, yeah—they called it a 'whistle' deformity because you were supposed to be able to whistle through it when you didn't want to. He sure needed to avoid that problem here.*

He worked on in silence, concentrating on closing the muscular layer of the lip. He was by himself, so he had to lay down the needle holder after completing a stitch and cut the suture himself, cutting it close to the knot so the free ends did not protrude through the skin and cause a local infection.

Once the muscle layer was closed, Anders tightened and tied the suture holding the junctional border of the lip together, leaning back on the field stool to make sure the alignment was satisfactory. *No, not just satisfactory, it has to be perfect.*

Satisfied, he began suturing the pink part of the lip with silk sutures that wouldn't irritate the captain when he ate, and nylon sutures for the white lip skin. It was closing nicely, Anders decided, relaxing almost visibly.

"Looking good here, captain. After it heals, I don't think you'll hardly be able to see the scar. I'll give you some oral antibiotics for a few days, just to cover the possibility of infection in these conditions, as well as some ointment to apply to the stitches. Okay?"

The captain nodded, which caused Anders to lose his needle

positioning on a stitch.

"Sorry, sir, I shouldn't have asked you a question. Just hold as still as you can, please. I'm almost done."

Anders was thinking about this injury. He'd seen broken noses and black eyes from volleyball, but never a cut lip. It was almost as if one of the captain's own players had purposefully set up an elbow to catch the captain just so—giving someone a cut, 'fat' lip also has other social connotations, Anders realized. *I wonder if this captain is a prick.*

"Well, sir, just about done. You're going to have to curtail your athletic adventures for a couple of weeks so you don't get hit again." *And try to be a better guy, too,* Anders thought, but didn't say.

After he finished, Anders cleaned the outer lip with peroxide, removing the blood clots around the stitches and making the job look good. He surveyed his work—a neat row of stitches, perfectly spaced, with the knots all cut the same length. He enjoyed the machine-like quality of his work, satisfying his obsessive nature. If one had looked out of place, he would have replaced it with a perfectly matched one. After all, the patient only sees the skin stitches, not the deep ones, and the way it looks is almost your signature. Like an artist who signs a painting only when it's finished to his satisfaction.

He applied antibiotic ointment to the sutures with a Q-tip and helped the captain sit up. "Sorry I don't have a mirror, sir, but you'll see it when you look in your shaving mirror soon enough. Just try not to cut the stitches when you shave—and let me be the one to take them out, okay?"

"I'll need to remove the stitches in the top part of your lip in three to four days, and the rest in about five to seven days. So just drive on over here when it's convenient. We're going out on a few air-evac missions every now and then, but that's sporadic. I'm usually here, or will be back within an hour or two, anyway." Anders was cleaning up the residue from his suturing as he talked, careful with the needles so as not to accidentally stick his finger with one of them. Although all military personnel in the Persian Gulf had been tested for HIV infection before deployment and found to be negative, it was a habit of caution that all health care workers had developed over the past few years.

"Now, captain, the flight surgeon left me some signed

'flight duty slips' and I'll need to fill out a 'down' slip on you for three days until I check the wound on Friday.'' A 'down slip' was a grounding order for a flyer when they had a medical condition which prevented their flying or posed a risk or hazard to safe flight. When the risk was gone, they would be issued an 'up slip' and returned to flying duty. Only a flight surgeon (or the aviation commander) can control this grounding for health reasons and, because the nearest flight surgeon was over at the 13th Evac Hospital, Anders had been entrusted with some blank, signed slips to use at his serious discretion. It was a lot of responsibility for an enlisted medic, but the flight surgeon had had confidence in Anders' judgement and carefully reviewed the rules about when to use the slips.

Weatherby looked at the 'down slip' and shook his head. He was damned tired of doing administrative work and wanted only to fly. Flying was his 'release' from the bondage of human problems and only in the air did he feel truly free. No pilot likes to be grounded, not even temporarily, but he understood the need. It would be several days anyway before his swollen lip went down enough for him to be understood on a radio transmission. He didn't want any problems because of a miscommunication.

''Thank you, Sergeant Anders,'' he managed to get out, somewhat indistinctly, like a toddler first trying to talk. ''I'm sure you did a good job and I appreciate it.'' He held out his hand and shook Anders'.

Anders was immediately embarrassed and hung his head. ''Oh, that's all right, sir. Anyone could have done it. Be sure to come by on Friday, or sooner if it looks red or inflamed.''

Weatherby nodded and tried to smile but couldn't tell if he was or not because his whole lower lip was numb.

Weatherby walked toward the tent flap to find the other flyers who had waited outside. He turned as Anders called to him one last time.

''And one more thing, sir. I may be out of line, and if so, I'm sorry. But if this injury wasn't an accident, then you need to figure out *why* it happened. Might be important to you.''

Weatherby stared intently at Anders for a minute, then nodded and left the tent.

* * *

Lieutenant Porter was dreaming. He was running along the

beach at sunset, frolicking near the water's edge with a young woman who resembled Cathy Long, but who wasn't really quite her. He and Cathy had had a brief fling one summer after graduation from high school in Augusta, before he went off to West Point. That summer he had lost his innocence to Miss Long, and, for that he was eternally grateful. In the dream, they had stopped near a rock outcropping and he was watching her remove her shorts and halter top when suddenly he was awakened with a start.

"Lieutenant," Sergeant Lopez said quietly, "it's time to get ready." It took several minutes for Porter to pull himself out of the surrealism of his dream and to become aware that he was here, deep inside enemy territory, not back on the beach at Charleston getting ready to explore Cathy Long's hidden assets. He loved women, as did any red blooded American fighting man, but Porter also loved adventure, and where better to be in a war than where he was right now. So, he tucked Cathy back into the recesses of his memory and crawled out of his sleeping hole to make supper.

The meal tonight was pretty much like it had been for the past week—a choice of MRE's. Their food cache was built into an elevated crevice in the rock, lined with a poncho and containing a large airdrop plastic container where the food was stored. They always ate on the opposite side of the crater from their sleeping holes and were very careful about cleaning up their crumbs and debris and burying it away from where they slept. Because rodents and snakes were attracted to food residue, they didn't want any company in their sleeping bags, so each man was very careful.

The problem was that the MRE entrees, usually some meat, contained enough liquid fat to keep a cardio-vascular surgeon in business for a career, and it was very difficult to keep that fat from spilling, especially when the meal was hot. Besides, there wasn't any place to wash up after a meal, so the men relied on a special, biodegradable, disposable cleaning cloth developed for special operations forces by Johnson and Johnson. Similar to the popular "Handiwipes" of civilian life, the special ops version was dark brown, contained no scent that would alert an enemy or a guard dog, and would even clean dried blood off a commando knife. After use, the wipes were buried in the ground or in the sand where they decomposed over a few days, leaving no residue.

Since their job tonight was to be a long 12-hour

reconnaissance mission, Porter chose a ham omelette from the MRE cache, his favorite. Using a special sterno stove that gave off very little heat and was a totally enclosed unit, he warmed up the entree and poured off the excess fat from the pocket into a ziplock bag for storage and disposal.

Porter thought the best part of the MRE was the peanut butter and jelly. He had always loved it when his mother put one in his school lunch, especially when she used her homemade stone-ground wheat bread. His mind wandered back to the many times when his father was away from home on an assignment, and his mother would hand him a lunch pail, pat him on the head, and send him off to the school on whatever military post they happened to be living at the time. He wondered briefly (again, for he thought about this more as he got older) whether he would have any children of his own, and if so, whether he would be around more for their growing up than his own father was for his. He loved his father, but had known the loneliness of a military son far more often than he had cared to, although he could not have shown it in those days.

He put the family thoughts out of his mind and finished his supper. He took the meal residue out to the waste burial area, about 100 meters from the crates, and used his entrenching tool to dig a small crater about a foot deep, then deposited his waste. It had to be buried deep because the 'shamal' wind storms could easily blow an inch of sand off the desert floor. The men did not want their MRE debris to come sailing into an Iraqi camp where the enemy might figure out that they were too far from Saudi Arabia for this to belong to Americans from down there. Their lives depended upon camp security and avoiding detection.

Tonight's patrol was important. Three of the team, Porter, Master Sergeant Lopez, and Sergeant Miller, would locate the Iraqi's Jalibah airfield and carefully recon the site, observing types and number of aircraft, location and types of antiaircraft artillery and missile emplacements, and vulnerable areas for future air strikes by Coalition aircraft.

Miller was the communications specialist and he would be able to transmit their findings by short-burst transmissions, either from the desert near the airport or preferably from their base camp after they returned.

This mission would take at least two days—a night march to

the site, a day for observation under camouflage and cover and a night march back. From the meal just eaten, they would only eat special high-protein, high carbohydrate energy bars that were light-weight and had a low residue content, thereby alleviating the need for defecation during the observation period. They would carry plenty of water in their collapsible canteens, because the march would tend to dehydrate them unless they replenished their water.

Tonight, each man would be carrying only his personal side-arm, which in their case was the Beretta 9mm automatic. Their mission was not to get into a fire-fight with the Iraqis, but rather to avoid one at any cost. The weapons were merely to ensure no one fell into enemy hands to be tortured into revealing sensitive information. Every special forces team member carried a 'Top Secret' security clearance and certain ones like Lieutenant Porter actually had an 'Eyes Only' level. It would not do for these men to be captured.

As the glow of moonlight settled on the camp, it began to look like a moonscape—some meteor-spawned crater in a sea of sand, reminding Porter of his first view of the moon when Neil Armstrong had climbed out of the spacecraft and set foot upon its peculiar soil. The moon seemed larger than life here in the desert, and its heightened clarity was probably because there were no city lights to diminish its intensity.

Tonight, after Porter replaced the batteries in his powerful Datascope, he had turned the scope toward the moon on a whim and gazed at its visible topographic features. He had long admired the Apollo astronauts who had risked their lives on a journey that was no less important than Christopher Columbus'. In fact, there were times when he had considered applying to NASA for an astronaut position—after all, he did have an engineering degree, and he was a glider pilot with well over 1,000 hours. His health and physical conditioning were excellent. He didn't think his father would mind such a career, because it could still be done as a military officer, returning to line duty after eight to ten years with NASA.

The thought always seemed attractive to Porter except when he realized there was a *fundamental* difference between him and the other military men who had gone on to become astronauts. Almost all of them had been pilots, and some, in the course of his career had likely dispatched another airplane in a dog fight or perhaps bombed an enemy position on the ground. But this was an *acceptable* way to take another human life, even if aggrandized a bit. But how many of them had actually terminated a man in a one-on-one encounter, either by blowing off his head with a silenced 9mm Beretta, or by cutting his throat with a stiletto? Porter had already done that on a number of occasions. Killing someone facing you is a very personal form of dealing death, and he realized the NASA psychiatrists would likely be very uncomfortable recommending someone with his violent and deadly skills.

Oh, well, he sighed. *Maybe I can fantasize tonight that I'm embarking upon an exploration of some distant planet. I guess it takes as much courage to cross the desert into an enemy camp as it does to explore the moon.*

He tucked the Datascope into his right breast pocket and shouldered his ruck. By Special Forces standards it was light and they should have no problem making 5-6 kilometers an hour. He removed the last item for the mission from its protective Cordura nylon case: the Magellan NA V100 MGPS. He had been impressed with his first use of the device and was more comfortable in its ability to show him the course to the predetermined targets. He powered up the unit and confirmed the battery strength. There were extra batteries in the case. Porter accessed the code for their objective and noted the indicated direction and distance to the site on the display:

Target: Code E

Jalibah Airfield

86.32 DEG MAGN

24.561 Kilometers

He marveled at the device and how it would advise him on their march if he strayed from the prescribed course. The Magellan was similar to the cockpit display during an instrument approach at an ATC airport. He was glad he had taken a number of computer courses in his engineering curriculum at West Point and so could use this navigation device to its full potential. However, as a man who never left anything to chance, especially when men's lives depended on him, he checked to make sure he was carrying his M-2 compass, too. Although a 'back-up' compass to the Magellan, the M-2 in its own right was sophisticated as compasses go. It was said to be the finest precision compass ever made and included horizontal and vertical angle measurement, jeweled movement and prismatic in-line sighting for superior accuracy. Its lightweight titanium alloy case and body were of Swiss-like precision. He had even taken this compass on hunting trips back in Germany and had become proficient with it.

Satisfied he was ready, Porter gathered his two men and left the camp with little acknowledgment from the rest of the team. He had placed the executive officer, CW02 Billy Nichols, in charge of the team in his absence. Mr. Nichols was fully qualified to lead if Porter should become compromised and he knew the frequencies and call signs to get the team extracted if need be.

Reconnaissance of the enemy, especially right under his nose, was known to be perilous, and these men of the military's elite special operations forces, including the Army's Green Berets and the Navy's SEAL's, voluntarily accepted the risk. Everything good in life has some sort of trade-off, and for the exciting and challenging lives Porter and his men lived, there was the risk of losing theirs. But Porter had always felt you can never really *appreciate* life until you have put it on the line or hung it over the edge. If you live after that, then life is all the sweeter. Over the past five years, on many occasions, Porter had put his life over that line.

Through his night-vision goggles, CW02 Nichols watched the recon team walk across the desert. He knew their mission was dangerous, but also vital to the success of any air war launched against the Iraqis in this AO. He silently wished them Godspeed and a safe return.

CHAPTER FIVE

MAJOR TOM NEEL was bored as well as frustrated. It had taken only about a week of inactivity at Khobar Towers to thrust him into this frame of mind. The war had not started, there was no indication the Coalition forces were ready and no definite plans had been passed to the medical professionals that their skills would be needed any time soon.

Normally, Neel's life back home was filled with some sort of activity from early morning until some time in the evening, more likely late evening than early. His professional life had been busy ever since medical school and he was not usually given to taking 'restful' vacations. The longest he had been away from his medical work (other than reserve activities) had been their honeymoon, when he and Marty had spent a week at the Castle Harbor Beach Hotel in Bermuda. Even then, he had become restless and anxious to get back to work. It wasn't that he didn't enjoy the honeymoon (he most certainly did) - it was just that he enjoyed medicine so much he didn't want to be away from it very long. An ideal vacation for Neel was three to four days of relaxation (usually skiing or Scuba diving) to 'replenish his batteries,' then a return to work with renewed vigor.

So it was particularly difficult for him to sit around Khobar without any medical responsibilities, trying to keep his mind and body occupied. But, one day an incident occurred that gave him the idea and impetus to change his static situation.

He was returning from the makeshift headquarters area at Khobar designated as a mail drop after posting a letter to Marty, when he noticed a heavy-set young male trooper hobbling across the compound. The soldier was obviously in pain when he walked, reflected by the grimace on his face at each step.

Quickly, Neel caught up with the soldier and asked him to stop. ''Good morning, private. Looks like you're having a tough time walking. What seems to be the problem?''

The private drew up as straight as possible and offered the

major a half-hearted salute. ''Mornin', sir,'' he responded, with a drawling accent Neel recognized as either from Alabama or Mississippi. ''I surely am having trouble, sir. I was just issued these desert boots two days ago, before I had to go and unload supplies at the docks. I had no time to break 'em in and had to walk all over kingdom come to do it. My feet have got blisters you wouldn't believe and they've been bleedin', too.''

During the brief exchange, Neel could tell the private was not likely one who complained or whined, so he must have a serious problem with his feet.

''Where are you going right now?''

''To the first aid station, sir, to see if someone there can help me with my feet.''

''Here, let me walk over there with you,'' Neel said as he took the man's rucksack off his shoulder and placed it on his own. *Man, this ruck must weigh 40 pounds,* Neel thought. *No wonder he was hobbling on his sore feet.* ''I'm a doctor, and I'll be happy to look at your feet at the aid station and see what I can do.''

The soldier's face broke into an expression of sheer relief. ''Oh, thank you sir, I would be mighty grateful to you if you could do anything for me.''

Neel walked across the compound with the man toward the makeshift aid station which had been set up by one of the medical clearing companies on an 'unofficial' basis. The Army had not planned very well for this transient housing as far as medical care was concerned, apparently forgetting that 15,000 people, even reasonably fit ones, develop health problems that need attending to. Consequently, the commander of the medical clearing company at Khobar had received tacit approval to open a sick call at a temporary location. Neel had no idea how the aid station was run or who was staffing it, but he would soon find out.

They located the appropriate building (not easily, though) and walked inside to the first floor receiving area. There were men and women everywhere! They were standing or sitting wherever they could find room, waiting to see someone about an ailment or complaint. Neel estimated nearly a hundred patients were there and surmised there must be four or five physicians seeing them.

He found a small area on the floor where the private could sit and rest his feet, and went back to find the physicians. What he located was one lone doctor, a pediatrician for goodness' sake, who was the only physician seeing the sick call patients, with the assistance of several corpsmen.

The young physician was Captain Raul Torres and he had been activated out of his senior year of residency at Galveston, and placed in a medical clearing company as a GMO (General Medical Officer). The captain looked tired and harassed and his frustration was written all over his face.

''Good morning, major. I'm sure happy to see you this morning. Did you come over to help?'' Torres inquired expectantly. ''I've been working here practically non-stop for a week and I could surc usc somc.''

''Where are the rest of the physicians in your company, Raul?'' Neel asked.

''They're down at the dock, sir, looking after the sick there. Apparently, they've got nearly 50,000 people stuck in warehouses at the port and they're trying to see those folks at sick call. They're probably worse off than we are here.''

Typical military screwup, Neel thought. *Line commanders do a great job working out the complex logistics of housing, transportation, and food for over 60,000 individuals and don't even think how to take care of medical problems. They simply ignore or figure the doctors will work it out somehow.*

''Well, I really just came over here to see about a soldier with bad blisters, but I can see I might be of some help here, if it's okay with you.''

Torres' face beamed with relief. ''Yes, sir, you bet it's all right with me. I've never seen some of these things they're complaining about, and I'm especially uncomfortable with the orthopedic-type injuries. I'd be very pleased for you to help out.''

For starters, Major Neel asked a corpsman to bring in the private with the bad feet and get him ready to be examined. The private's name turned out to be John Turner and he was from Enterprise, Alabama, not far from the Army's Aeromedical Center and Fort Rucker, where Neel had taken his flight surgeon training.

Turner was lying face down on a canvas litter, his boots off, but socks still on. Neel could see the socks were stuck to the back of the private's heels by bloody drainage and the private cried out when Neel tried to remove them.

''Corpsman, get me some peroxide so I can soften up this crust, please.'' The corpsman soon returned with a brown bottle of peroxide and Neel poured it over Turner's heels. The peroxide began to bubble fiercely as it contacted the dried blood in the crust. Neel knew it would be painful for Turner to have the socks removed, but he had to do it. He removed his ever-present bandage scissors from the pocket of his BDU's and cut off the sock, gently teasing it off the raw skin of Turner's heel. When the sock was off, Neel found a mass of infected, draining tissue that looked pretty bad.

He leaned over to talk to Turner. "John, these blisters are infected. I can see now why they are so painful. Why didn't you tell someone about them sooner?"

"Well, sir, there was so much work to be done, I couldn't just leave afore we finished it."

Typical hard-working southerner, Neel thought. *Would drop in the fields or on the job before he'd ever quit.*

"I'm going to have to work on this pretty extensively today, John, to try to remove the infected tissue so we can get this mess cleared up. Then I'll have to bandage your feet and get you some crutches to get around with. It may take me a week to get you on the road to healing, but it may take longer to heal totally."

Turner nodded. "Just do what you got to, sir, and I really appreciate you taking the time to help me, I really do."

"I know that, John, and I'll do my best. It's going to be pretty uncomfortable today because I'll have to cut away the infected tissue. I can't inject any local anesthetic into the area to numb it because I don't want to run the risk of spreading the infection, so it may hurt. I'll be as gentle as I can, okay?"

"Yes sir, go right ahead. I can take it."

I'll bet you can, Neel thought, wishing he was back home in Kansas City where he could do the debridement under intravenous Diprovan sedation and with demerol or morphine to help kill the pain. *But you're not in Kansas City—you're not even in the western hemisphere, so you've got to use what is available and just do your best.*

The corpsman found him a sterile (hopefully) suture set after rummaging through the meager supplies for about ten minutes. Neel inserted a number 15 scalpel blade onto the scalpel handle and picked up a pair of forceps. The necrotic and infected tissue looked a lot like a second degree burn and he proceeded slowly to excise it to healthier looking tissue. He knew he was hurting

Turner, but there was no choice. Turner was not making a sound, but his hands were gripping the litter sides so tightly his fingers were white. There were no sterile gloves or masks to be found, so Neel was particularly careful only to touch the wound with the instruments.

As he worked, he talked to Turner to help keep Turner's mind off of the pain. "John, are you a fisherman?"

"Yes, sir," Turner grunted.

"You know, when I was at Fort Rucker in the 70's, I used to go fishing on a lake about 20 miles north of town. Big lake, about 500 acres. Ever been there?"

"Yes, sir. It's called Lake Oglethorpe, after ... uh, that hurts, sir ... after some Civil War general who grew up on that land." Turner was talking through clenched teeth, which, with his Deep South accent, made him somewhat difficult to understand.

Neel had removed a fair amount of devitalized skin and was blotting some bleeding areas with a sterile sponge. *That's a good sign. Where the tissue bleeds it will probably heal all right.*

"What kind of fishing do you like to do, John? I'm a trout fisherman myself, particularly the rainbow trout down on the Eleven-Point River in south Missouri."

"Well, sir, I guess trout is okay, but I mainly love to fish for bass. Small-mouth mostly . . . ow, dammit . . . I mean, sorry, sir."

"That's all right, John, I know it hurts, but I'm just about done. Do you fish from a pier or do you have a boat?"

"Oh, sir, I've got the sweetest little bass boat in Alabama. Eighteen feet with a hunnert-fifty Merc outboard. She'll jump right outta the water, if I ask her to. I enter them bass fishin' contests all the time and got me a table full of trophies. Also, not bad prize money, either."

The infected tissue was nearly all debrided, but since Neel was getting close to the more sensitive perimeter of the wounds, where the junction with normal skin was, he decided to stop. The young doctor, the corpsmen, and even some patients had walked by during the procedure, all curious about what Neel was doing.

The cleaned, raw tissue area was about four to six square centimeters on each heel, with only a thin layer of fibrous tissue left covering the Achilles tendon. *Please don't let that tendon get infected,* Neel worried, *or it will rupture for sure.* He applied Betadine-soaked gauze sponges to the wounds for about 10 minutes to get a local antiseptic effect. During that time, he looked over the small pharmaceutical supplies that were available and chose some Darvocet N 100's for pain relief and Staphcillin 500 mgm tablets for an oral antibiotic. He got the corpsman to package and label them for Turner and set them down on the litter next to him.

"All right, John, I'm going to dress the wounds now. You can't get these dressings wet and I want you to do your best to keep them as clean as possible. The medicine is labeled and tells you when to take the oral antibiotic as well as how frequently you can take the pain medicine."

Turner nodded.

Neel dressed the heels with an antibiotic ointment, bacitracin, followed by the application of a Telfa bandage to keep the dressing from sticking to the raw wounds, which would make future dressing changes less uncomfortable for Turner. He then wrapped the ankles and feet with bulky Kerlix gauze to protect the wounds from accidental injury. The corpsman found and properly measured a pair of crutches for Turner, and Neel showed him how to walk with them so the nerves in his armpits would not be injured. Turner was instructed to return each day at 0800, after chow, for a dressing change.

"Will you be here, sir, when I come back for my dressing change?" Turner asked.

Neel looked around him at the sick or injured service members waiting in line to be seen. There was no way he could walk away from this and not help these people, he realized.

"Yes, John, of course I'll be here. That's why I'm here in the Persian Gulf, to help people. So I'll see you here at 0800. Come back sooner if you start running a fever and they can ring me up over at Building 310 if I'm not here. You're a tough man, and I think it won't be as painful in future dressing changes."

Turner's face flooded with relief. "Sounds great, sir. When do you think I'll be back ready to work?" he asked.

"What sort of work do you do here?" Neel inquired.

"I drive a water truck here, sir, to supply drinking water to the desert units. Back home, I'm a trucker and drive all over the South. I got me a nice 18-wheeler."

"Well, John, you're not going to be driving for at least two weeks. I could probably get you air-evaced back to Germany to heal up if you want.''

''No, sir,'' Turner replied emphatically, shaking his head. ''Us Turners have been answering the call to arms for our country since the Civil War and I'm not about to back out on this one!''

''We need more Americans like you, John,'' Neel said as he patted Turner's arm. ''Yes, sir,'' Turner responded with pride. ''My pappy, he lost both of his legs at Guadalcanal, and he's driving a truck yet, too. He got artificial legs from the VA, he does. He wants me to come back and join the American Legion with him. That'll make him plumb proud.''

Neel smiled as the simple, but genuine young man hobbled out the door with the corpsman's assistance, trying to learn to use the crutches and not doing a very good job of it. *Now there's a solid American,* Neel thought. *He's what the country's work force is built on and who the country relies upon when we go to war. Unfortunately, he's also the man who often doesn't return home.* He dropped his smile at that thought, and shook his head.

Neel walked back to Torres' exam room and found him resting on a short break. ''I'll be happy to help out here, if you'll have me,'' Neel offered. ''It's been a while since I was a GMO, but I think it'll all come back.''

Torres stood up, offered his hand, shook Neel's and said simply: ''You're a God-send, Major Neel. Of course you can help.''

The years Neel had spent as a general surgery resident treating everything from sprains to intestinal parasites began to come back. There were cases of sinusitis, pharyngitis, staph skin abscesses, coughs, wheezes, abdominal pains, twisted ankles and low back pain, diarrhea and the whole spectrum of disorders that occur under conditions of physical and emotional stress. It was good therapy for Neel as well, making him feel useful helping others. While it was different from his practice in the ultramodern trauma center back in K.C., it was equally satisfying, and helped him combat the daytime doldrums that had threatened his composure only days before.

Private Turner healed well, and after ten days was back on his feet and assigned to driving his water truck from the port to bases being established along Tapline Road, the major east-west Saudi highway. Turner came by the clinic for Neel to give him a 'return-to-duty' slip.

"I'm very obliged to you, sir, for the fine job you did taking care of me," Turner said in gratitude. "If you're ever in Alabama, you be sure to stop by home and we'll go fishing. Okay?"

"I'd really like that, John. Now you take care on that highway out there. I hear it's very dangerous and the Arab drivers are crazy. You just be safe." Neel shook hands with Turner, and silently wished him a safe journey for the future.

* * *

The morning Private Turner left the clinic on his final visit, Sergeant First Class Trinidad Gonzales was summoned to brigade headquarters in a building next to the V.I.P. quarters where Neel and Gonzales were staying. Gonzales' platoon commander, Lieutenant Rick Hanes, was present, as well as the company commander and the division S-2 (intelligence), Lieutenant Colonel Samuel Johnson and his staff. Gonzales and Hanes had no clue as to why they were there.

The room was small, with crates for seating, and with the windows boarded shut. Colonel Johnson stood up next to a large map of the Dhahran area, including the port of Ad Damman and the narrow channel between Dhahran and Bahrain. There was a large 'S' drawn on the overlay with a red wax pencil near the location of the city of Manama, on the northern edge of the island-country of Bahrain.

"Gentlemen," the colonel began, "you're here because of a terrorist threat which has been called to our attention within the last 12 hours. Somewhere near Manama, two parachutes were seen last night hitting the water in the Gulf of Bahrain. The incident was observed by three coastal watchers in a small patrol vessel, but by the time they got to the location, no sign of the parachutes or the possible jumpers could be found. An alarm was sounded and the Bahrain authorities conducted an immediate search of that sector of the island, but to no avail."

The colonel stopped to take a drink of coffee from his mug, which read '3rd Armored Division, Heads the Rest.' Then he pointed to the map again, at the region of Al Khobar, where they were currently housed.

"The point of sighting is only twelve kilometers from our location, six of that distance being the Gulf of Bahrain. It would not be difficult for a team of commandos to swim or scuba to the coast and be on the Saudi mainland by now. About two hours ago, we had a report of some fishermen seeing some dark shapes rising out of the water about three kilometers south of here. We cannot confirm the sighting by any other observers, but the Saudis seem to think these men should be believed.''

Colonel Johnson removed the pointer from the map and held it behind his back as he paced the floor in front of the men with his head down. Momentarily, he stopped and looked directly at them.

''Our limited intelligence network in Iraq has indicated Saddam is going to try to carry out some acts of terrorism against American military personnel. The analyst says he feels a number of dead soldiers would turn the American public's sentiment against the war, just as it did in Vietnam. He is reported to have said that if the American people will not support this effort, then he can win.''

Hanes and Gonzales looked at each other and frowned. Gonzales had experienced such lack of resolve by his country in the past. He certainly did not want to experience it again.

Just then, the closed door to the room opened and a short, sturdily built, balding (too much testosterone, it was rumored) officer entered the room and walked to the front, near Colonel Johnson. ''Good morning, Sam,'' he said, then he turned to the rest of the men ''And good morning to you, gentlemen.''

Colonel Gerald ''Bull'' Durham was S-3 of the 3rd Armored, its chief operations officer. His job was to carry out the action plans decided by the commander and to issue the orders to be carried out by division personnel, under the name of the commander, of course.

''I was just briefing them on the situation, Bull, when you came in. I was getting into telling them that CENTCOM is worried that a terrorist attack might be directed toward Khobar Towers, because of the dense concentration of troops in a small area.''

Durham walked to the front and turned to the men. In effect, he took over the briefing and Colonel Johnson moved quietly to one side of the room, leaning against the wall and bouncing the pointer against the toe of his boot.

''Men, we're taking this threat seriously. We've got nearly 10,000 3rd Armored Division personnel here now, and have been tasked by CENTCOM to assist the MP company in providing security for the over 15,000 total troops located there. All indications point to the fact, as Colonel Johnson has told you,'' he nodded in Johnson's direction, ''that Iraqi commandos may have landed in the Gulf last night, and are very likely in this immediate vicinity even as we speak.''

He pointed to a tall, athletic officer standing in the back of the room. ''This is Captain Schaeffer, commander of the 3304th MP company at Khobar. His job is mainly perimeter security and law enforcement, but elements of our division will work with his men not just to protect the compound from terrorists, if there are any, but to seek out these commandos outside the compound and deal with them. The Saudi military here has no indigenous special operations units and all of ours appear to be occupied at the moment.'' The men in the room assumed this meant they were in Iraq, possibly to assassinate Saddam Hussein.

''Therefore, we will send out armed patrols to seek out these terrorists and capture or kill them before they cam harm American service members. You, Lieutenant Hanes,'' he said, pointing at Hanes in the front row, ''will place your platoon under Captain Schaeffer's direction and patrol the most likely areas for the terrorists to attempt an attack. I would recommend 24-hour patrolling, with the patrols ranging outward about 2,000 meters. The main threat appears to be from shoulder-held Stinger missiles, which the Iraqis could have obtained in Kuwait, or a satchel charge of high-explosives, to be placed on an occupied building. Captain Schaeffer will brief you on the characteristics of an Arab that might lead you to be suspicious of him or her, for that matter. Any questions?''

Lieutenant Hanes raised his hand. ''Do you want them dead or alive, sir, if we find them?''

''Preferably alive, lieutenant. I'm sure Colonel Johnson would agree that they could be a valuable source of human intelligence for our people.'' Johnson nodded silently in agreement.

''However, lieutenant, we just want them, period. And before they do any damage. Understood?''

''Yes, sir,'' Hanes responded eagerly.

Gonzales had no real stomach for the mission. He had been on combat patrols before, plenty of them, back in Vietnam. It was always exciting at first for the inexperienced, but then everyone gradually came to realize that on just about every patrol, someone was going to die. It might be an American, or it might be a Vietnamese but someone would die. And, if you were a good Catholic and were taught the value of a human life from childhood, any death was upsetting.

"Now, we want the patrols to commence immediately, and you will take all of your platoon, Lieutenant Hanes, except those men guarding the V.I.P. billet, and form four-man patrols. You may enlist the help of your platoon sergeant," he said, looking directly at 1SGT Gonzales, "who has had considerable combat patrol experience. Listen to him, Hanes, and he'll keep your men from getting killed. Any questions?"

No one asked any. Both colonels left the room and Hanes, Gonzales and Schaeffer shook hands all around. They agreed to not intermix men from the armored and MP units because they would be used to working with their own. The MP patrols would be responsible for the 500 meters immediately outside the wire perimeter, while Hanes's short-handed platoon would range between 1,000 and 2,000 meters from the perimeter.

Hanes and Gonzales returned to the platoon building and briefed the men. Gonzales spent nearly an hour reviewing patrol tactics under the circumstances and in the suburban setting of Khobar Towers. He then assigned the men to patrols and made up a simple schedule. He decided to form eight four-man patrols, with four taking one twelve-hour shift at a time. Each of the four would be assigned a 90º sector of the compass, based on 0º (due north). The daytime patrols would be very visible, so they would merely walk the territory as a display of intent. At night, when the terrorists would likely strike, the men would wear dark green tanker coveralls, darkened flak jackets and helmets and practice stealth and sound and light discipline.

The first day's patrol was uneventful, as was the first half of the second day. The daytime patrols were casual-appearing and did not raise to any significant degree the concern of the residents. At night, no one suspected or noticed the patrols and no alarm was raised.

Gonzales had decided to go out at night, rotating his presence among the four patrol teams. The men were young and inexperienced in a firefight and he felt his presence could be of benefit. The first night's patrol was uneventful, and the second night was starting out the same.

Gonzales had deployed the men into a rather tight group, trying to avoid scattering the patrol with its attendant risk of misidentifying a friendly figure in the dark. The five men were walking slowly in line with Gonzales at the rear, when the point man, Corporal Tommy Adkins from Atlanta, Georgia, held up his hand. For a big city boy, Adkins had a very good sense of awareness on patrol, as well as excellent night vision. Gonzales quietly hurried to the point, looking at Adkins for further information. Adkins held up two fingers, pointed first at his eyes and then to the right at about 20º from their present position indicating Adkins had seen two figures off to his right.

Gonzales peered off in the indicated direction, sweeping a small arc with his eyes, knowing that at night one's vision is sharper when you're not looking directly at an image. He thought he saw a slight movement next to a clump of low bushes, and stared just to the left of that site for several minutes. His patrol was about 100 meters south of the possible intruders and were well camouflaged. He did not believe they had been detected.

There it is, he thought. *A man . . . no, two men moving slowly along beside that clump of bushes. Appears like they're low crawling.* He held up his right hand and repeated Adkins' gestures, indicating to the patrol that he, too, had seen them. In the dark, he didn't want to take his eyes off of their location for fear he might lose sight of them. No night-vision goggles were available at Khobar, so good night vision tactics were mandatory. He motioned for two men to move to each flank, to try to keep the intruders from either getting past them to the perimeter, or escaping toward the Gulf.

After the men had reached their flanking positions, he motioned them forward on-line—he didn't want to allow any of his men to get ahead of the others, or they might accidentally be caught in friendly cross-fire.

As he softly walked directly toward the intruders, he recollected the memory of such patrols in the jungles of Vietnam. Gonzales felt the same sense of excitement, fear and anticipation, all at the same time. He knew that the minutes before a fire-fight were the most intense emotional experiences anyone could experience, and felt his heart racing in his chest, the knotting in his stomach, and the tendency to breathe fast. Memories of Vietnam, including sounds, smells, people, explosions, places, all came back in a rush, but Gonzales tried to push them back into the recesses of his mind, where he had successfully stored them for so many years, in order to concentrate on the moment.

Gonzales stopped and listened for sounds of movement from his men—he heard none. Fortunately, the ground beneath their feet was a sandy loam and neither cracked nor slid when they walked. He maintained his gaze on the clump of bushes where he felt the intruders were hiding. He was now about 25 meters from the spot and opened his mouth to breathe more silently than if he breathed through his nose. He also ever-so-slowly moved the selector of his M-16 to the 'AUTO FIRE' position. He knew that it would be best to capture these intruders for questioning, but wasn't sure quite how that could be done under the present circumstances.

If he hollered to them to give up at this point, it would give away his position and he didn't know what kind of weapons they possessed. If they had automatic weapons, they could mow down the entire team. They might even have grenades or rockets which could certainly injure or kill his men and himself.

On the other hand, he couldn't see sneaking up on them and getting the drop on them from ten yards away in the dark. They would likely see him too, and start shooting. If he startled them, there's no telling what they might do. He had a real dilemma on his hands.

However, as often occurs in these situations, the circumstances did not remain static. One of the figures stood up and started running toward the perimeter fence, followed by the second. They both appeared to be carrying long tubular devices under one arm, which Gonzales thought he recognized as the FIM-92 Stinger missile. In the other hand they carried what was unmistakably an AK-47 assault rifle. *Damn, these dirtballs are serious. The kind of damage those missiles could do to one or two of the densely occupied buildings would be a disaster.*

Realizing he really had no choice, Gonzales dropped to one knee and brought his M-16 into firing position. Taking a deep breath, and hoping the other patrol members were on their toes, he hollered out a loud "Halt, you're under arrest." The loudness of his voice in the silent night came like an unexpected clap of thunder.

The two dark figures whirled and dropped the missiles. They quickly turned their rifles toward the shout and fired. Gonzales could feel the bullets whipping around his helmet like angry bees, but concentrated only on the two figures before him. He pulled the M-16's trigger and emptied a 30-round banana-clip magazine at the commandos. He saw them both fly backwards, with their rifles sailing off in opposite directions.

He waited a few seconds in a frozen position, then changed the magazine in his rifle. Slowly, he rose from his knee to a bent position and walked toward the figures, rifle at the ready. The closer he got to the men on the ground, the more cautious he became. He circled them and collected the two AK-47s. Still no movement from the fallen men.

Just as Gonzales started to approach the commandos directly, Corporal Adkins came up from the west side and walked up to the closest man. Before anyone could react, the wounded commando rolled over halfway onto his back, exposing an automatic pistol which he fired, hitting Adkins in the right thigh. As Adkins fell, screaming, Gonzales shot the commando in the chest, firing from the hip, watching the man's body jump. He then fired into the second commando's body, on the chance that he, too, might still be alive and dangerous.

''Wilson, get over here and put your rifle on these two bodies while I tend to Adkins.''

Gonzales ran to the wounded G.I., knelt beside him and laid both their weapons to one side, on safety. Adkins was writhing in pain and his wounds were bleeding profusely. Quickly, Gonzales opened the first aid packet attached to his web gear and wrapped the dressing as a tourniquet above the wounds, twisting the knot with a pen from his pocket to maintain pressure.

''Here, Tommy, hold this with your right hand and keep it twisted.'' Adkins grabbed the pen and did as he was told.

Gonzales then opened Adkins' field first aid packet and placed another tourniquet just below the wounds, having done that in Vietnam to keep the venous blood from coming out below the level of the arterial tourniquet.

By now, the MP's at the perimeter had heard the shots and had sent out two of their perimeter patrols to assist as well as two MP Hum-Vees with communications equipment. Gonzales had them radio for an ambulance crew for Adkins and made sure he was comfortable. While the ambulance was loading Adkins on the stretcher, he talked to Captain Shaeffer on the Humm-Vee radio and briefed him on the event. Schaeffer said he would be out with a special investigative team; and told Gonzales not to touch any evidence or move the bodies.

Gonzales walked slowly over to the dark figures lying sprawled on the sand. He unclipped his flashlight from his right chest web strap and shone the light onto the commandos' faces. The men's features were blood-spattered, as was the ground around them, but they could easily be recognized as Arabs - Iraqis he assumed. As he looked at them, he began to see more and more in their features, the faces of so many Vietnamese and Viet Cong he had shot and killed in what seemed like another life ago. But here it was happening again, and there was nothing he could do about it this time, either. Feeling tired, and old, and disillusioned, and somewhat ill, Gonzales sat in the sand next to the bodies and looked at the moon with burning eyes.

* * *

Tom Neel was lying on the beach at South Padre Island, Texas, relaxing in the sun and enjoying the scenery of bikini-clad women. One very special-looking beauty, with blonde hair and a great athletic body saw his interest and turned to walk toward him. She walked slowly, as if prolonging his anticipation of meeting her, her gait in the sand causing her hips to sway from side to side. She reached his lounge chair and smiled at him, putting her hand down on his leg and . . . . . .

''Major Neel, wake up, we need you right away at the aid station,'' Corporal Petty said, shaking Neel's leg vigorously. ''Wake up. Please, major.''

Neel's vision faded from his dream and he came rapidly to wakefulness, as he had so many times in the past in a hospital call room. Neel recognized the soldier as one of the building guards, a member of the 3rd Armored.

''Yes, yes, what is it?'' Neel sat up straight on the cot and swung his legs to the side. ''What's happening?''

''Sir, one of our patrols with First Sergeant Gonzales just found and wasted a couple of Iraqi commandos who were trying to blow up this place,'' the young man said excitedly.

Neel stood up and looked the young man in the eye. ''Is Sergeant Gonzales all right? Did anything happen to him?'' Neel and Gonzales had become regular running partners and had developed a sincere friendship in the process.

"No, sir, he's okay, I guess. But Corporal Adkins, Tommy Adkins, one of us, got shot several times in the right leg by one of the Iraqis before Gonzales finished him off. He's over at the aid station and they want you to see him, now!"

Grabbing his helmet, LBE and gas mask, Neel sprinted out of the room, down the stairs and outside. The corporal couldn't keep up with him. Running at full speed in combat boots, Neel reached the aid station in less than two minutes and rushed through the door, barely out of breath.

"Good to see you, sir," Captain Torres said. He was examining Corporal Adkins and appeared to be about ready to loosen the upper tourniquet.

Neel held out his hand. "Don't loosen the tourniquet quite yet, Raul. Let's get him stabilized and evaluated before we upset the applecart. Go ahead and start two large bore catheter IV's with Lactated Ringer's and let them run wide open."

Torres moved to get the catheters and alcohol while a corpsman retrieved the IV tubing and solution. As they were starting the IV, Neel stood at the foot of Adkins' litter and gently removed his boots. Adkins moaned loudly when Neel lifted his right leg slightly to slip the boot and sock off.

"Sorry, Corporal, I know it hurts a lot. I'll give you some pain medicine after I know you're stable and O.K." Neel inspected the color of the toenails on the right and felt the temperature of the foot, comparing it to the left. "Does anyone know how long the tourniquets have been on?" he asked.

A lanky corpsman, who was in the ambulance on the pickup said, "about 15 minutes, sir, give or take a few." Neel nodded.

The IV's were in place and the intravenous solutions were running quickly into Adkins' vascular system, to expand his blood volume after losing what Neel estimated at about two units.

"Vital signs, anybody?"

A corpsman looked up from his position at Adkins' left side, just finishing taking a blood pressure reading. "Sir, I've got 90/64 for BP and a heart rate of 138."

"Okay, thanks. That doesn't sound too bad. Let's get about a thousand c.c.'s of fluid in him, before I release the tourniquets."

Neel began to cut and remove the corporal's clothes, as he always did in trauma cases. He knew he had to see the entire patient so he didn't miss an injury or other problem that might otherwise be overlooked.

Neel kept looking at Adkins' face and checking his breathing to identify any change in his physical status. He didn't want Adkins losing consciousness, so periodically Neel talked to him and asked questions. So far, Adkins was stable, alert and oriented.

After Neel felt comfortable with the amount of intravenous fluids delivered, which had improved Adkins' blood pressure to 110/72 and his heart rate to 96, he decided to remove the tourniquets. He judged the tourniquet time was no longer than twenty-five minutes, an acceptable period for the lower extremity. All the supplies were open and laid out on a sterile towel, ready for him. Neel donned sterile gloves and asked Dr. Torres to cut the tourniquets and remove the rest of Adkins' trousers. Eventually, Neel could see four entrance holes in the upper thigh, all oozing blood, but no pumping hemorrhages. Quickly, he applied dressings and wrapped the entire upper thigh firmly with ACE wraps, creating a pressure dressing. He rechecked the distal pulses at the inner ankle, top of the foot, and behind the knee and found them all intact. Thank goodness, Neel thought, at least there's no vascular injury.

"Corporal, I'm going to give you some morphine now. It'll make you rest better and allow me to check the bone in your thigh." He turned to the corpsman. "Ten milligrams of morphine IV now." In a few minutes, Adkins was clearly resting more comfortably.

Gently, Neel took Adkins' right knee in his left hand and the right ankle in his right hand and began to move the leg up and down and from side to side. He then rotated it first inward and then outward, and felt no evidence of a fractured femur. Adkins appeared to rest well during this examination, but would not have taken it as well if the thigh bone were fractured.

"Raul, where's the closest Army facility with orthopedic surgeons?" Neel asked.

"Sir, the 85th Evacuation Hospital is over at the International Airport, about fifteen miles from here. They've got orthopods and a CAT scanner, too."

"A CAT scanner?" Neel whistled through his teeth. "Right here in the middle of nowhere? I'm impressed. Well, let's get him loaded back into the ambulance and take him to the 85th. I'll ride over with him and I'll take Smitty here with me.'' He motioned to one of the corpsmen who had impressed him with his competency and knowledge.

''We'll get back somehow. Maybe we'll catch a ride with the ambulance if they'll wait for us.'' Neel started to gather his gear and walk out with the stretcher when Sergeant Gonzales suddenly appeared.

''Major, how's Tommy doing? Is he gonna be all right?'' Gonzales was wet with sweat and his uniform and hands were splattered with blood. Neel wondered if it was Iraqi blood or Adkins' or both.

Neel walked over to Gonzales and put his hands on the man's shoulders. ''Sarge, he's going to be fine. The thigh bone is not broken and there's no damage to his major blood vessels. We're taking him over to the 85th Evac where I can pass his care over to an orthopedic surgeon. Adkins will go back home to recuperate in Germany, probably in a week or so.''

Gonzales had been looking at Adkins and, reassured, glanced back at Neel, holding his gaze. He touched his hand to Neel's arm in a quick gesture. ''Thanks, Doc, I can't tell you how much I appreciate you taking care of him. It was probably my fault he got shot tonight.''

Neel smiled. ''Listen, Sarge, from what I hear, you saved a lot of us from getting killed tonight, so you don't have anything to feel bad about, okay? Come on, you can go with us to the 85th in the ambulance. Maybe we can talk 'em out of some real food over there, who knows?''

The remaining corpsmen and Captain Torres watched with understanding as Major Neel and First Sergeant Gonzales walked out of the aid station together, arms on shoulders, unabashed.

* * *

An orange sun was rising directly in front of his Datascope range finder, but Lt. Porter was oblivious to it. He was focused on the structures and positions of the Jalibah military airfield directly in front of him. He had drawn a fairly accurate map of the airport on special graphics paper and was now determining the bearings and distances to various structures. The airport was laid out routinely, with both north-south and east-west runways. The runways were about 6,000 meters long, so they would accommodate just about any type of Iraqi aircraft, both tactical and transport.

Porter identified five concrete/sand hangars with MIG-21 fighters, two hangars with Su-20 Fitter fighters and at least one with the hot MIG-25 Foxbat, a converted interceptor that performed mainly reconnaissance missions for the Iraqi Air Force. Later, the team would have to carefully infiltrate the airfield and obtain a more accurate accounting of the aircraft, their numbers and locations. Security did not seem to be a problem; apparently, the Iraqis did not expect a visit this far into their country by Coalition special operations agents.

Porter also wanted to know more about the radar capabilities and the antiaircraft emplacements that could be a threat to Coalition attackers.

The three Green Berets waited out the day in their hidden locations, about 1,000 meters from the perimeter wire fence. Each of the men had quietly dug a trench that night after their arrival and set up the specially designed one-man low-profile polyester tent cover in desert camouflage, which included synthetic 'sand.' When viewed either from ground level or the air, they could not be spotted. The trio had chosen a site at 45º to the north-south landing strip so they would be less likely to be overflown by aircraft (prevailing winds were from the west.).

After nightfall, Porter and Lopez darkened their faces and hands and strapped on their Berettas. They would wear no other gear, save a 'SWAT' vest in which they would carry additional 9mm ammunition, a compass, and a special red laser light source. They needed to know how close they would be required to get to the targets at the airfield to 'paint' the target with their lasers so the smart bombs from the Air Force could home in.

They crossed the moonlit sand to the perimeter wire quickly, to avoid prolonged exposure to any inquisitive guards. When they reached the fence, Lopez removed an ammeter from his vest and touched the two posts to the fence to see if it was electrified. It was not, and without difficulty they quickly scaled the six-foot chainlink fence.

Because of the intense exterior lights the airfield used to light the tarmac or for maintenance illumination for crews working outside instead of within the hot hangars, the two men wore goggles with infra-red filters to reflect most of the high-intensity incandescent light. The glasses maintained their night vision, giving them an advantage over the Iraqi personnel.

The brilliant exterior lights also cast innumerable deep shadows around the airfield buildings and across the irregular surface of the surrounding desert. The shadows gave the agents plenty of places for concealment as they reconnoitered the airfield at close hand.

Because they were only a pair, Porter decided not to split up. The mission would take longer with a team of two, but would be safer - besides looking out for each other, one might be able to get the information sent to CENTCOM if the other were killed, wounded or discovered.

Porter led the way, with Lopez a few meters behind. First, they slipped into the shadows along darkened sides of the hangars to get an accurate count of the aircraft and their location. Porter tested the laser rangefinder and was able to pinpoint a minimum distance location from each hangar if it became necessary for his team to 'paint' the targets for Coalition raiders. He didn't think it would be a problem reaching the sites to shine lasers on the targets. He was concerned however, whether they would be so close to the targets that his men might not survive the bomb blasts. That was not a decision he could interfere with, so he resigned himself.

The mission had gone well and Porter felt there was still time to have a look at the radar and antiaircraft installations before retiring for the night. As they circled around the inside perimeter, they found an improved-Hawk missile battery at the end of each runway, which surprised Porter because the Iraqis were not known to possess the I-Hawk. Porter surmised that these Hawk batteries had been in Kuwait and were moved out of that country by the Iraqis to protect this vitally important airfield so close to the Saudi border.

The Hawks were formidable surface-to-air missiles (SAMS) with a range of 25 miles. They were effective at all altitudes used by tactical fighters and could be equally effective on low-flying aircraft and those approaching from higher altitudes. These batteries could certainly place Coalition pilots at risk if they were allowed to lock-on to their targets. They must be dealt with early in the attack, perhaps even by the SF team using Stingers. The special operations teams had once deployed with Dragon M47 antitank rockets, but they required a more extensive setup mechanism, including a tripod support and the need to fire the missile while sitting on the ground. But the Stinger weighed only 24 pounds and it had an optical aiming, infrared guidance system. It could be fired from any position and carried a high-explosive warhead, sufficient to devastate an I-Hawk battery.

Using fluorescent ink from a tubular cartridge, Porter made careful notes on his polyurethane note pad describing the deployment locations of the I-Hawk batteries. Satisfied they could be knocked out early either by a ground-launched missile (his team had six Stingers at the basecamp) or by an E-4G Wild Weasel using air-to-ground Shrike or HARM missiles, Porter decided to cap the night's mission with a look-see at the radar installation. He knew a lot about Soviet-type radars and felt he could decide how best to eliminate its effectiveness once he knew more about its power supply and capabilities. Every radar was vulnerable and he intended to find out what this one's was.

The two men moved silently and surely toward the radar tower. As they had become familiar with the airfield layout that day, and especially with the terrain features at night, they were trying to keep within the shadows of the sand dunes and bushes. Lopez was running in a crouched position ahead of Porter when suddenly he fell behind a sand dune, very clumsily. Not knowing exactly what had happened, Porter ran to the rise and saw an Iraqi soldier, his fatigue pants around his knees on top of Sergeant Lopez. Realizing Lopez must have stumbled over an Iraqi out taking a crap in the desert, he knew they were in dire peril. The Americans were so close to the radar tower that if this soldier cried out, he would be heard by someone.

Not wanting to risk leaving blood stains in the bright sand and knowing he could not give the Iraqi any chance to cry out, Porter swiftly moved up behind the soldier and, reaching around to the front of his neck, grabbed his larynx in his powerful right hand, squeezing and crushing it in his grip. The Iraqi could neither yell nor breathe and soon went limp in Porter's arms. He held the pressure on the throat until he could no longer feel a carotid pulse, then lowered the man to the ground. The action had occurred so quickly Sergeant Lopez's mind had not caught up with reality until Porter eased the man onto the ground.

They both looked at each other, slowing their breathing as the adrenaline level abated to the point where they both regained their composure. *I knew this thing had gone too easily,* Porter thought. *Now what do we do with this guy? Well, all we can do is pack him away and hope the Iraqis think he has run off or defected.*

While Lopez hefted the body to his shoulder, Porter took off his own camouflage cap and threw sand over the man's excrement. Then he brushed the sand to confuse any searchers and to alter the appearance of a struggle. They moved back to the fence, threw the body over, crossed the fence themselves and again lifted the body for the trip to their concealed observation post. They buried the Iraqi in a deep grave close to their position (they would have used one of their trenches but they still needed all three) and covered it completely with packed sand. Fortunately, the winds blew nearly continuously on this plain of the Arabian desert and the shifting sand would soon erase evidence of their intrusion.

Porter spent the rest of the night in his trench unable to sleep. The thought of the man he had killed being buried not 50 meters from where he lay was disconcerting. *This wasn't fair. If you kill somebody in a war or on a mission, you really shouldn't have to sleep next to his body. It just wasn't civilized.*

* * *

Jay Anders loved to fly in helicopters, especially with the side doors open during low, nape of the earth flying. The hot wind in his face, the rush of the landscape passing beneath the aircraft, and the feeling of freedom, all combined to make flight enjoyable for Anders. He never failed to accept a ride in a chopper or to volunteer to fly, no matter where an aircraft was going. When he wasn't working at the desert aid station, he was up flying with the pilots on their many missions, with most of them not really needing the skills of a medic, but requiring one by SOP.

This morning, Anders was accompanying a patient on a flight to the 214th Evac Hospital at KKMC (King Kahlid Military City). The patient, a young female soldier, had developed an acute inner ear infection, probably due to a virus, and needed the care of an otolaryngologist at the 214th. She was nauseated and occasionally vomiting. Anders had started an IV and was infusing normal saline solution to keep her hydrated. The flight surgeon at battalion headquarters had not been able to see her at their remote airfield's aid station and had told Anders to evacuate her. The flight surgeon would contact his friend the otolaryngologist, and alert him to accept the patient.

The young lady was weak and couldn't focus her eyes. Anders was sitting next to her litter, holding her hand, both to comfort her and to check her pulse rate. She had not done well in the early part of the 60-minute flight, but seemed finally to have settled down. *Perhaps the Phenergan medication had finally taken effect on the nausea,* Anders hoped. She was a quiet and pleasant young woman and his heart really went out to her, getting sick in this setting and under these circumstances. But, one good thing for her, he decided, was that she will likely be leaving the Persian Gulf for Germany or England as soon as she can tolerate an Air Force Nightingale evac flight.

Anders looked out and saw they were approaching KKMC. They began a descent from the mandatory ceiling of 2,000 feet in the final approach to the heliport next to the 214th Evac. Anders could see double rows of Temper tents housing the hospital wards, as well as the air portable metal 'boxes' that served as operating rooms and x-ray facilities.

Having landed in a helicopter hundreds of times, Anders had developed a subconscious sense of the proper sounds of the aircraft engine and rotor blades that occur when the landing is normal. Suddenly, that subconscious sense of the ordinary and expected was violated by the high pitched whine of the engine that sounded ominous. He looked at the crew chief who had held his earphones closely to his ear and looked at the pilot with a startled expression on his face. *Oh-oh,* Anders thought. *Something very bad is going on here.*

Anders had not kept his headset on during the flight because he needed to listen for the patient's blood pressure sounds (very difficult in a helicopter) and besides, he wanted to talk to his patient. Without a headset, he couldn't possibly know what was happening for sure, but as he glanced out the open door, he saw the ground coming up faster than it should - which meant the helicopter had lost lift and was dropping like a rock toward the earth.

Power failure! The words echoed through Anders' mind and left him in temporary shock. *What to do?* he asked himself. *It's all happening so fast.* He glanced at the crew chief who had slid down into the closest available sling chair and was strapping himself in. He saw Anders and made a motion to him where he forcefully brought his left fist down into the open palm of his right hand. *Crash landing!!* Anders understood and moved quickly. He whirled in his harness and grabbed hold of the patient's litter, which was suspended from the aircraft's roof by nylon straps. If the straps broke or gave away, she might be thrown out of the aircraft. He braced his feet against the side wall and held on to the litter with all his strength. This position made him much more vulnerable to personal injury in a crash, but he knew he could protect his patient better.

Upon impact, only seconds later, it felt as if he had been riding a piano to the ground, and it didn't even bounce when it hit. Anders was thrown toward the bulkhead, but managed to slow his movement with his legs and keep the patient from falling out of her litter.

Everything was unearthly silent for a few long seconds, until the crew realized each was still alive. They had survived a helicopter crash! Anders looked over at the patient, who was crying. He was afraid she was injured and in pain. But, as he put his face near to hers, he saw she was crying just from the joy of being alive.

Somehow, Anders unfastened his harness and stood next to the litter. The helicopter had crashed and come to a stop at a 20º list toward starboard. Anders had trouble keeping his balance at that angle, but held on to the litter straps as he checked his patient for injuries. Fortunately, she appeared to be uninjured and completely oriented.

Suddenly, several figures appeared in the doorway of the aircraft and began assisting the crewmembers out of the chopper. While unlikely, there was still some risk of a fire or explosion, or both. Recognizing that, Anders helped lift the litter from the retaining straps and began to help lift the patient out of the helicopter, when a burly corpsman put his hand on Anders chest and shook his head. He took Anders by the waist, nearly lifted him off his feet and walked him to the waiting ambulance. From there Anders was taken to the emergency medical triage section of the hospital to be evaluated.

As he was placed on a litter and carried into the tent, he kept admonishing himself - *don't black out, or they'll ground you from flying*. To prevent that, he dug his fingernails into his palms and the pain kept him alert.

Later, after he had checked out all right, they admitted him for an overnight observational stay. *Might as well,* he thought, *I can't ride that helicopter back to base tonight.* He laughed at his own joke, which made him realize he wasn't *quite* back on an even keel yet.

Almost immediately after his head touched the bed, he was asleep, probably due to acute fatigue reaction after the crash. He was totally unaware of the hourly vital signs and neurological checks the nurses conducted throughout the night.

When he awoke the next morning, he felt as if he'd had gone 10 hard rounds in the boxing ring. Every bone, muscle and joint ached and throbbed - there was not a doubt in Anders' mind he had been dropped very hard from the sky yesterday.

Slowly, he made it to the vertical position, and with some help from a female nurse (to his eternal embarrassment), he used the urinal at the bedside. He knew he should move around to loosen up the muscle spasms, so he smiled and conned the young charge nurse into letting him walk around the tent wards.

He found his former patient and fellow crash victim in the female intermediate care ward, sitting up in bed drinking some canned orange juice. She smiled when she saw him, but replaced that with a frown of concern when she saw his painful limping gait.

''Are you okay, Specialist Anders?'' she asked with concern. ''You look horrible.''

They both smiled when the impact of her last statement struck them.

''No, I don't mean you look *horrible* in a bad way, but . . . but . . . well, you know.''

''No, I'm fine, really. Just a little sore here and there. But, how are you today? You really do look better.'' He smiled at her and realized she was no longer his patient so there was nothing wrong in being friends. ''Isn't your name Becky?''

''That's right. But you know my first name and I don't even know yours,'' she answered demurely.

''Oh, well, I'm Jay. Jay Anders, from Wisconsin.'' He stuck out his hand to shake hers, but stopped short, realizing an IV needle was in the back of her right hand. She touched his fingertips with hers anyway and he felt himself blushing. He might be a lot of things, but one thing he *wasn't* was a 'ladies man.'

Just then she looked over his shoulder, dropped her hand, and got a serious look on her face. "Good morning, sir."

Anders practically jumped to one side as he turned around quickly and saw a colonel standing behind him, with several aides in attendance.

"Good morning, Specialist Gold," he said to Becky. "I'm Colonel Rush, the commander of this hospital. And I gather you are Specialist Anders."

Becky had said, "Good morning, sir," again at the exact same time Jay said "Yes, I am, sir," and the colonel smiled at the awkward moment.

"My doctors tell me you both will do fine and can return to your duty soon. You, Miss Gold, will not be returning quite so soon, but you will be able to stay in the theatre of operations. Dr. LaFere says your inner ear infection is responding well and you should have no long-term effects."

Then he turned to Anders and put his hand on Jay's shoulder. "Son, I have also heard a lot about you. The investigating officers indicated to me that all of the occupants in that aircraft, except for you, have testified that your actions to protect this young lady here, your patient at the time, not only placed your own safety at risk but also likely saved her life or significantly reduced her likelihood for serious injury. For this reason, this command has initiated a recommendation to higher headquarters that you be awarded the Soldier's Medal for your heroic action. If and when it comes through, I hope I can be the one to pin it on you. Congratulations!"

Anders was stunned to speechlessness. *How could they give him a medal for doing only what he was supposed to? Wouldn't everyone have done the same?*

He started to open his mouth to say something to the colonel when he looked at Becky and saw her wink at him, then smile. *Hmm, she's really very pretty,* Anders thought, *and the colonel just said she would be staying in the theatre, maybe even back to the desert. On second thought, maybe I will take this medal if they give it to me. And I'll ask them if Becky can be there at the ceremony.* He returned her smile.

CHAPTER SIX

THE FIRST AND second times Neel tried to use the telephones at Khobar Towers to call Marty back in Kansas City, the power went out after he had waited in line for over three hours—so no call. The installation of the phone banks in an underground garage had been a long-awaited event. Mail from the states simply was not getting to the service-members at Khobar Towers—there was some speculation that either the sheer amount of mail was overwhelming the fledgling mail service or that mail was being delivered or held for the destination APO's, that is, the area in the desert a unit was destined to be occupying.

It could even be a combination of those factors. Now it was Christmas time and the articles in the infrequent Stars and Stripes newspaper seemed to indicate the American people were responding to the massive deployment of military men and women to the Persian Gulf by massive mailings of their own in the form of packages and letters. They were sent not only to specific soldiers, sailors or airmen, but also addressed to "any service member." While it was still a real treat for the men and women to receive a letter or package from anyone, the Armed Forces postal system in the theatre of operations simply could not handle the volume.

For Neel and the others at Khobar Towers, it was a daily anticipation-discouragement cycle when they failed to receive mail. Thus, the arrival and installation of a bank of 100 telephones from AT&T was a blessing. Rumors abounded freely in the temporary military community at Khobar, and, in keeping with the usual military policy of 'keep 'em guessing,' the date for the opening of the telephone bank kept changing. When it finally did, mechanical failure of the power supply left many 'line-waiters' disappointed.

Determined to call home, even if he had to wait for a whole day, Neel got up at 0500 the third day of the alleged 'opening' of the bank and filled his canteen with bottled water. Slipping an MRE into his left BDU thigh pocket, and a paperback novel to help him pass the time in line in his right pocket, he set off by flashlight to the parking garage that housed the telephones. He was surprised to find others had been even more dedicated than he and the line had already grown to about fifty standees. By sunrise, there were fully five hundred. Conversations in line were sporadic, tending to reflect the frustrations everyone was feeling at that time, mainly due to their inactivity and a murky expectation for the future. Woven into the frustration was an acute sense of separation from jobs, loved ones and personal interests that many had not yet resolved. Because of the lack of alcohol, which for many was a major aspect of coping, outward manifestations of frustration were beginning to appear.

As a physician and keen observer of human behavior, Neel was fascinated by the conversations he overheard. He knew most soldiers were being helped to cope by friends, and a few others seemed to have become more inwardly focused. Certainly, spending Christmas away from home acutely aggravated the separation frustrations.

Neel tried to read his paperback, but found it too hard to concentrate. He had formerly been an avid reader of military adventure novels (at least in what spare time he had had over the past ten years), but for some reason, had no real stomach for them now. Maybe it was the frustration and constant exposure to active military things. At any rate, he had widened his scope and was reading *Talking God* by Tony Hillerman. Neel had always enjoyed archeology and physical anthropology, and Hillerman's novels of native American history and mystery set in the southwest, were fascinating and a welcome diversion from anything military.

Unlike the Vietnam conflict, Neel noted, studying the soldiers in line, where most of the participants had been young males (except for the older, career officers and NCOs), the composition here ranged from eighteen year-olds only six months out of high school to men and women fifty and even sixty years old, many with well-established careers—some even grandparents.

The hallmark of participation in the Vietnam conflict had been the draft call, while reactivation of the reserve components was a major aspect of the deployment of sufficient troops to the Gulf. Very few Reserve and Guard units or individuals had been called up for Vietnam; but nearly 250,000 were already out of their civilian lives and back into uniform in the U.S. or overseas. Clearly the 'citizen army' that was visualized by our forefathers was going to make the real difference in the outcome over here.

These were Neel's thoughts while he was standing, waiting and hoping to talk to his wife back in Kansas City. He knew she would still be angry with him, and hurt that he was away. Very likely she still blamed his continued participation in that very same 'citizen's army' that was a mainstay of the country's Bill of Rights. One of his personal heroes, Harry S. Truman, from Independence, Missouri, had gone to Europe in WWI as a young officer with a National Guard field artillery unit. He had always admired Truman's forthright and level-headed approach to problems, a no-nonsense man who could cut right to the core of any matter with his clear insights. It was obvious to Neel that if Truman had been a physician he would have been a surgeon—one of the 'fighter pilots' of medicine.

One of Marty's problems and a clue to her poor appreciation of the situation (at least in Neel's view) was that her own father had avoided military service and never had served in uniform. He tended to be a political 'dove' and likely it was that outlook which had strongly influenced Marty. Ted Schaefer had been too young during WWII, too old during the Vietnam conflict, and had possibly pulled some strings during the Korean War so he could stay in his management position with the family-owned textile mill. Neel and Marty's father no longer discussed politics where the military was involved, because of their widely conflicting views. In fact, Marty and her mother had called a moratorium on those discussions because they tended to heat up too rapidly, with neither man willing to concede points to the other.

As he neared the front of the line, Neel began to feel nervous about his call. It was nearly a month since he had last talked with her or even received a letter. He didn't know what her frame of mind was, or even if she would talk to him. She was a fine woman, but she could be very stubborn if she felt she had been wronged or her views hadn't been fairly considered.

What if she had moved out of the house and had already gotten an attorney to draw up divorce papers? She is not very forgiving and I could certainly see her doing that. What if there is some male professor at Rockhurst College who is preying upon her vulnerability, sympathizing with her, gently encouraging her to drop this uncaring bastard, and then positioning himself to be available to 'fill the void?'

Dammit, I'll kill him when I get home, Neel vowed. *Just let me get my hands on the bastard and he'll run like a scared cat. But, wait a minute. I could be here for a year! My God. A year. In that span, Marty could divorce me, marry someone else, have the baby, and my child would already have a new stepfather. I couldn't stand the thought of another man raising my son or daughter.* Neel was practically distraught by now, worried about talking to Marty and desperate about what he might find out in their conversation. Not usually given to wild speculations or fantasies, Neel was nevertheless a victim of the uncertainty, the acute separation, the boredom and frustrations of the situation and they all acted to cloud his usual clear judgment.

As Neel entered the underground garage/ telephone bank, he was pointed to a vacant telephone by a young, black female soldier. He noted she was wearing a wedding ring and wondered just how understanding her husband had been. Somehow he began to doubt he was the only one who had a problem with his spouse.

He sat down in the small, makeshift wooden booth and tried to rearrange his gas mask and web gear more comfortably. He placed his Kevlar helmet on his lap. Before leaving Fort McCoy, Neel had obtained an international telephone calling card and had memorized the number. When he lifted the telephone handpiece and dialed the number handwritten in black ink on the wall in front of him, he felt very nervous indeed. *Just like the first time he called a girl for a date,* he thought. *Except this time it's a lot more important, with more at stake.*

A pleasant female voice came on the line. "Yes, this is AT&T Saudi Arabia, may I help you?"

"Yes, yes, please. I want to make a call to Kansas City, Missouri, in the U.S.," Neel was surprised how shaky his voice sounded.

"May I have your AT&T calling card number please, followed by the number you are calling, with the area code first.

Neel gave her the numbers, realizing this operator was his "angel" today, bestowing upon him the near miracle of being able to talk to Marty from this soon-to-be combat zone.

It was amazing—the telephone connection seemed to Neel to be so good that he almost imagined he was calling from the next city, not halfway around the world.

The phone rang five, then six times and no answer. Neel's heart skipped a beat and he flushed. *What if she's not there? Where could she be this time of night?*

Then the sound of the phone being picked up. ''Hello?'' came a soft, unsteady voice. Neel had heard Marty's voice like this before when she had been awakened from a deep sleep. ''Hello, who is this?'' she croaked.

''Marty, it's me, Tom. Can you hear me?'' Somehow Neel always had a tendency to talk loudly over long distance phone connections. It might have been because he'd grown up with the phones of rural south Missouri, where the operators (and many of those receiving the calls) were older and hard-of-hearing.

''Tom? Oh, Tom, is that really you? What time is it?'' He could hear her fumbling around on the nightstand next to her side of the bed, looking for her watch. She always laid it neatly on her night stand before she went to sleep, claiming her hair often got caught in the band when she slept with her hand close to her face. ''Just a minute. Let me turn the light on.'' Click.

He could visualize her squinting at the watch, not really awake enough to comprehend the time. She was really not a good person to awaken in the middle of the night. Marty hadn't undergone the many years of constant calls that woke him at all hours, nor did she have to come instantly awake to respond to a difficult medical question or to look after some patient with a problem. ''Marty, it's about nine a.m. where I am, so it must be about two in Kansas City.'' There was a seven hour difference between Central Standard Time and Dhahran, Saudi Arabia.

''Tom, are you all right? Why are you calling me?'' *Typical female worry,* Neel thought. *They think you only call to talk to them when you have bad news.*

"I'm okay, Marty, I'm just fine. This is the first telephone I've seen since I got here, and they're only allowing us to talk for ten minutes. So if we get cut off suddenly, that's why."

"Tom," his wife asked, "just where are you?"

"I can't tell you that honey. We have to practice communications security—I can only say I expect to see Lawrence riding by in his robes most any time." Neel and Marty had gone before his deployment to see the movie "Lawrence of Arabia," which had been redone to improve its color. He thought that would give her a clue that he was in Saudi Arabia. There were signs all over the telephone bank indicating that military personnel should be careful about telling where they were. The enemy might use that information to bomb the compound.

"Tom, how come I haven't heard from you in two weeks? Why wouldn't you call me?" Her voice was strained, showing anger mixed with concern.

"Honey, I *couldn't* call, it wasn't that I wouldn't. They just got telephones installed today for the first time. I've been waiting in line for four hours to call you."

"Oh, Tom. Your mother calls every day and I have to tell her I haven't heard a peep from you, not a word." Marty was *definitely* upset.

"You mean you haven't gotten any of my letters? I've written you every day."

There was a silence on the other end of the line. *Either she thinks I'm lying to her, or that confirms what she already thinks of the U.S. Army. Either way, I'm in trouble.*

"Marty, how are you feeling? Are you going to Dr. Williams for your checkups? Does she say you're doing okay?" Neel really *was* concerned about his wife and their unborn child. He was going to be a father for the first time and he was both excited and a little worried.

''Yes, Tom, we're doing fine. Nice of you to ask,'' she replied coldly.

''No, Marty, I really mean it. Are you eating okay and not having nausea or bleeding? Talk to me, please, tell me how you are.'' Neel was pleading now, afraid his wife had pulled into a shell and would refuse to let him in. And here he was, thousands of miles from home with no way to physically break her shell.

''Tom, you needn't worry about me, I'm doing fine all by myself. Every time I turn on the television, there's some reporter talking about the crisis in the Persian Gulf and when are they going to start the war and isn't it just a matter of time? And the same thing when I read the newspaper or listen to the radio or talk to a friend. I can't escape from the fact that I'm here, pregnant with our first child, and you're over there and there's a war coming.'' She was almost crying.

''Honey, everything's going to be fine. Just relax and think good thoughts about me and you and the baby. We'll all be together soon and we'll have a great life.'' He heard her blowing her nose and waited a minute before continuing. ''What can I do to help you? What can I do to make it right again? Talk to me, Marty!''

''Well, you can start by coming back to me from wherever you are, so you can be here when the baby comes.''

''But, Marty, you know that—'' click. The line went dead. ''Time's up'', hollered the bored-looking sergeant in her tan T-shirt and helmet.

Neel just stared at the dead phone, unwilling to believe the conversation had ended so badly. Slowly, put on his helmet, stood, and made his way outside to wait for the war that threatened to rip his marriage to shreds.

* * *

Forced to become more aware of the susceptibilities of the Apache's instruments to the harsh desert conditions, Captain Weatherby kept a more watchful eye on them. The air speed indicator malfunction seemed to have been taken care of by the staged replacement of the pressure lines that in some cases had become blocked by sand, as well as by the interposition of a replaceable filter in the line. Light maintenance on the aircraft was being required after every ten hours' flight time, with heavy maintenance after fifty.

The most difficult problem his unit had was obtaining parts for their Apaches. The helicopter had not been in the Army's inventory long, and the subcontractor had not been able to gear up to produce the component parts fast enough to support the massive buildup in the Gulf. Weatherby was forced to curtail the flight schedules of his troop in order to maintain aircraft that were safe.

He felt that he had learned a terrible lesson from the fatal Apache crash, and although the Aviation Safety Board had not yet released its findings, he was certain it had been due to instrument malfunction from airborne sand. He felt real remorse for the aviators who had been lost and was having a few bouts of depression. In the past, he would have shrugged off the accident and even exaggerated his air of non-concern and bravado. But this time it was different; he felt a loneliness he had never experienced.

Tonight, Weatherby was flying reconnaissance along the Saudi-Kuwaiti border. He was joined in the cockpit by his weapons officer, CW02 Roger Garner, a calm and dedicated pilot, whose retiring demeanor was a direct antithesis to Weatherby's. The two loved flying the aircraft anywhere, even in Saudi Arabia, and had developed a "feel" for its capabilities.

Weatherby loved the low frequency vibrations from the twin General Electric T700-GE-701 turbines as they forced 3600 horsepower of rotation to the four-blade main rotor. The Apache could attain a maximum ground speed of over 150 knots with a ceiling of 20,000 feet. On a fully loaded attack mission, with eight Hellfire antitank missiles and three hundred and twenty rounds of 30 mm cannon ammunition, the Apache could fly for over two and a half hours at more than 140 knots.

Unlike his earlier days in the old AH-1 Cobra attack helicopter, Weatherby felt a lot less vulnerable in the Apache. Its survivability was said to be enhanced by a "fly-by-wire backup control system (BUCS)," which could be turned on if a combat hit debilitated primary flight controls. The crew cockpit was sufficiently armored to prevent injury to the pilot or co-pilot by any munition up to a 23-mm high-explosive or incendiary round. The high-impact landing gear and a crash-resistant (self-sealing tank) fuel system gave crew members a real chance for surviving a crash, either from a non-combat accident or by being shot down.

Even so, Weatherby concluded, everything really depended on whether your number was up. Even with these crash survivability features, he believed when it was time for you to check out that's when it would happen. He wasn't particularly religious (although he secretly hoped he could get to Heaven, if there was such a place, despite his many transgressions), but he did have a deep sense of destiny, bordering on fatalism. Deep within his soul was a decent man; his wife had seen it, and others could too when he was around his family. *Yes, they bring out the best in me,* he mused, *and the rest of me only comes out when I'm around other men. I've always been too competitive,* he thought, *and maybe I just come across as overly aggressive.*

Introspection was not a frequent companion of Weatherby's—maybe because he could become remorseful when recalling past situations where he might have reacted differently. *Maybe when all of this is over . . . .*

"Captain, I see movement on the ground at 2 o'clock." Garner was serving tonight as the observer for the mission while Tex was flying and watching the instruments. Both were wearing pilot night-vision sensors (PNVS) but their field of vision was so constricted the pilot simply could not divert his attention from flight operations.

They spoke to each other on the aircraft's helmet-to-helmet intercom system: "All right, Roger, what's the distance?"

"About a thousand meters starboard and moving to our six."

Weatherby made a slow banking turn to the right. Their altitude was about 2000 feet and they were flying without lights. Other aircraft in the vicinity would pick up their transponder signal (as they did theirs) and identify them as friendly.

Weatherby and Garner were flying as a two-bird team with an OH-58D Kiowa Warrior Scout helicopter, piloted by First Lieutenant Terry McGuire from San Carlos, California and his weapon's officer, Second Lieutenant Santiago Menache from New York City. This Kiowa was a modified version of the helicopter that had served so well over the past two decades, and it bore only a faint resemblance to its predecessor.

McGuire's helicopter had a mission equipment package that included a laser range finder-designator as well as all-weather, day or night target acquisition sensors that were used to acquire a target and to guide the Apache's weapon's systems to the proper target. These sensors were mounted on the rotor mast, well above the blades. Their navigation system allowed target data to be transferred to another aircraft or even to ground weapons systems the so-called "airborne target handover system." The Kiowa was scheduled to be fitted with air-to-air Stingers, but was deployed to the Gulf before new hard points could be installed.

Both aircraft were now flying NOE (nap-of-the-earth); about 75 meters above the terrain at a cruising speed of 150 knots. The mission was very straightforward—to patrol the Kuwaiti-Saudi border, north of the forward-deployed troops, looking primarily for troop or vehicular movement or evidence of radar or missile installations dangerously close to the border. Most tactical target identifications and positioning data came from JSTARS (Joint Surveillance Target Attack Radar System), the tri-service tactical multisensor image intelligence processing and exploitation capability.

This system primarily processed information obtained for the airborne JSTARS radar on E-8 Joint-STARS aircraft. Its data on enemy positions and assets were integrated with the computer analyses obtained from the multispectral imagery generated by LANDSAT and INTELSAT geostationary satellites, producing a reasonably accurate means of identifying Iraqi troops, materiel, and weapons. However, it was too hard to focus on every acre of desert north of Saudi Arabia, hence the helicopter reconnaissance.

Some information had been sent to brigade headquarters about the possibility of a small hostile radar unit operating in the sector of desert now being overflown by the two helicopters. This was first reported by VII Corps artillery, which utilized the Guardrail signal intelligence system to discover radar emissions. Guardrail had not been able to pinpoint the radar's location because it was obviously a mobile unit, and no additional information had been requested of or received from the satellite communication operators.

If there was a mobile radar so close to the forward-deployed troops, there might well be a mobile rocket or missile launcher along with it. The radar could certainly be a stand-alone sensor, to identify locations of Coalition air fields and aircraft flights, but, more worrisome, could be the guidance for an enemy rocket launcher.

The main threat to the Coalition troops from such a situation would be the presence of an Astros II SS-60 300-mm multiple-rocket launcher. This surface-to-surface rocket had a maximum range of 60 kilometers, and could easily reach such forward-deployed units as the 82nd Airborne and the 1st Marines. Another threat could be surface-to-air missiles like the SA-6 Grail with an effective range of 27 miles, or the SA-13 Gopher, a heat-seeker with low-altitude capabilities and an effective range of 5 miles. The SA-13 was mounted on a tracked vehicle and highly mobile.

Saddam Hussein had not yet agreed to remove his troops from Kuwait as required by resolutions passed by the U.N. Security Council. Current intelligence assessments of the likelihood of Iraqis leaving Kuwait by January 15, 1991, indicated it was highly probable a full-scale military action would be required to bring about such a result. Meantime, it was clear the Iraqis were strengthening front-line fortifications and pouring supplies into Kuwait through the nearby Iraq city of Al Basrah. There was also concern in CENTCOM that if the Iraqis were to score a successful attack on American servicemen where the casualty toll was high, conservatives in Congress might not allow the President to conduct this action in the proper military fashion. No one in CENTCOM, including General Schwartzkopf, wanted another fiasco like Vietnam, where civilians micro-managed all military activities to the detriment of everyone.

While Weatherby's orders, and those he passed on to each flight commander, had been of a general nature regarding reconnaissance of their assigned sector, he had not been ordered specifically not to engage the enemy, especially if, in his opinion, the target represented a clear risk to the safety of any ground troops or aircraft in the vicinity.

These thoughts were in Weatherby's mind as he approached the objects CW02 Garner had spotted. He kept a reasonable distance away until he could identify them.

"Talk to me, Garner, what's going on down there? What do you see?"

The two aircraft were about 500 meters from the objects before Garner could identify them.

''Jeez, Captain, looks like a big radar dish mounted on a truck. It's covered with camouflage and I probably would have missed it if I hadn't been looking right at it. Pure luck!'' Garner was leaning against the starboard window.

Weatherby turned his head slightly to the right, and tightened the collar on the collective so he could raise his hand to the long-distance, high frequency radio. He turned to the proper channel for brigade commo and hit the ''audio'' button to activate his helmet-mounted microphone. The Bendix/King AN/ARC-199 radio was one sweet piece of communications equipment, offering an ''easy-to-use, menu-driven software program and a one-button operation control display unit to minimize head-down input.'' Weatherby used its automatic link establishment (ALE) capabilities to bring brigade headquarters on line as well as to network the QH-58D Kiowa into the link as well. The ARC-199 could also use a digital-burst information transfer by modem, but Weatherby would use it now only as a secure line of verbal communication.

''Bird Dog One to CC Six; Bird Dog One to CC Six, come in.''

The command and control center came on-line almost instantly. ''This is CC Six, Bird Dog One, proceed with transmission.''

Weatherby was circling the vehicle with the Kiowa on his tail about 50 meters away. ''CC Six, Bird Dog One here. We have a mobile radar dish on a five-ton truck under camouflage netting at the following coordinates.'' Weatherby punched the button to send the stored coordinates of their position from the inertial navigation system on the aircraft. Brigade would see their location on an electronic grid map right away.

''Bird Dog One, this is CC Six. We have your location identified. You are one kilometer north of the Kuwaiti border. I repeat, you are one kilometer north of the Kuwaiti border. What are your intentions?''

Weatherby didn't know what his intentions were until he could see exactly what he was dealing with. He banked the aircraft to the right and came into a tighter circle around the radar truck. He felt that there was a lot of camouflage for one radar dish and worried he was missing something important.

''CC Six, this is Bird Dog One. I am going in for a closer look and will . . . Oh, hell, they've got a SAM launcher down there, I repeat, a SAM launcher.'' Weatherby jinked the helicopter back to the left and tried to gain altitude as an Iraqi SA-13 Gopher missile launcher backed quickly out from under the camouflage. He hurriedly called McGuire on the air-to-air net to warn him away to safety.

''McGuire, McGuire, get the hell out of there. There's a SAM and he's tracking on us already. GET OUT OF HERE!''

He couldn't look back in the cockpit to see whether McGuire was moving to escape the missile launcher because of the confines of the cockpit and the restrictions of the night vision goggles.

Tex was watching the instruments and jinking along when Garner sang out: ''Missile launch, right on our tails.'' There was virtually no way to protect a helicopter from a heat-seeking missile fired at such close range. He yelled at the Kiowa: ''McGuire, we have a missile launch. Throw chaff, throw chaff and jink the hell out of the sky.''

Just then he turned slightly to starboard in an evasive movement to confuse the missile when he saw McGuire's Kiowa suddenly come into view at the 5 o'clock position of his own aircraft, obviously having cut back behind the Apache. A split second later there was a brilliant light, followed by a thunderous explosion. Foreign objects seemed to rain upon their aircraft in a pinging chorus.

''God-dammit, those bastards shot McGuire and Menache right out of the sky,'' Tex said. ''Right out of the damn sky.'' He turned the Apache in time to see the remains of the Kiowa burning on the desert floor. As long as they stayed behind the burning wreckage, the heat-seeking Gopher missile would not likely be able to identify their engine's heat signature.

Weatherby forgot about his communication with brigade, he forgot about the safety of his own aircraft and crew and he forgot (or put out of his mind for now) the crew of the destroyed helicopter. He was focused on the radar unit and the SAM launcher that was trying to train its sights on his Apache. He was mad, but he had his anger under control—it was channeled into a cold fury and an intense desire to destroy the Iraqi vehicles.

''Tex, let's get the hell out of here,'' Garner pleaded. Garner was a fine man, with five children back in Utah, but he lacked the killer instinct that was brought out in Weatherby by situations like this.

The captain's voice was cold and hard. "Roger, we can't let those bastards get away with that. You want McGuire and Menache to die for nothing? What about the guys this launcher could kill if it fired at our lines close to here? Arm the Hellfires and we're gonna get a lock-on here right now!"

Weatherby quickly banked the Apache to the left of the fire and smoke and climbed steeply. He temporarily left the undersurface of the aircraft exposed to the Iraqi launcher but he was confident the SAM couldn't track them quickly enough at this range.

"Where's the launcher?" Weatherby asked, as he came over the crest of his climb and started a quick dive at about 1,000 feet.

"It's at our 4 o'clock and starting to swing toward us." Garner said excitedly. He realized what Weatherby planned to do and felt it just might work.

Weatherby set the Apache on its nose and headed straight for the radar dish on the 5-ton truck. The truck was essentially defenseless and he didn't think the Iraqi SAM crew would fire on their own radar crew. He suspected the Iraqi commander of this small unit was in the module of the radar unit and would not willingly order his men in the launcher to destroy his position.

Tex picked up speed and reached the radar dish plenty of time before the SAM launcher had turned the missiles through a 180º swing toward the aircraft. *Good,* Tex thought to himself, *I've got a few seconds while they ponder the decision to fire at their own radar dish.*

He placed the helicopter directly behind the radar dish, with his rotors just above the top of the dish.

"Roger, light up the laser, I want to pop it on that SOB. We'll get one good shot before he gets wise to us and blows us and his own radar away."

By now, Garner had seen the inevitability of Weatherby's actions and had decided to do his best to see that they were successful. He powered up the laser unit until he got a green light on the laser-rangefinder "POWER" display. "She's hot, boss, show me the target and I'll paint it for you."

Weatherby nodded and quickly brought the aircraft up in a higher hover, just above the radar dish.

Garner acquired the display of the missile launcher on this

display, now just under 1000 meters away. Weatherby guided the helicopter's nose until the beam appeared to be directly on target. "We've got a lock-on," Garner cried.

The Hellfire missile is 64 inches long, weighs 99 pounds and has a single 7-inch-diameter warhead. The missile is guided by a laser seeker that can be projected on the target by another aircraft (such as the Kiowa), by someone on the ground, or by the Apache's own laser designator. The missile was first used successfully in Operation Just Cause in Panama by Weatherby and his troop of Apaches, and he was about to fire it for the first time in the Persian Gulf. But Weatherby wasn't thinking of that, nor of the possible political ramifications of his actions. He was thinking only of pure revenge and how he had to keep this launcher from causing any more casualties to Coalition forces.

The repetitious sound of the target acquisition alarm sounded as loud in his ears as Tex's own heartbeat. He flipped up the arming switch for the Hellfire missiles on his cyclic and, holding the aircraft as steady as a rock, pressed the firing button for the port weapon pad once, then again. The Apache bucked slightly as the missiles leapt from their carriers toward the target. He and Garner were rewarded in a few seconds by the sight of the missile launcher exploding, spawning a series of fiery secondary blasts when the missile fuel tanks also blew.

Not a word was said, but both men felt a sense of due retribution for the lost crew members of the Kiowa. Weatherby lifted the Apache well above the radar dish and truck and flew north several hundred yards, then made a quick turn and hovered 25 meters about the desert, pointed at the radar dish. They watched as the doors to the radar truck and module flew open and Iraqi soldiers spilled out like ants out from a disturbed mound. Waiting until the Iraqis had left the radar unit, Weatherby began firing his 30-mm cannon at the radar dish and truck, destroying them with several dozen of the cannon rounds and setting the entire unit on fire.

Circling the Iraqi troops, then, he made sure none was carrying any weapons, or had a shoulder-mounted SAM before deactivating his weapons pod.

He keyed back into the ARC-199 and linked again with brigade headquarters. "CC Six, this is Bird Dog One, over."

"Bird Dog One, this is CCS. What is your status there? We

have reports of explosions in your sector. Please respond."

"CC Six, this is Bird Dog One," Weatherby replied wearily. This was a secure radio frequency so he did not need to utilize COMMSEC in his description of the events. "We just found a SAM launcher and radar truck. The launcher was concealed and before we could react, McGuire and Menache got hit in their Kiowa. Immediate destruction of their aircraft, no survivors. The SAM was ready to fire on us, but we hit it and the radar truck with Hellfires—both destroyed. We now have some dozen or so Iraqi military personnel on the ground, essentially unarmed, ready for rounding up. Will need troops to fetch the Iraqis plus an accident team out here now. We'll stay around until the infantry arrives. Over."

"Bird Dog One, this is CC Six. What is the status of the crew members who were shot down? Do you need an aeromedical evacuation bird for them? Over."

There's nothing anyone can do for them now, Weatherby thought, but I guess we have to take care of their bodies properly. "CC Six, roger that. Please send dustoff bird for remains of crew members. We have fuel for one hour's wait. Over."

"Bird Dog One, be advised assistance is on the way. Stay on orbit until airborne infantry arrives and then return to base for debriefing. Command out."

Weatherby hovered the aircraft near the Iraqi soldiers who were looking nervous enough to bolt for the open desert. He slowly circled them, with the nose of the aircraft pointed toward them, indicating he wanted them to get into a circle. It took two revolutions before they finally got the message and formed together in a tight circle, squatting on their haunches like scared animals.

Only after he was certain the Iraqis were going to stay in one place did he turn his attention to the smoldering helicopter wreck. The flames had nearly burned themselves out and the smoke had been blown away from the wreckage by the wind of the Apache's rotor blades.

Feeling guilty about his observation, nevertheless Tex thought the charred wreckage of the Kiowa resembled a burned whale. The rotor blades were partially imbedded in the sand and looked like the ribs of a cetacean carcass. The tail and tail rotor of the aircraft could have been the whale's tail and the cockpit its proboscis. He saw no evidence of living crew members, but supposed their bodies were inside the cabin.

His rage at the Iraqis had subsided totally and now he just felt *tired.* Very. And very sad for the families of these young men who had had their futures ripped asunder by a missile no longer than they were tall. For the first time in his adult life, Tex had a lump in his throat he couldn't swallow.

* * *

The call from the 2nd ACR Brigade HQ to the operations room of the 428th Air Ambulance company was placed just minutes after Weatherby concluded his report on the action. Brigade wanted a Blackhawk with a medic and an additional pilot to secure the bodies of the (presumed) dead aviators and to assess the situation for a report back to their headquarters. Specialist Anders was asleep on his cot in the adjacent tent when Sergeant Tom Doerdorf shook him awake.

''Wake up, Anders, you gotta go out on a run. Wake up.'' He continued to shake Anders until he sat up.

''Huh? What . . . what's going on?'' Anders asked as he swung his legs over the side of the cot, looking for his boots. He usually slept in his aviator jump suit, just in case.

''I dunno. Alls I know is there's a chopper shot down and burned up just over the border into Kuwait. We gotta go get 'em and investigate the thing.'' Sergeant Doerdorf was the crew chief for the on-call aero medical evacuation team tonight.

Anders quickly found his gas mask and MOPP gear, helmet and handgun, putting them on while running for the aircraft. He had forgotten his protective vest but no one else had one on so he didn't go back to get it.

The helicopter was 'hot' and lifted off as soon as Anders was strapped in. His aid kit was already in the aircraft along with two rolled-up rubber containers.

''What are those?'' he asked Doerdorf as they got their helmet microphones plugged in.

Doerdorf looked at him strangely in the flashing red glow of the rotating beacon light. ''Body bags,'' he hollered, and then looked away, uncomfortable.

The rest of the fifteen-minute flight was made in silence. Anders had never seen an aircraft shot down by hostile fire. Sure, he had seen photographs and news coverage of crashed jet liners, nothing left but charred remains of what used to a huge airplane containing maybe hundreds of passengers. The sheer magnitude of such an event tended to defy one's grasp of understanding. However, the destruction of a helicopter just slightly smaller than the one he was currently flying, with only two aviators in the cockpit he could appreciate. In fact, Anders was worried it might be too easy to grasp and he might never let go of the reality of what he would see and do.

It was easy to spot the crash site. Anders could see two, no, three smoldering structures in the desert, one appearing to have been a large saucer-like object. Probably a radar unit, he surmised. The second he wasn't sure of maybe some sort of an artillery or antiaircraft weapon.

As the Blackhawk circled the third object, it was not hard to see it had once been an aircraft, but he couldn't positively identify it from the remains. Off to the north, he could see an Apache helicopter apparently guarding a small group of Iraqi soldiers from the air. *Now that's a new twist to the sheep dog rounding up the sheep,* Anders thought.

The pilot set the Blackhawk down upwind from the smoldering wreckage so the debris would not enter his engine's intake. As the rotors slowed their revolutions to a complete stop, the crew chief opened the sliding crew door and Anders and the investigating pilot exited. They walked hesitantly toward the wreckage, and a number of odors could be distinguished from the smoke—burned fuel, oil and the unmistakably pungent odor of burned flesh. Anders stomach immediately began to react to this olfactory insult and threatened to empty itself in the sand. The pair walked over to the port side and peered into the cockpit, shining flashlights inside.

The helicopter had crashed upside down, and the two bodies were hanging out of their seats, still buckled in place. Both their helmets had been lost in the process, and the copilot was headless. Blinking in disbelief, Anders looked down to the side of the aircraft, and, on the ceiling of the cockpit was the head of the copilot, still in its helmet.

The sight was too much for Anders. He spun quickly away, walked several feet, sank to his knees and vomited until his heaves were without substance. The vomitus increased the tearing in Anders' eyes, but wasn't the sole cause for it.

He felt a hand on his shoulder and turned to see the investigating pilot on his left knee next to him. Chief Warrant Officer Four Harvey Bradlee was a grey-haired, kindly and quiet man who served as the 'father' figure to many of the younger aviators and enlisted men. With over 30 years of combined active duty and reserve time, he had come out of flying Hueys for medical evacuation missions in Vietnam and had joined the unit in 1971. In civilian life he ran a barber shop and knew just about every male in Madison, Wisconsin. Jay had known him for several years and always enjoyed flying with him on weekend drills and during annual training in the summer.

"Son, you've got to get hold of yourself. We've got a job to do here and we're the only ones right now who can. I know this is a terrible thing, and I know you'll never forget it, but we've got to get those boys out of that wreckage and get them back so their families' can lay them to rest. You'll help me, won't you?"

Jay nodded. This was no place for a dead American, out here on foreign sand with the enemy not a hundred meters away. He'd do it for them and for their families.

He stood up and wiped his mouth and nose on his flight suit sleeve. While Mr. Bradlee searched the wreckage and made mental notes of the findings at the crash, Jay went back to the Blackhawk and retrieved the body bags. He also found two pair of surgeon's gloves, and two surgical masks, to reduce the hand contact and the odors.

Anders brought the bags and other supplies back to the wrecked helicopter and cleared an area on the sand nearby. He unrolled the long rubber bags, which resembled thin 'mummy-type' sleeping bags. *If only these men were sleeping,* Anders thought to himself. He put on the surgical gloves and mask, took a deep breath and walked toward their charred remains.

The pilot's cockpit door had been sprung open either by the explosion or by impact with the ground. It was bent at a 45-degree angle and the plexiglass windows were partially melted. Anders braced his left foot against the frame of the roof and pulled the door forcibly off its hinges—it came off with little resistance. Jay knelt just inside the cockpit and inspected the situation. He would have to cut the four-strap harness and then ease the body onto the roof. He looked at the roof (which was now the floor in the upside-down position of the aircraft) and realized it was littered with debris. It just didn't seem right to drag the pilot's body through the debris and over the threshold. It actually might ''fall apart'' if the limbs were as brittle from the fire as they appeared to be.

He returned to his Blackhawk, noticing that Sergeant Doerdorf, the crew chief, was standing guard by the open cabin door with an M-16 cradled in his arms.

''How's it going, Anders? You about done?'' he asked. The pilots and Doerdorf were equally nervous about the Iraqi soldiers in the sand nearby, as well as by the prospect of carrying out the bodies of two fellow aviators in their aircraft.

Anders sighed and coughed. ''Just about, Sarge, only I need some blankets.''

Doerdorf blinked twice and looked at Anders with a frown. ''They're, uh . . . uh, dead aren't they? Why do you need blankets?''

Anders grabbed several patient care olivedrab wool blankets from their storage compartment in the helicopter and tucked them under his arm. As he turned to walk back to the wreckage he said, ''Yea, Sarge, they're dead all right. I just want to handle them as gently as possible.''

Doerdorf nodded. That's the way he'd want someone to handle his remains in the same situation.

Anders took one of the blankets and spread it out as best he could on the roof of the cabin. He then removed his Champion Swiss Army Knife from the velcro sheath on his web belt and unfolded the largest blade. He kept this blade very sharp to cut away web belts, trouser belts, helmet straps or any other piece of clothing or equipment that would need to be removed from a casualty in the field so he could begin first aid. Tonight, his knife would cut the harnesses that held the burned remains of the aviators in their seats.

Just then, Mr. Bradlee (warrant officers are called 'mister' in the Army) having completed his inspection of the wreck, appeared behind him. ''I can help you here, son, just tell me how.''

''Okay, sir, if you can grab hold of his shoulders, and hold him up until I cut the straps, then I think we can ease him down onto the blanket.''

Mr. Bradlee squeezed in beside Anders and started to grab the shoulders. ''No, sir, here, put on the gloves. They'll keep your hands from getting . . . well, getting contaminated.'' Anders didn't know what to say about that; he just felt that there was a chance some of the pilot's skin might fall off into their hands.

Bradlee put on the rubber gloves, having some difficulty in doing so because his hands were damp with sweat. Then he held the pilot's shoulders up as Anders squeezed past him and, with some difficulty, cut the four straps.

In fact, Bradlee need not have held the body up—its Nomex flight suit had not burned, but had ''melted'' in spots and sealed itself to the nylon mesh of the seat, in effect ''gluing" the body to the seat. With some difficulty, the two men tugged on the body and finally it fell onto the blanket with a ''sucking'' sound. Anders swallowed hard when he saw that pieces of the aviator's suit with attached charred skin was left behind on the seat. He knew he was close to vomiting again.

Steeling himself, he grasped the blanket, pulled it up around the body, and began pulling the body out of the cockpit, with Bradlee helping.

Why did I ever think that it was a ''glorious'' job to take part in victim retrieval after an accident or disaster? Anders worried.

They picked up the ends of the rolled blanket after the body was out of the aircraft and struggled to carry it to the body bags. *I never knew a dead body could be so heavy,* Anders thought as he nearly stumbled walking backwards. *I guess that's where the term ''dead weight'' comes from.*

They laid the body, blanket and all, on top of one of the body bags Anders had unzipped and opened. They were able to fold the rubber bag around the body and zip it up. Finally, they stood up and viewed their work.

Anders looked at Mr. Bradlee and lifted his mask off his lower face to get a breath of ''fresh'' air. He looked at Bradlee. ''Sir, have you ever thought about when a person's soul leaves their body to go to Heaven?'' Anders knew Bradlee was a religious man, and may have read some particularly salient scripture passages about it in the past. In fact, over the past weeks, Anders himself had felt a growing need to return to the Bible of his childhood and youth and had found that reading scripture was a real comfort. ''I mean, are we interfering with that happening by putting this . . . this man into the body bag?'' Anders had never thought about it before, but he was concerned about it now. In fact, he was very concerned.

Bradlee also removed his mask and looked up at the stars in the dark sky. In the desert at night, it was amazing how bright the stars shone, how bright the moonlight was. It was not hard to imagine, standing in the starlit night of the Arabian desert, the brightness of the Star of the East, which led the Magi to worship the newborn Christ.

''Jay,'' Bradlee began, calling him by his name for the first time, ''I don't think anything or anybody can prevent a soul from ascending to Heaven if the Father calls for it. I just feel it's going to happen. Maybe it's already happened for these unfortunate men, but I think there's a better world waiting for them than what they saw here tonight.''

Jay nodded and looked down at the body bag. Somehow, even though he had not known this man, these men, he felt he had become a part of their exit from their mortal lives. That somehow he was assisting the Lord's work here tonight, and that his life would be forever a part of their deaths. He had only a vague feeling about his and would explore it in his thoughts later, when he had an opportunity to get away by himself and think.

They returned to the wreckage with more blankets and removed the headless body of the copilot from this seat. Bradlee felt that a section on one of the rotor blades must have penetrated the cockpit on the copilot's side and decapitated him, probably at the time of impact with the ground. The stump of the neck was black with charred skin and boiled blood. Anders was again overcome with nausea and vomited near the broken tail of the aircraft.

The only remaining task was to retrieve the head of the aviator from the cockpit. ''Do you want me to do that, son?'' Bradlee asked. ''I will if you want.'' His experiences in Vietnam had hardened him to such sights, but he knew Anders should do it himself, in order to undergo the necessary process of personal detachment while performing the task.

''No sir, I can do it all right,'' Anders answered. He took another blanket, unfolded it and knelt inside the cockpit. Fortunately the helmet was turned sufficiently so that the pilot's face was only partially visible from this approach. He wrapped the blanket around it, and lifted it out of the wreckage, surprised how heavy it was. Cradling the helmet in his arms, as one might a baby or some fragile possession, he carefully carried it to the full body bag and returned it to the rest of the aviator's remains. After zipping up the bag, Anders stood and removed his mask and gloves, relieved that the task was over.

As he stood staring at the remains of what once were thinking, feeling, caring men who must have enjoyed life and were looking forward to whatever their future might be, he felt a sudden urge.

''Mr. Bradlee,'' Anders said, looking around the surreal site in the desert of this recent firefight, ''do you think it would be okay if we said a prayer for these men right now?''

Bradlee could see the distress on Anders' face and actually felt it himself. He knew a prayer might help them as much as to pay homage to these two brave young men. ''I think that would be real nice, Jay. Go ahead.''

Sergeant Doerdorf watched as the two men stood solemnly over the body bags with their heads bowed and hands clasped behind their backs. He couldn't hear what they were saying, but figured they were praying. A rough and casual man from Chicago, Doerdorf had nonetheless been brought up in the Catholic Church, serving as an altar boy. The ways of the Church had drifted away from him over the years, but he still maintained a sacred appreciation for death and the soul. He set down his M-16 rifle on the wheel strut of the Blackhawk, pointed it away from the aircraft, and removed his flight helmet. As he bowed his head, he made the sign of the cross and tried to remember some of the Catholic prayers that might be appropriate at a time like this. The praying men were only vaguely aware of the sound of approaching helicopters.

* * *

As his Chinook transport helicopter approached the scene of the fire fight, Sergeant Tatum strained to get a view out of the small, circular window. He saw the smoking wreckage of what must have been the Iraqi vehicles, and he spotted the Apache helicopter, sitting on the sand with its rotors slowly turning, its nose pointed at a group of Arab soldiers (he supposed they were Iraqis) sitting in a circle on the sand. As the Chinook turned and banked, he noticed the remains of the destroyed American helicopter, surprised to see two men in flight uniforms with their heads bent in seeming prayer over two long, dark objects in the sand.

Wondering about the scene, he looked over at the Blackhawk medical helicopter nearly and saw another man in a flight suit with his helmet off, similarly with head bowed. Suddenly, he knew what was happening down there on the desert floor, and was struck with a pang of human emotion that gave him a pain in his heart. *Dear Lord,* he thought, *take those unfortunate men up into your arms. They surely do deserve it.* Just then, an image of his mother crying at the funeral of his father (Lucius was only six at the time, but could periodically recall that event quite clearly) when they closed the casket and the choir began to sing "Amazing Grace." He had loved his father, as he knew his children loved him, and couldn't understand why his father was taken from him by the cruel carelessness of a hit and run driver. All those emotions flooded back into his mind as his gaze was fixed on the touching scene in the desert.

The jar of the Chinook's landing brought Tatum back to the reality of his mission. His platoon of paratroopers had been called up from their forward-deployed base camp about 20 kilometers south to take charge of the enemy prisoners. He guessed they couldn't be called "prisoners-of-war" yet because "war" had not officially been declared. But the scene before him looked like a battle zone, so he guessed, at the very least, they had an "unofficial" war here.

The Chinooks had been dispatched from the nearby aviation transportation unit and each carried a squad of paratroopers. Tatum led his men out the open rear cargo door of the Chinook over to where the Iraqi soldiers were squatting. While in Saudi, he and his men had been instructed on proper PW procedures, so they formed a circle around the enemy soldiers. Lieutenant Ted Knapp, the platoon leader, walked toward the group of prisoners, with a Kuwaiti soldier accompanying him as an interpreter. Through the interpreter, Knapp ascertained the group was to have fired its missiles at the 82nd base camp and at any aircraft that flew over their positions.

Although visibly calm, Knapp was angry inside at the intent of these Iraqi soldiers. He turned to the squad leaders and told them to move in and check the prisoners for weapons and documents. Using the Kuwaiti interpreter, Tatum and the others got the prisoners separated and spread-eagled on the sand. While two troopers stood guard, a third checked their bodies for concealed objects. After a thorough body search, the Iraqis' hands were bound in front of them with plastic strip cuffs and they were marched toward the aircraft. They all seemed to go willingly and, according to the interpreter, were all disavowing the Iraqi president and stating their support for the Coalition. *What liars*, Tatum thought. *They'd sell out their mothers if they thought it would help them personally.*

No matter what the Americans thought personally about the Iraqis, they were under orders to treat them fairly and civilly and did so. They even had to strap them into their seat harnesses themselves. The prisoners were headed for a makeshift prison compound near Log Base Alpha.

After the prisoners were loaded onto the Chinooks, Tatum's men took their assigned positions as guards in their Chinook, training their rifles on the Iraqis to let them know they would be shot if they got loose from their harness. No one thought the Iraqis would try to "escape" from a helicopter flying at 500 feet, but the Americans were concerned the Iraqis might attempt to cause the aircraft to crash, killing the Americans and ensuring their own place in Muslim "Paradise."

As Tatum started up the ramp to the inside of his assigned Chinook, he saw the medivac helicopter begin to lift off. When it circled back around the Chinook, Tatum stopped walking, stood straight at attention and gave the helicopter and its tragic contents a perfect salute.

* * *

In the medivac, Anders was looking out the window, alone in his thoughts, when he saw Tatum give his salute. He nodded, looked over at the body bags and thought. *Yes, men, there are those who care.*

Although there might have been some aviators and crew members who would have felt that it was bad luck or an evil omen to carry the dead bodies of two aviators in their aircraft, the crew of the Blackhawk Medivac chopper did not feel that way. Bradlee and Anders had made peace there in the desert with the remains of these men and they felt as if they were helping take the bodies to their final journey's end.

Anders was pensive as he sat in the darkened aircraft,

leaning back against the engine firewall and feeling the vibrations of the dual engines. The two body bags were strapped to the floor of the aircraft and were very still. Anders had realized tonight, perhaps *really* for the first time, but at least as strongly as ever before, just how fragile human existence is. These two men were doing no more nor less than what he had done on many occasions. He knew that Army aviation, even in a non-combat situation, was dangerous, but until now he had not seen the results up close.

Anders thought of his own life and how fortunate he was—a good home, loving parents who gave him the important things he needed in growing up, a good education, the ability to think for himself. He silently said a small prayer of gratitude to the Lord for what he had received. He also asked Him, if it was His will, to allow him the chance to live through this situation in the Gulf, so he might help others in some way.

When the aircraft landed at an airfield different from their own, Anders was thinking about his future. He leaned forward in the harness as the pilot first hovered, then taxied toward a soldier with a red hand held light, indicating where the helicopter should park. There was a Humm-Vee ambulance parked close to the location with two litter-bearers alongside.

While the rotors were still turning slowly, the two bearers left their positions next to the ambulance and ran in a crouch with the litter toward the open Blackhawk cabin door. Anders had unstrapped himself from the seat and loosened the tiedowns that bound the body bags to metal rings on the aircraft floor.

The two litter bearers began to lift the first body out of the aircraft. Once out, they started to place it on the litter, but one man lost his grip on the rubber bag, and it fell to the ground. Anders leaped from the aircraft in an instant and grabbed the front of the offending soldier's BDU shirt. He yanked the man roughly to him and stared into his eyes. ''If you do that again,'' he hollered so the man could hear him, ''I'll rip your head off, do you understand? Those are men in there, just like you and me.''

The rage in Anders eyes convinced the soldier. He swallowed hard, blinked and nodded. Anders didn't let him go until he calmed down, then he loosened his grip on the man's shirt. He turned and helped them load the first, then the second body gently onto a litter. Bradlee had joined him to watch as the graves registration unit placed the bodies into the ambulance, took the paperwork Bradlee had completed and drove off.

Bradlee put his hand on Anders' shoulder. "There, son," he said, "but for the Grace of God go we."

Anders nodded. He knew that was right. But would it last?

* * *

The prison camp had been hastily built by the Saudi military in an old business compound consisting of two buildings, one for administration, the other to house Saudi soldiers who were the Coalition PW guards. The PW area was walled off by a double fence of six-foot chain link with concertina wire on top. Four large American GP (general purpose) tents had been erected in the compound for the prisoners as well as two latrines made of wood and screen wire.

Tatum and his men waited until it was their turn to escort their prisoners into the administrative building, where they would be processed and questioned. As he saw the Saudi soldiers handling the Iraqi soldiers, it was apparent that they all looked alike—dark hair, swarthy complexions, prominent noses, moustaches, and thin physiques. He wondered if the Saudi soldiers had any regrets about going to war against their fellow Muslims? Tatum realized it would probably be easier for him to kill a white enemy soldier than a black one and wondered if that made him a "racist"?

After the prisoners were thoroughly searched, their hands were untied. They were given water and bread and expressed their thanks to the Saudi captors. *It was obvious there would be no serious trouble from this bunch,* Tatum thought. *They're probably thankful they got out of this mess alive.*

As Tatum followed his men from the compound and back up the ramp of the Chinook, he felt weary. *It hasn't even started yet,* he thought, *and I'm already tired. I've seen so much conflict between men, between brothers on this earth, and it's not over yet.* He slumped into his seat, strapped himself in and took off his helmet to wipe the perspiration from his brow. He looked around the aircraft at the young men in his squad—all healthy, all in top physical shape, all with some future in their dreams beyond tonight. All wanting to get this over with and go back home. *But who in this aircraft won't be going home? At least not alive.* He cradled his head in his hands and prayed for all of them. And for himself.

* * *

The lights of Dhahran were visible to Sergeant Gonzales as he sat on the roof of the VIP building in Khobar Towers. He had come to the roof with an urge just to think, to be by himself. There was a sandbag bunker, unmanned right now, and he leaned against it to contemplate the night. He had often done this back in El Paso, especially after he had returned from Vietnam and left the Army. He had tried to cope with the anger he felt toward those who didn't support the effort over there or the troops who served, and usually he did a pretty good job, with help from his wife, America. She was Godsend to him, he believed, and he worshiped her. But not even America could ease his anguish all the time, and so he had taken to the mountains over El Paso, to one particular spot where he could see both the desert on one hand and the city on the other representing his loneliness as well as his need for human company. Over the years, those trips to the mountain had helped him cope with his memories and his anguish. So, now in his loneliness, he again returned to the mountain, in the form of the building roof, to think and sort things out.

It wasn't as if he was at the end of his rope. No, he knew he had things well in hand with his military responsibilities. He was a natural organizer and leader of men, and that was going well.

His real problem had begun when he killed the two Iraqi commandos. Sure, he had probably saved a lot of American lives, even though one of his men had been wounded. He wasn't especially remorseful about killing the raiders, although he knew that act was basically counter to his own understanding of Catholicism.

No, the problem was he had actually *enjoyed* the experience—the excitement, the danger, the "high" of another life and death confrontation. In Vietnam he realized he seemed to thrive on the patrols and missions and periodically had actually missed the rush of adrenaline he felt when on the edge. *There's nothing quite like it,* he realized, *when your life hangs in the balance because of the way you conduct yourself and use your own abilities. Could it be the ancient Indian blood in him, that made him continue to want to hunt, to kill? The other side of the coin, though, was that he wanted to be a peaceful man, not a killer. He wanted to be the kind of man his children would respect and admire, and one his wife would be proud of. What would they think and feel if they knew he enjoyed the danger of the manhunt and that he enjoyed the kill, too. It didn't matter that he was remorseful afterwards, did it? What really counted was that he enjoyed it.*

Was he any different than a crazed killer of helpless victims? Yes, he thought, *I don't go out looking for it, it just seems to come to me. And during a war, it's acceptable to kill. Maybe that's what is wrong with things. Men have the authority, even the encouragement, to kill during war, but they have to turn off those finely honed skills and instincts the minute they return to their homelands. So, am I a killer or not?*

He watched an aircraft land at the nearby airport and wondered if it was bringing more men and women to the impending war. *Are there any others like me on that aircraft? How about here in this compound? If only I could find one and talk to him I'd understand myself better. Sure, I knew killers over in Vietnam; most grunts like me did kill, but, we never talked about whether we enjoyed it.*

He stood up and went over to the side of the building. Looking down, he could see the drop was about a hundred feet. *Could I do that?* he asked himself. *Could I solve my problem by just stepping off this roof? Maybe, but what kind of a problem would I be leaving for America and the kids? They all need me and I need them.*

He stood looking down at the ground until the guard below happened to look up and see him. The guard turned and stepped back a few feet.

"Hey, Sarge, what you doin' up there? You gonna jump?" The guard said it in an uncertain voice, as if the possibility were real.

Gonzales stared at him for a few seconds, then looked at the stars. So bright and so beautiful, just like his children.

He looked back down at the guard. "No, I'm not going to jump. I just came up here to check on you, to see if you were asleep."

The guard snorted, laughed and turned back to his post. Gonzales took a deep breath, stretched his arms, smiled to himself and headed back downstairs.

PART TWO

DESERT STORM

CHAPTER SEVEN

THE JANUARY 15 United Nations deadline for the removal of Iraqi troops from Kuwait had come and gone. Most of that day, Neel had listened to his Sony shortwave radio, tuned to the BBC in London, hoping for a diplomatic solution to the conflict, but realizing that would likely not happen. A further confirmation for him of the potential for impending war had been the fact that the troops at Khobar had been served a hot steak dinner that evening - a certain omen of a coming battle. Such rituals had occurred for centuries and it even reminded him of the pre-game steak dinners back when he was a high school quarterback in Joplin. Men have many strange rituals associated with games and fighting, he supposed, but somehow the rituals were almost as important as the actual fighting or the conduct of the game.

Sporadic gunfire could sometimes be heard outside the military compound, but Neel could find no one who knew its origin. There were no definite restrictions to travel, although transportation outside the compound was scarce, because many troops were still being transported each day to positions elsewhere in Saudi Arabia.

Neel heard about an opportunity to visit the 85th Evacuation Hospital at the nearby International Airport and had boarded the truck at first light that morning in order to visit and talk with other physicians. He had always taken for granted the opportunity to interact with other medical professionals, and he missed it.

The airport was fiercely busy and was occupied mainly by U.S. Air Force troops. The 85th was physically unpretentious: simply a large number of sand-colored tents, neatly set up in rows, with concertina wire outlining their perimeter. Personnel tents were set up nearby on bulldozed and flattened areas of sand. As Neel prepared to enter the central triage tent, he caught sight of a bespectacled physician sitting just outside the tent on a wooden bench, reading Stephenson's *Textbook of Emergency Surgical*

Resuscitation. Correctly figuring the man must be one of the 85th's surgeons, Neel introduced himself. The reader was Major Carl Patterson from Walter Reed Army Medical Center in Washington D.C., and he was a general surgeon. Patterson had finished his surgical residency six months earlier and was on the active duty teaching staff at the Army's largest medical center. The young man stood up and shook hands with Neel. He had a pleasant smile and a quiet demeanor.

They sat down together on the bench and Patterson told Neel they had been at this site for six weeks, but had only been open for patients for two. Most of the work was minor emergencies and trauma, as well as a large sick call, owing to the large troop concentration at the airport as well as in many locations in and around Dhahran.

As Patterson talked to Neel, he kept looking at his name on the BDU blouse and seemed to be thinking about it. Finally, his eyebrows lifted and he smiled as if he had suddenly made a mental connection.

"Say, I know who you are now. I've been trying to connect in my mind where I have seen you before. You're from the Maryland Trauma Center, aren't you?"

"I used to be," Neel smiled, pleased Patterson had heard of him, "but I recently moved to Kansas City to head the trauma unit there. Actually, I had barely gotten settled in when I got called up to come out here."

"Ah, that's too bad." Patterson shook his head. "It's bad enough being on active duty and over here, let alone giving up what you did when you got called up."

"Well, I'm all right about it, but my wife's not—she's really upset." *Now why did I say that,* Neel thought? *I guess I figured another surgeon would understand the strain the demands of our profession can place on a family.*

"I know just what you mean, Tom," Patterson replied, confirming Neel's belief. "My wife was sure that with my general surgery residency over, we would have a chance for a normal family life. Then all this started up." He shook his head and stared at the book. Then he looked up and smiled. "I saw you last year at the College of Surgeon's meeting in Chicago where you helped teach that postgraduate course on revascularization of the extremities. In fact, I was just reading Stephenson's textbook, trying to find some information about vascular surgery in contaminated wounds. Now that I've got an expert here, maybe I can ask you some questions?''

''Well, I'm no expert,'' Neel replied, ''but we certainly saw our share of farming accidents at Missouri and industrial injuries at Maryland. Some of the wounds we might see here if a war occurs could be similar, so I guess that experience will come in handy.''

They sat on the wooden bench for over an hour, discussing the clinical aspects of vascular surgery in contaminated wounds. It might have been any hospital setting back home but it wasn't. There were too many reminders that this was different, but for that brief time, the two men lost themselves in their professional discussion.

Finally, Patterson had invited Neel to ''lunch,'' which consisted of an unlimited supply of bread, peanut butter and jelly, apples, oranges, and citrus drinks. There were even picnic tables in the mess tent where they could sit comfortably. Neel had enjoyed his visit with Patterson and was depressed when he had to return on the truck to Khobar. They shook hands and vowed to stay in touch.

When Neel got back to the VIP building at Khobar, the guard on duty informed him the compound was on ''Threatcon C'' - a high level of security for possible terrorist attacks. No one could leave the compound and P.T. in the streets was forbidden. Full combat gear was to be worn to the chow line and everyone was encouraged to stay in their rooms. The roof guards had obviously been doubled. Tension and anxiety were evident.

Neel went to his room and changed into his Army P.T. gear, then proceeded to perform a series of strenuous exercises - pushups, situps, active stretching, calisthenics and isometrics. Exercise had always been a catharsis, a way to rid himself of tension, stress and nerves. It seemed to work again, and after toweling himself dry, he lay down on his cot to rest. He couldn't sleep and his thoughts kept returning to Marty and what she was doing. He looked at his watch, saw it was two o'clock in the afternoon, and after calculating the seven hours' time difference between Saudi Arabia and Kansas City, realized that she was just awakening and getting ready to go to work. He envisioned her starting her bath water and removing the long, silk pajamas she liked to wear in the winter. She had a habit of indulging in a long, languid stretch before stepping into the bath, which never failed to get his attention. He wondered how she looked now, in the first trimester of her pregnancy, and whether her tummy had begun to bulge. Realizing he couldn't stand those thoughts much longer, he sat up and found his writing tablet. As he leaned back against the wall, the words flowed easily onto the paper.

January 16, 1991

Dearest Marty:

I was just thinking about you, and wondering what you might be doing so I thought I would write. I hope you are feeling well and that you are having no trouble with the pregnancy. Can Dr. Williams hear any heartbeat yet? If not, it won't be long, I'm sure. Have you started to "show" at all? Be sure to go down to Crown Center and find some really nice maternity clothes so you'll feel good about how you look, O.K.? You'll look beautiful in whatever you wear, including maternity clothes!

How is work going? Has the second semester already started? Are you taking any classes for your Ph.D. this year? Don't let it go, because I know it's very important to you.

I visited a nearby Army hospital today and had a good talk with a general surgeon from Walter Reed. I always took it for granted when I talked to other surgeons about cases and treatment, but this made me realize how really special it is to be able to interact with colleagues. Especially since I've been isolated here from anyone other than general medical officers. I'm seeing sick call, if you can believe that, and acting like a G.M.O. myself. Funny, tho, it really is rewarding, but makes me feel like an intern again.

I'm safe here, so don't worry about me. I miss you terribly and hope you feel the same way. I know

> *there's a real strain between us now, but please try to keep positive thoughts about me. Right now, I guess both of us really needs the other, and since we can't be together in fact, we have to be in each others minds and hearts. I know I'm not given to sentimentality as a rule, but I'm lonely and miss you a lot and look forward to when I can come home. Please keep your spirits up and write me as often as you can. The letters are bound to catch up with me sometime.*
>
> *I.L.Y., Tom*

Neel read and reread the letter to sense the mood and effect and judge how it might strike his wife. *Darnit, who knows what she will think? I just hope she gets over this problem before I come home, so we can get on with our lives.* He groaned and lay back on his cot, lost in worry.

Somehow he had fallen asleep and when he awoke, it was dark. For a second, he was disoriented. Then, regaining his bearings, he found his way to the light switch. He addressed the envelope, dressed quickly and donned his combat gear and set off for the headquarters building to mail the letter. Along the way, he was impressed with the high level of activity. Large buses and trucks were being crammed with men, gear and duffels for transfer to the desert. Columns of military vehicles rolled out of the compound accompanied by armored personnel carriers, light tanks, or armed Humm-Vees. The military police were working hard to control the exiting traffic and still provide tight security for the compound.

Something's going on, Neel thought. *I haven't seen this much activity since we've been here at Khobar. I had better go and listen to the shortwave when I get back.* He posted his letter, then stopped by the mess hall - "mess garage" to be exact, because food service was in the underground parking garages for the Khobar Towers complex. He noticed the lines were shorter, surmising that was because of the numbers of soldiers deploying into the desert. He wondered when his unit would leave.

Back in the VIP quarters, he met SFC Gonzales coming out

the door.

''Evening, Major. I was just heading over to 3rd Armored intelligence briefing. Care to come along?''

''That might be real interesting, Sergeant. Any problem with my tagging along?'' Neel asked.

''What sort of a security clearance do you have, sir''?

''Well, it's TOP SECRET.''

''Yo, that ought to get you in the door, all right,'' Gonzales answered with a laugh. ''Most of the unit commanders around here don't even have TOP SECRET, so you'll be O.K.''

The two men walked across the sandy field to the 3rd AD headquarters building. Apparently, a sewer had flooded or backed up into the ground floor of the building. The stench was disgusting and they had to pick their way through liquid and semi-solid debris to reach the third floor conference room.

''Glad we're staying at the VIP, Sir?'' Gonzales asked, when Neel slipped and almost fell into a puddle of God-knows-what on the floor.

Neel smiled and shook his head. ''You know, Gonzales, I've been in deep crap plenty of times, but never shallow.''

The men stopped laughing just before they entered the apartment which had been converted into a briefing room for the division S-2. The entire room had a ''barnyard'' odor, but the men quickly got used to it. They found a corner of the room unoccupied and sat on a makeshift bench.

The audience was a varied group, many assigned to the 3rd AD. Since first-hand tactical intelligence information was hard to obtain at Khobar, other units sent representatives to these briefings in an attempt to keep informed.

The briefing officer, Captain Jesse Moss, stood up. A compact, athletic-appearing black man, Moss was polished and competent.

''Ladies and gentlemen, for the commander, Third Armored Division, I'll detail the available information about Iraqi units in Kuwait and Iraq, which our forces will face in the event of war, and I'll also show you the current and future positions of our forces with respect to the front lines.''

Captain Moss moved to a large map of the tactical area in the Persian Gulf and with a wooden pointer touched the southern half of Iraq and then Kuwait. ''In all, there are thirty-three divisions of Iraqi troops along the so-called 'Saddam Line,' which we'll have to deal with. The divisions are arranged in three tiers, with pure infantry troops, mostly conscripts, comprising the front. These troops are essentially locked into position, with no way to advance, due to the trenches and berms to their front, and they cannot retreat because of orders to the mechanized infantry and armored units in the second tier to shoot any front line troops attempting to flee. This second tier is mostly entrenched and in revetments, so we feel their mobility for launching an attack is low."

"It is obvious that if these troops do not withdraw voluntarily, we will have to take the battle to them with our own offensive. Behind the mechanized and armored troops are eight divisions of the Republican Guard, located here, and here." Moss pointed to their locations at the northern border of Kuwait with Iraq. "These units are currently felt to be located in large protective underground bunker complexes, but we are awaiting confirmation by special operations units on the ground in that locale."

"Those special forces guys are really in the frying pan," Gonzales whispered to Neel, who nodded, comprehending fully the risk those men were taking, as a result of his own experiences with special operations.

Neel felt a pang of envy for the men in that dangerous job, although he knew he had lost his own edge for such a mission.

Moss continued. "There are four other Iraqi divisions being held in reserve, presumably to bolster defenses in southern Iraq or western Kuwait. In all, we estimate nearly one point two million men are in position or moving into position in the potential battle area. Also, they have had the past three months to build defenses." Moss paused to let that fact sink in to the men and women in the room. "Any questions so far?"

A major from an air artillery unit asked, "Where are the Iraqi SCUD missiles now, with respect to the deployment of the divisions?"

"It appears, sir, that the SCUD launchers are either hidden at fixed positions in southern or western Iraq or on mobile launchers that could be anywhere in the desert. They are an unknown factor at this time and we're working hard to get satellite fixes on as many as possible."

The same major spoke up again, looking around the room. "You all know that we're sitting ducks right here in Khobar Towers, with perhaps twenty-five thousand personnel in a one-square-mile area. There's a lot resting on the Patriot missile units out back." He nodded toward the south edge of the compound where one could see the strange, box-like units mounted on truck beds that were Patriot anti-missile launching sites. All in the room murmured their agreement.

"Now," said Moss, tapping the pointer in his hand and walking again to the large tactical map, "let's look at the deployment of Allied troops."

"The non-American Coalition forces comprise the majority of the troops in the forward area. They include the Joint Forces Command East, made up of Saudi, UAE and Omani mechanized infantry. Across here," Moss said, pointing to the vast northern Saudi desert adjoining the Iraqi and Kuwaiti border, "we have the Joint Forces Command North, with armored and mechanized brigades of Syrian and Kuwaiti troops. Egypt has placed a number of troops in the desert, approximately three divisions, along with a Ranger regiment. Additionally, the British have two armored brigades and the French a light armored division near the border. As far as U.S. troops are concerned, we have elements of the 82nd Airborne Division located here and here," pointing to the map, "and elements of the 1st Marine Division located here, near Khafji."

Moss turned to the audience. "All totaled, we have fewer than seven full divisions in strength against more than forty Iraqi divisions already in place. We can respond to a localized Iraqi attack in just about any sector of the border, but we might have some difficulty with a major Iraqi offensive until our troop strength is significantly built-up along the front."

Most occupants in the room looked around at each other, shaking their heads. They hadn't known the situation was so fragile with respect to Coalition defensive capabilities.

"However," Moss smiled and continued, "we are pouring troops into the desert by the thousands each day. You've noticed that units are leaving Khobar in increasing numbers, and the same thing is occurring at the Port of Damman, at KKMC, and at Riyadh. Soon, and I don't know exactly when, the 1st and 2nd Marine Divisions will be in place near Kuwait, the 2nd Marine

Expeditionary Force will be on board ships in the Gulf awaiting word to invade Kuwait, and the entire U.S. VII and XVIII Corps will be at full strength and ready to attack. Until then, we will have to rely upon the air assets of the Coalition forces to take the battle to the Iraqis and to protect us from attack.''

Moss stepped away from the map and walked up to the edge of the audience. ''At this time, we do not feel Saddam will voluntarily withdraw from Kuwait. The U.N. deadline has come and gone and there is no evidence of withdrawal activity by satellite recon. Something will happen, ladies and gentlemen, and probably soon. Our primary concern is that the Iraqis will send missiles. It is almost certain, in our estimation, that if SCUD missiles are launched against us, they will contain chemical weapons, probably nerve and blood gas, so keep your troops tight about their chemical protective gear.''

With that, Moss concluded the briefing and began to answer specific questions from individuals in the group. As Gonzales and Neel left the room, there was not much to be said, but plenty to think about. They walked back in silence to the V.I.P quarters where they stood in the hallway together for a minute.

''Well, sir,'' Gonzales said, as he shrugged off his Kevlar vest and removed his helmet. ''I'm on watch tonight, so if anything happens, you'll be the first to know, after me, of course.''

Neel turned and walked toward his room. ''Well, I hope I don't see you tonight sergeant, because if I do, it will probably be bad news.'' He turned his head and grinned at Lopez. ''You know, they used to shoot the bearer of bad news, don't you.'' Both men laughed.

Neel went to his room, removed his combat gear, and turned on his shortwave radio, looking for any news of the diplomatic negotiations. The information he could gather indicated negotiations between Iraq and the U.N. members had been fruitless and were now being pursued only by France. *Fat chance that will go anywhere,* Neel thought, *if the Soviets and others can't work out an agreement.* He was torn between two opposing thoughts. As a physician and a human being, he abhorred the thought of many men, women, and children being killed and wounded in an armed conflict of the magnitude possible in the Gulf. On the other hand, growing up in the Midwest, he had been taught a sense of fairness and the difference between right and wrong, and he knew this aggressive act of Saddam Hussein could not be tolerated. His thoughts drifted back to his father, killed in Vietnam while fighting in a conflict that was neither supported by the American public nor had a decisive ending. It was sometimes difficult for him to remember his father's appearance, so he carried an old photograph in his wallet that he had laminated in plastic for preservation. He sat down on the cot and took it out. He saw a tall, tanned and athletic soldier dressed in tiger jungle fatigues with his arms around two combat buddies in front of a tent. They were smiling and appeared happy, but that appearance contrasted with the deadly paraphernalia of war that could be seen all around them—rifles, grenades slung from LBEs, helmets, and for his father, an aidman's medical pack. He had always felt that although his father was smiling, there was no happiness in his eyes—the eyes were sad, for they had seen too much pain and suffering ever to be the same.

Neel always became melancholy after he looked at his Dad's picture, but couldn't or didn't want to escape those thoughts just then. He closed his eyes and tried hard to remember his father before he went to Vietnam. They were pleasant memories; his father had been active and fun-loving, with a constant smile and a gift for jokes. He was a very "people-oriented" man, with a soft place in his heart for animals, children and older people, which was obvious to everyone who knew him. But, there was also a more rigid side to him as well, which he was as carefully guarded and controlled.

Neel's father could never tolerate the bullies, foul-mouthed men cursing in public, anyone who threatened or insulted his family, or any acts of unfairness or unkindness to others. He had a powerful awareness of what was right, and whenever he witnessed a wrong, his family could see a change come over him that made him a much colder and more calculating man, until he had the perpetrators or brought the situation back to its proper equilibrium. Neel had witnessed his father boldly approach a small gang of motorcycle riders who were causing trouble in town and somehow order them to leave before they received the fury of his cold wrath.

Neel knew that that same trait had been passed along to him, although perhaps somewhat diluted by the calmness and equanimity of his mother. Neel, the physician, was also a kind and caring man who chose the medical profession because of its potential for serving others. But, he also had an alter ego, one that compelled him to risk his life jumping out of airplanes and participating in special operations missions or clandestine activities.

He, too, had a problem walking away from any situation where he witnessed an injustice. Characteristically, he felt compelled to intervene when obnoxious teenagers cut into a line waiting for movie tickets or when an angry man was badgering an airline stewardess because he was caught smoking in a non-smoking section of an aircraft. He had never actually gotten into a physical altercation in those situations, not yet anyway, but he realized he would not mind if a situation ever came to that. Marty always thought he was crazy to get involved in anyone else's business, but clearly he could not do otherwise and suspected his father would have approved.

Neel had laid back on his cot with his hands behind his head and had nearly drifted off to sleep when suddenly, the Klaxon sounded outside in the compound, accompanied by shouting, the sounds of men running in combat gear, and hard footsteps on the stairways. Neel sat bolt upright in bed and ran to the only window in the room. The lights in the compound were rapidly being extinguished and he could see men running into buildings. In an instant no one was visible anywhere. Neel became aware of the thunderous sounds of military jets taking off from the adjacent airport in rapid succession.

The next words he heard made a cold chill course through his body. A military police vehicle was driving through the compound with a loudspeaker on its roof. The message was produced with distinguishable yet unforgettable robot quality: "SCUD LAUNCH - MOPP 4. SCUD LAUNCH - MOPP 4." The vehicle was warning them that SCUD missiles had been launched at the compound by the Iraqis and each individual was to put on the full complement of chemical warfare protective gear.

As Neel moved to don his MOPP suit and gas mask, his thoughts were racing. *What's going on?* he wondered. *Are we at war? Is this a preemptive strike by the Iraqis or one preceding an attack by ground troops? Just how effective is this chemical suit anyway? What if the missile hits this building and rips my suit -- will I be conscious enough to use the medical auto-injectors? What if the filters don't work on the gas mask?*

But he set his mind to the task and began laying out his

chemical warfare suit. Quickly he pulled on the trousers over his BDU uniform and tied the loose waist securely with some extra string he found in the chemical bag. Then he put on the outer jacket, zipped it up and snapped the buttons. Instantly, he was too hot in the suit and began to sweat. He opened the big rubber boots and tried to pull them over his military boots - but they wouldn't go. *Damn, Neel, settle down. You've practiced this a hundred times and you know they'll go on.* He took a deep breath and concentrated on working the rubber boots on until they were in place. He tied them securely with the long, black laces and pulled the plastic cuffs of the chemical suit down as far over the boots as they would go.

He could still hear the Klaxon alarms and the monotonous sound of the SCUD launch warning outside, which hastened his preparations. He realized even the potential use of deadly chemicals in warfare possessed far more capability to generate fear than would be rational. In fact, the response to a threat of an unseen, odorless chemical that could kill you by virtue of a small leak in a gas mask or a bad seal was so devastating to some they were incapacitated just by the threat.

Neel removed the gas mask from its bag and placed it on his face as he had been trained, immediately inhaling the dry rubber odor. He adjusted the scalp straps, then tested for a good seal. His face and neck were already sweating and he was so concerned he would not have a good seal, he tightened the straps even more. Then he pulled the mask hood over his head and neck and tried to find the small velcro straps to tighten under his arms. His field of vision was so restricted by the eye pieces of the mask that he couldn't see the tabs, so he had to complete the task by feel. Once done, he located his inner cotton glove liners, put them on, and with some difficulty pulled on the large black latex rubber outer protective gloves.

He stood and walked back to the window, but was unable to see any activity outside. Just then he heard the door to the room crash open and turned to see a similarly suited apparition walk clumsily into the room. Everyone looked alike in the suits, so he had to get up very close, almost mask-to-mask, before he recognized the figure as Sergeant Gonzales.

"*Buenos tardes,* major," Gonzales said. "You look divine in your new suit. Care for any company while we see what's going to happen?''

Neel was relieved. ''You bet, sergeant. It's always more fun to share a foxhole with someone, isn't it?''

Gonzales nodded. He had felt the same need to be with another person when under attack in Vietnam.

Neel picked up his radio, and walked over toward the window, the only source of light. He had to hold the radio directly up in front of his face to see the frequency numbers as he tuned to the military station of the U.S. Central Command, not an easy chore with the large rubber gloves. He was more used to operating with thin, sensitive surgical gloves on his hands.

The radio message broke the dark silence and they sat on the floor to listen. The announcer was repeating her message: ''The U.S. Central Command, has just confirmed that a massive air attack has been launched against Iraqi military positions in Kuwait and in Iraq itself. Baghdad is currently under heavy attack by Coalition aircraft. Other sites are also being targeted by the massive air strikes, but no further details are available at this time. There are also unconfirmed reports that satellite reconnaissance has detected the launching of what are believed to be SCUD missiles toward targets in Saudi Arabia. The Central Command has informed us that the Coalition military action is called Operation Desert Storm.''

Neel and Gonzales looked at each other but could not read the other's expressions behind the masks. They sat quietly for a few minutes, listening to, but not really hearing the radio reports, until Neel spoke up.

''Let the games begin,'' he said, in a voice that sounded both grim and unearthly in the gas mask.

* * *

The Jalibah military air field in Southern Iraq was a primary target for destruction by American Air Force attack aircraft that first night of ''Operation Desert Storm.'' The word had come to Porter in the desert several days before by encoded rapid radio transmission and he and his men were excited about the prospect of finally seeing some action after weeks of waiting and preparing. Their team's mission would be to guide the aircraft to the targets already predesignated for destruction by Porter's reconnaissance and to ''paint'' them with the laser range finder. The Air Force pilots would then use the laser beams as guides for the paths of their "smart" bombs.

Porter, Sergeant Lopez and Sergeant Miller had set out for the Iraqi air field the night they received the message, anxious to be in place and ready when the attack came. They had arrived at the outskirts of the air base in the dark, and, as before, had waited in the relative obscurity of new slit-trenches for the time to pass. Torn between not wanting to compromise their position and yet interested to know whether the Iraqis had changed any of their defenses or positions, Porter finally decided to make a one-man quick reconnoiter of the base. He did that himself, unwilling to put his men at risk for a job only he really thought should be done. To his relief, nothing on the air base had changed since their previous visit.

Back at the hidden site in the desert only about two thousand meters from the southern perimeter wire, the men discussed the mission in hushed voices.

"Lieutenant, how many planes do you suppose the Air Force will send out when they attack?" whispered Sgt. Miller.

"I figure a flight of four, probably F-16s, Miller, because they've got to come from KKMC and they can carry a hell of a lot of armament." Porter replied.

"How do you figure the kinds of armament they'll use here, Lieutenant?" Lopez was lying on his side in the slit trench, behind a sand dune, cleaning his M-16. He looked up at Porter.

"Well, each of those F-16s can carry up to eight Maverick missiles, several CBU canisters and two of what the Air Force calls their "smart bombs." I've never seen the smart bombs in action, but back at Bragg they showed us a film once showing the bomb guided into a target the size of a basketball by a laser. It was amazing!" Porter was eating an MRE fruitcake slice and was talking with his mouth full, which his mother had always abhorred. He took a swig of water from his two-quart canteen and continued.

"They'll probably use Mavericks to take out the radar dish and control tower. However, they'll be coming in so low and fast that their accuracy with those missiles will be reduced. We have to be prepared to finish off with our Stingers anything they miss." Porter looked over at the beige Cordura nylon travel cases which housed the six shoulder-fire missiles they had brought. "But our first task with the Stingers will be to knock out those two I-Hawk batteries the Iraqis have on the runways. We'll do that just minutes before the F-16s show up, so they won't be jeopardized. The F-16s plan to drop the CBU clusters on the runways on the first pass, so the Iraqis won't be able to launch their aircraft. After that it ought to be a turkey shoot.''

Miller looked at Lopez and raised his eyebrows. The lieutenant was a man of confidence, not given to uncertainty. Yet they all knew that hardly any special operation ever went according to plan and that occasionally something went terribly wrong. Success depended upon carrying out the mission despite the unexpected. That's why special ops members were specially picked for intelligence, flexibility and their ability to think and react under pressure.

''Say, boss,'' Miller asked, ''how do we plan to handle it if one of the aircraft gets shot down and the pilots bail out over the desert?''

Porter thought about that for a while. He and CWO2 Nichols had certain information the others were not privy to, and it was his decision, as the local commander in the field, when to divulge that information. Now was obviously one of those times.

''Good question, Tom. Our primary mission is to support the destruction of military targets of opportunity assigned to us by CENTCOM and only as a secondary mission do we become involved in search and rescue operations for downed pilots. We've got other A teams over here in southern Iraq whose primary mission is SAR. Remember Captain Charlie Cleaton, who was with the 7th group and ran the Seaspray Operation down in Central America a year or so ago?''

The other two nodded.

''Well, he's about fifty kilometers from here in the desert and I suspect, unless a pilot just dropped into our laps, that his team would be assigned the job of pickup and evasion until they called in the SAR choppers. They've already got the radio frequencies set for SAR on their cammo gear - we'd have to rely upon contacting any helicopter that happened to be in the area for a pickup - and that's pretty chancy.''

Porter thought about Cleaton for a minute. A clean-cut man, he represented the best of the Green Berets. Porter had seen Cleaton fracture his heel on a jump into the jungles of Honduras along the Coco River, and still carry out a week-long mission without complaint. Charlie had told him before their deployment to the Persian Gulf that he had applied to and been accepted by the medical school at Chapel Hill. *He'll make a fine doctor*, Porter thought, *if he returns from this alive.* Shaking that depressing thought about his good friend, he returned to the subject.

"It comes down to a real judgment call whether an entire Special Forces A Team with an important mission like ours should compromise itself on a search and rescue mission for a single Air Force pilot. The higher Army commanders were apparently willing to say no, that it wasn't worth the potential loss of an A team, but the Air Force felt so strongly about getting its pilots back, that they got the Army to agree to leaving the final decision up to the A team commander in the field."

For Porter, that decision was easy. He would not be able to stand by if he knew a pilot was down and not go to his rescue. He'd put Nichols in charge of the team and go to the pilot by himself if he had to. But, knowing his men as he did, he figured there would be no shortage of volunteers.

"Now listen, you two. When we go in to paint the targets and finish what needs to be done, I don't want any heroics, OK? Just in and out quickly. Don't go being a Rambo and try to wipe out the whole air base on your own, got it?"

Lopez and Miller grinned and nodded. For all the concern their leader had for his men, they knew it was more likely *he* would be the one to be the aggressor, not them. "Sure, Boss, if you'll follow your own advice for a change," Lopez replied with a grin behind a black, bushy moustache. "We figure we'll have to rein you in when you get to putting the full court press on the Iraqis!"

Porter grimaced. They sure had him figured. Whenever he got into a firefight, he became very aggressive and forgot about concerns for his own safety. But tonight would be different. If any of them were killed or captured, it could compromise the whole team and their future missions.

"All right, then, let's make a deal. We all do our job quietly and efficiently and pull out before anyone ever knew we were here. In fact, let's let them think the Air Force pulled off the whole job by themselves, OK?"

The other two nodded.

"Agreed, then." Porter checked his watch. "If they come tonight, it could be anytime after 2200 hours, so I suggest we get some sleep. We may be awake all night. I'll take the first shift and wake you up, Tom, in about three hours, OK?''

The men settled into their makeshift trenches and prepared to rest. Porter wrapped himself in the desert camouflage poncho and crawled to the rise of the sand dune, to scan the horizon for threats. Each was left alone with his own thoughts.

Later, Porter was soundly sleeping in his trench when Miller shook his leg. Porter slept with his Ka Bar knife at the ready, but his subconscious mind recognized Miller's voice and realized he was no threat. It was dusk when Porter sat up in his trench and dug his fingers through sleep-tousled hair.

''Sir, we just received a burst from headquarters. It's decoded on the digital display monitor on the commo set.'' He handed the small lap-top to Porter, who adjusted the screen.

COMMENCE OPERATION
0030 HRS. 4 AIRCRAFT
ON SITE 0100 HRS.
RADIO FREQ - 1305.2
CODE: LONGHORN.
CONFIRM ASAP

Porter looked at his watch. It was now 1045. That gave them only a little more than an hour and a half to get into position to destroy the I-HAWK.

''Tom, confirm their transmission receipt with 'CODE: CHAROLAIS'. Then let's get our butts in gear.''

As Miller prepared to send the burst transmission that they were ready for the mission, Porter awoke Lopez and they donned their combat gear and checked their weapons. Tonight, they would carry M-16B models, more reliable than the A-model, with 30-round banana clips taped together for more sustained fire power.

Quietly, they removed the six Stingers from their nylon cases and each took two. They also carried a personal 9mm Beretta apiece with five spare 15-round magazines, as well as a Ka Bar and four high-explosive grenades hooked to their LBE chest straps. Because of the virtual one-hundred percent chance of fragments from bomb explosions, they added Kevlar vests and helmets for protection. Lopez also had five pounds of C-4 plastic explosive stashed in his right trouser pocket, with two detonators in a metal-polymer composite protective case in his breast pocket. They were ready.

As they approached the air base in the shadows, they used the same routes they had become familiar with on the last visit. Their faces were darkened with camouflage paint and all of their metallic equipment, including the Stingers, had been sputter coated with a low gloss titanium-cobalt alloy for protection from the sand and to decrease light reflection from sources at the airfield.

Porter and Lopez were to get within range of the I-Hawk missile batteries at the end of each runway, and destroy them with a Stinger—hopefully one each would be adequate. Miller would go directly to the radar/control tower to stand by in case the Air Force fighter-bombers were unable to destroy them. He had the laser guidance unit that would "paint" the target for the F-16s. The other two would perform the same role at the Iraqi hangars.

Porter ran in a stoop, a very efficient run in the desert where there are no trees or fallen branches. He approached the I-Hawk battery from the south as planned, at a perpendicular to the east-west runway. He was pretty sure the F-16s would follow standard bombing procedures for air base runways, flying directly up or down the runway to unload their cluster bombs. At ninety degrees from the bomb run, it was less likely Porter would be injured by friendly fire.

Fortunately, the moon was covered by high, dense clouds. That would help both him and the F-16s. Porter dropped to his knees and crawled forward slowly, until he was behind a low rise. With his left hand, he scooped out a six-inch diameter notch in the sand at the rise, just sufficient to receive the Stinger missile carrier, yet not enough to change the smooth profile of the dune. He unslung one of the Stingers from his back and extended it to its full length, placing the bottom of the barrel in the notch. Porter flipped up the night optical sights and focused on the conspicuous outline of the I-Hawk battery. *No way to miss from this distance*, he thought, then realized he couldn't 'knock on wood,' so he mentally retracted that thought. He lifted the nylon wrist cover over his field watch and saw that it was 0025 hours -- just thirty minutes more before destroying the Iraqi missile battery to protect the F-16s.

His mouth was dry and his lips were chapped - he seemed acutely aware of that. Slowly, he pulled out his canteen, took several silent drinks and replaced it. Then he found one of his large supply of Chapsticks in his pocket and lubricated his lips. That helped some, but he still felt dehydrated. This was the time he disliked most before a battle - the waiting for an hour or less, which became an eternity. He always felt a little jittery. The thought of death usually didn't dwell with him, but tonight for some reason it invaded his thoughts. He really didn't have anyone beside his family who worried about him so he guessed they would be upset. *But,* he thought, *what better way to go than here and now, a fighting man in a battle. I think I'd like to be buried in Arlington Cemetery,* he thought, immediately regretting that thought. *Hey, I'd better concentrate on staying alive and doing my job well; that may save other American lives as well as my own.*

0045. Only ten more minutes. What I'd really like is an ice cold Diet Coke. I'd hold the cold can up to my forehead to feel the soothing coolness before I popped the top and slowly guzzled it.

0052. Time to arm the Stinger. He flipped the 'ARM' switch and saw the fluorescent reticles in the eyepiece came alive. The small missile was shorter than the Remington Model 1100 shotgun he used to hunt quail, but was ungainly and poorly balanced. However, with the front end resting on the sand, he could wriggle into a reasonable firing position by moving sand aside with his elbows and legs.

0055. Hot damn, time to fire. He held his breath and centered the reticle on the base of the missile battery, where it joined the transportation vehicles. He reasoned that the main missile engines would be located near the fins and would provide secondary explosions.

WHOOSH! The missile left so quickly he thought he had accidentally touched the trigger before he was ready. The little projectile spanned the one hundred and fifty meters in less than two seconds. Then was a huge explosion that temporarily left Porter with 'whited-out' night vision, followed by three other explosions in rapid succession. As he quickly replaced the Stinger carrier in its case, he realized the last explosions were probably from Lopez's missile exploding the other I-Hawk battery. *Great,* he thought, as he got to his feet and ran past the burning missile battery on his way to the aircraft hangars. *I have to cross this runway before the F-16s arrive or I'm lunchmeat.*

He found an area of the runway completely darkened with shadows and decided to sprint to the first hangar. Exhilarated by pumping adrenaline, he ran swiftly and almost effortlessly. Just as he reached the safety of a small out building, the alarm was raised at the air base. Lights came on in buildings and doors were thrown open as men looked out to see what was happening.

Just then, Porter heard the first high-pitched whine of approaching aircraft. Traveling at nearly Mach 1, the F-16s suddenly rushed down the runway behind him, engines screaming. He saw the cluster canisters spill out from under their wing pods, tumble toward the ground and then open to propel the bomblets the length of the runway. He averted his gaze just in time to avoid the brilliant flash of thousands of small explosions. When he turned back after a few seconds, the runway appeared to have been excavated - *there would be no aircraft taking off from this air base tonight,* he thought, relieved the F-16s were now in little danger.

Although he could not see the aircraft in their wide turn-around and return to the target, he could still hear the changing roar of their engines as they made another approach. Porter quickly removed the laser guidance unit from its pack and powered it up. The unit was a small, black rectangular box, with hand-grips and a technetium-painted sighting system for night use. The spotting laser beam was a light green and allowed the operator to aim the beam precisely where he wished the aircraft bomb to hit. Porter stabilized the unit against a building and aimed the beam high on the center of the large hangar door. Shortly afterward, the unit emitted a soft beeping sound, indicating an aircraft had picked up the beam and was homing on it. Holding the beam as steady as possible, he was nonetheless surprised to see a bomb fall out of the sky toward the hangar. He was so close he could see stabilizing fins. The bomb pierced the hangar door neatly, punching a hole in it the size of a small desk. Almost instantly, the hangar door and roof literally exploded away, raining shards of metal fragments on Porter's position. He ducked behind the small building and ran toward the next hangar, about a hundred meters west.

He repeated the same maneuver at the next hangar, and it, too, was penetrated precisely by an F-16 bomb. He recalled reading that the bombs were called "Paveways" and were one-ton, general purpose bombs outfitted with control fins and laser-seeking guidance units. *Great technology*, he thought, as the third hangar was destroyed.

He could see other fires and explosions, which would have been Lopez's and Miller's designated targets. He had heard no small arms fire and guessed the airbase personnel thought they were under air attack only, never suspecting special operations forces were aiding in the attack. As Porter ran toward the radar installation, to see if any important buildings were still unharmed, there was a tremendous blast that lifted him into the air and threw him backwards onto the sand. Momentarily stunned, he looked around for his rifle, found it, and reslung the Stinger cases around his back. He was sore in his lower back and neck, but could still run awkwardly without too much pain. Approaching what was left of the radar complex, he saw the outline of a figure on the ground. He flipped the safety off of his M-16 and approached carefully. It was Miller, lying in the sand with a significant amount of blood where his left lower leg used to be. He looked unconscious.

Glancing around and finding no threats in the immediate vicinity, Porter quickly knelt by Miller's head and felt for a neck pulse - it was fast and weak, but present. There were no other obvious wounds and Miller's helmet was still on his head. Quickly, Porter opened his field dressing kit and applied a tight tourniquet just above the knee, noting the time by Miller's watch. Then he removed Miller's dressing kit and wrapped the stump of the amputated leg as best he could to keep sand out of the tissues.

Miller stirred and moaned, but did not awaken. Porter retrieved a morphine stylet from his inner breast pocket and gave Miller a ten milligram injection right through his BDU arm sleeve. *It must have been the C-4 charge Miller set,* Porter thought. *Must have blown off a large piece of shrapnel that severed Miller's leg as he was running away. I've got to find that leg and take it with us. We can't leave any evidence behind that there are Americans on the ground here.*

He quickly surveyed the sand, able to see fairly well from the flames, and he spotted the severed limb about twenty-five meters away. He ran over, retrieved it without really looking at it and ran back to Miller. *I guess this will hit me later,* he thought, *but now I've got to get us out of here.*

He stuffed the severed limb remnant and boot into the back of Miller's pack and retrieved Miller's M-16.

The base was chaos. Fires and secondary explosions were threatening to engulf the whole place. The sirens had apparently been silenced, or the electrical power was totally cut off, because the only noise were men shouting and explosions. Porter feared he and Miller would be seen if they remained any longer, so he gently picked Miller up, threw him over his shoulder and began running toward the dark safety of the desert. Miller moaned when Porter fell to his knees once, and that was heartening to the lieutenant.

Miller was a short, wiry man, all muscle, but fortunately not too heavy. Porter was used to carrying up to a hundred pounds of equipment on long jungle or mountain treks, so the load was not too much for him. He still had the Stingers slung over his other shoulder, as well as the two M-16s and his other combat gear.

It was hard to run where the sand was soft and shifting, but he managed to stay on his feet when he came to the runway. The shortest way to their temporary base camp was across the runway, rather than around it, but Porter would have to risk stepping on an unexploded cluster bomb, which all too commonly occurred. He looked to his left as he paused at the runway and saw the burning I-Hawk battery; too risky to go around the short way, there he thought. Might be Iraqis still alive. To the right was more than three thousand feet of runway, and he didn't want to take the time to circle. The heat of the burning building to his rear seemed to be burning his back, moving him forward, so he took a deep breath and plunged into the relative darkness over the bombed runway.

He did the best he could, dodging craters in the runway surface and carefully avoiding any object that was even close to the size of a cluster bomblet. He was very concerned about Sergeant Miller, and thought of Miller's family back in Germany. His wife was a small, quiet, pleasant woman who had loved to fix supper for Porter at least once a month, telling him he needed a good woman to settle down with. Their two children were well-behaved, athletic and totally devoted to their father. The remembrance of the Miller family pushed Porter onward. *If anyone deserves to live,* he thought, *it's this fine man I've got on my back.*

He had just crossed the runway without incident when a dark figure suddenly loomed before like an apparition. Startled out of his personal thoughts, he almost dropped Miller trying draw his handgun.

"Lieutenant," the figure whispered, "it's me, Lopez. What happened to Tom?" There was strain and obvious concern in his voice as well as tiredness.

''Hit by shrapnel as best I can tell,'' the lieutenant quietly replied. ''I put on a tourniquet, but we've got to get back to the trenches to release the tourniquet and check on him.''

''Here, let me carry him for a while, sir.'' Lopez lifted Miller off Porter's back and almost effortlessly placed him on his own. *That man is amazingly strong,* Porter thought, as he suddenly felt weak and drained. They moved quickly to the site of their temporary camp and placed Miller in one of the trenches. Covering themselves with a poncho, Lopez shined a red lens flashlight on Miller while Porter checked his vital signs. ''His breathing's slow and deep and his heart rate's about a hundred,'' Porter said. Most A Team members were cross-trained as medics and had to be relatively self-sufficient in their often isolated assignments.

Porter then loosened the tourniquet, he saw blood immediately saturate the bandaged stump. Reapplying the tourniquet, he noted the time and reinforced the stump dressing with one from Miller's first aid kit. The two men looked at each other and saw the concern reflected in each other's eyes.

''Sir, he's gonna die unless we get him out of here to a hospital. We can't let that happen,'' Lopez said.

Porter looked at Miller, and thought about the risk to their operations that would occur if he called for an air evacuation mission. However, he didn't hesitate long. ''Screw it, let's call for Dustoff. We've got to get him out of here. Let me see the map.'' Lopez removed an area map from inside his BDU blouse and unfolded it for Porter. He shined the flashlight onto the area of the air base so Porter could see the grid markers. 46622958. After copying the numbers onto the back of his hand, he removed a powerful transmitter from his belt pack. He entered the codes for the team's identification, punched in the codes calling for an air evacuation mission to pick up a severely injured team member, and then input the grid numbers for a location he had picked approximately five kilometers southeast, well away from the burning air base as well as from their main camp to the west. He hit the SEND button and watched the digital readout as it told him when the transmission was complete. He waited impatiently for several long minutes until the unit received a return signal and processed the codes.

REQUEST CONFIRMED.

AIR EVACUATION APPROVED.

ETA 0430

Zero four-thirty. Porter checked his watch and saw they had a little more than ninety minutes to cover the five-kilometer trek to the pickup site. He looked at Sergeant Lopez. ''Let's do it, sergeant.'' Porter picked up Miller while Lopez piled all their extraneous gear into the trenches and furiously filled them in with sand using his entrenching tool. Lopez kept a Stinger for contingencies. The rest of their gear could be retrieved later.

The two men set off quickly toward the southeast, plunging into the darkness of the desert night, not even looking back at the destruction of the Iraqi base. That was history and they were walking into the future.

* * *

The mission of the 2nd Armored Cavalry Regiment the first night of Operation Desert Storm had been one of vigilance and preparedness. It was not yet time to bring the attack helicopter battle to the Iraqi tanks - that would come later. It was, however, important that the 2nd ACR be prepared to defend the border and to protect the exposed logistical elements of the Seventh Corps that were isolated in the desert from enemy counterattack. The ACR was highly mobile and its recon and attack helicopters could respond to threats hundreds of kilometers from their base camps.

Captain Tex Weatherby and CWO2 Roger Garner had already flown their Apache on one mission to check on reports of an Iraqi tank column in movement near the border. That had turned out to be wrong information and the men were back at the squadron headquarters tent, nursing cups of coffee and monitoring the radios. The coffee they were drinking did not come from the MRE ''accessories'' package, but from Garner's wife, who had sent him a large metal container of gourmet coffee packets, all very rich, aromatic and sweet. The men were savoring this fine coffee out of heavy ceramic mugs with the emblem of the 2nd ACR blazoned on the sides.

''Sounds like we're really popping the Iraqis' bubble tonight, captain,'' Garner said, as they listened to reports of the bombing of Baghdad on the powerful shortwave. ''Maybe he'll surrender after a few nights of this.''

Weatherby glanced at Garner. *How did such a gentle man ever become a weapons officer on an attack helicopter,* he wondered?

''I don't know, Roger. The Iraqis have had a long time to prepare their defenses against air attacks. We'll just have to see how much they can take.'' Weatherby sipped his coffee, enjoying the aroma as much as the taste. ''The only problem is that some of our pilots won't make it back in one piece. Did you hear that CNN reporter who described the antiaircraft fire over the skies of Baghdad? It must be like a quail flying through a 12-gauge shotgun pattern up there. I'd rather take my chances in the helicopter.''

Garner nodded, admiring the courage of the Air Force and Navy pilots who threaded that gauntlet to drop their bombs on Baghdad.

On a rare impulse, Weatherby decided to change the subject: ''Roger, what do you hear from your family back home?''

Garner was a bit taken back. The captain was not normally one who showed much interest in other people's personal lives. He didn't even realize Weatherby knew he had a family, even though they had been flying together for nearly six months.

''Doing well, captain, thanks for asking. My wife wrote in her last letter that the river was frozen in places and the kids were iceskating on the pond behind the house.'' Garner was a Mormon from Utah and he had been on an unaccompanied ''short'' tour to Germany when the 2nd ACR was deployed to Saudi Arabia. The father of five missed his family severely and took his solace in Bible study and discussions with other committed Christians in the unit.

The radiotelephone rang so suddenly both men were startled, almost spilling their coffee. Tex was first to reach the set. The call was from regiment. Garner saw him nod several times and take notes on the pilot's kneeboard pad. When he hung up, his face was grim.

''Saddle up, Roger. We get to nursemaid an air evac mission into southern Iraq to pick up a wounded Special Forces trooper.'' The two men quickly drained their coffee cups and ran out into the cold night air toward their aircraft.

* * *

Specialist Anders was in the moving aircraft, checking his medical kit and gear for the third time. He didn't have any idea how badly wounded the Green Beret was up there in Iraq and he wanted to be prepared for any contingency. He was completely oblivious when the Blackhawk air ambulance he was in crossed the Iraqi border traveling at top nape of the earth flying speed toward the pickup point.

He was also oblivious when they passed near several Iraqi troop emplacements as well as some enemy tanks in defilade. In the desert at night with no moonlight, there was little to see. Fortunately, the Iraqis seemed to be asleep in their bunkers, because no hostile fire was directed their way.

His headset crackled in his ears. The metallic sound of the crewchief's voice was distant and slightly garbled, because of turbine noise and the usual chopper vibrations. "ETA in two-oh minutes, Doc. You ready?"

Anders looked up at the crew chief and stuck up his thumb. *As ready as I'll ever be,* he thought, trying hard to swallow the lump in his throat. It would not go down.

CHAPTER EIGHT

THE CHEMICAL SUIT was hot and uncomfortable and the head straps of the gas mask gave Neel a terrific headache. Breathing in and out through the filters was laborious and he needed to exert some effort even do it. Neel had tried to lie down on his cot and sleep, but just couldn't - he felt better sitting up. For about the tenth time in the past hour, he clumsily opened the drinking port on the front of his mask near the speaking valve and inserted it into the receptacle on the cap of his canteen. That was a difficult task since he couldn't see the connection in the dark and had to do it by feel. He knew he was becoming dehydrated in the suit and needed fluids. He twisted the lever to bring the rubber "straw" inside his mask so it could be grasped by his tongue and pulled to his lips. Holding the canteen upside down above his head, be took several big swigs.

"It's sort of like milking a cow with your mouth, major," Sergeant Gonzales said from across the room. Neel had thought the sergeant was asleep, as they both waited quietly in the dark room, listening to the shortwave for news of the air war. There had been several more warnings by the loudspeaker in the compound about Scud missile launches, but no word on any explosions nearby.

"It's amazing to have TV reporters right in Baghdad, reporting live from the heart of the bombing, isn't it?" Neel said. "I'd love to see all of that on TV live. Hope my wife is taping it at home so I can watch it someday."

Gonzales nodded. His thoughts were in a different time, a different war, when the American public did not want to see or know anything about what was going on in Southeast Asia. Now, here, the whole world is on the edge of their seats, listening to the opening events of the war, live from Baghdad.

It was a surreal experience for the men, here in this darkened room, sitting in awkward, hot, and ridiculous chemical suits, waiting for that possibly inevitable moment when a Scud missile would hit somewhere close to them, perhaps right on them.

There was no maneuvering of the building away from a torpedo as a ship could, no evasive action they could perform like a tactical aircraft, and there was no counterfire they could utilize to protect their building. It was as if their lives were completely in the hands of fate, or as Gonzales said, in the "hands of Jesus." Waiting for fate to come to them was difficult for these men of action, but what else could they do?

The radio reporter was describing the bombing of Baghdad, when suddenly they could hear air raid sirens in the distance from Dhahran. Then came what sounded like a series of explosions just outside the compound. The room rocked with the reports. Neel jumped up and went to the window. He couldn't see anything unusual and turned back to Gonzales.

"Do you suppose those were missiles that hit close by?"

"I don't think so, major. That might have been the Patriot missiles firing at the Scuds overhead. There's an anti-missile battery just outside the compound and they warned us that they sound just like an explosion when they're launched." Gonzales stood up and walked over to the window next to Neel.

"They're supposed to find these Scuds by ground radar and then launch the Patriot when the Scud is only a few miles away." He used his hands to show how the Patriot rose to meet the incoming Scud missile. "The Patriot uses its own radar to locate the Scud when it gets close and then detonates its warhead near enough to the Scud to destroy it or cause it to veer off course. I guess it doesn't really hit the missile directly."

"How successful are Patriots against Scuds?"

"Well, sir, this is the first time Patriots have been used in combat so they don't really know."

"Oh, great," Neel muttered. "I hope honest defense contractors built them, not some company that left off a valuable part, just to steal money from the government."

The radio announcer interrupted a review of events leading up to operation Desert Storm to notify listeners that Scud missiles had reportedly been blown up over Dhahran, but it was unknown whether there was any damage or injuries sustained, either directly or from falling debris. One reporter from a hotel in Dhahran said: "We are here in the basement of the hotel after the air raid warnings sounded. We are in a sealed room wearing our gas masks, but we can still hear the air raid sirens and sounds of explosions outside. The main concern of everyone in this room, as well as everyone here in Saudi Arabia is whether the Iraqi missiles that are being launched toward us contain lethal chemical gas. We were told by unnamed military officials they were one hundred percent certain Hussein would use chemical weapons in his missiles to achieve an early psychologically devastating advantage in hopes of turning the commitment of the Coalition forces away from any invasion. While there is obvious concern about chemical weapons among those of us in this room, and likely in thousands of similar rooms throughout this port city of Dhahran, we feel the use of chemical weapons would only increase the resolve against Saddam Hussein. This is Roy Johnson, live from Saudi Arabia.''

''You know, sergeant, I could really get to dislike that Saddam Hussein,'' Neel said. ''Here he is, playing games with all our lives and there's not a darn thing we can do about it.''

Gonzales nodded. ''Well, sir, all we can hope is that we get a chance to return the favor.''

Both men were becoming increasingly uncomfortable and restless in their chemical suits. They were sweating heavily, both from the heat of the suits as well as from the stress of waiting for the Scuds to land.

''You were in Vietnam, weren't you?'' asked Neel.

Gonzales nodded.

''My father was over there, too,'' Neel added.

''What unit?''

''82nd Airborne. Kind of older when he went over. Not a young man. Turned down a commission to become a medic.''

''Good for him,'' Gonzales said, but added quickly, ''no offense to you major, but some of the officers over there were not too well liked.''

''I know, but he would have been a good leader, I think. Trouble was, he just couldn't bring himself to accept that he would send enlisted men to their deaths in battle, so he chose to become one of them.''

''What was his name, major? I might have heard of him because I was with the 1st Cav and came across a lot of 82nd troopers when we had joint operations.''

Neel hesitated for a minute. ''His name was Sergeant Samuel Neel, but they all called him 'Red Neel' because of the color of his hair.''

Gonzales thought about that name, as if trying to place the person. Then he said, "Say, major, your father was Red Neel? The Medal of Honor winner? I've heard stories of him off and on for twenty years. About how he was wounded three times, wasn't it, and still crawled out into a rice paddy to pull his half-dead platoon leader back to safety? Am I right? And then, didn't he get the Medal for jumping on a grenade to save a bunch of wounded paratroopers?"

Neel nodded and looked at the window. *Where are you now, Dad, when I need you? Were you also scared of dying when you were in danger? Or is it just me not being as strong as you were. Talk to me, Dad, tell me how you felt and what I should do.*

"Sorry if I brought up unpleasant memories, major," Gonzales said.

"That's okay, Trinidad. I guess I ought to think about him more than I do. It's just that I have always wondered what he thought and felt when he was there. How he felt just before he died; even whether he thought of his family just before it happened."

"Well, major, I'll bet he did. A man like that would have known he was giving a lot up to do what he did, but look at what he gave the families of the men he saved. You should be proud of what he did."

"I am, I really am. But it was tough growing up without a father. I don't want my kid to have to do that."

"That's right, sir, you've got a niño on the way. Say, you'll really love those kids. My wife, America, has given me three beautiful daughters, and, with God's help," he crossed himself at this, "I'll make them a good father. You'll do the same, major. I made it back from Vietnam because the good Lord wanted me to do something good in this life, and taking care of my family is one of them. He's got the same plans for you, too. He won't take two fathers out of the same family, you gotta believe. Just trust in Him, and He'll take care of you." Gonzales pressed on the front of his MOPP suit and could feel the crucifix he wore around his neck, cool against his sweating chest.

Neel nodded and both men became lost in their personal thoughts.

Just then they heard and felt an explosion that seemed like it was right next door. It was the loudest sound Neel had ever heard.

The explosion was followed by a few moments of silence, and then considerable yelling and screaming could be heard. The door to the room was suddenly flung open and two chemical-suited soldiers rushed in.

"Sarge, Doc, a missile just hit the apartment building next door, and they got some bad casualties, I think. You gotta come and help!"

"Any indication of chemical gas out there, soldier?" Gonzales demanded.

"I didn't see anything, Sarge, but I'll go open my detection kit and check before you go over if you want."

"We can't wait for that," Neel said, as he pushed past the men and grabbed his field first aid pack. "We've got to go now, gas or no gas." He ran out the door toward the front entrance.

Gonzales looked at the major's disappearing back. *Yes, he's his father's son all right;* then he ran after him.

As the men exited their building, they could see the damage to the apartment house next door. A three-story structure, the entire top floor was nearly gone, with part of the roof blown away, and one whole side split open. A few chemical-suited men looked up at the building from below, but it appeared no one had begun rescue operations.

As Neel ran up to the building, he pointed to a group of men. "You, men, follow me up there." He pointed to another man, "You, go run to the dispensary and get the ambulance and every available medic over here on the double. Then tell them to call the MP's to get this area cordoned off." The man gave a short salute and ran off toward the dispensary in a strange kind of gait, slowed down by the wide MOPP boots.

Neel and Gonzales, followed by five men from outside, entered the building and stopped at the first level. "You two," Neel pointed, "check this floor and take everyone out onto the sidewalk outside, whether they're injured or not. Start an assembly area and keep it tight and secure. The medics can use that as a field base. You other two men, do the same thing for the second floor. You," he said, pointing to the remaining man, "you come with me and Sergeant Gonzales to the top floor."

They climbed the stairs until they reached the landing on the third floor. Much of the concrete was gone, and there were no doors to the two large apartments on that floor. "Let's check this side first,'' Neel said, pointing to the left. ''It looks the worst.''

''I don't think the missile exploded in here, Major,'' Sergeant Gonzales said, as they picked their way through a hole in the wall. ''Otherwise we'd have a major fire. May have been just a big piece of a missile that hit and pushed its way through these thin walls.''

Neel nodded and bent down to lift a piece of wall, revealing the motionless form of a soldier. Neel started to take off his gloves when Gonzales stopped him. ''Sir, we don't know if there's chemicals in here, yet.''

''Well, we'll soon find out, sergeant, I can't work on these people with this crap on me.'' He removed his gloves and gas mask and took several deep breaths, half expecting to die right on the spot.

''I think it's safe, sarge.'' Then Neel lifted the man's head and neck and felt a large, bloody defect on the back of his head. There was no pulse and the eyes were glassy. Neel gently replaced his head on the floor after clearing away some debris under it. He looked up at the third soldier. ''Get a blanket or something and cover this man, please. He's dead.'' Gonzales and the soldier looked at each other, and Gonzales nodded for the soldier to comply.

Neel then went from room to room, looking for survivors, and finding none. They uncovered the bodies from the room debris sufficiently to check for a carotid pulse but did not completely uncover them—that would be done by a subsequent graves registration team.

Gonzales stood up from a body and said to Neel, ''Major, we're not going to find anyone alive here. What about going to the next apartment? It may not have been as badly hit.''

''You're right, sergeant. We're not doing any good at all here.'' His face was wet with perspiration and his hands and face were smeared with dirt and blood from the victims' bodies.

Quickly they made their way through the debris, stepping over scattered gear and equipment, as well as pieces of walls and roof.

As they entered the second apartment, they could see it had been spared extensive damage. ''Over here, Doc, I think this one's alive,'' the soldier yelled.

Both Neel and Gonzales rushed to him. Neel knelt beside a

man who appeared unconscious, but who had a strong neck pulse. His left ear had been partially severed and his right arm had an obvious fracture at the mid-forearm that was bent at an unnatural angle. There was still active bleeding from the ear injury.

Neel carefully felt the victim's neck and back and elicited reflexes from his legs and left arm.

''All right, it doesn't appear his neck or back are broken, but we'll need to take him downstairs in a stretcher.'' He looked at the soldier. ''Go down and see if the ambulance is here yet. Bring up as many litters as they have to this apartment first.'' The man started to leave.

''Wait. Let me have your bandage packet before you go.''

The soldier quickly removed the package from his LBE harness and handed it to Neel. Then he raced out of the room.

''Here, Trinidad, you hold the back of his head and neck like this with both hands and lift gently.'' Neel showed the sergeant how to cradle the neck of the victim to protect the cervical spine (in case of injury), while Neel, at the head of the patient, wrapped the left side of the head where the ear was missing.

''We don't have time to look for the rest of the ear right now, sarge, but maybe we can after we've taken care of everybody. If we don't find it, then someone will have to do some plastic surgery on him later.''

Neel then used his flashlight to check the victim's pupils, finding they responded normally.

''I think he's got a mild closed head injury but it could get worse, so we need to get him to a neurosurgeon ASAP,'' Neel said.

He asked Gonzales to find two flat pieces of wood or some material strong enough not to bend. While Gonzales was looking around, Neel placed one hand in the victim's elbow crook and then grabbed his wrist with the other hand. He suddenly pulled firmly, and the angulated fracture of the forearm was reduced into place. He felt the wrist pulse and was satisfied the blood supply to the hand was not compromised by the fracture or the reduction he had just performed. ''Okay, sarge, let's put your splints on either side of the forearm and give me your bandage dressing.''

The sergeant held the makeshift splint of two wooden arms from a chair onto the victim's arm as Neel wrapped the cloth dressing around them, securing the fractured arm in a stable position. Neel then removed his chemical suit jacket and rolled it into a pillow, gently placing it behind and around the victim's head and neck both for comfort and stability.

"I think he'll be okay now, sarge, so let's look around. We'll keep an eye on him every so often, though, until the ambulance arrives."

They moved to the next room, where they heard some faint moaning. There were two soldiers in the room, both lying in a heap against the far wall where they must have been thrown by the force of the missile impact.

Neel and Gonzales moved quickly to the next victim. When Neel checked, the soldier appeared to be semiconscious and responsive, but he continued to moan softly and clutch his abdomen. Neel found no fractures or evidence of head injury but saw the man was cold, clammy and shivering.

"I think this man has internal injuries, sarge, and he's in shock. Let me have your jacket and try to find some blankets around here if you can."

Gonzales searched the room and found an army-issue poncho and a field jacket. They covered the man to keep him warm, while Neel exposed the man's arm, rolling up his sleeve. He felt his wrist pulse and estimated its rate at over one hundred and forty per minute.

"This man needs an IV fast," Neel said softly to Gonzales. "Or else we're going to lose him. They placed the victim in a head-down position when two medics and the soldier entered the room with two stretchers and a field medical kit.

"Over here, first," Neel hollered. "Get out two bags of D5LR and a couple of large bore needles. We've got to start IV's on this man right here.

The two medics appeared to be frozen in place - they had never seen a situation like this.

"Now, damn it," Neel barked. That got the medics attention and Neel soon had two needles inserted and intravenous fluids flowing into the victim's body, working to combat the shock.

"This man gets priority for evacuation. I want a chopper here ASAP to take these men to the 85th Evac Hospital. Take him down on the litter now, call in the medivac request and send another team up for the soldier in the next room. And tell them to put a cervical collar on him and to watch that neck. You two stay with this man outside until the chopper comes. Got it?''

The medics nodded. ''Yes, sir, will do.'' They loaded the victim gently on the litter and the three men made their way out of the room and downstairs, with the soldier holding the IV bags.

Neel then moved over to the third victim, whom Gonzales had been comforting. This one appeared conscious, but he was obviously scared to death.

''All right, son, you're going to be just fine. I'm a doctor, and'' he said, winking at the victim, ''this beautiful young sergeant is my nurse.'' He looked at Gonzales, who didn't see much humor in the line.

''Now tell me where you hurt.'' The soldier, who didn't appear much older than seventeen or eighteen, pointed to his left ankle. ''It hurts like crazy, Doc, and I can't move my toes at all.''

Neel gently cradled the young man's boot in his lap and withdrew his Swiss Army knife from its sheath on his belt. The victim's eyes opened wide, but relaxed when Neel said, ''Son, I'm just going to take your boot off to look at your ankle.''

The sharp blade cut through the boot laces quickly and Neel gently pulled off the boot. The young man's sock was bloody, and Neel knew what lay underneath. He cut away the sock with the scissors on the knife and confirmed his suspicions. There was an open, compound fracture of the ankle, with several bone fragments sticking through the skin. The skin looked devitalized in some areas.

Neel changed his grim look to a forced smile and told the youth, ''You're going to be fine. What's your name?''

It's . . . it's Roy Huffmeyer, sir.''

''Well, Roy, you just got your ticket back home - one of those injuries that will get you back to Germany for sure, and maybe all the way back to the States.''

The young man appeared relieved, and rested his head back down on his hands. ''Can you fix it, Doc?''

''Well, I'm going to dress it now, and give you a pain killer so it will feel better when we take you downstairs. How does that sound?'' The young man was visibly relieved and tried a tentative smile.

Neel rummaged through the field kit until he found what he needed sterile gloves, Betadine antiseptic, non-adherent gauze dressing, Keflix wrap, tape and a morphine stylette. He then decided to give the injured young man the morphine shot first, to ease his discomfort during the wound dressing and subsequent travel. It took less than five minutes for the shot to take effect.

"Sarge, can you help me with this dressing?"

"Sure, Doc, just tell me what to do."

"Okay, clear an area here, and lay out these supplies on a clean bandage sling. Then when I point to something, open it up for me. I'll have on sterile gloves and I don't want to get contaminated."

Gonzales nodded and unconsciously wiped his own hands on his trousers to clean off some of the dirt from the search.

They made a good team, but Gonzales was particularly impressed with the speed and efficiency with which Neel bandaged the injured ankle, taking care to completely soak the exposed bones in the Betadine solution before protecting them with well-placed supportive dressings. The foot and ankle were encased in a big, clean dressing within two minutes, protecting the compound fracture from further injury or contamination.

By then, the second litter team had arrived, along with a number of military personnel, who were either curious or investigating the accident.

"Listen, you'll have to talk to these injured men later at the hospital, "Neel told an MP captain, as they were loading the last of the injured men onto the litter. "We're taking them to the 85th Evac Hospital. You can see them there, once they're stable."

"But, major, I've got to make a report right now," stammered the captain.

"Well, just look around and figure it out, because you're not going to bother these men for a while." Neel's voice and the hard look in his eye convinced the MP.

Neel and Gonzales helped carry the litter down the two flights and outside to the makeshift medical assembly area. The ambulance crews had loaded the first two victims and they placed the third victim inside.

Neel turned to Sergeant Gonzales. "Well, Trinidad, I'm going to ride with the most seriously injured men to the hospital. I don't know when I'll be back. Thanks for all your help—it was really great."

"Well, Doc, that's okay, I just realized that if I ever get hurt or wounded, I hope you're around to take care of me."

Neel thumped Gonzales lightly on the shoulder. "You're too tough to get hurt. But you know I'd take good care of you if you did, don't you?"

Gonzales nodded silently and watched Neel climb into the ambulance and shut the doors.

* * *

It was frustrating for the men and women of the 82nd Airborne Division elements at the forward base camp when news of the start of Operation Desert Storm reached them. They were so close to the action, but still so far away. Clearly this was not the time for an airborne operation against the Iraqis - in fact, some were predicting that air strikes alone would win the war.

First Sergeant Leroy Washington was in his characteristic position with his feet planted on his field desk, which looked as if it would collapse from the weight of his massive legs. Staff Sergeant Lucius Tatum was perched on a stack of MRE ration boxes. Both men were outfitted in their chemical suits, but without masks or gloves, listening to the news reports on a shortwave radio.

"So, like I was saying, Lucius, I think the Navy and Air Force are going to pour it to those miserable SOB's so heavy that it'll knock all the fight out of them. Just listen to the radio: we're killing 'em."

Tatum contemplated his fingernails, and, finding some sand under several, took out his pocket knife and began cleaning them for the umpteenth time.

"I don't know, Leroy, those Iraqis have had months to dig in and prepare their defenses. And you don't know where they've hidden their chemicals and all the other bad stuff they said they'd throw at us." Tatum looked up at Washington. "They hate westerners as bad as Iran does. I just think we'll end up having to fight 'em real personal like."

Washington opened his drawer and took out an MRE. He cut it open and dumped out the contents on his desk, rummaging through the packets. "You want something to eat, Lucius? Lots of good stuff here."

"No, Leroy, you eat enough for both of us." Tatum watched the big man pick out an orange nut cake. "If you're not careful, man, you're going to need your own C-130. They'll have to rig your parachute like they do when they drop a truck."

Washington laughed heartily, licking his fingers clean. "I surely do like to eat, and my wife Sissy, does like to feed me. She says I'm at my best when I'm full and happy."

Lucius couldn't help liking the big man. He always seemed to have a positive attitude, never down or depressed. But, he could also be the meanest bastard in the company when someone stepped out of line in a major way. Consequently, the first sergeant kept things under good control through a well-orchestrated combination of friendliness and implied and real intimidation.

Washington looked at Tatum seriously. "You having any more trouble between those white boys and black boys in your platoon, Lucius?"

Tatum stood up and began pacing.

"I don't think so, Leroy. That last problem with the smoke grenades seemed to be it. I privately cracked a few heads over that one and everything seems under control. I just don't see why those boys get so fired up over little things. I think it's the stress of being bored and yet scared of what's facing them in the future."

"Well, we've had a problem since Vietnam, though. I can remember trouble over there that I was real ashamed of, really on both sides, black and white."

"I know, I heard about that stuff. But I just can't keep from thinking we've come a long way in the United States since then. There's no formal segregation any more. The courts have been more fair on issues than every before. And yet ...." Tatum's voice trailed off.

"Yet, what, Lucius."

"Well, Top, I still, myself, get some hard feelings about things. Take the Army officer corps for example. You still don't see many black officers, they just don't seem to get promoted, and they don't seem to get the responsible assignments."

"What about General Powell?" Leroy asked.

"Yeah, I know he made it to the top, and rightly so. He's got everything it takes to be chairman of the Joint Chiefs. But look further down the line. Out of hundreds of generals, I'll bet there are only a few that are Hispanic or Black. We still have a long way to go."

"Well, why don't you go back to college, Lucius, and apply for a commission? You'd make a good officer."

Tatum looked up and smiled. ''You sound just like Mary, my wife. She's been bothering me for years to do that, and I'll admit it's been more on my mind lately, too. Maybe after this is over, I'll apply for one of those 'bootstrap' army scholarships and go back to someplace like Georgetown University. I've always been interested in economics and business. But, I'd need to get it done before the kids get older, because I'll need more money, like on an officer's salary, to send them to college.''

''You're a mighty good man, Lucius, and I know that somehow you'll get those kids sent off to college all right, whether you're an officer or not. Remember, the Lord will provide.''

''I believe that, too, Leroy. He's got a plan for each of us, and we'll find out what it is someday. I just want my children to get educated so they'll have the best chances against the odds.''

Both men were silent for a while, lost in their own thoughts, half-listening to the radio.

Then Washington spoke up. ''How about opening that other MRE box, Lucius, and let's see what's in it?'' They laughed heartily.

* * *

Porter and Lopez were almost exhausted. They had taken turns carrying Miller through the dark desert night, while the other navigated to the medivac pickup site with the Magellan. Five kilometers is a long haul when you're carrying a wounded man who was only half conscious, even for men in superb physical condition.

Porter put his hand on Lopez' shoulder. ''We're here,'' was all he said. He unrolled his poncho and laid it on the ground, making a comfortable place for Miller to lie. Then they covered him with every extra piece of clothing they could spare.

''How is he doin'?''

''Well, sir, he's still pretty much unconscious, but that helps against the pain, I think. Here, let me check his pulse.''

After a few seconds, Lopez stood up. ''Its about a hundred and thirty. He's lost a lot of blood and needs some IV's ASAP. We'll just have to pray that dustoff chopper gets here fast.''

Porter rummaged in his small field pack and came out with a strobe light about the size of a pint can of orange juice. He checked his watch again and then walked fifty paces to the south, placing the strobe light where he had stopped. He turned it on and watched the red, flashing burst of light. That would mark the site if the helicopter got within visual range. He wanted to avoid any more radio transmissions if at all possible.

* * *

In the Apache, Weatherby was on the lookout for the medical evacuation helicopter. His mission was to escort the chopper into and out of enemy territory and to ride ''shotgun'' for protection during the pickup of the wounded Green Beret. Whether the landing zone was 'hot' or not was unknown. The Iraqis might be there and that's what Weatherby was doing as his part of the mission.

''Captain, I've got friendly aircraft transponder at two-oh-oh.'' The medical evacuation helicopter was emitting a signal only another American aircraft could pick up.

''Got it, Garner. Let's go see.'' Weatherby banked the Apache to the left and headed on an interception course toward the other craft.

In few minutes, Garner had the aircraft on his radar scope, and Weatherby tuned the radio transmitter to the predetermined frequency for this mission.

''Angeldust one, Angeldust one, this is Gabriel One, do you read me?''

''Gabriel One, this is Angeldust One, I read you five by, Over.''

''All right, good buddy, let's get on with this pickup. I'll lead the way and you tuck in behind me. Okay by you?''

''Wilco, Gabriel One. Pickup site will be marked with red strobe, I repeat, red strobe. We'll land to the south of the strobe, over.''

''Sounds fine, Medivac. I'll keep a watch over the area while you go in for the pickup. If we run into trouble going in or coming out, I'll stick around to protect your six and you hightail it home, got it?''

''Roger, Gabriel One, we're noncombatants, remember? You guys get to have all the fun. Out here.''

They flew in radio silence for another fifteen minutes when Garner picked the flashing light out of the desert. *I'll never know how he got such good eyes,* Weatherby mused. *I sure wouldn't have seen that myself. And he doesn't even hunt.* Weatherby banked the Apache and flew a short radius circle around the light, but couldn't see anyone on the ground in the dark.

"Any ground traffic on your radar, Garner?" he asked.

"Nada, captain. No ground or air blips at all, just us."

"Okay, Roger, we'll circle while the medivac goes in. Keep your eyes peeled for visitors."

"Angeldust One, this is Gabriel."

"Gabriel, this is Angeldust. We see the strobe, over."

"Angeldust, go ahead and park it. Keep your flight lights on so I can monitor your position and give me two minutes before you lift so I can get on the heading back home, over."

"Roger, Gabriel. Going in for the pickup. Out here."

* * *

Porter and Lopez saw the two helicopters approaching their position and knelt to block Miller from the sand turbulence. They heard but did not see the medivac chopper land, standing and turning when the distinct winding down of the rotor blades began. After a short time, the sliding side door of the Blackhawk opened and two dark figures emerged, one carrying a medical kit bag. Porter motioned to them with his red-lensed flashlight and they ran over.

Porter shone the flightlight on the men's breast tags on their flight suits. "Anders and Smith, welcome to nowhere. We're glad to see you." Anders knelt quickly by the wounded Miller and looked at his bandaged leg.

"How long has the tourniquet been on?" he asked Porter.

"How long, sir," interrupted Lopez.

Anders looked up. "Sorry, sir, I couldn't see your rank in the dark and they didn't tell us who was going to be here."

"No offense, Specialist. It's been on roughly thirty-five minutes," Porter said after checking his luminous-dial watch.

"Okay, sir, I've got to loosen it for five minutes here, so can you two hold this dressing to the stump and apply pressure while I do?"

Lopez and Porter compressed the stump with a bulky dressing to retard the wound bleeding while Anders released the tourniquet. The return of blood to the injured leg was obviously painful to Miller and he began moaning.

Anders quickly checked Miller's blood pressure, and after he was convinced it was high enough, gave him a shot of morphine. He then opened two bags of intravenous fluids, and with the crew chief's assistance in holding the bags, started two IV's. He then reapplied the tourniquet and rebandaged the stump. All of this took no longer than three minutes.

Porter and Lopez were impressed. They were also comforted that this young medic would do what he could for Miller.

Porter put his hand on Anders' shoulder. "Anders, not only is this man a real live hero, he's also our friend. Be sure he's taken care of right, okay? We're counting on you."

Anders swallowed hard. He knew how close these Special Forces team members were to each other. "Yes, sir, you can count on me. I think he'll make it fine. We'll take him to the 13th Evac Hospital down at the Saudi-Iraqi border first, but I figure he'll end up in Germany after that. I don't know when you'll get to see him next."

Porter knelt beside Miller. He was unconscious, but Porter put his hand on the man's chest and whispered in his ear. He stood up again and looked at Anders.

"We'll see him somewhere, sometime. We just don't know where or when."

They all gently lifted and carried Miller to the waiting stretcher and helped load him and the IV bags into the special litter rack inside the aircraft. Porter and Anders shook hands, then Porter slid the helicopter door shut. He and Lopez backed away from the chopper and shielded their eyes from the sand spray as the rotors gained speed and the helicopter lifted.

Once they were gone, Porter retrieved his strobe, turning it off and repacking it, hoping it would not be needed again. They listened to the sounds of the helicopters until they were gone. The night became quiet and dark again, and reluctantly, the two men turned to make their lonely way back to the base camp.

* * *

Anders was concerned about Miller's blood volume, so he monitored the heart rate and IV fluid rate. It was impossible to use the stethoscope for blood pressure readings in the noisy helicopter cabin, so he used the palpation method to check the systolic blood pressure level. So far, Miller was stable.

Weatherby had decided to fly the return mission at two thousand feet, to avoid the intense air traffic at higher altitudes from air force and navy fighters and bombers. He hoped they wouldn't get in the way of some stealth fighter, because he wasn't sure he could pick up the fighter on his radar, and the fighter might blow by before he realized he was a friendly. But the return flight was uneventful.

"Angeldust One, this is Gabriel, over"

"Gabriel, this is Angeldust. Time to part sweet company?"

"'Fraid so, Angeldust. We're at the border now, so we've got to go to our separate beds. How's your fuel supply, over?"

"Gabriel, we're okay, not great, but we'll make it. The 13th Evac is only about eight klicks ahead."

"All right, Angeldust, we'll see you again, probably. By the way, who's your medic on board tonight, over?"

"Gabriel, medic is Specialist Anders, you know him?"

"Yeah, I do. Tell him that his patient is keeping a stiff upper lip. Out here."

The medivac pilot wasn't sure he knew what that meant, but he relayed the message to Anders over the intercom. Anders laughed softly to himself. *I think there's hope for Captain Tex Weatherby yet,* he thought. Then he turned his attention back to his patient.

CHAPTER NINE

THE WORD TO deploy to the desert came unexpectedly. As with most things involving the army, it was "hurry up - wait - hurry up."

Neel was writing an entry in his daily diary when a captain from the administrative section of the combat hospital came looking for him. "Major, we're going up to the front today, so you'd better get your gear ready."

"Captain, I've heard that sort of thing before in my previous life as a real soldier. Now, tell me what the true odds are that we'll move out today?"

"Well, sir, like I said, we're supposed to have our gear packed and ready to go in two hours, then load up on a Saudi bus for the ride up to the new desert camp."

"Just how long a ride will it be?" asked Neel.

"Near as I can tell, sir, about eight to ten hours."

"Great, that means at least twelve hours in a crowded bus with your gear sitting on your lap. I'm all packed up except for a few things to put into my Alice pack, so I'll be O.K. Just send word to me when you're ready."

"Right, sir." The captain left to find the next medical officer who was billeted apart from the rest of the group.

Neel was keeping a daily diary partly because he was an inveterate writer and enjoyed putting his thoughts and feelings down on paper, and partly because he felt it would be an important document for his children to read. They would be able to understand better his feelings and thoughts under the conditions of combat. The stress, the isolation and the loneliness were difficult to put into words, but easier to describe on paper. At any rate, he hoped to be able to write each day of his experiences and thoughts and the pages were filling up.

Neel closed the scientific data notebook that was his diary and stowed it in the back of his Alice pack, adding his personal toilet kit and several other items he kept out for daily use. In the remaining space in his pack, he tucked MRE meal packs wherever they would fit. Then he filled his two-quart canteens with bottled water and laid them next to his pack. Essentially, he was ready to go whenever the word came. He had the Alice pack to put on his back and the duffel bag to carry and that was it. The sleeping bag and ground cover were strapped to the Alice pack, so he was completely mobile.

Maybe I ought to call Marty, he thought. *This may be the last phone call to her for sometime. They probably won't even have phones anywhere close to where we're going - she'll be worried sick and also angry with me if I don't let her know what's happening.* His decision made, he strapped on his LBE web gear, hooked the gas mask and chemical suit to his waist and grabbed his helmet. He left the apartment and walked quickly toward the phone bank.

When he arrived, he was dismayed to see a long line of men and women waiting. He wasn't sure exactly when his unit would leave Khobar, but he hoped he would have time. As a field grade officer, he could have made his way to the front of the line, pulled rank, and gotten in sooner. But that was not his way. In fact, he became angry whenever anyone tried to cut into lines anywhere. To Neel, that just wasn't "American."

So he waited dutifully. He had left a message on his cot back at the room telling where he was, and he kept glancing around, half expecting to see a runner coming to pull him out of line.

However, when his turn came to enter the telephone bank, he made his way to an empty station. He had already concluded that Marty was probably at work (it was 0900 in Kansas City) so he decided to call her office first. Hoping she wasn't teaching a class or in a meeting somewhere on campus, he dialed the math office at Rockhurst.

The phone rang several times before it was answered. "Good morning, Department of Mathematics," said a pleasant voice. Mary Brown was the departmental secretary, whom Neel had liked from their first meeting.

"Mrs. Brown, this is Dr. Neel, can you hear me?"

Mrs. Brown was slightly hearing impaired and Neel always felt he had to speak louder when talking with her.

"Dr. Neel, is that really you? Where in the world are you, Dr. Neel? Are you back in Kansas City?"

"No, Mrs. Brown. I'm afraid not. I'm still overseas. Is my wife around? I'd really like to talk to her, and my time on the phone is running out."

"Oh, yes, I understand. I'll go get her right away. And by the way, Dr. Neel, all of us here think what you people are doing over there is wonderful. We support you one hundred percent!"

"Thank you very much, Mrs. Brown. Can you please get my wife for me?"

I don't think there is really a total consensus on that support, Mrs. Brown, Neel thought to himself. *I know one person in the department who isn't too happy with the situation.*

It seemed to Neel a long time had passed before Marty came on the line, but in reality it wasn't quite a minute.

"Tom, is that you? Where are you?"

Why does everyone want to know where I am? Neel wondered. *Don't they watch CNN and read the newspapers?*

"I'm where I was before, honey, but I'm fixing to move to the desert any minute and I wanted to talk to you before I left."

"What do you mean 'to the desert,' Tom? Just where are you going?"

"I can't tell you, Marty, but where I'm going they

probably won't have any phones available, at least not for a while. So I really had to talk to you today.''

''Well, naturally I'm glad to hear from you, Tom, but I don't really know what to say.''

''Well, then, tell me about you,'' Neel responded. ''Are you feeling O.K., and getting enough rest and good food?''

''Well, I don't really have anything else to do except go to work, come home and work on my dissertation. The weather's been so bad I can't get outside much so I've been going to the mall on weekends just to walk and get some exercise.''

''That's good, Marty, real good. Keep on exercising and you'll feel better. Just don't overdo it. Are your checkups with Dr. Williams going O.K.?''

''They're just fine, Tom. Angie says the baby is growing and I can feel a lot of kicking or whatever in my stomach already. You could probably feel it too, if you were here.''

''Honey, I really would rather be there, and I will, just as soon as this thing is over. Have you been watching the news on the air war?''

''Tom, there's nothing else on TV but the war. I see it morning and night, and it's on every radio and in every newspaper. I will say that everyone here, and really in the whole country, is really going all out to show their support for the troops. I guess it's hard not to get a little wrapped up in it myself.''

Hot damn, Neel thought. *That's the first positive thing she's said since I found out I was called up. But I had still better tread softly.*

''Well, we're all hoping here that Iraq will give up

without a ground war, and it looks like the Air Force and Navy are giving them quite a beating.''

''Tom, we heard that a SCUD missile had hit an army barracks and killed and wounded some soldiers. I was worried sick about you, until they gave the names of the victims and you weren't one of them. Was that anywhere close to you?''

Uh, oh. What do I say now? ''I heard about that, too, Marty, but it wasn't even close.'' *Only about a hundred yards. Forgive me, Lord, for lying to my wife, but I just can't tell her the truth, not only for security reasons, but because it would only make things worse.*

''Well, they said there was a doctor right on the spot who gave them almost immediate medical care, and that's why the survivors lived. I just thought of you when I heard that.''

''Marty, you know I'm just trying to stay out of trouble and get home as soon as I can.''

''Sure, Tom, and I'm Harry Truman, too,'' Marty said wryly.

''Listen, honey, I love you and miss you something terrible. I think about you night and day, I swear. Just keep on taking care of yourself and the baby and maybe I'll be home sooner than we think.''

''All right, Tom. But don't you do anything foolish and get hurt or worse, you hear me? You've got a family back here who needs you and you had better come back to us soon, preferably in one piece.''

''I will, Marty. Love you and take care of the baby.''

''All right, Tom, we love you, too. Bye.''
Neel sat in silence for a minute, staring at the phone. She

wasn't as negative as she had been before, and he was grateful for that, but her softened feelings only served to make him feel more homesick and lonely. He hoped this war would be over one way or the other and if he was to have an active role, then let's get to it.

As he was walking back to his room, he was met by an out-of-breath enlisted man from his CASH, a medical supply corporal.

"Major," the young man said, breathing hard, "you gotta get your gear. They're gonna take us out of here by helicopter in about fifteen minutes and we've got to get all of our gear outside the gate right away and load the aircraft."

Typical Army B.S., Neel thought. *Completely change the whole plan and expect people to respond right away. Why didn't I expect this? I've been in the Army long enough to know better.*

"All right, Karnes, I'm packed and ready. Just tell me exactly where to go."

"Just outside the front gate, sir, in that open field area to the east of the MP tank emplacements. They've got four Chinooks that just showed up looking for us and no one knew anything about it."

"That's typical military planning, Karnes. Stick around and you'll see a lot more of it in the future. Let's go."

Neel sprinted the remaining distance to the VIP quarters and up the stairs to his room. He was struggling out of his room with the big Alice pack on his back and the stuffed duffel bag in his hand, when Sergeant Gonzales stepped up to him and grabbed the duffel.

"Looks like you're headed out, Doc."

"That's right, Trinidad. I was hoping to see you before I left. We're flying up to the front somewhere in the desert, but I have no idea where."

"Well, we're moving out early in the morning ourselves. Our tanks have already been trucked up Tap Line Road, and we're going to join them at the base camp. Looks like we're both going to be busy from now on."

"Yeah, I guess so."

"Here, Doc, I'll carry your duffel and walk you out to the front gate, okay with you? Don't know when we'll see each other again."

"Great, Sarge, but I can carry my bag. You don't have to."

"My privilege, sir, my privilege, after all you did for us

here."

They walked in relative silence to the front gate, occasionally commenting on the frenzied activity level of the compound as units and troops began leaving for their next location to prepare for the possible ground war.

As the two men stopped at the MP-guarded front gate, they shook hands warmly.

"Take good care of yourself, Doc. There are a lot of people who may need your skills in the times ahead. I've been honored to know you, and I wish you the best."

"No, Trinidad, the honor has been mine. You're a true warrior and a fine man. I hope if you can get to Kansas City with your family someday that you'll stay with me and Marty. We'd love to have you."

"Well, sir, I just might take you up on that. The same goes for us and El Paso."

Neel picked up his duffel and began to walk toward the waiting helicopter, when he stopped and turned. He pointed his finger at the sergeant.

"Remember, I don't want to see you in my hospital, you got that? You stay healthy and don't get hurt!"

Gonzales gave the major a 'thumbs-up,' but suddenly had a funny feeling in the pit of his stomach. *I don't know, Doc,* he thought to himself, *I don't think I'm going to come out of this one without getting hurt.*

He watched the major load into the back of the Chinook and gave one last farewell wave. The Chinooks lifted and were soon out of sight. Gonzales turned and walked slowly back into the compound, wondering if he would ever see his new friend again.

* * *

The helicopter flight to the front was relatively uneventful. A combat support hospital is normally fifty-percent air mobile and the 252nd CASH had been downsized and reconfigured to more closely resemble the MASH—the mobile army surgical hospital that was one hundred percent airmobile.

In the desert war, the theory was that there existed the possibility for very fluid troop movements, especially in large numbers, and the medical care should more closely support them and their movements. Because of sandstorms and rain, air evacuation by helicopter could not be relied upon, and ground transportation might be too slow. Thus, there was a need for medical assets that could either be moved quickly or broken into transportable detachments that could keep up with the action.

The 252nd CASH was such a hospital. It could be established in two parts: one, a standard hospital that was stationary near the southern Iraqi border to receive casualties and handle them in-place; and the other, a mobile detachment that could relocate a hundred kilometers deep into enemy territory, if necessary, to provide surgical resuscitation capabilities. Neel was in charge of the small mobile detachment for the CASH.

All the CASH personnel and their belongings were contained in four Chinook helicopters --more than 150 individuals. The Chinooks were reliable cargo and personnel carriers, but it was still unknown how their engines could tolerate sucking the sand into the intake for hours on end without seizing up. The Alice packs and duffel bags were stacked in only a loose semblance of order in the middle of the cargo bay, the personnel strapped into narrow, cramped web seats. The inside of the aircraft was cold and breezy. It was apparent to each passenger that their equipment was only loosely tied down and if the load shifted, it could crush the occupants on that side of the aircraft as well as destabilize it enough to crash. However, the crew members seemed unconcerned about such a possibility, so the passengers kept their worries to themselves.

Because of the threat of enemy fire from ground-launched rockets or surface-to-air missiles, CENTCOM policy had dictated that all helicopter operations and flights be conducted under two thousand feet. The helicopter pilots interpreted that as a green light for nape of the earth flying. This type of low-level, terrain-hugging flight was always exciting, even in the desert, but even more so in a huge transport helicopter like the CH-47 Chinook. Neel felt he was riding a huge roller coaster as the giant aircraft swung from side to side and up and down. He could never figure what terrain features were being followed with such an erratic course, because all he could see out the window were sand dunes. The aircraft was too noisy inside for talking and too shaky to read anything, so he just tried to keep warm and sleep. Unfortunately, he couldn't and his thoughts turned to his wife and the future.

Neel had faced the risk of death in his past adventures in almost a cavalier fashion. When he went to airborne and special forces schools, when he participated in clandestine missions in Central America and other parts of the world as a Green Beret, he was single. Except for his mother and sister, he had no legacy to protect, no one who would be directly affected by his death, as he had been by his father's.

But now, everything was different. Now he was married. He loved his wife, and wanted to spend a long enjoyable marriage. She was definitely the best thing that had happened to him. Then there was the matter of his unborn child and of other children in the future. Partly because he loved kids, partly because of the loss of a father he had suffered in his own life, he was keen on being there for any children he and Marty might have, now or later. He knew the personal drawbacks of medicine with its time commitments and dedication, but he was determined to do his best as a father.

As Neel sat in the drafty Chinook, flying toward the uncertainties of war, he felt strong feelings of insecurity, even some fear. His job demanded his professional expertise right up close to where the battles were fought. He and the other members of his detachment would likely be exposed to the same risk of artillery and rocket fire, chemical or biological warfare, and capture as the line combat troops.

Neel's past experience with the special forces would serve him well if he was captured - he had taken the Survival, Escape, Resistance and Evasion (SERE) course at Fort Bragg, but that was not what bothered him.

Considering the recent history in this part of the world of taking prisoners and hostages, particularly westerners, and holding them for years - that was his concern. That he might be killed was less troubling than the risk that he might be captured and kept away from his family indefinitely. His life and his family's life would be in limbo then. No, he couldn't handle that. He had always had definite conclusions to events in his life - he was goal-oriented - and being captured simply would not do. He vowed to avoid capture at any cost.

Night was descending upon the desert when the helicopters finally reached their destination. Typically with the Army, the coordinates the pilots had been given were wrong and it was only sheer luck that one of the pilots had seen a campfire and a handful of tents in the distant dusk.

As the choppers landed on a makeshift LZ hastily identified by a cross design of red flares, a cold rain began. Neel was surprised because he had assumed the desert was always dry and hot. But that certainly had not been his experience so far in Saudi Arabia—there was more rain here than in Southern California.

The hospital personnel unloaded their Alice packs and duffel bags in the rain, then stood around, becoming more and more miserable, until someone told them what to do. Neel found Major Ted White, the medical service corps officer who was the unit's exec and discovered that only four large GP tents had been available in Riyadh and everyone would have to sleep in them until more tents arrived. There were no heaters, no latrines, and only the food and water each person carried.

Neel and White began working to get everyone out of the rain and into the tents set up by the advance party, designating tents for male officers, female officers, enlisted females and enlisted males. Each person carried his or her Alice pack into the tent, but for lack of space, they covered the duffel bags with the outer covers of the now-erected tents.

Neel was the last to bed down that night, having checked on everyone to make sure his detachment was secure for the night and accounted for. He found a spot in the male officers' tent, unrolled his ground cover and laid the styrofoam sleeping pad on it to keep dry. He then laid out and unzipped his sleeping bag, taking off his wet boots and outerwear, and crawling into the warm, winter bag in just his shorts and T-shirt. His last thoughts were of sleeping with Marty in his warm, king-size bed at home in Kansas City and wondering if he'd ever do that again.

* * *

Specialist Anders was in a quandary. As long as he kept busy on medivac missions or at the airfield dispensary, he was fine. However, when he was left to his own thoughts, they kept coming back to Becky Gold. He thought about her a lot. He had seen her several times since her release from the hospital and had gotten to know her a lot better.

She was a student at a state university in California and came from a family whose patriarch was a retired air force colonel. They had lived all over the world and she had many tales to tell about the exciting places she had visited. Anders, on the other hand, had barely been out of Wisconsin, so he was enthralled by her stories.

Becky was helping pay for her education by serving in the army reserves, and she was assigned to a field hospital designated to care for Iraqi prisoners. Becky wanted to be a child psychologist and she was planning to go to graduate school for a Ph.D. when she finished her degree.

None of that was a problem for Anders, nor was it the source of his dilemma. He respected the right of women to pursue any career, and even understood that the new family dynamics with two working parents were here to stay. He respected a woman who knew what she wanted and was willing to work hard to get it.

The problem was, Becky was Jewish. Anders came from a long line of Lutherans, strong in their Protestant beliefs and not merely a little rigid in their views on Baptists and Jews. Anders was open-minded, but he knew his family and all of the other Lutherans in his county were likely to be close-minded about a Jewish woman.

Regardless, Anders had fallen for Becky. Even in desert BDU's and LBE, she was a beautiful young woman, witty and intelligent. Her perfect smile and complexion were framed by a full head of dark brown hair. Her eyes were large and brown and seemed to sparkle when she talked. She always displayed a slight, permanent smile and she would laugh heartily at Anders' attempts at humor. She was very quick, but never made Anders feel uncomfortable, even though he knew he was not much of a conversationalist. She seemed to bring out the best in him.

Once, when he had made a surprise visit to see her, during a well-planned trip to the PW camp, she had been working in the patient administration tent in just a T-shirt and BDU trousers. That vision had cinched it for Anders - what a fine figure of a woman.

He was hooked, but he was also practical. He couldn't help fantasizing about the future, but no matter how he studied it, the problem of religion remained. Eventually, Anders knew any relationship between a Christian and a non-Christian had to resolve that issue, and while he felt comfortable talking about it, he had yet to do so with Becky. The biggest unknown was what his family would think if he announced he had fallen in love with a Jewish woman.

He had to find a Lutheran minister somewhere here in Saudi to talk to. His minister back home, Reverend Soderstrom, was a kind man and good leader in the community, but was also pretty rigid. Maybe even old-fashioned. He needed to talk to someone more open-minded and understanding.

Anders was thinking about all that while sitting on his cot in the tent. Rain and winds had temporarily grounded the helicopters and he was not scheduled to work in the dispensary for nearly four hours. He was trying to read a new adventure novel, but his thoughts kept returning to Becky. Finally, he closed the book. He laid back on the cot and began to wonder in earnest what the future might hold for him and Miss Becky Gold.

Becky's field hospital was far south enough into Saudi Arabia that a threat of attack by the Iraqi army was not very great. It would take a major offensive to reach that area. Anders was more concerned, though, about the Iraqi PWs, whose number was growing daily at the adjacent PW camp. Some sort of an uprising there might jeopardize Becky and there was nothing he could do about it.

As far as his own safety was concerned, Jay certainly had a dangerous role. Although a non-combatant, he and his fellow medivac crew members were continuing to fly dangerous missions, mainly into southern Iraq to pick up downed pilots. He had not thought much about risks in the past, willing to do his job and leave his chances to the Lord. But now, things were different. He really had someone he cared about.

Thinking about the future always forced him to consider his old nemesis from the depths of his mind and reexamine it. Could he or should he become a physician?

Anders sat up on his cot, preferring not to think about his career puzzle, but somehow drawn by the direction his thoughts were taking him. He reached over to the packing box that was his container for personal items and found an MRE cherry nutcake, one of his favorites, which he had saved for a snack. Then he reached under his cot and found the prized item he was searching for - a can of Pepsi. Soft drinks were very scarce and he had scrounged this one earlier in the week from the 2nd ACR airbase during a maintenance helicopter ride. Captain Weatherby was away, but Anders left word at the ops tents, inquiring about his lip. It was important for medical personnel to learn about their efforts and work through close followup of patients, but it was nearly impossible in the desert, owing to activity levels and shifting assignments.

Anders opened the nutcake and slowly began to eat it. He knew he would probably not give this nutcake a second look back in Wisconsin, there were so many really great treats available from the pastry cooks of the region (including his mother). However, in times of relative deprivation, something like this was delicious. And there was the Pepsi, too. He had always figured soft drinks were available everywhere, but in the desert, they were coveted items. He took a sip, savoring the cool, tart taste, and swore never to take a Pepsi for granted back in the real world.

Okay. Now if I get back in time to start fall semester, I can go ahead and finish next spring. But what about the medical school application? I've got to make a decision. I owe it to my parents to tell them why I don't feel I can be a physician. What do I say? That I have no confidence? Well, that's the truth, isn't it, and doesn't the truth hurt? They won't understand and they'll try to talk me into changing my mind. They'll say: 'Look, son, at how well you did in the Persian Gulf War.' Well, mom and dad, I haven't really saved anyone's life here, so it's not been all that great. Sure, there's Becky, but all I did was hang onto her litter when we crash-landed—really no big deal. And the Green Beret's leg was already treated with a tourniquet. And the poor souls in the helicopter crash and fire were too far gone for anyone except St. Peter. So, I haven't done anything here to convince me I'm good enough to be a physician.

Maybe I'll take Dr. Fletcher's offer at Minnesota and do research there with him. I could go to Minneapolis and enroll in graduate school—I could get a Ph.D. just like Becky plans to, and do research. Would she come to Minnesota for graduate school in psychology? The thought excited him so much he sat upright in bed again and combed his fingers through his hair. *Man, she was something else. I've never felt this way about anyone before. I wonder what she's doing now? Is there a possibility she's sitting on her own cot, thinking of me? I wonder if the guys in the commo tent could patch through a line to her hospital? I could tell them I need to check on a patient. That's not too far off, actually she was my patient for a while, wasn't she?*

Driven by this new-found notion, he put on his boots, donned his LBE and gas mask carrier and ran out the tent into the drizzle without his rain gear.

* * *

Sergeant First Class Trinidad Gonzales finally felt settled. He was sitting atop his Abrams M1A1 tank, awaiting his turn to fire up the behemoth and drive it off the flatbed trailer, parked at the platoon's new desert staging base.

After an all-night and part of the next day ride across Saudi Arabia on the notorious 'Tap-Line Road,' Gonzales felt he was 'safe' again. Sitting in the cab of the big 18-wheeler carrying his tank, he had seen acts of daredeviling and sheer stupidity driving along that road made the L.A. freeways look like kiddie park rides.

The Arab and Coalition drivers had turned the narrow, two-lane highway in the desert into a massive six-lane raceway-to-the-death in an attempt to get supplies and equipment delivered for a ground war against Iraq. A bottleneck at the port of Damman delayed off-loading of ships and that had caused CENTCOM commanders to call for an all-out effort to get the vital materiel to the staging areas in the desert.

Consequently, all rules of the road Americans were used to obeying at home were virtually non-existent along Tapline Road. You did whatever you felt you needed to do to get where you were going in the shortest possible time. Couple that with exhausted drivers and the Arab philosophy of "as Allah wills it" and you had disaster waiting. Gonzales had been told by his rig driver that twenty-three people had already been killed along the notorious highway and countless others injured. Gonzales couldn't sleep a wink in the truck during the entire trip.

Now he was sitting atop his own tank once again, back in his element. His crew was preparing the M1 for startup and he had no specific tasks in that, so he was taking a relaxing break. High atop the tank on the flat bed, he could survey the desert scene around him. As far as he could see, tanks and armored personnel carriers were being fired up and moved off to one of several brigade encampments. The division area, it was said, stretched over twenty-five square miles of desert, the size of a whole city back in the States. So, there was activity everywhere—trucks hauling POL (petroleum, oil and lubricants) for the hundreds of vehicles starting up, Humvees driving wildly and seemingly aimlessly from nowhere to nowhere.

Once the platoon's vehicles were off-loaded, checked and fueled, they were instructed to follow a guide vehicle to their tactical assembly area, nicknamed Camp Henry. There they would set up platoon tents and begin the daily training exercises designed to prepare them for the ground assault.

As much as anyone in the brigade, Gonzales knew what the forthcoming ground assault would be like. He had never participated in a desert tank battle, but he had studied doctrine and examples from the Israeli-Egyptian tank battles. That knowledge, coupled with his armored combat experience from Vietnam, gave him a sense of foreboding and gloom that was hard to shake. By all reports, the Iraqis were well-entrenched in their revetments and barricades. It would not be easy to breach their defenses and fight tank-to-tank, head-on. He knew many American soldiers could lose their lives in a ground assault—in fact, there were predictions of up to five thousand coalition casualties a day!

Ruefully, Gonzales shook his head and looked around. Of the men he could see, walking around on the ground, clambering onto their tanks, standing and joking with others, which would survive? Gonzales had already met death and faced the fear that comes with it. He was less concerned about himself than he was about the young men he was charged with leading (and protecting), and how they could be helped in their forthcoming dance with death and fear.

He had hated to see men killed in battle in Vietnam and he felt no differently now, despite his own experiences. He thought of the families and friends and futures that belonged to these young soldiers, and his stomach turned sour at the knowledge that for some of them, their futures could be measured in weeks.

He felt the sense of responsibility to his men so keenly it transcended his own thoughts of safety and his role as head of his own family. He was a man who accepted responsibility without questioning and he would do his best. *That's all a man can do,* he thought. *And if I do my job well, I'll have the rest of eternity to spend with my family in Heaven.*

He was startled by the sound and vibration of the big tank's gas turbine roaring to life. Corporal Ron Jennings, the affable driver from Manchester, New Hampshire, stuck his head into the turret.

"Hot damn, Sarge, the old girl still runs. We're ready to rock and roll. Let's get this baby off the truck and get along to our new home, okay?"

Gonzales smiled. *I really love these guys. They're like family.* He looked over at the loadmaster, who was motioning to Gonzales to off-load his tank from the flatbed. Gonzales threw a wave of the hand to acknowledge and tapped Jennings on the head with the other hand.

"Come on, cowboy, drive this little dogie on outta here. It's almost supper time and I'm getting mighty hungry."

The tank gave a lurch and eased down the ramp and onto the sand as easily as driving a car going down a driveway. Jennings guided the huge vehicle into a near-right-angle turn and, following Gonzales's directions, drove the tank toward Camp Henry and their destiny.

* * *

Captain Tex Weatherby was not usually introspective. He had led his life pretty much as it confronted him and tended to take things in stride. Sure, he had feelings (most of them strictly masculine) and periodically he was aware of them and thought about them. He had special feelings about his family at Christmas and Easter (although he wasn't particularly religious), and certainly at Memorial Day, Veterans Day, and the Fourth of July. He felt proud of his sons and the young men they were becoming, and, of course, he loved his wife. But to analyze his feelings about anything was rare for Tex.

He and CWO2 Garner were supposed to be flying a routine air recon mission along the Iraqi border, looking either for enemy movement or damage assessment after attacks on the front-line Iraqi troops. But the unpredictable Arabian desert had suddenly produced a rainstorm, so no routine missions were being flown.

He was not in the mood for cards or socializing, so he had sought a place of solitude where he could be alone. That was hard on a day like this, when nearly everyone in the camp was in their tents. But, he found the empty cab of a five-ton truck and climbed in, huddling under a wool blanket for comfort.

Water streaming down the windows made it impossible to see any of the camp clearly, so Tex arranged his long legs in the cab and lighted a cigar, one of the few treats he allowed himself. He puffed hard on the sweet smoke and then cracked the side window. *I love a good cigar, but it's even better mixed with some fresh air.* The monotonous patter of the rain was mesmerizing, reminding him of the incessant sound on the metal roof of his family's ranch back in Texas.

He had come a long way from that back-country ranch, but, life there had been simple, and hard physical work had made the Weatherbys successful. On the other hand, once he went to college at A & M, he found himself ill-prepared for some of the more subtle aspects of human relations. He had done all right in the environment of the Corps of Cadets, mainly because of its emphasis on manly traits and behavior, but when dealing with others outside the Corps, he was often ill at ease. He also knew when he tried to meet with others, he tended to be seen as arrogant and self-centered. He didn't consider himself to be like that, but there had been enough unpleasant episodes in his adult life that he was tending to believe the rumors.

It wasn't as if he acted that way on purpose. It was just that the only people who had influenced his personality development as a child and young man were his parents and the ranch hands, and they all tended to be the same.

At A & M, when he had first met Nancy, his wife, she had been immediately turned off by his braggadocio and refused to respond to his attentions. However, he had tried very hard to be nice and had gradually won her over. *At least, she knows there's more to me than I project, and for a long while, I believed I didn't need other friends. But now? Now I'm not so sure. I'm thirty-five, and I've got very few friends I could really count as true, not like old Raul, the mestizo foreman on the ranch.* They had developed a fine close relationship before Raul had developed lung cancer and died in the VA hospital in San Antonio.

Where am I really headed in life? Sure, I've got a good place here in Army aviation and I know I'm a good pilot. But, I'm not a leader of men, despite my rank and position. The men follow me only because I'm in charge, but they don't like me for myself. That never used to bother me, but somehow, here in this desert, I'm coming to some new realizations. Back in Korea and in Panama, I flew to beat hell out of the bad guys, but now, I wonder if it's all worth it.

What's my life going to be like in ten or fifteen years, when I'm retired from the Army? What kind of work does a "has been" helicopter jockey do? By then, the boys will be ready for college and they'll leave. Just when I'm starting to get to know them. The cigar suddenly started to taste bitter so Tex tossed it out the window onto the wet sand. He sucked in a deep breath of cool outside air and closed his eyes.

The only person recently able to see past the exterior of Tex Weatherby and to understand more of the man inside, had oddly enough been that medic, Anders, the one who had sewn up his lip. It was strange for Weatherby to have felt so relaxed and natural in the young man's presence. Normally, doctors and medics caused him to be wary, and he never felt at ease around them. But, this young man was different. Tex listened to what he had said and even thought about it later on. Much of what Anders implied was true, Tex believed. *I do bring a lot of my own problems on myself. But, it just seems to happen and I don't really know how to control it. Hell's bells,* he thought, *it would be silly for me to talk about this with anyone, but I really believe I could with that kid if I ever get a chance.*

Tex thought about the forthcoming ground war. He knew it would come. The air war was going well, but Hussein would not give up easily. He knew his squadron would be called upon to play a major role in the ground assault, as they had in Panama. The new Apaches had yet to be proven in combat against tanks. And, since the desert ground war would be primarily a tank battle, the Apache's anti-tank capabilities would be tested to the limit.

He never thought of being a hero, even thought he had received his share of medals for valor and hazardous duty. He just tried to do his job and see that his men did their's.

With a sigh, Tex checked his watch. Almost twenty-two hundred. Nearly time to call brigade for an updated weather and ops report for tomorrow. Reluctant to leave the protected truck cab, he nonetheless opened the door and stepped into the blowing rain.

* * *

The men of the 82nd had done a fine job turning the large GP tent into a battalion chapel. The altar had been hand-made from 2 x 12 rough-hewn planks brought from the dock area at Dhahran by Merlie Hawkins, the chaplain's assistant. Merlie was a master carpenter (a gift he felt was of divine origin) and he had constructed a beautiful piece of work. The large cross had been carved in relief into the front of the altar and the craftsmanship was superb. A simple purple cloth had been draped across the top of the altar, and only three objects were laid on it: a Bible, a silver chalice, and a silver paten, the latter two for communion.

Lucius Tatum was sitting on one of the twenty "pews" made from discarded weapons boxes, a strange but symbolic use for them. The chapel tent had been rigged with red lighting so it was possible to hold services after dark. However, the tent was completely buttoned up to comply with night blackout orders.

The chapel was a place of solitude and solace for Tatum. He came often to the tent to meditate and to read his daily Bible lesson.

Tatum's company had just received word to expect the ground war at any time. They had their tentative battle plans and were to beginning to plan for an airborne assault on a vital area in Iraq near the northern Kuwaiti border where there was a large concentration of Iraqi Republican Guards. The drop zone was near an Iraqi city called An Nasiriyah, close to the south bank of the Euphrates River. Apparently, 18th Corps was going to block any possible retreat by the Iraqi army to the north, catching the enemy in a giant pincers action. All the plans were confidential, and Tatum only knew of them because of his friendship with First Sergeant LeRoy Washington, who knew Tatum would keep the information to himself. Besides, Washington thought Tatum could be of valuable help in getting the men ready for the combat jump.

Tatum had just finished reading the 27th Psalm, and he reread the beginning:

"The Lord is my light and my salvation
whom shall I fear?

The Lord is the stronghold of my life
of whom shall I be afraid?

When evil men advance against me
to devour my flesh,

When my enemies and my foes attack me,
they will stumble and fall.

Though an army besiege me,
my heart will not fear;

Though war break out against me,
even then will I be confident."

Tatum closed the small New Testament supplied for the troops in the Persian Gulf by the International Bible Society of Colorado Springs. It had a desert camouflage cover and fit nicely into his BDU breast pocket. Tatum's was already well-thumbed.

He knew death awaited them all—that was inevitable, but the Lord alone chose the time and place. Tatum would try his best to prepare and protect his men in the forthcoming ground war, but he knew that some would die, perhaps even him. A man had to be prepared to die, if he was a soldier, and Tatum had long since made his peace. In fact, every time he jumped out of an airplane, he put his life in the Lord's hands.

But it took a war, a battle of men against men, for someone to understand how tenuous life is. If he died, then so be it. His only regret would be losing his family. As he thought of them, Tatum gripped the Bible tighter. *How would they manage without him? Who would pay for the kids to go to college? Mary was certainly resourceful, but even that wouldn't suffice in this day and time, with college costs what they were. And the servicemen's life insurance was only $20,000, a real drop in the bucket compared to living expenses these days.*

Fleetingly, Tatum wished he had taken that post office job years ago, but he knew he wouldn't have been happy. He enjoyed the challenges of an airborne infantryman and he did not regret that choice. But, he also knew his career was not financially sound until he had made his twenty and had a nice retirement pension to count on. He would be eligible for retirement when Lucius Junior was finishing college, so his retirement check would help put Samantha and Jessica through school. *If the good Lord lets me live through this, I might consider a transfer out of the airborne into a less risky unit. Maybe I owe it to the kids to try to guarantee that retirement money for them.*

Tatum tucked the Bible back into his breast pocket and walked to the rear of the tent, where there was a picnic table that served for Bible classes and where the chaplain conducted counseling sessions. Save for Tatum, the chapel was empty, so he sat down to write his family. Taking out lined notebook paper that had been sent to "any service member" from a well-meaning American citizen, he sat with his pen poised, but didn't know where to start. He had never written a letter like this before. But somehow he knew he had to. He took out the picture of him and his family that he kept in his wallet and laid it before him, gazing at his loved ones for a moment.

Dear Mary, Lucius Junior, Samantha and Jessica:

If you are reading this letter, then you know something has happened to me over here in the Persian Gulf, and that I'm not coming home. Whatever has happened to me, don't be sad. I was a soldier because I wanted to be one, and I died in the service of the United States of America. I loved our country. And I want you to love it also.

Honey, I want to be buried in Arlington Cemetery, in that quiet, beautiful place we often visited in the past. I'll rest there fine, knowing I'm with so many good men and women who felt the same way I did about America and who gave up their lives for their country. Please be proud of me and come to visit me there whenever you can.

Mary, you've got to take care of the kids now, but you don't have to do it by yourself. I'm releasing you of any obligations to me, so you can get remarried. The kids need a father real bad and I want someone who will be nice to them and help you take care of them. I'll always be their father, no matter what, but you'll need someone. It's O.K. But, you can always still love me, and I'll always still love you. Make sure the kids grow up to be the kind of adults who would make us proud. They've just got to go to college and become educated. Education is the key to success and the only way to make something of yourself, so make sure they get educated, please.

Junior, Samantha and Jessica please be good to your mother and to each other. Help each other and take care of yourselves. Don't worry about me 'cause I'll be in the hands of the Lord and He'll take care of me now. Just make sure you all become the right kinds of people—no drugs, no lying, cheating or stealing, no being mean to each other or anyone else. Just remember that I'll be looking down at you and watching everything you do, so be a good person. I had dreams for you three kids I wanted you to get your education and make something of yourselves. Without a college degree you just don't have a chance. So be the very best you can be, promise me that. And, sometime in the future, you'll need to find a way to serve your country. You don't have to be a soldier, but somehow you need to give back something to America for the privilege of living in the best country on earth.

Kids, if your mother remarries (and I've given her permission to do that) I want you to treat the man right. She'll pick someone who will love you all and also her, so you can love him right back, it's O.K. Kids need a dad to look after them, and I'm sorry it won't be me. But, I was blessed to have the time I did with such a beautiful family.

I want all of you to go to church regularly, and to say your prayers. Study real hard in school and make me proud. When you have a tough decision to make, just think of what I would have told you about it, or what you would have done to make me proud. Also, remember that no one is perfect and you need to love your fellow man. Be good Christians. Also, look after Grandma Tatum 'cause she'll take this real hard and will need your love.

I have loved you all more than anything in this world. But it's God's Will that this happened and so some kind of good must come out of it. Don't ever forget me and I'll be waiting for you when you join me in Heaven.

Love for all times,

Dad

It had been many years since Tatum had cried, but he was now. Tears were streaming down his cheeks as he addressed and sealed the letter. He would send it in another envelope to the Reverend Ebenezer Oates, pastor of the church in D.C., where he had been baptized and grown up. Reverend Oates would see that the letter got to his family if something bad should happen.

Tatum felt relieved as if a heavy load had been lifted from his shoulders. If the Lord let him live, then when he got home he'd pick up the letter from Reverend Oates. Maybe he'd read it sometime, to remember what he was feeling and to remind him how important his family was to him, now and in the future. Pocketing the letter, he put on his poncho and opened the tent flap. Looking back at the altar with its crude, but beautiful inlaid cross, he realized God had listened to him tonight, even in this desolate desert on the other side of the world from home. God is certainly where your heart is. He left the tent at peace.

* * *

Lieutenant Porter was dead tired. He and his team had just returned from a desert meeting with the Iraqi resistance group they had met what seemed a year ago, but was in fact only a few months earlier. He had received a communications burst from CENTCOM that the team should proceed to a certain coordinate to meet with the rebels and develop a plan for moving Coalition airmen who had been shot down over Iraq along the resistance network to Porter's team for final safekeeping and pickup.

The meeting had gone well and Porter found himself continuing to like and respect the resistance leader, Hussein. The two men came from completely different cultural backgrounds, but each was a leader and appreciated those qualities in the other. The specific routes and call signs had been agreed to and committed to memory. Hussein had some ability to communicate directly with CENTCOM, but Porter did not ask how. The less each knew of the other's operations, the better.

The men had shared a thermos of strong Arabian coffee, laced with pungent goat's milk and plenty of sugar. The mixture gave Porter a potent caffeine surge and he had felt tireless during the return trek across the desert. But now, as he ate a warm MRE, he was tiring fast. For some unknown reason, Porter began thinking about his father, the general. Major General Nathan Porter had never really been a very emotional man, aside from his temper outbursts when Porter (or his brother) had made what the general felt was a monumental mistake. Porter remembered every single time the old man had said he loved him—six, to be exact. Over a whole lifetime. Porter vowed that if he ever had children, he would tell them every day that they were loved.

Even so, he knew, his father felt something strong for him. Maybe it was fatherly pride, or perhaps the kinship of a lineage of Porter military men stretching back to the Revolution. The two men had enjoyed sports, games and hunting and had even enjoyed working on the old family estate near Augusta. But there was always that distance between them, as if the father was holding something back, not quite giving everything of himself to his surviving son. That might have had something to do with his brother, John, who was killed in Vietnam. Scott was only a kid, but he knew how terribly John's death had affected his father. He had grieved for months.

Porter wondered if his father would grieve that much for him if he was killed in this war? His father always kept his innermost feelings to himself, making him almost impossible to read. Whether that made his father a better leader or not, Scott didn't know, but it certainly didn't work for him. Porter was open with his men and they usually could tell what he was thinking and often what he was feeling, too. Scott thought he had inherited his esthetic traits from his mother, but, he also believed he was just as patriotic as his father and could be just as courageous, feelings notwithstanding.

Scott Porter had tried to prove himself to his father time and again, from his earliest recollections. But now, it was hard to separate proving his worth to his father and his own need to prove his worth to himself. Somewhere a transition had been made—maybe in Panama. Scott had begun to realize that he was capable of doing his job well and of taking care of his men, particularly under hostile fire and in hazardous circumstances. His loyalty to them and his assumption of responsibility had begun to lessen the desire to please his father. In fact, he wondered just what it would take to please his father. There had never been any finality to that process between them. His father had never said, "Son, I'm proud of the man you have become." If that ever did occur, then Scott's quest would end, and the father-son relationship could assume a new maturity. Until then, Porter was uncertain how his father felt about him.

He finished eating and dumped the scraps into a zip-lock. He was about to get up and walk out to the desert "garbage dump," when Master Sergeant Lopez slipped over and took it from him.

"Let me take that for you, sir, I'm going that way myself. Why don't you hit the sack and get some shuteye?"

Porter could barely make out Lopez's features in the dim moonlight. *The man is as tired as I am, but I don't feel like putting up a fight tonight. Suddenly, I feel about fifty,* he thought. "Right, I'd really appreciate that."

He watched Lopez disappear over the crater edge and turned to his sleeping hole, already cooling down from the night air. *Well, dad, wherever you are, goodnight. I'll do my best to make us all proud of me, even if I never hear you say the words.*

CHAPTER TEN

STAFF SERGEANT LUCIUS TATUM stood in the door of the aircraft, waiting for the jumpmaster's order to jump. His fear had returned, but he couldn't give in to it, at least not yet. It had begun again at the airfield in the northern Saudi Arabian desert, getting rigged up with his parachutes. It always came back then, while he was putting on the big parachute and strapping it tightly to his body; so tightly, in fact, that he couldn't really stand up straight, so he had to walk to the airplane sort of hunched over. It always occurred to Tatum that he and his men looked like some sort of upright man-sized turtles with their protective shells of parachutes strapped to their backs. *And don't forget the reserve in front. That's been a life-saver more then once when I had a "Mae West" twist to the main parachute and had to deploy the reserve. Man, that jump into Grenada with the Ranger unit had been hairy - low level, from 500 feet, we only jumped with our main chute, not the reserve, because it wouldn't have had time to deploy. The chute barely had time to open, and pow! I was on the ground. My mother told me I was crazy to go airborne and right about now I think she was right.*

The day had begun when Tatum's battalion commander received the official order that they were going to jump into southern Iraq to block the Republican Guard from running away from the fight. He knew they had been planning this blocking maneuver for some time, but the CENTCOM commanders had been hampered by incomplete intelligence on the Guard and he didn't think they were sure even now how much resistance the Iraqi elite force would muster once the 82nd hit the ground.

You fool, he thought to himself as he looked into the swirling night - *you could have taken the civil service exam in D.C. and been walking a nice safe postal route along some street lined with sedate brownstones. But no, I had to join the army and be an airborne ranger. Well, at least I can't see the ground, so my stomach won't be heaving and churning when I look at the DZ. In fact, we could be over the ocean right now instead of the desert for all I know they both look the same at night. Man, I hope that Air National Guard crew knows what they're doing. Where are they from? California? I'll bet they've been smoking pot or something all day. Hey, wait a minute, these guys are professionals, and you're a professional, too, so stop that line of thinking. Just stand here and jump when it's time and you'll be all right.*

Tatum's starboard stick of jumpers were all his own squad members from the 503rd of the 82nd Airborne. They had been garrisoned in a tent city near the Iraqi border for over seven months and now, finally, they were going to get a piece of action. It had been crazy when they had loaded themselves and all of their combat gear onto the dirty Saudi buses for the short ride to the air field staging area yesterday. In typical army "hurry up and wait" fashion, they had stood around for hours in the sun, then crowded into too few buses, jamming rifles, knives, gas masks and all into a seat made for two small Saudis, not a large black soldier. Then more waiting. He never understood why there was always the waiting. *Why couldn't they make the decision to do something and just do it. There's always this waiting around—probably been this way since General Washington wintered at Valley Forge. Waiting is just the army way, followed by a mad headlong rush into whatever had been decided.*

After arriving at the airborne staging area, they had taken their gear to an open-sided tent that kept the sun off of them but did little else to make them comfortable. He had spent most of the time checking his men's equipment, making certain each of them had a clean rifle and a sharpened bayonet. They had been in the desert so long, waiting for combat with the Iraqis that it just didn't seem possible the time had finally come.

They had been issued ammunition and MRE's at the same time, so he had sent two details to bring them back to the tent. He thought it was too careless to eat and load their ammunition magazines at the same time so he had let them eat first while he kept an eye out on the ammunition cases. Things had a way of disappearing over here unless you watched them like a hawk.

It was while they were loading ammunition clips when he saw the first breakdown of the false bravado of some of the men. PFC Billy Harper, from Moline, Illinois, had joined them as a replacement for Leeds, after Leeds had gotten appendicitis and was air-evacuated back to Germany. Harper had just finished jump school and had been assigned to the 82nd replacement company only two weeks before being sent over. *Man,* Tatum had thought, *he had only made his five qualifying jumps at Fort Benning one month before, and now here this boy is, trying to load his M-16 magazines to go into battle. And not doing a very good job of loading,* he noted, as Harper had kept dropping the shells from his ungainly trembling hands. *Scared people always have a way of looking around at others to see if they're being watched and to find out if someone is on to them,* considered Tatum. *For goodness' sake, man, I do the same thing when I'm on that aircraft, waiting to jump, so why should I put down this kid?*

Slowly Tatum had made his way over to where Harper was sitting on an MRE box and knelt beside him. "How's it going, Harper?"

"Fine, Sarge, just fine. No problem as soon as I get these slippery shells put in. Must be the heat makin' my hands slick."

"Yeah, it makes it hard, Harper, but don't screw up your loading or you'll regret it later. Pay attention, relax, and it'll be fine."

Harper nodded, looked down at the sand and began scraping at it with his heel.

"Sarge, what's going to happen to us today?"

Now it was Tatum's turn to look at the sand, wondering what he should say to this young trooper and how much of the truth to tell him.

"Son, there ain't nothing you or I know about that. All you got to do is to do everything I tell you to do, remember your training and for God's sake, keep your head down. These Kevlar helmets are high-tech, but your face is still open - so keep it buried in the sand until you need to fire or you go on the move. You hear what I'm saying?"

Tatum was remembering the fiasco in Panama when they jumped onto the airfield and no one knew what the hell was going on. *Man,* he thought, *I hope this goes according to plan and we don't get caught out there in the desert with our pants down. If we do, kids like Harper are going to die unless I can keep them rounded up and under control. I hate being responsible for these kids—I've got enough worry with my wife and the kids and their college and how do I pay for it, and how do I stay alive myself to look after them. Who's going to do it if not me?*

But the doubts and fears inside Sgt. Tatum stayed there, and there was no discernible change in his face as he and Harper looked at each other intently.

"Okay, Sarge, I'll be fine. You see me doing something dumb, you just holler at me. My daddy used to do that all the time until they took him off to jail, so I guess I'm pretty good at doing what others tell me to."

Tatum unslung his two-quart canteen and took a long swig of his fruit flavored water - today was cherry, his favorite. The powder came out of the MRE packages, and with some sugar added, almost made the potable water from the water buffalo tasty. Almost. He recalled how his three children always used to love cold Kool-Aid when they went on picnics back at Fort Bragg - of course each wanted a different flavor, so his wife had wisely settled on fruit punch, which contained just about all the flavors there were.

Looking back at Harper, he saw the boy was still gazing at him. They stared at each other for a second, each wondering if the other could read his thoughts, then looked away, as men do when looking at each other becomes uncomfortable.

"Sarge, where you gonna put me in the stick when we jump tonight?" Harper was new enough that his position in the line of jumpers inside the aircraft was still important.

"You'll be right in the middle, boy, just in front of Kerwowski." *If Harper balks in the door that big pollock from Detroit will just dump him out with a flick of his arm.*

Harper thought about that a minute until he realized what Tatum was really saying. "You don't think I'll hang up in the door, do you?"

"Harper, you can close your eyes tonight, 'cause it'll be so dark you won't know the difference. Just shuffle up to the door behind the guy in front and jump when you get to the door. Close your eyes for all I care, because you'll go out one way or the other. Just like buffalo in a stampede." He smiled.

Harper seemed to be doing better. He filled most of his magazines without dropping any more .223 shells onto the ground. "Won't pay to get sand in your magazine, son, so you be real careful to wipe off your hands so the sand don't stick to them and the shells, OK?" Tatum smiled as he said this, and softly hit the young paratrooper's knee with his hand as he rose from a crouch. "That M-16 don't like sand, so those shells had better be as clean as a baby's butt, you hear? Clean that rifle once more. And be sure to put a condom on the muzzle to keep out the sand when we board the aircraft. There will be a lot of sand flying when those C-130's get cranked up."

Tatum took one more look at Harper before he moved on.

"Yeah, Sarge, I got 'ya. I'll be okay."

You better be, boy, 'cause I don't want anyone in my platoon getting killed on me. That thing in Panama was bad enough, but the Republican guards are ten times better than the PCDF and I just know someone's going to get killed. Oh, why couldn't I have been a mailman?

Tatum resumed his rounds, watching his men prepare for battle, like men had done for hundreds of decades. Each man acted a little differently, depending on his personality and his reputation in the unit. Corporal Tom James from Cincinnati, Tatum's right-hand man, was solid as the Rock of Gibraltar, with an athletic grace unusual in a white man. He was the epitome of the airborne soldier. *Should be on a recruiting poster, except for that crooked nose. Supposedly James got it when he took on five drunken leg soldiers at a bar in Columbus, Georgia, when they were fooling around with a girl who didn't want to be fooled around with. His nose was broken, but I'll bet at least two guys ended up in the hospital. James won't talk about it, and I don't ask him. To him, doing what was right just came natural. Got to admire a man like that, although it's a real burden to carry, always trying to do right and stick up for others. Probably going to get him killed some time. Not me,* thought Tatum, *I learned to mind my own business in D.C., and I'll do that except when I have to do different while I'm doing my job for Uncle Sam.*

James had been a real source of encouragement for the men during the long and hard time in Saudi. He never seemed to "lose it" and always had a smile and encouragement for the men who got homesick or depressed or discouraged. *I wonder what makes him so stable?* Tatum thought. *Probably just grew up in your basic WASP family, learned those midwestern work and moral ethics early in life and went to church every Sunday. Be nice to have a son or son-in-law like him someday. But, a black boy with his personality would be better than a white one.* He smiled at the thought of showing his new white son-in-law to his mamma in D.C. Poor woman, she'd faint dead away.

Tatum returned to the small area in the tent he had "staked" out to deposit his belongings. Laying out his poncho on the sand to keep things clean, he proceeded to clean his rifle, sharpen its bayonet, checked his compass case and made sure the lanyard was tightly attached to his LBE. He then rechecked his helmet webbing and straps. *No one wants his helmet to tear off in the jump or at landing, or else he'll get one hell of a headache. It's bad enough anyway. Oh no.* He realized he was starting to think about the 'actual jump' and was getting that bad feeling in his stomach again. So he busied himself with the mechanics of preparing for combat and tried to get his thoughts off the jump.

James walked over to him with the easy gait of a mountain lion. "Sarge, any idea when we'll get our mission briefing?"

"Won't be long now, Tom. First Sergeant figures we'll brief about 1400, but you and I both know that the army being the army, it'll be more like 1500. You ready?"

"I'm so ready I could have gone last night," James replied. "Some of the men are getting kinda squirrelly, Sarge, but I think I've gotten them talked down okay."

I'll bet you have, James. I saw you when we went into Panama and you were still a PFC. Even then you had that air of confidence that gave the other men strength. I hate to ever think this, but you'd make a great officer. Tatum knew the NCO corps felt the Army was 'really' run by them, not the officers. But, if you have to have officers, this young man was the kind they should have.

James stood there, almost at attention, but not really seeming to be. Tall, blond, and well-built, the desert camouflage uniform fit him perfectly, as if tailor-made. *He is the man those uniforms were made for, with those broad shoulders, thin waist and wide thighs. I'm in pretty good shape for my thirty-two years, but I look fat in these cammies, not like James, who looks like he's modeling them for Army Times. And that reminds me. We sure haven't been able to run as much over here as we did at Bragg. I sure hope our legs are strong enough to handle a combat jump with nearly 100 pounds. I'd better check with the doc to see if he's got enough stuff to handle more leg injuries than we've had in the past.*

"Tom," Tatum said quietly, "make sure Doc understands

that he needs to pack plenty of air splints and wraps for this jump. If he needs someone else to help lug 'em, tell Slaughter to pack some with him. If anyone injures a leg, it'll be Slaughter, so Doc might as well have the splints right there with him."

"Right, Sarge," James replied, as he turned smoothly and walked away to find the medic.

Doc was kneeling in front of a trooper named Miller who had a boil on his neck. "Dammit, Miller, don't go picking those zits with your dirty fingers like this or you'll get blood poisoning for sure," Doc said. Miller was the kind of man who had been plagued with acne ever since puberty, and would bear the scars forever. Maybe when he got married and got his hormones settled down, it would become quiescent. No matter how many times Miller washed his face and neck, it always looked like a pizza fresh out of the oven.

"Aw, heck, Doc," Miller retorted. "My hands ain't dirty."

Doc looked up at him and frowned. "Miller, you pick your nose, wipe your butt and dig in the sand with those fingers and you don't think they're dirty?"

Miller looked away. Doc sounded just like his mother, who had told him to wash his hands so many times he couldn't even begin to count them. *But, I'd give anything to be back home in Arkansas with Ma and Pa right now - I'd love to hear her tell me a thousand times to 'wash my hands.' At least I'd be out of this Godforsaken desert and be back home in the Ozarks. Man, I miss them hills.*

Doc was small and slightly built with an owl's face and horn-rimmed glasses to match. They always seemed to be sliding down on his nose, in spite of the black strap he wore to keep that from happening. Doc's looks were deceiving, because he had strength and stamina most of the men could never match. A competition cycler, Doc could ride 100 miles before breakfast and hardly break a sweat. He also seemed to have no fear of jumping out of airplanes, either. Something Sgt. Tatum just couldn't understand.

Doc would gripe and complain about the men's hygiene and personal habits, their apparent disregard for common sense in the things they did. But when it came right down to it, he felt a deep sense of concern and responsibility for each and every one of them. Of course, he didn't want them to know that and he went to great lengths to appear nonchalant toward them. But everyone saw through that because Doc's ministrations were too sensitive and competent for them to feel otherwise.

"Miller, I'm going to write your mother and tell her that everything she taught you is going to waste." Doc finished applying the antibiotic ointment and placed a thick dressing over the boil to protect it from the straps of Miller's parachute. "I ought to send you to the aid station, but we're going to need that M-60 of yours, so, I guess we're stuck with you. Now get out your canteen and take these Cipro tablets. I'm going to give these to you 'til we're done with this mission."

Miller simply smiled and nodded, taking out his canteen to take the pills. Doc grumbled as he stood to leave, but almost as an afterthought, turned and playfully punched Miller on the shoulder. "Just let that be the only thing I need to treat you for, okay, Bill? Don't be getting your ear shot off or something, OK?"

Miller nodded, but was left with that thought as Doc walked off to look for another 'victim' to give his attentions to.

As Doc approached, James raised his hand in greeting. Tom James was the only one that Doc let call him by his first name, as they had become friends in jump school, in what seemed like ages ago.

"Larry, the Sarge is concerned that you have enough leg and arm splints to handle more jump accidents than usual. He feels it's going to be a problem because we haven't been able to run as much here in the desert."

"Hey, tell the Sarge I've got it covered. It's my job to know this stuff and prepare for it. I've got plenty of air splints and bandages and I've spread them out among five or six guys who are close to me in the stick. My main worry is that we'll be sitting ducks in the air if the Iraqis see us coming. Even if they don't, they can tear us up by just strafing the air in our general direction. There's only one of me and I can't help everyone right away who gets shot or hurt. Damn, this could be a bad scene."

James read the concern in his friend's eyes and didn't know quite how to respond. They had been together in Panama during Operation Just Cause and there had been a lot of wounded men when the PDF had spotted them hanging from their chutes. "Well, we've got dark chutes and there are lots of clouds tonight, so we should be practically invisible unless they turn a spotlight at us,"

James replied.

"I hope you're right, Tom. But I've got a bad feeling about this one." The two men met each other's gaze for a long moment, then smiled. "AIRBORNE! ALL THE WAY!" they said simultaneously, using that phrase to bolster their frame of mind and lighten up the mood of the conversation. They gave each other a 'high five' for good luck.

"Right on, man, so let's get about business," Doc finished.

The rest of the day passed agonizingly slowly until the mission briefing was called at 1535 hrs. From then on it plunged quickly forward into history. The meeting was led by First Lieutenant Harry Schiller, the 2nd platoon leader, who had spent most of the day at battalion headquarters being briefed. He was assisted by Sergeant First Class Thomas "Pug" O'Reilley, whose nickname was aptly applied in this case. A big man, although not too tall, O'Reilley had grown up on Chicago's South Side where he had been destined to follow the family profession and become a policeman except that his name had just surfaced to the top of the draft list for Vietnam. The O'Reilleys suspect to this day, that some disgruntled citizen 'run in' by one of the O'Reilleys in the course of duty had taken an opportunity to even a score. However, it didn't turn out to be the coup they might have thought.

In fact, Pug O'Reilley found that being a warrior was his true calling (he had sensed that during his amateur boxing career as a teenager) and Vietnam proved it. With one tour in the Americal Division and a second in the 173rd Separate Airborne Brigade, he had earned his reputation as a real combat infantryman. That reputation lingered in the 82nd Airborne as well. Pug's only weakness (and of course he did not consider it one himself) was that he was born with a fondness for the 'fruits of the vine' and he had undergone some really tough times to comply with the general orders for the Persian Gulf banning alcoholic beverages. Consequently, he looked better and healthier than he deserved for his 45 years.

Lieutenant Schiller was a polar opposite next to the 1st Sergeant, although no less the warrior. Tall, and slender, wiry and strong, Schiller presented a perfect Teutonic figure right down to his prominent Teutonic nose. Although removed from his European predecessors by several generations that had been muddied considerably by the 'melting pot' gene pool of Cleveland,

Ohio, the lieutenant still periodically flashed glimpses of those familiar Hun traits.

Schiller looked around the tent. "All right, let's quiet down. We've got a lot to go over and not much time."

The large GP tent had been hastily supplied with a wooden floor, and since chairs were scarce, most of the men sat on the floor, their briefing notebooks out and ready. The wind would occasionally gust outside the tent, making a sudden audible "flap" in the tent walls, but the men were used to that.

The platoon briefings for a mission were usually attended by the platoon administrative NCO's and the squad leaders and assistant squad leaders. With Operation Desert Storm under such world-wide scrutiny each day on the television (it was almost as if the American people had inside information on the war's progress that not even the soldiers had) the importance of the 82nd Airborne mission was prime, so other interested observers as well as liaison and supply representatives were attending many of the briefings. There were about 30 soldiers, all male except for two women - a warrant officer Blackhawk pilot, and the battalion ammunition point NCO, a black female SFC.

Staff Sergeant Tatum was attending as first squad leader, first platoon; the acting assistant squad leader was Corporal James, who had been elevated to that position when Corporal Sammy Billings had broken his elbow falling off the back of a 5-ton truck. Billings was evacuated out because he was unable to put on his chemical suit and mask with a cast on his arm up to the shoulder.

Schiller stood in front of a large military map of the pertinent countries of the Persian Gulf War - shown were Kuwait, Saudi Arabia, Iraq, Israel, Jordan and Turkey. The map was covered with a transparent, thick plastic overlay containing a myriad of different colored arrays, military unit designations (both friendly and enemy) and sector delineations. Next to the large map was a smaller one of southern Iraq showing the area bounded by the Tigris and Euphrates Rivers to the north and Kuwait to the east. For all to see was the unit symbol of the 82nd Airborne division right in the center of that area.

Okay, Tatum thought, *I knew we'd be going into Iraq, but I didn't think we'd be going in that far. Are they going to have us drive on to Baghdad and get that screwball Hussein or what? What kind of resistance will we see? Will the DZ be hot?* Tatum's mind was racing, considering all the questions that would probably be answered by the briefing, but which were products of his experience. All the older NCO's were certain a combat jump into enemy territory was imminent and they had been preparing for months. Now the final details were about to be revealed.

"All right! Listen up!" Schiller's voice penetrated the nervous chatter. "I want to get started on this briefing because we've got a lot to do before takeoff." Several men cleared their throats and looked at each other while Schiller turned toward the large map.

"Our mission tonight is to jump into southern Iraq, form a half circle with battalions on line and block the supply route and exit for the Republican Guard divisions occupying the northern sector of Kuwait. CENTCOM has named this move 'Operation Hail Mary'."

Pointing to their present location, Shiller continued. "The brigade will stage at the airfield adjacent to this position tonight at 2100 hours. Our platoon will be located at tent number 5, where we will have a full equipment check, then strap on the parachutes at 2200 hours. We will march by squads to the tarmac at 2300 hours to await aircraft transportation. Our estimated time of departure from the airfield is 2330 hours. Any questions so far?"

One burly sergeant shot up his hand. "Sir, are we going to get a hot meal or do we have to eat that MRE crap tonight?"

"Sergeant, the U.S. Army has looked favorably upon us, seeing as how we are about to go save Kuwait and kick some ass, so we'll get a hot meal with bread and fruit at the equipment shed. Also, there will be latrines at the shed for use after the meal."

The sergeant dug his elbow into the man next to him and said in a loud whisper, "Them latrines is goin' to be overflowing with nervous runs tonight—I'd hate to be burning out those drums." A few nervous laughs burst out, but died quickly.

"Squads one and two will form the two sticks of jumpers in the first aircraft and the third squad will join the third squad of second platoon in the second aircraft. Squad leaders will jump first in the stick with assistant squad leaders bringing up the rear. We'll be jumping dark brown T-10B 'chutes tonight from 1000 feet, so we'll get to wear a reserve."

If those Air Force National Guard pilots can only read their altimeters right, Tatum thought. *Nah, I'm just starting to get that old feeling and I'm damn mad at myself. I've got to put it at the back of my mind and listen up to the lieutenant. Maybe if I take notes I'll be better off.* Tatum took out his squad leader notebook and quickly penciled in the important items the lieutenant had just covered.

"The operational order is being copied right now and will be passed to you to read when we're done with this briefing," Schiller continued. He walked over to a crudely penciled list nailed to the wall. "Have your squad armorer draw enough ammunition for each man to carry 500 rounds of M-16 ammo with 1000 rounds for the machine gunner. Spread the M-60 rounds out among two or three other people so the gunner won't be so weighed down. Each man will carry two HE grenades and two white phosphorus. Squad leaders and assistants will carry one each red, green and blue smoke flares for signaling for medivac pickups and close air support. Chemical suits will be worn over BDU's, but gloves, boots and masks will be stored in the butt pack. I repeat, we will not jump wearing chemical masks."

There was an audible sigh of relief from the audience. The chemical masks were tight, hot and increased the feeling of claustrophobia. *Thank you Lord,* Tatum thought. *I'd rather be gassed than wear that blasted mask on a jump. I just know I'd vomit into it before we jumped and wouldn't that be a sight?*

The lieutenant stepped back to the map. "Jumpmasters will be designated for each aircraft, but we will not use platoon personnel for this. Jumpmasters will be from headquarters company." *I just hope that desk pusher remembers how to jump us right. If he screws us up, I will personally throw him out of the aircraft.*

Schiller pointed to the map at a location approximately 100 miles due west of Basra, Iraq. "The drop zone is designated DZ Bastogne and is approximately two miles in length. It is bounded on the north by the Tigris River and the rest of the directions by sand." His attempt at humor was lost on the assembled group at this stage of the briefing. "The DZ will be lighted by a pathfinder team from the second brigade which is already in place. The area was previously reconnoitered and the enemy positions noted by a special forces team which has been in place for several months. They will guide in the air attacks before the jump to destroy the radar and antiaircraft positions and will direct the close air support to any threat to the safety of our jump."

If this goes okay, and those Green Beanies do their job, I'll buy them the biggest steak in Fayetteville and a whole keg of beer, Tatum promised himself. *It feels real good knowing those SF guys are down there looking out for us.*

"Our mission, as detailed in the OpPlan, is to link up with the other two battalions and to hold the position as a blocking force. We will be resupplied within 72 hours, or sooner if we need ammunition resupply before then."

The lieutenant moved closer to the men and leaned on his pointer as he might have on a putter at the Fort Bragg golf course in better times. "All right, now what are your questions?"

* * *

Staff Sergeant Lucius Tatum stood in the door waiting for the jumpmaster's order to jump.

The air was very cold at one thousand feet, and Tatum decided that had to be the reason his teeth were chattering. He could see fires burning in the desert and periodic explosions, which threatened to diminish the night vision that had slowly been improved by the red lights inside the C-130.

That must be the special forces team down there, Tatum thought, *destroying the radar and antiaircraft positions to make our jump safer. When I meet up with them, you can bet I'm going to show them my gratitude.*

The jumpmaster looked at Tatum and the rest of his stick and held up one finger—"One minute," he hollered, but no one heard him. They did see his finger, though.

Tatum turned and took a correct exit position in the door of the aircraft, feet eighteen inches apart, knees slightly bent, and outsides of the hands braced against the cold metal open door of the aircraft.

Tatum felt the bile rise in his throat, and the accelerating rate of his heart beat. *Dear Lord,* he prayed, *just get me to the ground in one piece, and I'll take it from there.*

Suddenly, the jumpmaster slapped Tatum's left buttock hard, and yelled "GO" in Tatum's ear. In an action born of reflex and without conscious thought, Tatum leaped out the aircraft door, falling toward his destiny at a rapid rate of descent.

CHAPTER 11

THE 3RD ARMORED was on the move! The tankers expected to begin their assault into southern Iraq on the 25th of February, but the VII Corps commander, General Franks, decided to push ahead by one day the assault by the huge armored force. Preceded by the armored cavalry regiments, the division was speeding through the desert toward the western flank of the Iraqi forces.

The decision had been made to avoid sending the division through the breach at the front lines of the Iraqi emplacements, but rather to produce an end-run around the enemy line to cut off their supply and escape routes. The maneuver was also designed to divide the Iraqi elements and isolate them from their communications and control.

Elements of the 1st Brigade were spearheading the main body run into southern Iraq, with the First Platoon of the 1st Battalion in the lead. It was now early dusk and the tankers had been on the move for over four hours. Sergeant Gonzales had maintained his observation of the attack from the main turret hatch, in constant contact with the rest of the platoon. The M1A1 main battle tanks of the platoon were all running abreast, ahead of the rest of the division, which was trailing behind. The entire division was driving up the Wadi al Batim, an ancient, dry river bed that accommodated the 15-kilometer-wide division, a huge armored force.

At mid-afternoon, First Platoon had left Phase Line Tangerine, their jumping-off point for the assault, and had met no resistance after passing through the sand berm. Although somewhere to the east was the 1st Armored Division and to the west, the 1st Mechanized Infantry Division, they occupied such vast areas of the desert no sign could be seen of the other forces.

Gonzales heard the call sign from Platoon Commander Lieutenant Rick Hanes, and he keyed the microphone at the front of his helmet. The rest of his crew were wearing chemical suits and gas masks inside the tank, where the masks fit into a special closed system, but Gonzales had not yet done so, preferring to visualize the desert ahead while it was still light.

"Green One to Green Two, do you read me?"

"Green Two here, Green One," replied Gonzales.

"Green Two, we're sucking fumes here in this tank, so I'm calling up a fuel truck to fuel us all up, over."

"Roger, Green One. Will notify the flock about the fuel. Shall we stop on-line at your command, over?"

"Green Two, we'll defilade just behind that long, low rise ahead, and start refueling from east to west, with the full tanks moving ahead 100 yards to wait for the others. Send ahead a scout tank to keep a radar eye peeled so we don't have any unexpected visitors, over."

"Copy that, Green One. Will relay. Out here."

Gonzales called up the rest of the tanks on the platoon net and relayed the orders. Soon the entire line had come to a grinding halt behind the natural concealment of the sand rise and the fuel truck had begun refueling. No one exited the tanks during the refueling and any one needing to urinate did so into his personal bottle. Meals and snacks were eaten on the run during the assault, although not many had gotten over their attack jitters sufficiently to feel very hungry.

Refueling an Abrams while the engine was running was risky. Any fuel spilled accidentally on the hot turbine could be ignited, but that rarely happened. Even so, the refuelers stood guard with large fire extinguishers just in case.

Soon the job was done and the platoon was ready to roll. Gonzales turned in his hatch and looked south through his armored binoculars. *No sign of the rest of the division, but they were surely behind somewhere.* There was considerable dust in the air to the south, which was undoubtedly created by a huge mass of tanks and support vehicles racing across the desert at speeds in excess of forty kilometers. Gonzales turned and gave the order to move out again to his driver, Corporal Ron Jennings. Jennings got a real kick out of driving the behemoth and harbored a secret desire to drive it down the main drag of his hometown some day in a victory parade.

The sky was growing dark, both from dusk and with what appeared to be an incoming storm front. The wind picked up and

Gonzales took one more look around the darkening desert before dropping into the tank and taking his position in the commander's seat. He put on his tanker's gas mask and hooked the hose into the receptacle next to his seat. Almost immediately he smelled and tasted the cool air entering his mask from the tank's hybrid closed air circulation system. That was a relief because it often became very hot in the tank when clothed in the chemical suit.

Sergeant "Bull" Jones was scanning the optical sights on the TAC, the target acquition console, looking for distant targets in a 245-degree arc. The platoon's scout tank had dropped back on line so any vehicle identified on the console would have to be an enemy. Jones was particularly anxious to get the first "kill" for the platoon and did not take his eyes from the console for hours at a time.

Suddenly, he hollered and hit Gonzales' leg with his hand. "Got a target, Sarge, looks like a tank to me."

Gonzales leaned down and looked at the screen. It was hard to do that from his position with the chemical mask, but he could make out a definite contact on the screen.

He hit the switch from internal intercom on this headset to platoon net and called Lt. Hanes. "Green One, this is Green Two, come in."

"Green One here, Green Two, what's up, over?"

"Green One, we've got a target bearing zero zero five five degrees at four thousand yards, moving this way. Believe this is a hostile target. Request permission to fire, over."

Just then, Jones cut in on the intercom. "Sarge, I've got two more, no, three more targets that just showed up. Hell, Sarge, they're coming in from all over the place."

"Green One, we now have multiple targets dead ahead, at least four. Awaiting orders, over."

"Green Two, this is Green One. We now have target acquisition. Give order to fire at will, I repeat, fire at will!"

"Roger, Green One, this is Green Two, out."

Gonzales hurriedly called up all the other tank commanders on the net and apprised them of the situation and order. Some tanks had not yet acquired the targets, being at the fringes of the laser range. "Green Flock, just keep on-line. If you stray out front, we may have an accident, I repeat, keep your position as you advance forward."

He kept the platoon net open and flipped the dual switch to intercom. "All right, Jones, let's see what you can do with this baby. Acquire targets and fire when ready."

The M1A1 tank uses a laser range finder interfaced with a state-of-the-art ballistic computer to acquire targets. Similar to what Lieutenant Porter accomplished at Jabilah airfield for the Air Force, Sergeant Jones could do against enemy tanks. However, the Abrams tank had a much more powerful rangefinder, capable of "painting" a target at up to four thousand meters. Unlike some of the enemy tanks, the Abrams could keep moving as the computer locked on to the targets and computed the range and trajectory of each.

Gonzales's tank was fitted with the 120 mm smoothbore automatic fire cannon and carried forty rounds of APDS. This round, the Armor Piercing Discarding Sabot, had an enclosed depleted uranium warhead that could pierce enemy armor at a high velocity, imparting a huge terminal energy to the round at the time of penetration. An Iraqi tank hit squarely by this round would certainly be disabled if not totally destroyed.

"I've got it, Sarge. Here goes!" Jones fired the first round about three thousand meters from the closest enemy tank. The huge 65-ton M1A1 was traveling about 35 kilometers an hour at the time, but was still rocked by the recoil from the stabilized gun. Gonzales looked out his viewing port, but could see nothing at first. Then, the desert horizon lit up with a huge spectacular fireball.

The crew all whooped and hollered and Jones raised his clenched fist in the air, then came down with an open palm, to hit the palm of his commander, in a "low five."

"Outstanding, Jones, outstanding, but don't forget that those guys can shoot back, so get another target," Gonzales said.

By then, the firefight had opened up. Jones had counted at least thirteen enemy tanks or vehicles on the screen and some of them were going up in flames as a result of hits by other platoon tanks. He had acquired another tank when the acquisition data blipped off, indicating the tank had been hit by other fire. He rapidly locked in onto another target and fired another round, this time making his second hit.

"Hot damn, Sarge, how many does it take to be a tanker ace, I wonder?"

''Just pay attention to your targets, Bull, because those guys are getting closer,'' Gonzales shouted. Just then, an explosion close to them rocked the tank and he heard metal fragments hitting the turret.

''Green Flock, this is Green Two. Anybody hit by that last round close by?''

An excited voice came on the net. ''Sarge, Price's tank just got hit and it's on fire. It's right in front of me, what do I do?''

''All right, nobody panic,'' Gonzales said. ''I'll call in a Bradley from the scouts to get over to Price and get them out of there. Just keep on toward the targets. Watch out, now, because they're in range now and you've got to keep moving and not give them a chance to acquire you. Next time, just identify yourself by name, and we'll keep this communication line simple. Gonzales out.''

He got on the scout network and called for a Bradley with infantrymen to go to the rescue of the damaged tank. It would take men to open the emergency hatch and get the tankers out of there, if they were still alive. The Abrams couldn't stop moving and firing until the enemy was all killed. It was a simple as that. Anyway, the M1A1's had an internal fire extinguisher that should take care of most fires--at least that's what they were told.

The firefight was becoming very confusing. The enemy tanks had scattered and were at many different locations. They were within their own guns' range now and shells were exploding in and around the American tanks. The Abrams had internal recognition systems for each other, but the problem was that if the enemy tanks got between two American tanks, there might be a direct hit on a friendly tank by mistake. Because it was dark, there was no way to identify the tanks by sight.

Radio communications was becoming more undisciplined. Tank commanders were trying to identify and assist their comrades, but that just seemed to make everything even more confusing.

''Smitty, watch out, one's coming up to your left.''

''Dammit, Rodriguez, you're right behind me. Move up farther so you don't blast me, man.''

''There he is, there he is, I've got him!''

Finally, Lieutenant Hanes came on the net and ordered commo discipline and control. But still, it was impossible to control the frenzy and aggression with which this firefight was being engaged. There was a real danger of friendly fire losses, which Gonzales and Hanes were trying their best to prevent. The First Platoon was finally into the fracas in a big way.

* * *

Two miles to the southeast of the tank battle, elements of the 2nd ACR, including four Apache attack helicopters and one OH-58 Kiowa scout helicopter, were racing to join the forward elements of the 3rd AD. Since the indigenous air cavalry assets of the 3rd AD had already leapfrogged over the First Platoon's current position, the brigade commander had called for assistance from Captain Tex Weatherby's unit. Tex and his weapons officer, CWO2 Garner, were directing the helicopters to the firefight to provide support from the air.

Tex was wearing the AN/AVS-6 Aviator's Night Vision Imaging System goggles for the flight tonight. He really despised them, because they severely restricted his field of view, but tonight he was operating under regimental orders and he had no choice. The night was closet dark, with no moon and in the presence of severely restricting cloud covers. Additionally, the northern wind was increasing and it was likely air operations would be shut down within several hours. Therefore, there was some sense of urgency in the minds of the aviators to join the battle before they were recalled.

Even fitted with the night vision goggles, Weatherby was having difficulty visualizing the details of the firefight just ahead. As he and Garner flew toward the battle, he could see the outlines of burning tanks and explosives, which caused a flashbulb-like phenomenon in the visual field of his goggles. Brightness, such as occurs with explosions and fires, plays havoc with the sensitive, low-light amplification mechanism of the goggles, and actually serves to diminish the effect of the goggles, rather than to enhance them.

"Talk to me, Roger," Tex said over the aircraft's intercom system. "What's going on down there on your screen?"

"Captain, we've got about thirty-five to forty vehicles in a square mile area, and they're all getting mixed up. I can sort out most of the friendlies, but some of the bigger T-72's look a lot like the M1A1 on my scope."

"Well, let's make sure we know what we're shooting at,

first, Roger. I don't want any accidents. I'll call up on the on-site commander to try to coordinate the attack."

Weatherby switched his radio set to the pre-designated air-to-ground frequency and glanced at the call sign for the tank platoon commander he had been given during the hasty briefing.

"Green One, this is Tango One, over."

A pause, then static.

"Green One, this is Tango One, over."

Finally, Lieutenant Hanes was on the line.

"Tango One, this is Green One, over.

"Green One, we are within one thousand meters of your position, directly to the south. I have four hot Apaches ready to help you get some scalps. But, we're having trouble making out friendlies, over."

"Tango One, we are now engaging the enemy at less than two thousand meters, and trying to keep on-line, but it's pretty confusing down here. The burning tanks are all enemy but one friendly is on fire. I have eleven, I repeat, eleven friendly tanks heading north or northeast. Enemy tanks are now in movement, attempting to break through our line and are swinging east and west, over."

"Roger, Green One, understand present status. What is your recommendation for us, over?"

There was a pause for nearly a minute. Hanes had called Gonzales on the radio and asked his advice.

"Tango One, we recommend a close fly-by to see if you can sort out the good guys from the bad guys. If not, then best if you leave the engagement to us, over."

Tex was inclined to agree with the fly-over, but knew his fellow aviators wanted a piece of this action, and felt that they could probably isolate some Iraqi tanks and attack safely. However, the commander on the ground was right, and they'd take a look first.

"Green One, will comply with your recommendation. Two aircraft will recon over the back of your neck and see what we can see. Tango One out."

Weatherby switched to the Apache air-to-air net and informed the pilots that he and Lieutenant Perez, his assistant flight leader, would take a low flight over the battlefield in an attempt to visualize the tanks and their relative positions. The other aircraft would hang back a thousand meters and await further orders.

"All right, Roger, keep your eyes peeled and let me know when you can positively identify the bad guys. I'll be looking out as well."

"Got it, Captain. Just don't skewer us on a tank cannon, O.K.? I like my shishkabob over a grill, if it's all the same to you." Garner had experienced Tex's love for low level flying and had never really gotten used to it.

Weatherby glanced over at the starboard side and could just barely see the outline of Perez's Apache about three hundred meters back. It was difficult to look around in the cockpit and even more difficult to scan the panorama outside the aircraft. When moving the night vision goggles rapidly, there was a sense of vertigo, not unlike moving a videocamera through a rapid arc. Tex was fully aware these goggles had caused a number of fatal aviation accidents over the years, and knew he had to be very cautious when pressing an attack at night wearing them. What was usually seen and processed very quickly with the normal field of vision had to be carefully observed and time taken to understand the images thoroughly. Too often, mistakes were made because the images were misinterpreted, then inappropriate decisions had been made.

The two Apaches dived to approximately two hundred feet above the ground and moved forward at one hundred and twenty knots. There was a certain danger to the low-flying helicopters either from the large caliber machine guns mounted on the Iraqi tanks or from turret-mounted surface-to-air missiles, but the reconnaissance had to be done.

Weatherby planned a quick survey of the battlefield with a back-and-forth sweep. On the first, he saw no moving tanks, but did see a burning hulk at the extreme northern boundary of the survey, presumably an Iraqi T-55. On the second sweep, both he and Perez overflew several large tanks with characteristic rounded front turrets--unmistakably Soviet-made T-72's.

However, Tex had just begun his turn for the return sweep, when an American tank suddenly raced into his view. At least he thought it was an American tank because it was headed in the opposite direction as the two Iraqi T-72's.

Perez came quickly on the radio: "Tango One, did you see that big juicy enemy tank back there? Let's go get it!"

"Tango Two, just hold up a minute. I thought it was a friendly, but which one did you see?" Tex was a little confused about Perez's identification.

"Captain, the one you just flew over was an Iraqi tank, no doubt about it. Let's make a go-around and hit it, over."

"Perez, we'll take a one-eighty on the same heading and head south again. Look for the single tank in front of the two T-72's. I think that's an Abrams heading north."

"Tango One, I think you saw another tank than the one I'm describing. It was clearly a single Iraqi tank, over."

Weatherby completed the northern turn and headed back south again, with Perez still at his aft and starboard side. He passed over the two T-72's again, but could not see the other tank in his field of vision. He looked around in as complete a scan as he could, but the tank was nowhere around his aircraft.

"Tango One, there it is, but it's now close to another tank that must be a T-72 also," Perez radioed, excitement in his voice. Perez had not been in a real firefight before, having just joined the unit from an assignment at Camp Stanton in South Korea, near the DMZ.

"Tango Two, I saw the two enemy tanks, but where is the other tank I thought was friendly, over?"

"Tango One, it must have gotten out of the way when they heard us come over. We need to get these guys before they get too far into the friendly lines." Perez really wanted to engage these tanks, and that was the attitude that made an attack helicopter pilot a warrior.

"Tango Two, wait one while I call up the ground commander. Keep on my four o'clock and don't arm your weapons until I give the order."

"Wilco, Tango One, but don't let them get away. We know where they're at right now."

Weatherby switched quickly to the ground frequency and called Lieutenant Hanes. "Green One, this is Tango One, come in."

Hanes responded immediately this time. "Tango One, Green One here, over."

"Green One, we visualize two hostile tanks at a heading of zero zero four two degrees. Both tanks were stationary and facing south. Do you copy that those are enemy tanks, over?"

A pause while Hanes conferred with his weapons sergeant.

"Tango One, we have confirmation of two enemy tanks in approximately that heading about fifteen hundred meters from our general platoon line. We have been receiving fire from them but they must be in defilade because we cannot get a laser fix with our rangefinder. If you have definite I.D. and can get a shot at them, go ahead. Use caution though, because I have eleven friendly tanks out there and they're moving in all directions, over."

Tex was thinking fast now. He felt reasonably sure he and Perez were talking about the same tanks. After all, they had passed over the tanks within several hundred yards of each other. He had not been able to make out that they were in defilade, because of the darkness and too-brief observation time, but they certainly looked like T-72's. After all, he had spent countless hours memorizing the flashcard silhouettes and skyward outlines of the threat armor, hadn't he?

The T-72 main battle tanks carried a 200-mm main gun that would not be a threat to the Apaches, but the optically sighted, turret-mounted missiles and the large machine guns on their hatches would be. Current doctrine indicated that if it was not possible to obtain a "stand-off" laser target acquisition for a hostile tank, then the Apaches should strafe the tank at low altitude, firing 2.75-in. rockets. The rockets were unguided, but with nineteen rockets to a pod, there would be a high likelihood of a hit on one pass. The fast pass would also reduce the risk from enemy fire at the helicopter and its crew.

Weatherby had to make a quick decision. The action on the battlefield was fast-moving, with tanks changing position with respect to each other every several minutes. Just then, Perez cut into the radio.

"Tango One, what's the decision? We can't let those guys just take shots at our tanks without at least hitting them with something, can we?"

At the very root of his professional aviation career Weatherby was basically an aggressive pilot, one who had already successfully applied his skills against the enemy. But Perez had thrown down the gauntlet and it was hard for Tex not to react. Feeling a sense of excitement brought on by the mere possibility of action, Weatherby made his decision.

"Tango Two, let's go for it. Follow my lead and use your

rockets. You take the starboard tank and I'll take the port one. We'll make one pass on them and fire when we sight them. Fire your rockets at the junction of turret and gun, if possible. On the second pass, we'll check for damage and prepare to use the guns if necessary. Arm your weapons.''

He then switched to the ground frequency and made the call. ''Green One, this is Tango One, over.''

''Tango One, go ahead.''

''Green One, will make one pass at the hostile tanks and fire rockets. Keep an eye on the field and tell me how we do, over.''

''Tango One, I hope you have a positive ID on those tanks because we've got several of our own pretty close together, too.''

Damn, Weatherby thought, *that's just great.* But he was committed to attack, and he had passed the point of no return. ''Roger, Green One, am certain of targets. Out here.''

Weatherby made the turn and armed his rockets. Although the fire power of the Apache was tremendous, it had only begun to be tested in actual combat. This would likely be the first time any Apache pilot had fired rockets against an enemy tank.

Suddenly, the tanks appeared in the distance. At their rate of speed, Weatherby and Perez only had time to align the optical sights on their assigned tank and fire. The Apache bucked from the release of the multiple rockets and suddenly they were over the tanks and speeding away.

What a thrill, Weatherby thought. *That must have plastered those Iraqis but good.*

''Whoopee,'' hollered Perez over the earphones. ''We got them all right, Captain.''

Weatherby was already thinking about how he could paint two enemy tank insignias on the side of his Apache when the ground-to-air radio crackled.

* * *

Gonzales had heard the conversations between Lt. Hanes and the helicopter overhead, but had focused his main attention on the evolving firefight around him. ''Bull'' Jones had acquired another target and blasted the enemy tank, giving them three ''kills.'' Several other American tanks had scored hits and only one of their tanks had been hit. Suddenly, a transmission from his platoon net radio burst into his ears.

''We've been hit, we've been hit. Good Lord, someone help

us, the tank's on fire. Help us!''

Gonzales quickly called up on the net. ''Who got hit? Who is that? Identify yourself to Green One or Green Two.''

Another voice entered the net. ''Green Two, this is Rodriguez. Smitty's tank and Washington's tank both got hit. Smitty's tank was hit real bad, but Washington's still moving. I saw it and I can still see both of them. Sarge, you won't believe this, but they got hit by our own choppers.''

Gonzales was stunned. At first he could not accept what the man had said. With all of this sophisticated weaponry in the U.S. Army arsenal, how could there be a hit by friendly fire?

''Green One, Green Two here, did you copy that last transmission?''

Lt. Hanes' voice was strained and broken. ''Roger, Green Two, I copied. Dammit, I told those pilots to be careful. I did.''

''Lieutenant, can you get the scout Bradley over there to get those men out of the tank?''

''Negative, Green Two. The scout has taken the men from the first tank back to the field medical area. I don't even know where Smitty's tank is.''

Gonzales made a quick decision. ''Green One, I'm going up for observation and will make visual contact with the tanks.'' He quickly disconnected his seat suspension belts and stood up, lifting the hatch to the turret. He flipped off his gas mask and left it hanging from his neck. He then powered up the SACMFCS (Small Arms Common Module Fire Control System) attached to the M2 .50-caliber machine gun at his turret and sighted through it, using its night-time low vision capabilities to search for the crippled platoon tanks. Rapidly scanning the battlefield, he picked out the two. One, probably Washington's, was moving north slowly toward the forward edge of the battlefield, possibly to provide fire and cover for the more badly damaged tank, because there were still enemy tanks firing at the Americans from stationary positions.

Washington's tank appeared to have thrown the port track, but was still moving ahead on the starboard tracks ''crabbing'' to accommodate for the missing one. What was obviously Smitty's tank was smoking and there was no sign of activity, nor were the hatches open.

Gonzales grabbed his headset and microphone again and tried to call Smitty on the platoon net. No response. Then he tried to reach Washington, but the damaged tank's radio antenna must have been damaged or a circuit wrecked.

He looked down into the crew compartment and kicked the metal plate next to Corporal Jennings' shoulder. 'Pick up the headset,' he signaled. Jennings nodded and put his headset back on. ''Jennings, get this tank moving dead ahead. I'll give you the directions, but just get it moving!''

The driver kicked the Abrams into gear and they lurched ahead, quickly gaining speed in the loose sand. Several enemy tank rounds hit within fifty meters of Gonzales' exposed position, but only sand was thrown his way. Gonzales ignored the remaining enemy tanks and focused intently on the smoking tank just ahead. He hollered to Jennings to stop about seventy-five meters short of Smitty's tank and told Jones to take command and protect their position. Also, Jones should tell the lieutenant that Gonzales had dismounted and to call for a medivac chopper ASAP.

After exiting the hatch, Gonzales slipped on the oily and smoky tank deck just below the gun and fell hard onto the sand next to the port track. He wasn't hurt and got up quickly, running toward the disabled tank. *If there had been any chemicals in the air, I'd have been dead by now.*

The tank hull was hot, very hot. The internal fire extinguisher must have been functional because only a little smoke and steam were coming from the vent ports. Gonzales climbed up on the turret from the rear and removed the big gas cans attached there, throwing them into the desert as far away from the tank as he could. But when he did he was splashed with gasoline from a leaking can. Disregarding that, he climbed to the main turret hatch and tried opening it. It wouldn't budge. He knocked on the hatch with the base of his flashlight and heard a faint return knock.

Mustering all his strength, he was somehow able to elevate the hatch enough to get his fingers under the rim. It was scorching hot and his fingers were seared. As he lifted the hatch, hot steam came rolling out, burning his eyes and temporarily blinding him. He could smell fuel inside the cabin and feared the tank would explode before he could get the men out. Diving in head first, he first encountered the tank commander, Sergeant Smith, who was hanging weakly in his seat harness. Using his Ka Bar knife to cut through the harness webbing, Gonzales awkwardly pulled Smitty out of the seat and onto the deck of the tank. Smitty appeared to be alive, but just barely.

Jumping back into the tank, feet first this time, he saw the other three crew members, all seemingly alive, but too weak to exit the tank by themselves. The cockpit floor was wet with fire extinguisher fluid and what might have been blood mixed with oil. Gonzales slipped, striking his right shoulder hard on an exposed metal pipe. He felt immediate pain but pushed it to the back of his mind. Bracing himself against the forward bulkhead, he pulled the driver out of his seat and pushed him up the hatch, leaving him just outside the opening. Then he pushed open the secondary hatch and got the loader/gunner out there. Finally, he was able to pull himself out the main hatch and hoist the driver onto his shoulder.

Slowly and painfully, he eased the driver off the deck and onto the sand, dragging him as far as he could to a safe distance away from the tank in case it exploded. Next, he went back to get the last man and succeeded in pulling him away from the vehicle. A third trip allowed him to retrieve the fourth crew member. Although exhausted and weak from blood loss from his shoulder wound, Gonzales climbed back up on the starboard track and tried to pull Smitty down to him. But Smitty's boot had somehow gotten caught in one of the viewing ports of the main body of the tank and would not budge.

Fearing an explosion at any time, Gonzales worked feverishly, cutting the boot off Smitty's foot. Finally, the boot came free and he was able to drag Smitty over to the front of the tank. Half-sliding and half-pushing the man over the edge, they both toppled to the sand, a fall of about three feet. With superhuman effort, Gonzales grabbed Smitty by the chest and hoisted the man's limp body over his shoulder.

The men were only about 25 meters from the tank when it exploded, showering them with hot pieces of metal and burning liquid. Gonzales fell on top of Smitty's body and sheltered him from the blast, but suddenly realized his own back was on fire. He pushed away from Smitty so as not to burn him and began rolling in the sand, as he had been taught. There was no pain until the fourth roll when it struck him like a lightning bolt. The pain was sudden, severe and nauseating, then there was only darkness.

* * *

Specialist Anders was on his way to the latrine when a figure with a blue-lensed flashlight came running up to him. "That you, Anders?'' The man shone the light in Jay's face.

Anders turned his head. ''It's me, all right, who are you?''

''It's Doerdorf, man. We've got a hot mission. Like, right now. Bird's ready and waiting.''

Doerdorf turned and began running toward the helicopter pad, with Anders close behind. The rotors were beginning to turn on the Blackhawk as they approached the cabin from the front. Anders noticed his field medical bag already strapped to the floor and saw there were six litters on board. He had barely gotten his seat harness locked when the chopper lifted off and banked sharply northward.

The ride was mostly in silence, although Doerdorf did tell him they had received a call from the 3rd Armored Division that there were friendly casualties from a tank firefight deep inside southern Iraq. No one knew how many casualties nor how badly the tankers were hurt. Anders began to feel nervous, as he always did when it appeared people would have to depend upon him.

As they approached the battlefield, the pilot circled, looking for the characteristic L-shaped flares that would guide him to a landing into the wind. As the Blackhawk circled, Anders could see the burning hulks of many tanks. He could also see a number of others, formed into a loose semicircle around their LZ.

As the wheels touched sand, Anders unstrapped himself and jumped up, grabbing his medical kit and hitting the ground. He was met by a young tanker lieutenant, who grabbed his arm and pulled him over to where a number of men were standing. He could see five bodies on the sand covered with ponchos, but could not tell if they were dead or alive.

He knelt by the first man, who was awake and alert. He was coughing a great deal, and Anders felt he probably had inhaled smoke from the burning tank nearby. He told a tanker to give the man some water for his throat and checked his vital signs. The heart rate was rapid and the breathing fast. However, he appeared stable so Anders reassured him and moved on to the next.

The second man was unconscious, but stable. His vital signs were not worrisome. There was a large smear of dried blood in and around his left ear, but his pupils reacted well to a flashlight beam. Anders suspected a closed head injury, maybe even a basilar skull fracture which would account for the blood. The man responded to a pinch by moving his arms and legs and moaning. Anders placed a cervical collar around his neck to protect it as best he could if a neck injury was present and helped the crew chief and some of the tankers load the two men on stretchers and into the Blackhawk.

Running on to the next two, he found the third one sitting up by then and able to talk. His name was Smith and he was the tank commander. He told of the tank being hit by unknown fire that came out of nowhere and that was the last he remembered until he woke up in the desert. Lieutenant Hanes placed a hand on Anders' shoulder and shook his head, indicating that he should not ask any further questions about the incident. Confused, but obedient, Anders helped the sergeant to his feet and the other tankers took Smith to the helicopter. The fourth tanker was stable and capable of walking without assistance.

Turning his attention to the last man, Anders at first thought he was dead. The man was lying on his side, and had a significant amount of blood over his left shoulder and chest. His tanker's coveralls were nearly burned off his back and legs and his hands were charred. Only burnt stubble remained on the back of his head. Anders listened to his lungs and heard and was surprised to hear both breath sounds and a heartbeat. He immediately cut off the burned coverall sleeves and with some difficulty, found a vein near the inside of each elbow. By flashlight, he started two intravenous fluid lines and began the fluids wide open. He was reluctant to give morphine to the unconscious man, but knew it was beneficial in burn cases, so he did it anyway. After wrapping the man in blankets from the aircraft, the chopper crew gently placed him on the litter.

After the aircraft lifted, not much more could be done for the casualties, save for monitoring their states of consciousness, breathing patterns, heart rates and pupillary activity. For the burn victim, Anders carefully watched the intravenous fluid rate and faithfully recorded the times, type, and amount of fluids given. The return trip to the nearest medical facility took only twelve minutes, so it seemed quick to Anders.

They arrived at the makeshift helicopter pad of the mobile surgical detachment of the 252nd Combat Support Hospital. Actually, it was little more that a flat area in the desert next to a half a dozen tents and modular containers. There were several litter teams waiting at the pad, alerted by the pilot after the hospital was selected to receive the patients by the area medical evacuation officer. Anders assisted the litter-bearers in transporting the patients to the triage receiving area, taking the burned patient there first. He was surprised to see a very efficient and quick triage team leap into action when they entered the tent.

* * *

Neel hadn't really been asleep, just lying in his sleeping bag, awaiting the first casualties to their surgical hospital. Of course, it wasn't a real hospital, but they had the facilities, the team and operating rooms to care for severely wounded casualties and stabilize them for transportation up the chain to the next hospital, usually an Evac, where there were more surgical specialists. Neel was worn out from the all-day forced drive into southern Iraq and from the extreme effort it required to set up and prepare the facility for casualties. Fortunately, this hospital had been designed with that in mind, and it "unfolded" into ready-made surgical suites.

When the triage NCOIC shook him and informed Neel of the incoming casualties, he sprang up at once. This was why he was here in the Persian Gulf and now he had a chance to be of some help to these unlucky individuals. He ran to the triage tent, laid his gas mask on the ground under the first litter position, and pulled on some sterile gloves.

His heart sank when the litter team brought in the first casualty. By all appearances, the man had suffered severe burns over nearly fifty percent of his body and, in addition, had a serious shoulder wound. He asked about the time of injury, and about the amount of fluids, so far and was surprised to be answered with exact information by the young blond medic who didn't look old enough to vote yet. The medic had a strong gaze though and appeared to have done the right things for these casualties. As he looked familiar to the doctor, Neel took a second look, seeing his face through the smeared blood and soot, and checked the nametag on his flight suit. 'Specialist J. Anders.' *Sure, I remember him from the flight over to Saudi and at the airfield.*

"Well, Anders, looks like we meet again," Neel said, not glancing up from the patient.

Anders looked confused. "Sir?"

"We came over on the plane together from Fort McCoy. Remember the girl at the disembarkation tent who had the status asthmaticus?"

Suddenly, Anders' eyes lit up. "Oh, yes, sir, I surely do

remember you. It's really good to see you again. I'm sorry it's under these circumstances, though,'' he said, looking sadly at the burned man on the litter.

That's right, son, Neel thought. *Life is tough, and it's going to get a whole lot tougher for all of us now.* He turned to the nurse and asked about the patient's vital signs.

''Well, Doctor, he's got a heartrate of one hundred and sixty-two and his respirations are labored at forty-four. I can't get a blood pressure cuff on him, because his arms are burned. I don't see how this medic even got IV's into him out there in the desert.'' She looked at Anders with admiration, and Neel saw Anders blush and turn from her gaze.

Neel had a dilemma. There were three other casualties, none as badly hurt as this man, and there were likely more on their way from other VII Corps firefights. To treat a burn such as this would be very time-consuming and he needed to help other casualties. He made his decision.

''Okay, keep this man on the litter, and keep giving him lactated Ringers. Insert a foley catheter and start intake and output recordings. I'll place him in the expectant category. If he's still alive when I'm done with the other casualties, I'll reevaluate.

Anders looked up sharply. *Set him aside for now?* Anders couldn't understand that. Sure, he had learned the categories of triage for wartime casualties, and understand their function, but he had never seen a decision made to withhold care from someone under that system. *What kind of a man is strong enough to make that kind of a decision about a person's life. I could never do that.*

Neel went from one casualty to another, assessing injuries and categorizing them by triage and treatment group. First, the patient who was unconscious with a possible basilar skull fracture required an x-ray of his skull and cervical spine. Their facility had a small, portable x-ray unit that could obtain these views with fairly good clarity, certainly acceptable under the circumstances.

Neel checked the other three casualties and tended to their wounds, none serious, while the x-rays were being processed. These men could be held by the facility for forty-eight hours and then either air-evacuated on low priority back to the rear, or sent by ground ambulance if one became available.

The radiology technician brought the films to Neel and he put them up on the field x-ray viewer. Most of the triage staff gathered around as he pointed out normal anatomy and assessed the films for injury. Anders was standing just next to Neel and was very curious about the loss of normal curvature of the cervical spine. Did that indicate a fracture, he asked?

"No, Anders, I don't see any fracture here. Notice how the anterior bodies of the vertebrae line up completely, with no overlapping or displacement. The cervical spine usually straightens out like that on an x-ray whenever there's been some sort of injury to the neck, like in a hyperflexion-hyperextension injury. The old "whip-lash." It's due to spasm of the paracervical spinal muscles and such an injury should be okay."

He turned then and walked back to the patient. He opened his eyelids and noticed the patient made a conscious effort to close them again. "Good," Neel said, to no one in particular, "looks like he's starting to come around."

"Hey, corporal," Neel said, looking at the two stripes on the tanker's collar. "Can you hear what I'm saying?"

The man moaned and moved his head a bit. Neel checked his reflexes and then turned to Anders. "Can your chopper transport this man to the nearest Evacuation Hospital on your return flight? I'm sure he's going to be fine, but he really needs a neurosurgeon to check him over. We can keep the others until ground transportation opens up or we can send them back to their unit."

Anders said he'd ask the pilot and scurried off to the aircraft.

As Neel was moving to the metal and plastic scrubsink to wash off the blood and charcoal from his hands, one of the wounded men called to him.

"Say, Doc, can I ask you a question?"

Neel grabbed a paper towel and walked over to the man. The patient's coughing and shortness of breath, probably due to acute smoke inhalation, had improved and he was able to talk without coughing. "Sure, what do you need to know?"

The man leaned over to him and then motioned with his head toward the burn patient. "Doc, is he going to make it?"

Neel shook his head. "I don't know, sergeant, he's in pretty bad shape and we really don't have the time or facilities here to work on him. By all rights, he probably won't. But, I was just going over to check him again. If he's still stable, I just can't let him go; I'll do my best for him, I assure you.''

The man grabbed Neel's shoulder. ''Doc, you got to save him. He saved our lives, pulled us out of that burning tank all by himself. Ain't no braver man than Sergeant Gonzales.''

Neel felt as if he had been slapped in the face. He stared hard at the man who had just talked to him. ''Sergeant Trinidad Gonzales?''

''Yes, sir, and he's the best.''

''How well I know, sergeant, how well I know.''

Neel moved quickly back to the burned man's litter. He looked again at the face, but still found it hard to believe this was Trinidad Gonzales. The man's face was swollen and dark with smoke and char. The eyes were swollen shut and a white eschar was starting to form on the neck.

''Lieutenant, what are his vital signs now?'' Neel shouted.

''Still about the same, major. He's starting to put out some urine now. I think we're not too far behind on the fluids.''

Neel went into action. *Damn the medical battalion policy. He was going to do what it took to keep this man alive and on the way to recovery. If he dies, it won't be my fault.*

''Sergeant Akins, get Captain Otto out of bed and tell him I'm going to take this patient to the operating room and I need his help. Also get the nurse anesthetist and the O.R. crew ready--we'll be there in five minutes. Oh, and one more thing. Call the corps medical evacuation officer and tell him we're shut down for additional casualties until further notice. It may be twelve hours before we're open again.''

Sergeant Akins whistled softly and shook his head. *This could mean a court-martial for the major; at least a serious reprimand. I'm glad I'm not in his shoes.* ''Yes, sir, you got it.'' Then he ran from the tent to find Captain Otto, the other surgeon.

Anders came back into the tent to report to Neel that the medivac crew just got permission to evacuate the head injury patient to the 13th Evacuation Hospital to see the neurosurgeon. As he walked up to Neel, he saw him gently place his hand on the hand of the burned tanker. When Major Neel looked up at Jay, his eyes were moist and he was blinking rapidly. Anders was immediately touched by the scene and turned his head out of embarrassment for Major Neel. But, on second thought, he looked up at the physician and smiled. He understood.

* * *

All the way back to the airfield, Tex Weatherby couldn't believe it. *How could those two tanks they fired on have been friendly? We got confirmation between the two of us, and then from the ground commander. Damn, could it have been another pair of tanks Perez saw instead of the ones I had seen? Maybe that Lieutenant Hanes in the tank thought we were talking about what he saw as two enemy tanks.*

If only I hadn't been so eager to get another kill, he thought. *I should have made a second recon run on that pair of tanks before hitting them. Maybe all of this wouldn't have happened. What am I going to do now?* he asked himself. *How can I live with myself after injuring my own fellow soldiers, even though it was unintentional and in the heat of a nighttime firefight?*

CWO2 Garner knew better than to say anything on the flight back to the base. Radio silence had been imposed by the captain after he ordered the flight of Apaches and Kiowas back. He knew Weatherby had a real temper if things didn't go right, and this was just about as bad as it could get for things going wrong. What Weatherby would do was anybody's guess. He sure didn't have the admiration of many people before this incident and now he doubted if even his mother would think much of him. Of course, Garner had to share in the blame, but he was the kind of man who could take it. But, everyone knew the aircraft commander called the shots and only took the advice of the weapons' officer when it suited him.

They landed at the air base in the dark, under a strong cross-wind. There was a desert storm in progress and sand whirled around them from wind and rotor action. After the rotors stopped, both men just sat in the cockpit, neither willing to get out and face the silent accusations of the rest of the squadron. Garner was sure the word had spread by now, as everyone back at the operations tent was well as regimental headquarters must have heard that tanker lieutenant's damning comments to Weatherby over the radio:

"Tango One, what in the hell did you do? You just hit two of my tanks. Didn't you see they were friendlies instead of hostile? You son of a bitch!"

Weatherby was too stunned to reply. He was hurt by the lieutenant's words. Somewhere beneath Tex's bravado shell, there existed a man with a lot of sentiment and decent values. But over the years he had been increasingly unable to express those feelings, and had turned himself into something of a cruel joke.

Finally, the two men left the Apache, walking separately and not speaking. When they entered the communications/command tent, the several aviators in the tent suddenly stopped talking. Weatherby crossed to a cooler and pulled out a cold Coke, pressing it against his forehead where his helmet had rubbed it raw. Then Tex turned to the men and addressed his squadron executive officer, Captain Hill. ''Ev, any calls from headquarters for me?''

Hill cleared his throat. ''Yes, Tex. The colonel called from brigade and asked if you could call him when you got back.''

Weatherby sighed and took a long swig of the Coke. ''Okay, get him on the horn for me, will you?'' He sat down in the chair next to the radiophone and crossed his legs.

Hill handed him the phone. ''Captain Weatherby here, Colonel.''

Colonel Smitts ran the battalion from brigade headquarters. ''Weatherby, are you okay?''

''Fine, sir, just fine. We just got back from the mission a few minutes ago. I guess you heard what happened?''

''Yes, Tex, I did. I'm real sorry and I know you are, too. Of course, we'll be conducting a full investigation. There will be a team coming over from the Aviation Safety Center at Rucker, but they're over in Riyadh right now investigating a Blackhawk that crashed into some high power lines. I don't know what the investigation will turn up, Tex, but as you know, they typically take months to complete. I could put you on administrative duty with no flying if you think I should.''

Weatherby didn't speak for a while. He knew he was physically fit enough to fly, but what about his mental state? He felt it would be worse if he just sat around doing nothing for months. Besides, he was the most experienced combat Apache pilot in the squadron and his men would be needing that experience.

''Sir, I don't feel grounding me would be of any help to anyone. I am the leader of this squadron, and if you'll let me, I'll continue to lead it.''

''Well, Tex, I'm going out on a limb for you, but if you think you can handle it, I'll trust your judgment. You may have some problems, but until now, there's never been any problem with your courage or flying skills. But you'd better remember, mister, there's more to being a good leader than hot flying. You've got to lead by example, and that example has got to be good. You hear me, captain?''

''Yes, sir, loud and clear,'' Tex replied, feeling red-faced and chastised.

''All right. Then go ahead with your job, but you will cooperate one hundred percent with the investigation and don't be risking yourself or your men on any action outside of your orders. I'll be in touch. Out here.''

Weatherby sat with the dead phone in his hand for several minutes before hanging up. *Well, I've got a second chance, or is it my third or fourth? This is it, Weatherby, you're flat out of chances. Either you straighten up or your career is finished.*

He turned and looked at the silent men in the room. ''Well, Colonel Smitts just told me I'm still the commander here and that I'm still on flying status. Roger, there will be an investigation team coming from Riyadh sometime soon. We need to be available to them and we will cooperate fully. Until then, we'll all do our jobs as best as we can and carry out our assigned missions. I'm just as sorry as hell this has happened, but I can't undo what was done. Much as I'd like to. You all will just have to trust me that things will get back on track again. I know I've been a real bastard sometimes; for whatever it's worth, I'm sorry. I'll take care of this by myself if I have to, but I'd certainly appreciate any support any of you wanted to give me.''

The men looked at each other, then at the floor. They really didn't know what to say. Weatherby had never, ever, apologized to anyone that they knew of, and had never asked for help.

''Ev, can you call and find out for me what happened to those tankers in the desert? I'd like to go visit them if I could.''

''Sure, Tex, I'll find out for you. Why don't you just go kick your feet up for a while. I'll take care of that and the debriefing with the other crews. I'll holler if I have any news.''

Weatherby nodded and stood up. As he walked toward the tent door, he stopped and put his big hand on Garner's shoulder. ''Roger, none of this was your doing tonight. It was my responsibility. So don't you be feeling guilty about it, you hear?'' Without waiting for a reply, Weatherby left the tent.

Garner swallowed hard and just stared at the doorway.

CHAPTER 12

"ONE THOUSAND ONE, one thousand two, one thousand three." Tatum counted the seconds as he had hundreds of times in the past. Suddenly, the parachute opened with a loud snap and his free fall stopped abruptly. He looked up in the darkness and saw the vague outline of his parachute canopy; it looked open and full. *Thank you God.*

He could not see the aircraft receding in the dark sky, but he could still hear the drone of its turbo-props. All above him were the mushroom-shaped outlines of hundreds of other parachutes from the dozens of C-130s and C-141s that had airdropped them on this assault. The descent was fast and quiet, except for the sounds of explosions and small-arms fire in the distance at the Republican Guard base.

Tatum turned his attention to the desert below and prepared for his landing. His M-16 rifle was in its canvas jump cover, strapped to his left side. The combat Alice pack was strapped to his lower legs below the knees and suspended from his harness with quick-release straps. It was difficult to judge height above the ground in the dark, especially in the desert with no trees to provide perspective, so he had to use his experience to tell when he was within a hundred feet of the ground. He reached down with both hands, pulled the pack straps and allowed it to fall to the end of its twenty-five foot cord below him. It would hit the ground first and warn him when he was about to land. With his hands on the parachute risers, he began to maneuver until the wind was in his face. He had preferred a right front parachute landing fall (PLF), and always tried to land that way whenever possible. In this instance, with his rifle strapped to his left side, it was preferable.

Avoiding the urge to look directly at the ground beneath him, Tatum tried to fix his gaze at what he estimated was maybe fifty yards ahead of his probable landing spot and let his reflexes take over. He pulled his body fully up into the risers of the parachute and tucked his helmeted head forward slightly, bracing it between the protective risers. As usual, when he landed, the PLF was automatic and over before he knew it. There was little breeze across the drop zone, so his chute collapsed quickly. He quickly surveyed his body and found no evidence of injury, a concern for all the paratroopers since they had not jumped in months. Although they had practiced PLFs with a makeshift Swing Landing Trainer at camp, that was no substitute for the real thing.

The desert sand was firmly packed, pretty much like the drop zones at Fort Benning and Fort Bragg. He had certainly landed on harder surfaces (like the airport runway on Grenada from five hundred feet), and Tatum was up on his feet in a minute. Pulling the wire ring quick-releases on his chest harness, he shrugged out of it and began wrapping the parachute shrouds around the harness arm over arm as he had been doing for fourteen years of jumping. Tatum deposited the bundle on a sand rise, where it could be picked up later if the division decided to, and ran to choose an assembly area for his squad.

Using low calls and whistles, Tatum located all of his squad but one. PFC Harper was nowhere to be found. Tatum sent Tom James and Doc out to scour the area, and they came back about five minutes later, carrying Harper between them. They gently sat Harper on the sand while Doc probed Harper's left ankle. He howled in agony as Doc tried to move the foot back and forth.

"Sarge," Doc said, without looking up, "Harper's got a busted ankle. As long as it's in his boot, he'll feel better and it will be as stable as a splint. I'll give him some morphine and splint it to his gun case to make him comfortable."

Tatum knew Harper wouldn't be able to complete the mission. "O.K., Doc, I hear you. Harper, you have to stay here. We'll go on, but they'll send a medical team to clear the drop zone of casualties, and they'll take care of you."

Harper nodded. He was relieved and chagrined at the same time. He knew he would no longer be in harm's way, but at the same time he hated to let down his fellow troopers.

Tatum stood up and moved closer to the rest of his squad. He could barely see them in the dark. "Listen up, men. We've got to stick together and link up with the rest of the platoon. That's due east over there," he said, pointing with his arm after checking his luminescent compass. "We'll be meeting the platoon at the northeast sector of the DZ, so let's move out."

He turned to Doc and Harper. ''Doc, you got him fixed up all right?''

''Yeah, sarge, I decided to put one of those pneumatic splints on his leg that you recommended I bring along. It'll work better than the gun case. I'm ready.''

Tatum leaned down and squeezed Harper's shoulder. ''Don't fret, Harper, you'll be okay. We'll come visit you when this is over. Every five minutes or so, just call out and the pickup team will find you.''

Harper smiled bravely. ''You all give 'em hell, for me Sarge, all right?''

''Right, son, we'll give them hell all right. Airborne, all the way!'' With that, Tatum turned and jogged with Doc to catch up with James and the rest of the squad.

It was easy to find the rest of the platoon. Lt. Schiller had posted a rear guard with a red flare, who was making circles in the air with it. As they arrived, Schiller called the squad leaders together and quickly reviewed the situation and the operational plan.

''The word is that there were fewer injuries on the drop than expected. We've got nearly 1200 men in the battalion ready to assault the objective and we'll move out in, let's see, about eight minutes. As you could see from the air, the SF guys and the Air Force have already worked the place over, but their current sitrep report is that the Guard is coming out of undestroyed bunker areas and forming a hasty defense. The primary assault will take place at the west side of the base, here and here.'' Schiller had drawn a crude sand map of the base, and pointed to the western perimeter.

''Alpha Company will handle the main assault, with Bravo flanking to the south and east. Our company will provide a blocking force to the north, to prevent the enemy from escaping across the river. We don't know exactly where the SF team is, so make sure you have a positive ID on anyone before firing. We'll move out in full platoon, column formation at double-time. Have your men load and lock, but keep safeties on until we receive fire. Any questions?''

The squad leaders quickly returned to their men and briefed them. Most were silent, engrossed in their own thoughts about what lay ahead.

With a hand signal, Schiller motioned the platoon forward.

They started off disjointedly, but after forming into column formation by twos, they got the hand signal for double-time. Picking up their legs to run in the desert, this platoon of physically fit men began covering the ground to the objective quickly and efficiently. All their movable gear had been taped or velcroed in place, so the movement was surprisingly quiet for fifty or so men and their gear. Rifles at port arms, these paratroopers looked every bit the fighting machine they had been trained to be.

As they approached the northern perimeter of the Republican Guard base, Schiller slowed the double-time and they walked slowly around the barbed wire fence. Beyond the fence was a tall sand berm and between the berm and fence was reportedly a mine field, which would be breached by shoulder-mounted rockets to create a wide swath of safe passage. The mine fields would only be cleared in the areas held by the U.S. paratroops, so as to control the exit of the Republican Guard elements from the base.

Schiller positioned the squads along a five-hundred-yard length of the perimeter, assigning a sector to each rocket team for destruction of the barriers on his command. Tatum divided his men into two-man teams and set them digging team foxholes in the sand. After less than thirty minutes, the platoon was entrenched in its sector of the perimeter, awaiting the Iraqi counter attack.

* * *

Porter was crouched behind a large piece of concrete which, until an hour ago, had been part of a guardhouse at one of the entrances to the Iraqi base. With a C-4 charge, he had blown it up by remote control just as a cruise missile slammed into the Guard bunkers. Porter didn't know the U.S. had a cruise missile that could be dropped from a B-52 bomber high over the target. Porter never even heard the huge airplane. The last transmission of mission orders to him in the desert had advanced the attack on the Republican Guard base in Iraq by nearly a full day and it had been a scramble for the team to prepare for their role.

The orders outlined a low-level attack on the base by fighter and bomber aircraft that would likely be detected by radar bases surrounding the area, so the Republican Guard would be prepared for an assault. It was not possible for the SF team to destroy all the radar installations in the remaining time, so it was apparently decided to use the secret cruise missile delivered by a high-flying B-52. Since B-52s had been flying over Iraq for well over six weeks now, the Iraqis no longer paid much attention to them.

The modified cruise missile, the AGM-86C, had been equipped with a two-thousand-pound concrete and steel-penetrating warhead. Intelligence compiled from satellites as well as through reconnaissance by special operations units in Iraq, had shown the Republican Guard bases were huge underground concrete bunkers. They had only one entrance/exit but many air vent shafts to filter gases and chemicals. A two-foot-thick concrete slab covered the entire underground complex, with at least three feet of sand plowed over the concrete roof. The living modules for the Iraqi soldiers were pressurized chambers connected to a central tubular corridor running the length of the underground complex. There were modules for a sick bay, kitchen, armories, food, and water, as well as a command center. The Iraqis thought them impenetrable.

All this information had been sent to Porter's modular display receiver by burst transmission two days ago. He had been expecting a mission involving the Guard, and had held some planning sessions with his team even before receiving the actual plans. He had originally worked out details for the entire team participating in the assault, but yesterday, Hussein and his men had brought a wounded Navy flier to their camp.

Porter had made the necessary arrangements by satellite communications with CENTCOM and two of his men were currently making their way with the flyer to a rendezvous point in the desert with a rescue helicopter team. That left him with only nine team members to coordinate and support this assault from inside the enemy base.

They had arrived early in the night and checked the actual layout of the base with the information they had been sent by CENTCOM G-2. Much to their relief, the information was surprisingly accurate. They had breached the mine field slowly, locating and deactivating each pressure-sensitive mine, using a state-of-the-art device that demagnetized the arming mechanisms and allowed them to dig up the devices and discard them. Once inside the perimeter, they donned desert camouflage-colored Kevlar ponchos and quietly set explosive charges on their targets. Although they knew the approximate time the B-52 would be over the base with its missiles, they wanted to get their jobs done and back out to the relative safety of the sand berm perimeter as soon as possible.

There was no warning when the two cruise missiles hit the bunkers. If Porter hadn't been looking directly at them through his night vision goggles, he wouldn't have seen the suddenly-appearing white ''telephone pole'' object that slid into the desert sand over the bunker's concrete roof. The resultant explosion was muffled, but it shook the ground like an earthquake. Seconds later, the other cruise missile penetrated the other bunker with similar effect. Secondary explosions occurred in buildings next to the bunkers, presumably from electrical fires and fuel ignition. They were followed by serial detonations of charges placed by the SF team members on selected targets. First, the radar dish exploded and toppled; next, the ammunition supply dump exploded in a spectacular series of fireworks. Then came the destruction of the lesser targets, including the guardhouses at the gates and the motor pool fuel tanks. By the time the paratroopers exited their aircraft for the drop zone a mile away, the base was in a state of self-destruction and mass confusion.

However, there was still a sizable resistance being organized by the Iraqis. Apparently, hundreds of soldiers were not killed or injured in the bunkers and they began streaming out of the exits. Those who were working above ground or living outside of the bunkers were still to be reckoned with as well.

Porter peeked around the concrete slab. Because of the light generated by the fires and explosions, he had put away his night-vision goggles and could still see pretty well. Each team member carried an FM transmitter/receiver with a ''hands-free'' microphone headset for communications during the operation. He voice-activated the set. ''Lopez and Santori, come in.''

''Yeah, boss, Lopez here.''

''Ditto, Santori in.''

Porter reactivated the mike. ''Did you account for all of the charges detonated? We can't have our airborne guys getting hurt with an unexploded charge.''

Santori replied. ''I'm not sure the charge went off at the big radio antenna. Could be I didn't set the high frequency RF low enough. I'd better check it.''

Porter thought a minute. ''All right, Santori, but be careful. Don't expose yourself yet. Wait five minutes, then crawl out. If the charge was bad, don't fool with it, just fire it with a grenade.''

''Aw, Lieutenant, that's cheating. I can fix it if it's bad,''

Santori boasted.

"You heard me, sergeant. Now wait five and go. The rest of us will hold our positions."

"Roger, LT."

Porter could see the Iraqis becoming more organized in forming a hasty defense for their base. The U.S. paratroopers had yet to show up and the Iraqis still unaware what was really happening. But Porter knew that wouldn't last once the airborne arrived.

He watched Santori quietly and stealthily slip along the shadows toward the RF radio antenna. But when he got within four or five feet of the antenna, there was a terrific white blast and Santori was thrown backwards about twenty feet. The antenna swayed and then came down right onto Santori's body.

Oh my God, Porter thought. *Is he still alive?* Porter was sweating and ready to spring into action when he saw Sergeant Lopez dash out. Lopez was bent over Santori when, somewhere from the right came a blast of automatic fire, cutting into Lopez and dropping him over the antenna. There was no movement from either man.

Porter called over the radio: "Lopez, Santori, are you all right? Talk to me."

Silence.

He repeated the call, but there was no response and no movement from the bodies.

From the corner of his eye, he saw two figures running toward his two men. Porter shouldered his CAR-15 and fired a thirty-round clip into both runners. They fell motionless to the ground. *All right,* he thought, *the shit has hit the fan.*

He raised up and dashed toward the antenna, his rifle ready and pointed toward the fallen Iraqi soldiers. So far, no other enemy soldiers had apparently heard the shots in all the confusion, but Porter knew that couldn't last.

When he reached the two men, Porter rolled Lopez's body over. Shot in the back of the head, he had two ugly exit wounds where his eyes had once been. Porter felt immediately nauseous and fought the urge to vomit. Lopez was the team "daddy." Santori was dead, too, although Porter could not tell whether the blast or the antenna had killed him. Taking what ammunition he could reach, Porter dragged Lopez's body back to the concrete slab and had turned to return for Santori when CWO2 Billy Nichols and Sergeant Willie Davis came running up carrying Santori's body.

"We've got to leave them here for now, Billy," Porter said, "They're going to tumble to us soon, so we'd better get back to the northern perimeter and wait for the paratroopers. We can observe the activity in the camp from the sand berm and pass along information to them from there."

Davis looked at Porter with anguish. He and Santori had been close friends. "LT, I just can't leave them here. I can carry both of them if I have to. They're my brothers, man."

Porter understood. It would slow them down getting to the perimeter, and make them more easily observed, but Davis was right. "You're right, Willie, let's take them with us. Call in the others, and we'll divide up the equipment so we can carry them."

The remaining seven men congregated at the stone slab and quietly shouldered the two bodies and the remaining equipment. Porter led them behind the burning motor pool into the desert toward the northern sand berm.

* * *

Lieutenant Schiller crawled over to Tatum's position. "Your men ready, sergeant?" he whispered.

"Yes, sir, we've got the blasting team up front, with the rest of the fire teams set up in a lazy circle next to them." Tatum nodded just ahead of his foxhole.

"Good. I just got an FM transmission from the SF lieutenant who's out there in the camp. He and his team are coming our way to set up just behind the sand berm. Don't shoot them, and don't blast the berm until we know they're clear, O.K.?"

Tatum nodded. He had a lot of respect for the special operations men, and although he didn't know a great deal about their current mission, he knew it had to be plenty dangerous.

He had his eyes trained on the sand berm about a hundred meters in the distance, when he thought he saw a dark object drop down behind. Then came another, and another, and finally, he estimated there were roughly nine dark forms there. *I hope those are the Green Berets, and I hope they see us, too.*

Tatum was worried about sand getting in his M-16, but there wasn't much he could do about it now. He had kept it as clean as possible before the jump, and had placed a condom over the end of the barrel after he removed it from the jump case. But there was no way to keep the sand out of the firing mechanism and no time now to field strip it. He'd just have to pray the Good Lord was looking out for him.

What were they waiting for? I thought Alpha company should have attacked across the western perimeter by now. Why didn't someone do something or at least tell them what was happening. The waiting was always the hardest, so Tatum decided to do something. He crawled out of his foxhole and made his way over to the left flank of his squad's position.

"Airborne," he whispered, not wanting to startle any of his men and cause an incident. "Oh, sarge, it's you," Private Miller said with relief. Miller looked about fifteen years old in his foxhole, with a helmet too big for his head, and all those pimples on his face. "Wha-, what's happening out there, sarge?"

"It's okay, Miller," Tatum whispered. "Something's going to happen soon, I think. Just stay cool, and keep your head down. Watch what James does and stick close to him." He nodded to James who had decided to team up with Miller. Tatum knew James was going to protect Miller if he could. He poked each of them on the shoulder. "Well, I'm going to check on everyone else, you all seem to be fine."

James grinned and nodded.

As Tatum went from foxhole to foxhole, he realized how much he cared for these men. They all came from such different walks of life--black, white, city or country, northerner, southerner. None of that mattered now. All that mattered was working as a team, getting the mission accomplished, and trying to stay alive. They'd protect each other.

When Tatum got back to his own foxhole, Top O'Reilley was waiting. Tatum was a big man, but Pug O'Reilley was bigger. There wasn't room enough for both of them in the foxhole, so Tatum crouched on the sand outside.

"Tatum," O'Reilley growled, "it's going to go down any minute now. Only we won't get into it unless the A-RAB bastards come our way." He pronounced Arab as if it were two words. "You saw that SF team out there on the berm ahead of us?"

Tatum nodded.

"Well, it's our job to get those guys out of here safely, if they get into trouble. I guess they know too much about top secret stuff, and the brass don't want them captured. Got it?"

"Got it, Top." *What was there to get? Everyone wanted out of there alive.*

O'Reilley stood up. Towering over Tatum, he looked like a huge statue in the desert. "All right, then, I'll let you know if anything else comes down." With that, he turned and walked away, not bothering to crouch or crawl. Tatum knew O'Reilley didn't particularly like Blacks; but then he didn't much like Protestants, Jews, Orientals or just about anybody else who wasn't Irish-Roman Catholic. He probably couldn't help it, Tatum thought, growing up with all those other O'Reilleys in Chicago.

But he never had caused Tatum or any of the other black NCO's any trouble, so they tolerated each other. Even so, Tatum felt a little angry whenever he was around such a bigot. *On the other hand,* Tatum thought, *I don't really like slick-talking, privileged white officers much either, so maybe Top and I are really more alike than different.*

Then all hell broke loose to the west. Explosions from the berm-blasting rockets created a sudden bright light, followed by small arm and machine gun fire. Each man in the platoon tensed up and looked away from the firefight so as not to decrease his night vision. The battle heated up with the firing of grenade launchers and shoulder-mounted Redeye missiles. Then, the attack came from the south by Bravo company and carried around to the east. The Republican Guard troops were being caught in a vise, with their only escape route right over Charlie Company and Tatum's platoon.

* * *

Porter watched the battle through his night vision goggles. Whenever the Iraqis seemed to be organizing their men for a counterattack, he called that information to the airborne company commanders. By direct observation, he could direct mortar fire from the airborne battalion's heavy weapons platoon, from about two thousand feet behind the western perimeter. With Porter controlling the mortars, they were severely punishing the Iraqi troops in the compound.

Porter sensed before he saw, that the Iraqis were moving the fight farther north, toward his sector. He radioed the Charlie Company commander behind him that he thought the Iraqis were going to attempt a breakout toward the northern perimeter, probably to reach the river. Then he keyed the team's FM radio and voice-activated it.

"All right, men, now listen up. It looks to me like the enemy is going to try to break out here through us any minute. Everyone agree?" There was muttered asssent. "They'll probably send a recon in force at us first, to test how strong we are. If we can knock them back, maybe the main force will stay in the compound and be captured. If not, they'll probably make for the river and head for Basra."

Everyone knew what to do. They laid all their weapons on their Kevlar ponchos. Grenades, automatic rifle ammunition, LAWs (light automatic weapon), and a variety of personal weapons. Normally, special forces soldiers did not make a stand-and-fight position; instead, they were hit-and-run or clandestine. Even so, they were all well-trained in weaponry and conventional warfare.

Porter saw a large group of Iraqi soldiers moving their way. He took off his night-vision goggles and set them aside--he wouldn't use them in a close-up firefight anyway.

When the Iraqis came within range, running quickly through the sand, Porter began the action by firing his CAR-15 at the center of the enemy cluster, taking down three men immediately. The rest of his team opened up, laying down a deadly hail that nearly wiped out the attackers. The few living Iraqis fled, leaving their dead and wounded on the sand in front of the Americans. Keeping a close watch in case any of the enemy wounded would fire again, Porter inserted a fresh clip and waited.

*   *   *

Tatum heard the firing, but could not see the enemy because of the sand berm. He was tensed and ready for action, but relaxed when the firing ceased. He understood the Iraqis were probing for a way out of the trap and would probably hit the northern perimeter again, but not directly against the Green Berets next time.

Suddenly, there were explosions over on the left flank of his platoon position, and he wondered who had given the order to the rocket team to blast a path in the berm. Then, he saw a large force of enemy soldiers coming across the perimeter east of the Green Berets, toward his second squad's position. He raised up in his foxhole and hollered to his own squad: "Up and out of your foxholes. Over to the left flank to support second squad!"

He charged to the left just in time to see at least twenty Iraqis running and jumping over the crushed barbed wire fence. Tatum ran up behind a foxhole and knelt behind it, firing full automatic. One Iraqi soldier went down, then another. Then men in the foxhole in front of Tatum opened up with an M-60 machine gun and several more Iraqis fell. By then, the rest of his squad had reinforced the line and were laying down heavy suppressive fire onto the advancing Iraqis.

There was a loud explosion to his right, and sand kicked up all around Tatum, covering him with a sticky wet substance. At first, Tatum thought he had been hit, but he felt no pain. He looked over and saw a dark crater where the adjacent foxhole had been, with two dark clumps alongside it. A grenade had landed in the foxhole and blown up its human contents.

"Doc, Doc, get over here right away," Tatum hollered, as he crawled over to the bodies, firing as he did.

Doc came crawling up quickly, his glasses almost sliding off the end of his nose. "Jeez, Sarge, these guys have had it." Tatum looked at the medic and then at the bodies. "I guess you're right, Doc. Sorry."

By then, more Iraqis had begun pouring through the breach in the perimeter, moving toward the second platoon. Third platoon had begun to move over from its westernmost position, but the Iraqis had blown an opening in the mine field over there, and were trying to exit their camp on both sides of the Special Forces position. The whole company was in a firefight with a lot of Iraqis who seemed to be increasing in number as they located more breaches in the perimeter.

Several Iraqis made it to the platoon's position. Tatum rose to his feet and charged an Iraqi soldier who had just shot an American paratrooper in his foxhole. Not having time to replace an empty clip, Tatum brought the buttplate of his rifle up into a vicious swing, hitting the Iraqi in the face. He dropped and did not move. Running to the left, where his men had deployed, Tatum ejected a 30-round clip, inserted a new one, and flipped his selector back to automatic.

He glimpsed a figure from the corner of his right eye, and turned just in time to fire from the hip at an Iraqi soldier coming directly at him, with his AK-47 raised. Without pausing to see if the man was dead, Tatum moved forward. He saw PFC Miller on his back in the sand, struggling with an enemy soldier who was trying to plunge a knife into the young man's chest.

Tatum made a diving drive into the enemy soldier, just as he used too as a star fullback on his high school football team in D.C. The Iraqi went down and lost his knife. Tatum grabbed the man by the throat and squeezed as hard as he could, crushing the man's larynx.

Miller was still on the ground transfixed. Tatum grabbed his LBE and yanked him to his feet. ''Get your rifle and come with me, Miller.'' Miller picked up his rifle, checked the clip and moved forward with Tatum, still trembling.

''Damn, Sarge, you saved my life,'' he stammered.

''Well, Miller, you can name your first son after me, if you're so grateful,'' Tatum replied, out of breath and pumped up with adrenaline.

Name my son Lucius? Well, O.K., I guess I can.

The two troopers came up behind Corporal James who had commandeered an M60 machine gun and was firing it standing up. ''Miller, get some more ammunition for this thing,'' James hollered. ''It's over there, next to those two bodies.'' The three men formed a strong point, firing on Iraqis coming through the breach by the scores. They were holding their own, but barely.

Back at the far right flank of the squad's position, Corporal Sly Rodriguez and Private Jesse Jones were waiting for the Iraqis to try to break past their foxhole. Just behind a portion of the barbed wire fence that had not been blown, the two men figured they could limit the opportunity of the enemy soldiers to outflank the American paratroopers and overrun them.

Jones and Rodriguez were complete opposites in this firefight; the former was in a state of frenzied hyperactivity and excitement, while the latter was as calm and under as much control as anyone could be under the circumstances.

Jones wanted to take the fight to the enemy, constantly urging Rodriguez to come with him and charge into the breach, while Rodriguez was satisfied to wait in the foxhole, observing the activity and planning.

Six enemy soldiers were making their way along the end of the intact sand berm, moving cautiously. One of the Iraqis had a large, hand-held radio and Rodriguez figured he was an officer. The other men were scooping out an area behind the berm to set up a light machine gun behind.

"Hey, man," Jones whispered excitedly. "What we gonna do about those guys? We can't hit them from here, and our grenades are going to fall short--they're just too far away."

Rodriguez was thinking. There was only open ground between them and the enemy soldiers, who had the sand berm for added protection. Trying to lob grenades would be a long shot all right. Since the Iraqis were on the other side of the berm, a grenade would have to hit very close to the top and roll down toward them. The only way that could happen was for someone to crawl over and toss the grenade exactly where it needed to be.

The enemy machine gun began firing, kicking up sand about fifty meters to their left at a group of Americans who had been firing from a prone position at the oncoming enemy soldiers. The men heard several screams of pain as the machine gun hit its targets.

Rodriguez made up his mind. He reached into his BDU pocket and pulled out a smoke grenade. "Here, Jones," he said, "when I say so, you throw that grenade as close to the machine gun as possible. Then lay down fire about four feet above the sand at where you remember the Iraqis are. I'm going to slip under the smoke and knock them out."

Jones stared at Rodriguez in horror. There was nothing to hide behind in that hundred meters between them and the Iraqi machine gun nest. Who knew how long the smoke would last or even if it might get blown away too quickly?

"Man, you can't do that, that's suicide. Let's get some mortar fire on it and let them knock it out."

"We don't have time, Jesse," he said, using the black man's first name for once. He put his hand back into the BDU jacket and came out with some black camouflage paint. After opening the lid, he placed two fingers in the paint and then made two streaks along each cheek. Turning to Jones, he grinned. "Just like when we used to get the white man circled in his wagons, hey?"

Jones couldn't help laughing at this crazy soldier. He grabbed the smoke grenade and pulled the pin. Just before throwing it, he looked over at the Indian and said, "Good luck, man, I'll come to you when you holler for me, okay?"

Rodriguez nodded.

Jones threw the grenade as far as he could toward the Iraqi

machine gun position. In high school, Jones had been an excellent athlete, participating in all sports. He had hoped to go to college on an athletic scholarship, but none had come his way. Probably no one had been too interested in a black kid from Harlem. But, after his stint in the Army, he was going to use the G.I. Bill and go to City College in New York. No one knew it, but he really wanted to be a high school coach. He hoped he got his chance.

The throw was true. The smoke grenade billowed dense white smoke just in front of the Iraqis and Jones followed up with three-shot bursts from his M-16, firing just four feet above the desert floor. He hoped Rodriguez kept his head down.

Rodriguez slipped out of the foxhole as soon as the smoke began to form, running in a very low crouch, bent almost double. He would run fast for a few steps, then slow down and repeat the cycle, making himself as unobtrusive as possible. He looked to his left and saw several Iraqi soldiers looking his way, which made him stop motionless. They made no attempt to shoot at him; maybe they couldn't see him.

Then Rodriguez was into the dense smoke and he increased his speed, running almost up onto the berm before he realized it. He flattened against the north slope, listening to the Iraqi machine gun firing very close to his right ear. This wasn't going to be easy. The only certain way to kill all the enemy soldiers was to climb the sand berm about fifteen feet west and throw his grenades where he could see them. Rodriguez rolled left and crawled quickly along the sandy slope for about fifteen feet. He dug his toes into the sand and charged.

As soon as he reached the top, Rodriguez looked and saw the enemy--just as their officer spotted him. Throwing a grenade with each hand, he yelled out an Indian war whoop that must have frozen the officer. Horrified, the Iraqis watched the grenades come their way and made no attempt to flee. Rodriguez's surprise attack had worked. When the grenades blew, the machine gun nest was gone.

Jones had heard the Indian whoop and the explosions. Quickly he rose out of the foxhole and ran toward the berm. Two other men from the squad joined him from the left. They had seen what Rodriguez had done and came over to help.

When Jones got to the berm, he couldn't see Rodriguez on the north side. Flipping the selector on his rifle to full automatic, he crawled slowly over the berm. All the Iraqis were dead. The machine gun was twisted. At first, he did not see any sign of his friend, but then he saw a dark clump to the east, along the peak of the berm. Running over, he saw Rodriguez was clutching his stomach. Jones was nauseated by the amount of blood on his friend and on the sand around him.

He kneeled down and cradled his friend's head in his lap. He no longer was aware of the firefight, only the face of his friend.

Not a word was said at first. Rodriguez's face was contorted in pain. Then, he seemed to relax and smiled, looking up at Jones. "Don't die on me, Sly, hang on until the medics get here!" Jones pleaded.

Sly shook his head. "My grandfather is here to take me home," he said. "We will ride the wings of the great white eagle to the high mountain summit. There, don't you see them?" The Indian gestured with his hand, then closed his eyes and died.

Jones just sat there, tears forming, wondering about the courage of a man who would risk near certain death to charge an enemy machine gun nest. The world was upside down for Jones and all he could do was stare into his friend's face.

"Come on, Jones, let's get out of here. I'll help you carry Sly's body back to the squad line," one of the other men said. "It's too dangerous out here."

Jones rose and lifted his friend's body onto his shoulder. "No, thanks, man. I can bring him back." Even in death, Sly felt light as a feather to Jones.

At the center of the American line, Tatum and his men were in the middle of an intense firefight. Two waves of Iraqis had come through the breach and were putting pressure on the paratrooper defense.

Suddenly, from nowhere, Pug O'Reilley began firing an old-fashioned .45-cal Thompson submachine gun that made him look just like some military hoodlum. "Tatum," he bellowed, "pull your men back in stagger about a hundred yards. They're going to send some helicopters to pull us out of here. We're going just up north to the river to join the 101st to block these bastards from escaping in force."

Tatum told James and Miller to move back and to get the rest of the squad started back to the pickup zone. As they left, Tatum turned to his right and shot an Iraqi who was hiding behind an American body and pointing a rifle their way. Tatum shot him, but not before the Itaqi got off several rounds. Tatum heard O'Reilley grunt and turned in time to see him fall backwards.

Running to him and kneeling beside the man, Tatum saw he had two spreading red stains across the front of his camouflage blouse and there was blood frothing from his mouth. Tatum knew it was bad.

''Top, you're going to be okay,'' he said, as he stuffed a large field dressing under his shirt where the bleeding was profuse.

''Bullshit, Tatum,'' the man rasped and coughed. ''I've had it and you know it. Do something for me man.'' He took another breath and coughed up a mouthful of bright red blood. ''Get my crucifix from around my neck.''

First, Tatum checked and saw no Iraqis in the immediate vicinity. He pulled Pug's shirt collar back and separated a chain with a crucifix on it from the man's dog tags and broke it loose, placing it in O'Reilly's big hand. The first sergeant put it to his lips and kissed it, leaving a blood stain on the cross.

''Tatum, you've got to do something for me. If you make it, give this crucifix to my daughter, Anita, in Chicago.''

Tatum took the cross and wrapped the chain around his hand. ''Sure, Top, I'll do that for you.''

Pug motioned for Tatum to put his ear close to his mouth. His breathing was labored and wet. ''Tatum, you're not bad for a ....,'' and lapsed into a coughing fit.

Okay, you're going to say 'for a nigger or a black man, aren't you, and I'm going to have to take it.

But O'Reilley finished his sentence. ''For a...a Baptist,'' and started laughing, a laugh that became a choking spell that stopped abruptly.

''Top, Top,'' Tatum shouted. He shook the man, but saw the unseeing glaze in the eyes and knew he was dead. Tatum felt awful thinking the worst of this man, who really wasn't as bad as he had thought. A man who, in his dying wish, had thought of his church and his daughter.

Tatum lowered him to the ground and grabbed him by the shoulders, dragging him along the desert sand toward the rear. He had gone about fifteen yards when an Iraqi suddenly appeared in front of him, taking aim at Tataum with an AK-47. Tatum's rifle was slung on his shoulder so he could get O'Reilley's body back to the helicopter and he was defenseless. Bracing for the bullets that would surely fell him, Tatum was surprised to see the enemy soldier drop his rifle and fall backwards, dead before he hit the ground.

Miller and James ran up, having just arrived, shooting the enemy soldier before he could get Tatum. "Does this mean I don't have to name my first son after you, Sarge?" Miller said with a chuckle.

That man was growing up fast, Tatum decided. "Thanks, guys. No, Miller, you don't have to worry about that any more, son."

"Well, Sarge, maybe I will after all," Miller replied.

The two young men took Top's body from Tatum and began to carry him toward the waiting helicopters. Suddenly, Tatum stopped short. *The Special Forces men! What was it Top had said to him back at the foxhole? Weren't we supposed to help them back to the choppers if we had to leave?*

He turned to James. "Tom, get the squad loaded on the chopper. I've got to go back and tell the Green Berets we're leaving and show them the way back here. If I'm not back in five minutes, go without me."

James started to shout a protest, but Tatum had already taken off back toward the berm.

Tatum jumped across several foxholes, tripping once over a dead Iraqi. When he stood, he faced two very lively enemy soldiers turning in his direction. They were as surprised as he. Bringing up the M-16, Tatum started firing before the muzzle was pointed in their direction. The first man fell in a heap, but the second crouched to one knee and fired a round that caught Tatum in the side. Burning erupted in his stomach, but Tatum managed to kill the enemy and resume his run toward the SF soldiers' last position. As he ran, he stuffed his last field dressing inside his shirt over the wound.

Still strong, but short of breath, he stumbled across the barbed wire fence and ran haltingly toward the sand berm where he spotted the Americans. When he reached them, they all looked dead. Around them were at least fifty dead Iraqis, many of whom must have been killed by hand-to-hand combat. *My Lord, those men really saw Hell before they died. Please deliver them in Your Hands,* he prayed.

He went from man to man, but found no one alive on the north side of the berm. Looking over the side to be thorough, he saw an American officer lying outstretched over two Iraqi soldiers, a bloody Ka Bar in his hands. Expecting to find him dead, too, Tatum rolled him over dejectedly. However, the officer moaned and jerked. Kneeling as best he could with his side wound, Tatum saw the man was a lieutenant. He couldn't make out the name because of the blood stains. The LT also had a large thigh wound on his left leg that may have been from an AK-47.

But, the man was alive, so Tatum did his duty. When he tried to lift him on the first try he fell onto his knees. Mustering his strength and grunting, Tatum was able to shoulder the officer, getting first to one knee, then the other. He staggered over the berm and nearly fell down the other side. Looking back, he noticed something was unusual about the Special Forces soldiers. Finally, he realized they had fought to their deaths wearing their green berets, the final symbol of the eliteness they all were and deserved to be.

Tatum struggled each step of the way, stumbling occasionally, but staying on his feet. At last he saw the helicopters. He tried to move faster, but the pain in his side was almost unbearable. The last helicopter was hovering about two feet off the ground and Corporal James and Private Miller were motioning with their arms, yelling at him to hurry.

Just then, several bullets whizzed past Tatum's head, so close he could feel them. He turned slightly, regretting the move and the pain it caused and saw about six Iraqis coming over a rise behind him. The men in the helicopter were firing back over his head and he kept it down as much as he could.

There, only ten more feet. Now just five. Then he had the lieutenant up off his shoulder, as James and Miller yanked him off his back. They laid the badly wounded officer on the floor of the helicopter and Miller reached out for Tatum, as James laid down suppressive fire at the oncoming Iraqis. Tatum was exhausted, but he stretched out his arms and opened his hands to catch Miller's. Just then something shiny tumbled from his right hand and fell to the ground. *What was that? Oh, no. That was the Top's crucifix. I've got to give it to his daughter, just like I promised. I promised a dying man.*

He stopped and bent over, looking for the crucifix in the

swirling sand of the desert floor. Just as he found it and grasped it in his hand, he was suddenly hit in the back and legs by many blows from a huge sledgehammer. He could stand no longer and sank down onto the sand, face first.

Tatum felt himself almost floating up to the helicopter as hands lifted him into the door. They laid him on the floor next to the unconscious Green Beret lieutenant. Tatum felt as if he were swirling into a dark, cold pit. He couldn't stop the sinking and the voices around him sounded so distant. Then he saw Mary and the kids in front of him. They were really there, running toward him, arms outstretched. But the faster he ran toward them, the more they seemed to recede. He felt himself coming to a halt and watching them disappear. The last thing he felt was the warm crucifix in his cold hand.

CHAPTER 13

THE PICKUP SPOT for the wounded Navy pilot was in the same sector as Tex's previous rendezvous with the Special Forces team. Weatherby rechecked the computer on the Apache's inertial guidance system and saw the same coordinates on the data screen that had been programmed there in the previous hour. The orders had come to the squadron from CENTCOM headquarters, which coordinated all SAR (Search and Rescue) efforts in the Gulf war. So far, only one crash had no survivors, a C-130 carrying a load of special operations agents and crew, which had crashed in the desert of southern Iraq.

Weatherby was still commanding the squadron. The investigating team had arrived at the helicopter firebase, and interviewed everyone involved, including a grueling four-hour talk with Weatherby. They had replayed the tapes of the mission and even talked to some of the men on the ground with the 3rd Armored. So far, no one had given Tex any idea what their findings might be. Trying to put the problem out of his mind, but never really able to forget it, Weatherby had decided that since he and Garner had patroled this sector on another medevac mission, he should escort the medical helicopter himself.

There were mixed sentiments around the attack helicopter base about the incident. Perez and his weapons officer felt as badly as Weatherby and Garner, and the other pilots generally supported Perez. On the other hand, because of Weatherby's arrogant attitude and his general disregard for the others, many were willing to prejudge him guilty of dereliction. Garner had tried to describe the confusing situation to many of the men, citing the frenzy of the firefight, the darkness, the bad weather, and the conversations with the ground commander, but most were willing to believe the worst about Weatherby.

Tex had spoken to no one about the incident, other than the investigators. He always felt he could handle his own problems and work them out without help from anyone else. However, this one was really hurting his gut...and his heart. There were times he thought about seeking out the battalion chaplain or the flight surgeon and asking for help.

But he was as strong as he was stubborn, so he was still keeping his feelings to himself. No one, even his old buddy, Ev Hill, could seem to get through that hard crusty shell Weatherby had erected after the incident. While some thought it was the same old Weatherby, Hill and Garner knew different; this was a reaction they had never seen in Tex Weatherby. Garner thought it was because he had been really hurt by the event and had trouble talking about it with anyone.

Garner was right. Weatherby was experiencing some serious introspection and had learned a lot about himself and what the others had thought about him.

Besides the medevac mission, the squadron had been assigned to support the 1st Armored in its drive up the eastern side of the Wadi al Batim. They would provide close air support of the lead elements, much as Weatherby's task with the 3rd, as the 1st Armored made its turn into western Kuwait.

Although Weatherby dearly wanted to lead that mission, he realized that until the investigation was over, some of the pilots did not have confidence in him as their leader. So he assigned Ev Hill to lead the squadron into the fight at Al Salmy, while Tex escorted the medevac.

The night was calm, with no storms or significant winds. The medevac, a Blackhawk from the 428th Air Ambulance Company, was about four hundred meters back. There were no threats on the radar, but Garner was keeping a sharp eye out, because there had been reports from special operations units in southern Iraq that the Iraqis had begun to mount helicopter gunship flights in order to capture or destroy isolated American units.

Sitting above and behind Garner in the armored cockpit, Weatherby could only see his friend's helmet in the dim light from the instrument panels. Just then, Garner cut in on the intercom. ''Captain, we're within five klicks of the pickup area. I should be getting a signal from the RF beacon anytime.'' The Special Forces men used a special homing device to guide the rescue helicopter to their position. It was tough to spot three men in the vast terrain, even with exact coordinates.

''Roger, Roger,'' Weatherby said, trying to joke as he used

to on tense missions. But somehow, it didn't quite come out right.

A moment of silence. "I've got them, Captain, at heading zero one five five, about three klicks." Weatherby turned to the new heading and they both looked outside trying to spot the men.

Weatherby switched to the air-to-air frequency. "Nightingale One, this is Tango One, come in."

"Tango One, this is Nightingale One, over."

"We have electronic contact with the signal dead ahead. Follow me in, but hang back about a click so we can recon the area first, okay?"

Weatherby and Garner were both straining in the dim light of predawn to find the men who had set off the signal. Just then, in his peripheral vision, Weatherby saw the three figures, with a small fire next to them. Must be cold in the desert this morning, Weatherby thought. He banked to the right to circle again and get a visual identification on the desert travelers.

* * *

Sergeant Ed Rafferty was a big man, tall and muscular. He had missed his daily routine of workouts on the fitness equipment and free weights back in Germany, as well as the unique high protein, high carbohydrate diet he had concocted for himself to keep up his muscle bulk. Unfortunately, all he could do here in the desert was lift sandbags filled with sand and eat MRE's. Although he felt himself getting somewhat "soft," to all outward appearances, he still looked formidable.

Rafferty and Staff Sergeant Otto Grestizsky had brought the downed Navy pilot, Lieutenant Bill Davis, from the Special Forces base camp to the rendezvous point with the additional orders that they were to use this mode of extraction from southern Iraq for themselves. The mission was over for the special forces unit and, while they would be exiting via medevac with Lt. Davis, the rest of the team would be linking up with elements of the 82nd Airborne Division at the Republican Guard base and would be extracted from there.

Unfortunately, the Berets had no way of knowing their team had been involved in the fierce fighting at the base and that Lieutenant Porter was the only survivor, although critically wounded. Radio contact had not been maintained between the two groups, because the team in the desert was on strict radio silence except for the final radio transmission two hours earlier, when they confirmed their arrival at the pickup. That call was to CENTCOM in Riyadh.

Lt. Davis was exhausted and hurting, but had not complained to the Green Berets. He had been flying an A-7D Corsair II aircraft, armed with SLAM missiles. Called the Standoff Land Attack Missile, it was a derivative of the Harpoon anti-ship missile, and Davis had been attacking targets close to Basra when his aircraft was hit by an Iraqi SAM. The Corsair's computer guidance system and the SLAM's computers had previously been loaded with the target location and mission data before takeoff and he had fired two of the missiles at known Republican Guard locations near Basra before the Iraqi SAM smacked the rear of his A-7. In the one-man plane, Davis had fought to twist and turn in the air, punching metal chaff to confuse the oncoming missile, but could not avoid the SAM. Davis had never ejected before, and he was surprised at the buffeting his body experienced from the two-hundred-knot slipstream. At some point, his right arm blew away from his body and his shoulder was dislocated. When he landed, the fall on the sand had further injured his shoulder so that he passed out right after releasing his canopy.

Fortunately for Davis, the first men to find him crumpled on the desert floor, were Iraqi nomads who had seen his chute opening. The nomads were tending sheep on a nearby grassy knoll and they ran to see what this strange sight was. They were not sympathetic to Saddam Hussein and were able to get word to the resistance movement that they were looking after an American flyer.

The nomads were kind to Davis, managing to reduce his dislocation through a series of painful manipulations that caused him to pass out again. Afraid they intended to hand him over to the Iraqi military, Davis thought about escaping, but he had no strength and no transportation. Only when the rebel leader arrived, a man by the name of Hussein, did Davis feel any relief, able to understand perfectly the man's English.

With his right arm secured tightly to his chest to prevent further movement at the shoulder, Davis bid his nomadic rescuers farewell, leaving them the only gift he had, the silver Rolex Mariners watch his father had given him after his graduation from flight school at Pensacola. It was a fair exchange for his life and he would have given them much more if he had it.

Hussein and his men had provided food and aspirin, making Davis as comfortable as they could during the long ride in the ancient Land Rover to the special forces camp. He had arrived without warning at the Green Beret camp, just as they were planning the mission to attack a Republican Guard target. Because of Davis, the Beret lieutenant had to report his arrival to Riyadh. Two of the Berets would help Davis evacuate via helicopter from a predetermined site about fifteen kilometers southwest of the base camp.

Normally, the two Berets would have covered the fifteen kilometers to the extraction site with no problem. But, Davis was in marginal condition for such a grueling hike, and the two Berets had reluctantly agreed to be driven in the Land Rover within two kilometers of the site by Iraqi resistance.

Hussein left them all in the desert with a smile and a handshake and drove off into the rising dawn in the ancient vehicle. Those were the true heroes of this conflict, Lt. Davis felt. They had to stay on in Iraq and continue to fight the daily battle against the oppressive regime of Saddam Hussein.

After Grestizsky made the contact with CENTCOM, confirming their arrival at the extraction site, Davis had been seized with chills. The excitement was almost over, and his body had reduced its production of adrenaline, increasing his shoulder pain and exhaustion began to take over. Unable to keep him warm, Rafferty had built a small fire, using available desert sticks and miscellaneous pieces of paper the men had with them. Davis was wrapped in Rafferty's poncho, sitting next to the small fire, when they first heard the helicopters.

Grestizsky had placed the small homing device about fifty meters to their south and the fire was due north of the beacon, easily seen from the air. The men on the ground first saw the Apache followed by the Blackhawk medical evacuation some one hundred meters to the rear. They were a welcome sight. Even the two Special Forces men were excited about leaving the desert and getting back to some form of civilization.

Rafferty keyed the ground-to-air radio. ''Tango One, this is Desert Rat. We have you on visual, over.''

The Texas drawl was unmistakable: ''Desert Rat, Tango One here. We also visual you. Nightingale will get down to your east. Secure the LZ, over.''

''Roger, Tango One, wilco.''

Grestizsky quickly extinguished the fire with water from his canteen and retrieved the beacon, tucking it into his Alice pack. The medevac, with its red cross on a white background, was a relief for Davis, who was shielding his eyes from the sand swirls caused by the rotor blades of the landing helicopter, but still looking at his final rescuers out of the corner of the poncho.

* * *

Specialist Jay Anders could see the two Green Berets, who had turned their backs to the landing helicopter, as well as the man on the ground covered by the poncho. His only information about the downed flier was that he had some sort of arm or shoulder injury. He had packed plenty of slings and supports in his field medical kit.

Although no one wanted to stay exposed in enemy territory, Anders and the crew chief waited until the rotor blades had slowed sufficiently to stop kicking up sand swirls, before exiting. Jay approached the Green Berets and extended his hand, shaking each in succession.

''Nice to see you, sergeant. It must have been real tough living out here in the desert.

''Oh, it hasn't been too bad, Doc, sorta like an extended stay at the beach, only without the water,'' Rafferty said with a grin.

Anders turned his attention to Davis, who was trying to remove the poncho, but having difficulty with only one arm to use. ''Here, sir, let me help you with that,'' Anders said. He removed the poncho and quickly surveyed the Navy flyer.

''So, how do you feel now, sir? I mean, what hurts or doesn't work right?

''I'm all right except for my right shoulder. I must have dislocated it in the ejection, but the nomads in the desert somehow knew how to get it back into place. The only other thing is that I just can't seem to get warm and stop shaking.''

Anders figured the flyer was probably experiencing some shock, so he needed to keep the man warm and get some intravenous fluids into him. He was probably dehydrated, too.

Anders checked the capillary return in the nailbeds of the flyer's right fingers and checked the pulse at the wrist. He looked at the shoulder sling and decided to rewrap it for the flight back to the hospital. Taking off the old sling, which looked as if it had been made from a woman's shawl, Anders tucked it under the lieutenant's arm, both to protect the nerves and vessels in armpit, and as a souvenir. He would appreciate that later, Anders thought.

Lt. Davis's arm was folded across his chest and tied with the field sling in a series of figure eight cross-overs. Then his elbow was secured to the neck, taking the weight of the arm off his shoulder so the torn muscles and ligaments would not be too painful during the flight. Satisfied, Anders turned his attention to the left arm, where he rolled up the sleeve, and applied a tourniquet above the elbow, looking for a vein to insert an IV needle. The flyer was more dehydrated than Anders thought and it took him several minutes to find a suitable vein and cannulate it. However, once the intravenous fluids began running, Anders secured the tubing with plenty of tape and placed the flyer's arm on a short board, to protect the IV.

As Anders was packing his field kit back, Sergeant Rafferty suddenly stood up, looking eastward. "Hush, everyone, I think I hear something."

Anders turned his right ear toward the east, but heard nothing. Maybe Rafferty had heard the changing sound of the Apache escort helicopter as it circled widely around the Blackhawk, keeping a close watch over the extraction site. But then, he, too, thought he heard another sound; no, perhaps two sounds, different from the Apache which was circling to the west of their position. "All, right," Anders said, "let's get the lieutenant into the helicopter fast, in case we need to get out of here."

The Green Berets sprang into action, grasping Davis's belt and hauling him gently to his feet while Anders protected the flyer's shoulder and left arm, holding the intravenous fluid bag in his teeth. The Blackhawk was more than fifty meters away and with the injured flyer the going was slow.

* * *

To the west, Weatherby and Garner had just completed a turn in their lazy oval overwatch of the extraction site, when Garner yelled, "Captain, we've got two bogies moving toward us fast from the east!"

Instinctively, Weatherby accelerated his turn and straightened the nose toward the unknown bogies. "How fast, Roger? Are they aircraft, or do they look like helicopters?"

"Definitely not fast movers, Captain. I'd say helicopters, but moving pretty fast, about a hundred and fifty klicks an hour.''

Roger and Weatherby were excited, but worried. There shouldn't be any friendly helicopters in this sector of southern Iraq. The 101st Airborne had already deployed to the north and this site was sufficiently far to the west of their supply route that only two aircraft way off course would be traveling their way. He had to assume the bogies were hostile.

''Roger, arm the Hellfires and activate the rockets. I don't know what we're up against, but let's be ready.''

''Yes, sir.'' Garner keyed his necessary switches to make their arsenal ''hot.''

Moving swiftly toward the extraction site, Weatherby could see the oncoming aircraft--Iraqi Mi-24 Hind D gunships with a formidable complement of missiles and guns that could wreak havoc on the unprotected Blackhawk and the men on the ground below.

It was going to be a close call as to who arrived at the Blackhawk first, the Apache or the Hinds, but Weatherby had a plan. His heart sank, though, when he saw the lead Hind fire a missile from a thousand meters, missing the Blackhawk, but hitting dangerously close to the men on the ground. He saw the men drop flat, halting their progress toward the Blackhawk, safe for now, but exposed to enemy fire.

''Get me a laser lock on the lead Hind, Roger, now. They're going to massacre those poor guys on the ground unless we do something.''

Only a few seconds passed while Garner worked the computer controls to the laser rangefinder and the Hellfire. It seemed like an eternity to Weatherby. Finally: ''Lock-on, captain!''

''Fox one,'' Weatherby said, as he fired the first Hellfire toward the lead Hind, now only five hundred meters away. The Hellfire was designed as an air-to-ground missile, but could be used as an air-to-air missile in a pinch -- which was what they were in now. Because the Hind was traveling faster than the usual tank target, there was less room for error.

Weatherby watched the missile jump from the port weapons pod and blast its way through the air toward the enemy helicopter, only about a hundred meters over the heads of the men on the ground below. At first he thought the missile had missed until the

Hind exploded into a giant fireball in the air, raining metal fragments all over the desert. *Great,* Weatherby thought, *one down, one to go.*

The second Hind had jinked out of the way of the fireball and was coming in fast from the north in a tight circle, beginning to fire guns at the Blackhawk. Tex could see the tracers coming closer to the medivac chopper and could think of only one solution. He banked left, then right, interposing the Apache between the Hind and the Blackhawk. Flying straight toward each other at a closing speed above two hundred knots, the two craft appeared to be on a collision course. Weatherby and Garner saw the rounds from the nose gun of the Hind walking up the sand toward their Apache. Because the weapons officer sat below and in front of the pilot, Garner was more exposed to the rounds and would likely be struck before Weatherby. Although the cockpit of the Apache was armored, it was no match for the high-velocity, Soviet-made cannon rounds. Garner closed his eyes and started to pray, knowing it was the end for them.

Suddenly, Weatherby flipped the cyclic stick forward, pushing the nose of the aircraft down toward the desert, bringing the portion of the cockpit where Garner was seated away from the stream of rounds about to hit the Apache. Garner heard the rounds hit the cockpit, just above him, where Weatherby was seated. He heard the windshield shatter, then heard Weatherby grunt sharply over the intercom. Unable to look above and behind him, Garner had no way of telling what sort of damage had been done to the aircraft or to the pilot.

All of this happened in a short tenths of a second. The Hind aircraft was right in front of them on a collision course, one instant, then in the next it was passing only a few feet away. Garner couldn't believe they were still flying, but they were. He glanced at the aircraft systems console and saw no major loss of power or hydraulics and it appeared Weatherby was still flying the Apache.

Weatherby didn't know what was wrong with him, but something was. Over half of the cockpit windshield in front of him was shattered, making it difficult to see through. The front of his sun visor was cloudy, with a red film. His vision was not too good either, but at least he could see well enough to fly. His worst problem was the pain in his face and neck. He had never known pain like this, not even after his emergency appendectomy. His face and neck seemed to be on fire. He was also having trouble breathing, as if something was slowly tightening around his neck, choking him. But he couldn't think about any of that. There was still an Iraqi Hind out there somewhere and the men on the ground below were helpless, more helpless than he and Garner.

"Captain, captain," Garner yelled over the intercom. "Are you all right? Talk to me."

Weatherby tried to speak, but all he could manage were some garbled, wet noises that made him cough. He thought he wasn't going to get his breath again. But when he tried to calm down and swallow, he was able to breathe a little better. He jinked the aircraft right and left, searching for the enemy. Quickly, his mind took in the scene ahead - the Hind was making a slow circle to the south, obviously setting up for another run at the Blackhawk. *This time,* Tex thought, *he's not going to come in close, he's going to go for a missile lock and fire, then pick us off, one by one.*

Almost without thinking, Tex straightened the Apache as best he could toward the turning Hind and twisted the throttle a full turn on the collective. The Apache leaped ahead, racing toward the Hind at full speed. Weatherby's only hope was to catch the Hind in its turn, when the rotors and engine would be exposed briefly. He flipped the cover switch over the 2.75-inch rocket pod trigger and lined up the nose of the Apache with the turning Hind. He depressed the trigger twice, loosing the full complement of thirty-eight rockets. The rockets were unguided, but he hoped he could score a few hits by the sheer numbers of them. But the rockets were designed for air-to-ground missions and did not fly far enough to maintain flight, dropping to the sand too soon.

Desperate, with the Hind widening its turn to avoid the fire from the Apache, he could only think of only one other thing. Swinging the nose of the aircraft in the same arc as he judged the Hind to be in, he squeezed the trigger of 30-mm chain gun. *Please don't let it jam up on me now, dear God, or those guys below have had it. Help me!*

The gun fired and he tried to lead the enemy aircraft just as he had been taught to do when hunting ducks south of Houston. As his father's friend, Don Joseph, used to say, 'shooting quail is reflexes, but shooting ducks is ballistics.'

At first, the Hind appeared not to have been affected by the chain gun rounds. Weatherby was feeling worse every second and knew he had nothing left except to ram the Hind. And that was not a decision he could make without Roger, who would also die in the crash. But then Tex saw some smoke coming from the engine of the aircraft. He kept depressing the trigger even though all twelve hundred rounds had already been fired.

Then suddenly and unexpectedly, the Hind exploded - vaporizing into nothing. Weatherby saw it smoking one moment, the next it was gone. He felt immediate and enormous relief, but then, as he turned his attention back to himself and the aircraft, he realized he was rapidly losing consciousness. He had to set down this aircraft before it crashed with an unconscious pilot. He owed that much to Garner and his family. With his visual fields narrowing, and his breathing becoming more labored and constricted, Tex struggled to focus on the desert floor. Twisting the collective and pulling up more pitch, the aircraft slowed and came almost to autorotation. Weatherby tried to hold it level as it descended, but it pitched backward slightly, bouncing the tail rotor on the desert floor. Recovering for an instant, Tex kept the main rotors from impacting and by rote found the main engine cutoff switch and flipped it down. Then he blacked out.

* * *

The men on the ground had witnessed the aerial battle with dread and anguish. There was absolutely nothing anyone could have done to help the Apache in its combat against the Hinds. It was an amazing series of feats the American pilot had accomplished, and now they saw his aircraft hit the ground hard, and suspected something was very wrong.

The Blackhawk pilots could not leave their aircraft. They had to keep it running and ready for the evacuation, so they did just that. But they had felt like sitting ducks and were greatly relieved. They were also worried about the Apache pilot. They could see damage to the front of the upper cockpit and the blood stains around him. They crossed their fingers.

Anders and the Green Berets reached the crashed Apache at about the same time. They didn't know how to open the cockpit from the outside, so they had to wait for the crew chief from the Blackhawk to come running up. Anders could see the weapons officer and he looked all right. But the pilot's head was slumped over the controls and he was not moving. *God,* thought Anders, *let that brave man be alive.*

Sergeant Doerdorf climbed onto the weapons pod and inserted a short, crowbar-type tool into a slotted receptacle just beneath the canopy rim. He quickly released the canopy lock, and tossed the tool onto the ground. Gesturing to Rafferty and Grestizsky, he began to open the canopy. It jammed, but the three men were able to lever it up enough so Garner could climb out. Then, the four of them finally were able to push it all the way open.

''Captain, are you all right?'' Garner screamed, as he leaned into the pilot's compartment and cradled Weatherby's helmet.

Anders pushed the warrant officer gently out of the way. ''Here, sir, let us get him out.'' The other men helped Anders release the unconscious pilot's safety harness and pulled him out of the aircraft. Weatherby was a big man, even heavier unconscious. Doerdorf slipped in the blood on the aircraft while trying to hand Tex down, but they finally managed to carry him over to the Blackhawk, where Anders could examine him. They placed the captain on a litter and covered him with a blanket.

Anders saw the pilot's name on his blood-soaked flight suit - 'Captain J. Weatherby!' *The pilot whose lip he had sewn up over a month ago. My God, this man was a hero and I know him. Now he's my patient again, and I'm responsible for his life this time.* Anders unstrapped the bloody helmet and gently removed it from the flier's head, avoiding twisting or lifting his neck too much.

What he saw was frightening. The man's face was covered with blood and multiple fragment entrance wounds. The eyelids were bloody, but after Anders wiped them with sterile gauze, he could see there was no injury, only blood from the forehead. Anders' main concern was swelling of the face and neck where some larger fragments had penetrated the skin. *There are so many important structures in the neck,* Anders thought, *that he could have damaged just about anything.* Checking the rest of his body quickly, he saw no other wounds.

Cutting loose the sleeve of the flight suit, he quickly started an intravenous line, using Lactated Ringers to combat blood loss and its effect on Weatherby's blood volume. He decided there would be no point dressing the facial wound; it was more important to get the pilot to a surgical hospital as soon as possible.

Just as he turned to pack up his field kit before loading the aircraft, he heard Rafferty call out: "Doc, I don't think he's breathing!"

Anders turned quickly and noticed Weatherby struggling to breathe, but no air was passing. His lips were turning blue and his eyes had popped opened, staring at Anders in terror. Anders knew immediately the swelling somewhere in his neck must have compressed the man's breathing passage, and he was asphyxiating. He also knew what he had to do to save Weatherby's life. Anders had only performed a cricothyrotomy on a goat during a military medicine trauma training course and it had not been easy. Another instructor had had to complete the procedure. Now that was the only choice he had to keep alive the man who had just saved all their lives.

Anders steeled himself and reached into the kit for the cricothyrotomy package. With shaking hands, he opened it up and extracted the disposable scalpel and blade. He laid the hemostat on the captain's chest and handed the short tracheostomy tube to the Green Beret medic. "You want to do this?" he asked Rafferty hopefully.

"No way, Doc, you gotta do it. He's your patient."

Anders nodded and leaned over Weatherby's neck. He felt for the thyroid notch, known as the Adam's apple, and then below it about a centimeter, where he thought he located the open space between the thyroid and cricoid cartilages of the larynx. He stretched the swollen skin and cut it quickly with the scalpel, startling slightly at the dark blood that formed at the incision. Then he cut deeper, plunging the scalpel through the membrane barrier into the open airway.

Quickly, he threw the scalpel to the sand, picked up the hemostat, and inserted it into the neck wound, opening it to allow air to be diverted into the trachea. Reaching for the small trach tube, he inserted it between the opening he created with the hemostat and pushed it into the slit.

Suddenly, Weatherby took a deep breath and air bubbled in and out through the trach tube. Anders withdrew the hemostat and tied the tube around Weatherby's neck with gauze, securing it in position.

Weatherby's color returned and his lips were no longer blue, but nicely pink. The pilot's eyes were closed, but his breathing was regular and unlabored. Anders was still shaking when he sat back on his haunches and rubbed his bloody hands on his pants.

"Great job, Doc, you did it. You saved his life!" cried Mr. Garner. "He's going to be okay now isn't he, Doc?" For the first time, Anders really felt good hearing himself called by the name 'Doc.' He knew he wasn't a real doctor, but he had saved the life of a man who would have died if he hadn't intervened. The feeling was indescribable. He hadn't known he could do it, but he had!

"Let's take him into the aircraft and get to the nearest surgical hospital," Anders said shakily. "He's still got a serious wound in his neck that's going to need surgery." The men lifted the captain's litter and carried him onto the Blackhawk, placing him next to the Navy pilot. The two Green Berets strapped in on the starboard side. While the crew prepared to take off, Mr. Garner disabled the Apache and set a delayed detonation device that would destroy the aircraft so it would not fall into enemy hands. When all were aboard, the Blackhawk lifted quickly off the ground, and banked to turn south, toward safety.

Everyone on the aircraft looked down on the scene they were leaving behind; two destroyed Iraqi Hind gunships with no survivors after they exploded, and a lone Apache helicopter, broken and awaiting destruction. Mr. Garner cringed when he heard the explosion and realized his helicopter was gone. However, both he and Captain Weatherby were alive, as were the other men in the Blackhawk. He closed his eyes and said a prayer.

Anders was monitoring the captain's vital signs. So far, so good, but he was concerned about the large hematoma in the neck. He hoped they were sent to a good hospital, where they had an excellent surgeon like Major Neel. Anders had done all he could, but a real surgeon was needed now.

A frustrating thing about the current medical evacuation capabilities for helicopters was that there was no way to transport and power a portable suction device. Anders saw Weatherby was producing a great deal of bloody mucus out of the trach tube and he was worried it might obstruct the tube. Rummaging through his medical kit, he attached a cut-off intravenous catheter to a large 20 cc. syringe. Anders inserted the catheter into the lumen of the trach tube and quickly pulled back the plunger, generating sufficient suction to clear the secretions, which he squirted from the syringe near the doorway. He repeated that every few minutes, to keep the airway open, yet not often enough to deprive Weatherby's lungs of vital oxygen.

Leaning back in his seat harness, Anders tried to relax for a moment. He reached over and without really thinking, grasped the captain's hand. He was surprised to feel the captain return his grasp, strongly. There was a bond between them, an unmistakable appreciation for what each had done for the other. *If this is what being a physician feels like,* Anders decided, *it must be the grandest feeling in the world.*

CHAPTER 14

AFTER TAKING A last brush at his fingernails, Major Neel completed his five-minute Betadine surgical scrub at the sink and threw the brush into the plastic bag. He pushed the water pump with his foot at the field scrub sink and rinsed the rest of the antiseptic from his hands and arms. Then, walking through the temper tent into the metal isocontainer that was the operating room, he stepped up to the surgical technician, Specialist Rose Ann Gurkowski. "Thanks, Rose Ann," he said as he accepted a surgical towel to dry his dripping hands. "Do you have the dermatome on the field? I think we may use it today."

"Yes, sir," Rose Ann replied. "But we haven't hooked it up to the power supply yet, so we're keeping our fingers crossed." The military's new DEPMEDS medical hospitals and supplies were designed to be completely outfitted for all needs and with components that would interchange among the Army, Navy, and Air Force. So far, the concept had been practical, but the problem was that many pieces of surgical or medical equipment had not been placed with a particular hospital, or the necessary connecting items were not working, so the surgeons and nurses often had to use their ingenuity.

"Well, Rose Ann, I'll take the skin grafts with a Padgett knife if I have to," Neel replied.

"Are your hands steady tonight?" asked Lieutenant Sue Wong, the circulating nurse for the case. "If not, you'll cut your own hands off as well as the patient's," she said with a laugh. Not shy by Oriental standards, Sue was a hard-working and aggressive nurse, new to the Army and still enthusiastic. She could prepare for a surgical case faster than anyone Neel had ever seen.

"Sure, they're just as steady as they usually are," Neel replied in a joking manner, holding his hands out and shaking them violently.

"Now Dr. Neel, how you do go on," Rose Ann said, as she held out a surgical gown. While he was gloving, Neel looked over at his friend and patient, Sergeant First Class Trinidad Gonzales, who was asleep on the operating room table with an endotracheal tube protruding from his mouth. The nurse anesthetist, Captain Tom Burns, was almost finished connecting several pieces of monitoring equipment to the patient and Lt. Wong was scrubbing Sgt. Gonzales' thighs with a Betadine prep. It was Neel's intention to harvest as many skin grafts as he could from Sgt. Gonzales' anterior thighs so he could apply them to the debrided areas on his back where the burns were full thickness and would not repair themselves well.

"All right, doctor, I'm done with the prep," Lt. Wong said. She had been chief surgical nurse at the hospital in Wichita, Kansas, when she was called back to active duty with a nursing detachment to deploy with the 252nd Combat Support Hospital. There were some critical shortages of personnel in just about every reserve component medical unit, and thousands of medical personnel had been mobilized and added to the units to augment them. Lt. Wong had been an excellent addition.

"I'll put towels over the thighs, Rose Ann," Neel said, holding out his hands. She began placing surgical towels in his hands, one after the other, as he carefully, but quickly isolated the skin graft donor sites from the rest of the nonsterile field. Using skin clips to secure them in place and long sterile surgical sheets, Sgt. Gonzales was soon completely covered except for his face, head and thighs.

Neel looked up at Burns. "Tom, is he all right? May I start the skin grafts?"

"He's doing fine, Major." Burns knew this patient was special to Neel. He suspected Neel knew him. "I've got him on Isofluorane, but no muscle relaxants because of the burns. That ought to be much safer for the sergeant."

"Thanks, Tom, I appreciate your taking care of him so well."

Neel turned his attention to the surgical site. Although Sergeant Gonzales was his friend, Neel put that in the back of his mind, as he became 100% surgeon and concentrated on the task.

"Hello, Captain Otto, welcome to the party," said Burns, as the assistant surgeon came into the operating room. He had just scrubbed and was waiting to gown and glove. Neel raised his head from the dermatome. "Hey, Randy, thanks for coming in." He looked at the patient, Sgt. Gonzales, and nodded. ''This man was burned in a battle in the desert about two hours ago when he rescued a tank full of men just before the tank exploded. I know you just got off ICU shift, but I really need your help here.''

''No sweat, major, I'd as soon work with you as try to sleep anyway. I figure we'll be so busy here for a while none of us will get much sleep.'' He walked over to the operating table and stood opposite Neel. ''How can I help?''

Captain Otto was a young family practitioner who had supplemented his income during medical school in the army reserve, liking it so much he stayed after his residency. Otto was practicing in Sikeston, Missouri, pretty small by anyone's standards, so it was a real hardship for the community , as well as for Captain Otto's young family, to have him deployed in the Persian Gulf.

As a family practitioner, Otto had been assigned the professional designation of ''field surgeon,'' which mean he was a front line medical doctor, assisting the surgeon at the combat medical detachment, and also in charge of the recovery room/ intensive care unit.

After Neel described the dermatome procedure, Dr. Otto nodded. He knew Neel was a 'hotshot' trauma surgeon, but he didn't have the egotistical manner like so many general surgeons seemed to. Neel was a real, down-to-earth guy, who also happened to be from south Missouri.

''Okay, Randy, I need you to take this tongue blade and moisten it in mineral oil. Hold it just above the knee, pushing down really hard on the skin to flatten it, so I can come along just below it with the dermatome.'' Otto did as he was instructed and pushed the tongue blade down firmly onto the anterior thigh. ''That's great, just slowly move it up and I'll follow.''

Neel depressed the foot pedal of the electrically driven oscillating blade, starting the cutter. He pressed the hand-held machine firmly onto the thigh and leaned into the field. As the two men moved upward on the thigh, a thin layer of skin slowly vibrated out of the opening on the top of the dermatome, as if being manufactured by the machine. When they reached the top of the thigh, Neel pulled up on the machine, neatly cutting the skin graft free from the rest of the attached skin. Where the skin used to be was a white layer, slowly oozing blood, which stood out in stark contrast to Sgt. Gonzales' darkly pigmented skin.

"Nice piece, Major," Otto said. When he took the skin from the dermatome and hold it up by forceps, it began to roll into a cylinder.

"You see, Randy, the natural tensions on the skin tend to make it assume a cylindrical shape, just like the shape of the thigh. Just because we removed the skin from the rest of the body did not abolish those tendencies. After they heal, the grafts will tend to contract and heap up, and that's where the hypertrophic scar can come from that characterizes burn grafts. To counteract that, we will compress the grafts with an elastic garment as soon as they heal. For this patient, it will probably be a long stocking setup and a torso or body suit. He'll have to wear it for months, to flatten and compress the scars."

"Here, Rose Ann, place this skin into sterile four by four gauze and keep it soaked in cool saline until we need it." Although the outside temperatures were beginning to climb, the combat hospital had capabilities for refrigeration, mainly for blood and medications that required lower temperatures. It could also provide ice for compresses and for chilling saline solutions.

The two physicians proceeded to repeat the graft harvesting procedure twice on the left thigh and then moving to the right, harvested three more. All the grafts were set aside in cool saline solution for safekeeping.

"All right, Sue, let's apply the dermal dressings soaked in topical thrombin. That will help stop the oozing from the graft sites and begin coagulation." After wrapping the thighs, Dr. Neel stood up and looked around. "Hey, everybody, what happened to the music. We gotta have music!" Neel had operated to music in the operating room for over six years and it was a habit and a way of life. He had brought along a battery-powered cassette player, but now that the surgical hospital detachment was set up, the generators were supplying AC for lights and medical equipment.

Lt. Wong walked over to the stainless steel cabinet near the wall and pulled out the cassette player. She plugged it into a floor socket and opened the cassette door. "What will it be today, Doctor Neel?"

"Sue, how could you have forgotten?" Neel asked in fake exasperation. "It's gotta be the best for this patient. Let's have . . . I know, Marty Robbins, and put on the side where he sings 'El

Paso City.' That's where Sergeant Gonzales is from.''

Dr. Otto looked up. ''You know this patient, Major Neel?''

Neel looked Otto directly in the eyes. ''Yes, Randy, I do. This man is a bona fide hero if I ever saw one. Do you remember the terrorists who almost blew up Khobar Towers while we were there? Well, it was Sergeant Gonzales who found them and single-handedly stopped them. It was also he who helped me evacuate and treat the men who got hit at the barracks by the Scud. Now I hear he rescued four men from a burning tank during a firefight in the desert with the Iraqis. On top of that, he's also a great person. So, yes, I know him.''

The men held their gaze for several long seconds. Dr. Otto knew what it was for a surgeon to operate on a friend. It was very tough to dissociate personal feelings from medical decisions and tasks. To perform the kind of radical surgery Dr. Neel would have to do on this patient - his friend - really took a lot of courage and dedication.

''All right, everyone, now comes the tough part,'' Neel said, pushing away the Mayo stand that held some of their surgical instruments. ''We need to turn the patient onto his stomach and expose the back. Tom, the most important thing is to keep that endotracheal tube in position and watch we don't pull out any of the IVs.'' Breaking sterile technique for this part of the procedure, the four members of the surgical team slowly lifted and turned Sgt. Gonzales onto his stomach, while Captain Burns disconnected and supported the endotracheal tube. Once he was safely onto his stomach, Burns reconnected the tube to the anesthesia machine and began breathing for the sergeant again.

''Tom, how much fluid has he had since he came into our hospital?'' Neel asked, as he changed his gown and gloves.

Burns looked at his worksheet for a minute. ''Just about four and half liters, Major, all lactated Ringers. His vital signs are really doing well and he's putting out about a hundred cc. of urine an hour.''

''Fine, just fine, Tom. I figured, according to the BAMC burn formula, that we should give him eight liters of electrolytes in the first eight hours, so we're right on target. Run it in about two hundred and fifty ccs. an hour, and get an hematocrit before we're finished to see if he'll need some packed red blood cells.''

''Right. We've got four bags of O negative and four bags of

O positive in the refrigerator. As soon as they give the hematocrit I can check it out. Let's see, he's O negative according to his dog tags, so we'll be okay if he needs it.'' Burns began adjusting the intravenous fluid rate to comply with Neel's orders.

Both surgeons surveyed the patient's back and legs, as Lieutenant Wong scrubbed the entire back half of Sergeant Gonzales' body with Betadine. Neel figured the areas that were likely to be full thickness burns at about twenty percent and the partial thickness burns as another thirty percent, for a total of fifty percent burns. Essentially, the entire back was burned to some degree.

''He must have been running away when the explosion occurred and he caught fire, don't you imagine?'' Captain Otto postulated. ''I guess it's a good thing he didn't get his front burned. Especially the face. I think that would be the worst.''

Neel nodded. ''You're right on both accounts, Randy. Fortunately, he didn't suffer much smoke or flame inhalation, or we'd have to do a tracheotomy on him as well. I checked the upper airway with Tom when he intubated him, and it really looked fine.''

Receiving the towels and drapes from Rose Ann. Neel again draped the surgical area.

''Randy, this is the part that is not fun about this kind of surgery. We actually have to cut off all the dead skin and debride down to viable, bleeding tissue so the skin grafts will take. Just try to think of it as a task, and not that you're doing this to a person, as hard as that might be. I've had to do this repeatedly to little children who were burned over ninety percent of their bodies in fires and believe me, you never get used to it.''

Otto saw the shadow of sadness in Neel's eyes as he remembered those cases that would haunt him.

''You almost wish they would die to spare those little kids the terrible pain they experience.'' Neel shook his head, trying to shake the recollections.

Neel and Otto picked up scalpels and forceps and began, first at the feet, and then worked their way painstakingly up the body, removing the dead and revitalized skin. The process took hours, and it was that knowledge that caused Neel to make the decision to close the small surgical hospital, so they would have enough time to complete the initial resuscitation and take care of this horribly burned man. When they finished, they would have to reopen the hospital.

The only other board-certified surgeon in the detachment, an orthopedic specialist, was busy operating on a patient with an open fracture of the leg in the next isocontainer OR, and he had several patients in pre-op waiting their turns. If this war ever turned into the high casualty conflict originally predicted, there was no way small surgical units like this could keep up with battlefield wounded. Further, Neel understood, if chemical casualties occurred, the whole process would fall apart, with no chance to recover. He hoped Saddam wasn't that crazy.

Despite the cool air entering the isocontainer from the portable air conditioning units of the MEDDEPS, both physicians were soaking with sweat. "Man, there's no way we could ever do surgery in a chemical suit and mask," Neel said to Otto. "That's pure fantasy. I hope when this is over, someone with some common sense sits down and learns a lesson from all of this."

"The Army?" Captain Otto said in a mocking manner. "Who ever said the Army had common sense?" Both men laughed.

The strains of 'El Paso City' were being sung by Marty Robbins. Neel stood up and stretched his back and thought about Trinidad Gonzales' wife back in El Paso. He knew that soon someone from Fort Bliss would call or visit her to inform her that her husband had been wounded in battle in the Gulf War and was burned. His doctor had listed him as being in 'critical' condition. Neel knew how much fear a burn can strike with a family member, and hoped that whoever notified her was compassionate and comforting. They certainly deserved that. When his thoughts started to drift to his own wife and his own mortality and vulnerability, he quickly pushed the thoughts from his mind, bending over again to concentrate on the debridement, not his personal problems.

Finally, the debridement of the burned skin was completed. Everyone in the operating room was tired and hot, but the procedure was long from over yet.

"All right, Rose Ann, let's see to those grafts now." She handed Neel a small basin full of gauze sponges soaked in saline, each containing a long strip of skin.

"Randy, we'll sew these on with chromic catgut, in a

running fashion. Just watch me start the first one and you'll catch on pretty quick.'' Neel laid the graft on the pinkish tissue of Sergeant Gonzales' back, then mentally measured the requirements for skin. ''Let's just graft the full thickness areas for now, and dress the partial thickness burns with Silvadene cream.'' He showed Captain Otto how the undersurface of the graft was white and glistening, and the outer surface was dull and darker.

With the skill of years of experience and thousands of surgical cases, Neel deftly began running the chromic suture along the perimeter of the graft, securing it. Otto watched in awe, then clumsily began his own suturing.

''Sue?'' Neel asked. ''Can you change the tape now to a nice soft jazz piece? Put on one of Bob James' tapes. I like him. Randy, did you know that Bob James grew up in Missouri? Right up in Marshall, along the Missouri River. The best modern jazz pianist in my book, and a native Missourian.'' The melodic sounds of a flute and piano came drifting toward the tired men, helping soothe their tense muscles and relax their spirits. ''I can listen to this when I'm coming home from an all night case and be relaxed by the time I hit the door. It's the greatest!''

''It is good, Major. I want to see the cassette cover when we're finished so I can look for it when we get back to the States.'' Then they were each taken up with the thought of what they would do first when they got home.

''Well, I'm going to hit the best steak house in Kansas City,'' Neel said, ''and to heck with my cholesterol.'' They all laughed.

''I can't wait for a juicy hamburger, with lettuce and tomatoes and onions and pickles, and a big order of greasy fries,'' offered Lt. Wong.

''It's a pitcher of beer for me, along with a huge bag of buttered popcorn,'' said Burns.

''My wife makes the best lasagna and Italian bread in all of Southeast Missouri. And her brownies are out of sight!'' added Randy Otto.

''I'll come to your house, Dr. Otto. I just love lasagna and I can't make it worth a darn.''

''You're always welcome, Rose Ann, and bring your husband, if he's still speaking to you.''

''Now, Dr. Otto. That wasn't very nice. You know perfectly

well he's going to jump for joy when he sees me back home again.''

''I know he will, Rose Ann. Who couldn't love you.''

Neel had finished this three grafts and leaned over Sergeant Gonzales' back to place the fourth one, then helped Otto with his side. Soon, all six grafts were in place and the Silvadene had been applied to the remaining exposed tissue.

''Tom, let's go ahead and give him another gram of cephalosporin, IV. His last was just before we started the case, so he's due another.

''Right, major, I'll start it now,'' Burns replied, reaching over to the medicine chest next to the anesthesia machine that held all the OR medications. He withdrew the antibiotic fluid and injected it into the intravenous fluid bag, so it would be circulated in the vascular fluids, targeted for the damaged tissue.

With some difficulty, the team managed to dress the burns, essentially the whole body, except for the head, turning the patient onto his back again without dislodging any tubing. At that point, Sergeant Gonzales had tubes up his nose into his stomach, in his mouth to his trachea, in his bladder, as well as two intravenous lines.

They transferred him, still asleep, to the litter, and the litter team carried Gonzales to the recovery room/intensive care unit, in an adjacent GP medium tent. Neel and Otto accompanied him. They were met by the head nurse, Major Jocelyn Oates, who was as efficient and friendly a nurse as a physician could ever hope to meet. It was a real treat for Neel to have both Oates and Otto in charge of the postoperative care of his surgical patients - he knew they would receive the best.

Neel placed his hand on Otto's shoulder. ''Randy, I'm leaving him to you for a while. Watch him like a hawk and keep that urine output up. If he needs pain medication, give him about five milligrams of morphine every four hours. I don't want him to hurt too much, okay? Just titrate it so he breathes well and doesn't get any fluid in his lungs. Also, when he's awake, call me, and I'll take out his endotracheal tube and we'll see how well he can breathe.''

''Yes sir, I can handle all that.'' Otto had spent weeks learning the nuances of postoperative surgical care and much of that learning had come from Major Neel and Major Oates. Within certain guidelines, he felt comfortable with the responsibility.

Neel went over to the litter and observe his friend's breathing. Steady and deep. Won't be long now until he's awake. Maybe I'll just stick around until he is.

Neel took a seat on a small folding chair and placed the medical chart on an empty litter in front of him. *I'll just write out my operative notes and finish my admission history and physical while I wait. Thank goodness the military doesn't require all the paperwork civilian hospitals do. This is about the only good thing about operating in a battlefield setting, except, of course, taking care of wounded soldiers.*

Just as he finished the operative note, he heard Sergeant Gonzales coughing around the tube. Neel jumped up and ran to the litter. The sergeant had opened his eyes and was looking around, searching for a familiar face, confused as to where he was and what had happened.

Neel leaned over the litter and looked directly at Gonzales. "Sergeant, I thought I told you I didn't want to see you in my hospital." Gonzales focused on Neel's face and then smiled with his eyes, nodding slightly. He relaxed.

"I've got to take this tube out of your throat, Trinidad, and then I'll tell you what happened and what's wrong with you, okay?"

Gonzales nodded.

Neel untaped the tube from Gonzales' chin and mouth. "All right, now take a deep breath." When the sergeant did so, Neel pulled the tube out smoothly and Gonzales began coughing. After he stopped, he tried to talk to Neel only no words would come.

"Listen, Trinidad, your throat is swollen from the tube and from breathing in some fumes. Whatever you did out there on the desert last night, you got burned doing it. Fortunately it's your back and the backs of your legs and arms and neck, but it's about fifty percent of your body. It's serious, but so far, you're doing real well. It's going to hurt a lot, because we took off the burned skin and replaced it with skin grafts from your thighs. Pretty soon, you'll begin feeling the pain. Just tell us and we'll give you a shot for it, okay? Don't try to be tough -- we expect you to ask for the medicine. Now, I can't guarantee anything, but I'm willing to bet that for a man as ornery as you, we can get you back to see your family pretty soon. How does that sound?"

Gonzales smiled and nodded.

"You'll be cared for in here by Doctor Otto and by Major Oates, the head nurse, as well as some other nurses and technicians. You're still in the middle of southern Iraq, but as soon as I think you're stable, we can airevac you out of here and eventually back to Germany." Neel knew he had done the right thing by deciding to operate on Sergeant Gonzales, even if he was court-martialed.

With some difficulty, Gonzales slowly lifted his hand and grabbed Neel's. He squeezed it tightly, looking at the surgeon with tears in his eyes. Neel thought he was going to cry too, and decided he'd better get out of there before he did.

"All right, you," he said, "let's let them start earning their combat pay and start taking care of you. I'll check on you every couple of hours to see that you're doing all right." With that Neel lowered his friend's hand onto the blanket and left.

The lab technician walking in the tent door thought he saw moisture in Major Neel's eyes. *Nah,* he decided, *it must just be the sand. Doctors never cry.*

* * *

Every time Captain Weatherby coughed, Anders thought the swelling in his neck was worse. There was certainly more oozing of blood from the facial wounds than before, and there seemed to be more bloody mucus coming from the tracheotomy site. Anders was worried.

He got on the aircraft intercom and talked directly to the pilot: "Captain Ward, I'm having some problems with one of the patients back here. Uh, I was wondering, sir, how much longer to the hospital?"

The captain's voice sounded metallic and unnatural in the vibrations of the helicopter. "We've been vectored to the 13th Evacuation Hospital, Doc, just at the Iraqi-Saudi border. Can he wait that long? If not, we can take him to the 252nd CASH. They're not expecting us, but I can call them up."

Major Neel again! Why not? If anyone can help Captain Weatherby, he can. "Yes, sir, I think we ought to make for the 252nd right away."

"Right, Doc, I'll see what I can do."

Anders turned to Captain Weatherby and suctioned the trach tube free of some bloody mucus, causing the captain to cough fitfully. The young medic was becoming more worried about the neck and didn't have the experience to know what to do about it.

"Doc," the pilot said over the intercom, "they've cleared us for the 252nd since its right here close to the battlefield. We'll be there in two mikes."

The Blackhawk slowly rolled and turned east toward the combat hospital. *Neel must have reopened for business,* Anders thought, *after taking care of that burned sergeant. I hope he did all right.*

Very shortly, the helicopter began its descent into the landing site next to the hospital. The CASH detachment was within fifty kilometers of the main battle front, so it could provide close support for wounded members of the VII and XVII Corps.

The litter team was waiting and ran to the open door as soon as the rotors slowed. Anders directed the unloading of Captain Weatherby first and followed him into the triage tent, while Sergeant Doerdorf helped the Navy flyer. Dr. Neel was in the triage tent, still in surgical scrubs and cap. He nodded to Anders. "Talk to me, Anders, tell me what's going on with this patient."

"Sir, he was in an Apache flying protective overwatch for one of our clandestine medevac pickups, when two Iraqi Hind gunships showed up. He managed to knock them both down, but took what Mr. Garner says were probably 23-mm. rounds into the cockpit. We were just about to load him on the chopper when he lost his airway. I had to do a cricothyrotomy. He's been breathing okay, but bleeding from the neck and face wounds and I think the neck is becoming even more swollen.

Neel looked from the patient to Anders and back again. "Good work, Anders. You saved this man's life, you know."

Anders looked away shyly, saying nothing.

"What's wrong with the other casualty?" Neel asked, nodding toward the Navy flyer sitting on a litter about ten feet away.

"Probably dislocated a shoulder when he ejected over Iraq. The nomads found him and fixed him up, but it's still pretty unstable and sore. He has a good grip and sensation in the hand, and his pulse is strong.

"Fine. Bobby, call Captain Collopy and see if he's done with his last fracture in the OR. See if he can come out and see our Navy friend and fix him up for evacuation back down the line."

The medic ran off toward the OR isocontainer to track down the orthopedic surgeon. Collopy had been an all-star collegiate baseball player at Marquette, and had migrated naturally into orthopedics. His father had been a surgeon in Vietnam and he felt compelled to do his part, too, leaving a lucrative practice with two other orthopedic surgeons in Minneapolis to come to the Persian Gulf with the surgical detachment.

Neel quickly surveyed Captain Weatherby's body for other injuries, but found none. "All right, start another 14 gauge I.V. in the other arm and check his blood type. Tell Lt. Wong we'll be back there in the OR in a couple of minutes. Bobby, you're back I see. Get a stat hematocrit on the captain, then draw enough blood for a complete electrolyte series and type and cross. Start a gram of cephalosporin in the existing IV bag and run it in full blast. Mary, start cutting off the captain's clothes and get him out of his boots and flight suit." The medics and nurses began their tasks efficiently and quickly.

Leaning over the litter, Major Neel looked into the captain's eyes. "Captain, can you hear me?"

Weatherby opened his eyes and nodded slightly.

"Specialist Anders saved your life with the airway, but we've got to go in and stop the bleeding in your neck. We'll put you to sleep with an anesthetic, so you'll be comfortable and in no pain. When you wake up, you'll be all patched up, but you'll still have the trach tube in your neck for a few days. Sound okay to you?"

Weatherby nodded again.

"All right, I'm Dr. Neel and surgery's my job. You're a pilot and obviously you do that very well, from what Anders told me. We'll take good care of you, don't you worry." Neel laid his hand on Weatherby's chest and patted it.

"Come on, Anders. We've got to scrub. Tell your chopper buddies you won't be coming back with them this trip. They can pick you up in a day or two when they return for the evacuation of these patients. I'm pulling rank and commandeering your services."

"But, but, I can't stay here, sir."

"Who's the ranking officer here, son? Do you see anyone around here higher than a major?" Neel pulled Anders out of the triage tent.

Anders knew he had no choice. "Sergeant Doerdorf," he hollered," tell Captain Ward I'll be staying here at the hospital. Tell him to get Sergeant Tillman to go up with you guys for a couple of days. If anyone says anything, tell them I was ordered by a higher authority, okay?"

Doerdorf just laughed and nodded.

Neel showed Anders where the scrub suits were kept and he changed out of his flight suit in front of the scrub sink, leaving his boots and equipment in a pile. They donned caps and masks and went into the operating room to talk to Captain Burns.

"Tom, we've got a flyer with a trach tube in place, courtesy of this medic here, with an expanding hematoma in his neck. I'll need you to hook up to his trach tube and put him to sleep. Then, we'll open his neck and control the bleeding. Run his IVs wide open and get the right blood in the room and hang it up just in case. If it's the carotid or jugular, there could be some heavy bleeding for a while. Then, once we have control of the vessels and have debrided the wound, we'll change the cricothyrotomy over to a formal tracheotomy with a bigger tube."

"Sounds fine, Major. I'll get ready." Burns left to check on the patient's blood type and to secure the blood.

"Rose Ann and Lieutenant Wong, this is Specialist Anders. He's our resident hero with airways today. Say hello."

"Hello, Specialist Anders," they echoed together. "Are you going to scrub in?" asked Rose Ann.

"I . . . I guess so," stammered Anders. "I don't know what I can do to help, but the major got me here, anyway."

"What size gloves do you wear?" asked Lt. Wong, as she began opening the sterile packs and instrument sets for the case.

"Seven and a half, please," replied Anders politely.

"My, isn't he a nice young man. We don't hear many 'pleases' around here do we Rose Ann?" laughed Lt. Wong. "If you're always this nice, you're welcome any time."

"Now, be careful, Sue. He's much too young for you. You need a more mature man, like Captain Collopy, for instance," Neel kidded.

"Now just you hush up, major. You know I'm married. Besides, Dr. Collopy is much too old for a mere child like myself." Lt. Wong was probably in her mid-forties, but had kept herself in excellent physical condition through an active aerobic exercise program. She did look twenty years younger.

The triage team brought in the litter with Captain Weatherby into the OR, setting it on the metal support 'horse.' After Neel and Anders helped Lt. Wong and Captain Burns transfer the pilot to the operating table, the triage team took their litter and left, wishing the captain good luck.

Captain Burns attached his anesthesia machine to the tracheotomy tube and turned on the oxygen and anesthetic gas to induce general anesthesia. After Captain Weatherby was asleep, Lt. Wong inserted a Foley catheter into his bladder. While she was doing that, Major Neel had quickly prepped the face and neck with Betadine and he and Anders had left to scrub. When they returned a short five minutes later, Rose Ann had draped the captain with sterile sheets and the field was ready.

"Very good, Rose Ann. I guess you finally figured out the way I like to drape the head and neck region," Neel said playfully, as he dried his hands. "All right, Anders just do what Rose Ann and Lt. Wong say, and they'll get you all decked out properly. Then come over here and stand on the right side of the operating table, keeping your hands at chest level, so you don't contaminate yourself. We've got to move ahead with this neck exploration."

Anders nodded and did what the two women told him to do to get gowned and gloved.

Because he was left handed, Neel moved to the left side of the table. Most of the hematoma was on the side of the neck and so were the facial fragmentation wounds. Neel took the point of a scalpel blade and lightly incised the skin of the left neck, making a faint curvilinear incision from just below the earlobe to the level of the trach tube. Captain Burns had extended his anesthesia tubing out of the field and what was in the field had been 'painted' with Betadine solution by Neel.

Neel looked up at Burns. "Ready, Tom? Got all the blood you need?'

"Right, Major. He was O positive, so I've got all four units up here in case we need them, but I can send all or some of them back to the refrigerator if we don't."

"Better to have too much, Anders," Neel said, as the young medic stepped up to the table. "If you don't have something ready, that's surely the one thing you'll need in a hurry. Remember that!"

"Yes, sir, I will."

"All right, Anders, have you ever assisted on a surgery case?"

"Well, just at the medics trauma course at Fort Sam, when we went into the goat lab and did procedures. But never on a person," Anders responded, almost guiltily.

"That's fine. All I want you to remember, is if I tell you to do something to help me, do it right away and without hesitation. Got that?"

Anders swallowed hard and nodded.

"I'll give you running commentary as we go along, but sometimes I may be too busy to talk. Just hold steady with what you're doing and I'll start up again when things are easier." Neel took two large cloth sponges and handed them to Anders. "Now, hold these on either side of this line here on the neck, pulling the skin apart. You put tension on it that way and it cuts easier. There, that's it."

Quickly, Neel cut through the skin in a single deft, arcing motion with the scalpel, exposing the underlying muscle. "All right, Rose Ann, let me have the Bovie cautery. Sue, set the cutting on thirty and the coag on thirty-five." The coagulation handpiece was capable of either cutting through tissues without much blood loss, or coagulating bleeding vessels, depending on which button was pushed. Because Neel feared further loss of blood and because he knew he needed to get to the vessels as quickly as possible, he used the Bovie rather than the scalpel and scissors, his usual surgical preferences.

"Hemostats please to Anders here. Just clamp any large bleeders, son, as I cut through the muscle. This coag unit won't cauterize vessels bigger than two millimeters in diameter, so keep a clamp in your hand and use it on them. We'll both work together as a team."

They soon got into the rhythm of cutting and clamping, with Anders learning how to hold the clamps upright so Neel could tie the vessels with silk suture. Anders was amazed at the speed and dexterity with which Neel operated. He was almost machine-like.

"Okay, Anders, this is the carotid sheath," Neel said, pointing to a white glistening structure that pulsated. "Inside are the common carotid artery and the jugular vein. Also the vagus nerve to the stomach and chest. I suspect we have a laceration of the external branch of the carotid, because the captain didn't have any neurological problems that would indicate loss of blood to the brain through a clotted-off internal carotid. Of course, it could be the jugular vein, which is always harder to control. I'm going to open the sheath and follow the vessels superiorly. Be prepared to suction a lot of blood if we get to a damaged vessel.''

Neel had Rose Ann set on the Mayo stand for ready use, if needed, the right angle and vascular clamps, along with the blue silicone vessel ties. Then he bent back over the neck wound and picked up the carotid sheath with long Cushing forceps and inserted a pair of Metzenbaum scissors into the sheath, neatly slicing it open up to the carotid bifurcation, where the external and internal carotid branches formed. Immediately, blood clots and bright red blood began pouring from the sheath.

''There it is everybody. Looks like the external branch, all right. Let me have the right angle clamp, Rose Ann.'' The technician handed the clamp to Neel, who swiftly spread the tissues around the vessel, bringing the clamp almost completely around the vessel from behind. ''All right, Anders, get that blue vascular loop on a pair of forceps and insert the end in my right angle when I open it up.''

Anders did as he was told, handing forceps with good coordination and placing the blue silicone loops into the major's clamp on the first try. ''Good job, Anders. Very good. Now, I'm going to cinch up the loop and constrict the base of the external carotid branch. That ought to slow down the bleeding while I find the laceration in the vessel.''

Dissecting carefully, Neel followed the vessel superiorly, while Anders suctioned the steady ooze of blood from the wound to enhance the surgeon's view. ''There it is,'' Neel finally said. ''And there's a piece of glass or plastic, probably from his helmet or cockpit windshield sitting in the laceration. Another pair of Cushings please, Rose Ann.'' He reached out his hand without looking, secured the forceps, and painstakingly removed the fragment from the laceration. ''There are probably more of these pieces in the neck and face, but we'll look for them later. I want to repair the tear in this vessel first.''

Neel placed another right angle clamp around the vessel above the laceration and Anders had another blue loop available, without being told to. ''Very good, Anders. I think you're trainable,'' Neel said with a chuckle.

With the vessel controlled above and below the laceration, Neel had a choice. He could simply tie off the vessel and there would likely be no consequences to the captain, because the external carotid supplied the face and part of the mouth and throat. On the other hand, Neel's training was such that if there was any chance for function of the vessel, it should repaired. Neel elected to.

"All right, Rose Ann, let me have some 8-0 Prolene suture on a cardiovascular needle."

Silence.

"Major, we only have 6-0. There's no cardiovascular suture packed in the isocontainer."

Neel felt his anger spout. "You mean to say we're a surgical combat unit, and whoever packed up this OR back in England or wherever, didn't think about seeing we had cardiovascular suture?"

"I guess not, major," Sue said ruefully.

Neel sighed. *No use getting upset. That won't get the suture here.* "Okay, Rose Ann, let me have the 6-0. At least I can see that without my loupes." Neel normally operated on blood vessels with magnifying glasses called 'loupes,' but hadn't thought to bring them to the Persian Gulf.

Although the suture was larger than he was used to, he handily closed the vessel laceration with a reverse running stitch, tying it securely at the end of the tear. "Okay, Anders, cut the tags about two millimeters long. Not three millimeters, not one millimeter, but two millimeters. Good, that's just perfect. You've got young eyes, haven't you?"

Now, thought Neel, as he released the vascular clamps and saw the vessel pulsating again without a leak at the repair site, *my only concern is the internal jugular vein. I haven't seen it and it could still have been injured. I'd better look.*

"Anders, we're going to look for the internal jugular. It's a much thinner-walled vessel and more easily injured. If it's cut, there's going to be a lot of bleeding until I can clamp it. So, if that happens, just keep up with the suction and keep the retractor exactly as it is now so I can see."

"Yes, sir," Anders replied, sensing the potential severity of the situation. He got a more secure grip on the tissue retractor with his left hand and placed the suction catheter tip in the wound, ready for use.

Neel carefully retracted the carotid arteries out of the way with a vein retractor and asked Rose Ann to hold it. He hesitated momentarily, then cut open a tissue plane over the general vicinity of where the jugular vein should be. The tissues were discolored and he was worried about trapped blood. Then, as he suspected, there was an immediate flood of blood into the wound. He pushed his finger into the wound, compressing the lower portion of the cut vessel that had begun bleeding again once the compressive tamponade of the blood clot had been removed.

"Tom," he said calmly. "The jug's cut and I've got my finger on the distal end. If you hear any air bubbles in the esophageal stethoscope, let me know and we'll have to turn him on his left side and aspirate the right atrium." Because the venous pressure in the internal jugular is well below zero, there was the possibility for air to be sucked into the cut end of the vessel and travel to the right side of the heart, blocking the blood return, and allowing air to get into the blood vessels to the lungs, a condition that was often fatal.

Anders was scared to death. He had never seen so much blood in his life. He didn't know how Major Neel could handle this situation, but he knew there must be some way.

"Rose Ann, let me have a Kelly clamp, please." Neel took it and placed it next to the finger that was compressing the lower end of the cut vein. "Anders, be ready to suction the blood so I can see what I need to clamp. Okay, now?" Neel released his finger and in an instant had identified the vessel and placed a clamp on it. He slowly lifted his hand, and there was no more catastrophic bleeding. Next he took another clamp and spread the tissues above that, looking for the upper portion of the vessel. Finding what he thought was the vessel, he hesitated for a second.

"Anders, we're right at the base of the skull, next to the jugular foramen. What we've got in this vicinity are the ninth, tenth, eleventh and twelfth cranial nerves. If I clamp one of them by accident, it could cause him a significant functional problem, such as a paralyzed vocal cord or difficulty swallowing. I have to be sure I only have the vessel in my hemostat. Understand?"

Anders cleared his throat. This was all very tense for him. "Yes, sir," he managed, staring at the area of tissue and wondering how Major Neel could tell for sure what was what in there.

With the forceps, Neel located and identified for Anders the four cranial nerves, and showed him how he placed the hemostat only on the vein stump. Then, while Anders carefully held up each hemostat, Neel placed two 2-0 silk ties around the vessel stumps, securing them from further bleeding.

''What about the blood return from the head, major, with the jugular vein on this side tied off?'' Anders asked finally, when the task was completed.

''Good question, Anders.,'' Neel straightened up and stretched out the tension in his back and shoulders. ''In most people, the right jugular vein is the largest and has the greatest blood flow, so this patient is better off than if we had had to tie off the right side. Second, there are collateral veins in the neck that will dilate and begin to take more return flow from the head than before. Finally, the vertebral veins in the spinal column will also take a greater share of the blood. His face might stay swollen for a while longer, but that shouldn't cause him any problem, as long as his neck doesn't get infected and rupture the weak vessels before they heal and seal off. So, we won't close the neck wound, just debride and irrigate it with an antibiotic solution and give him intravenous antibiotics. He's young and healthy and should heal up well, though, if I had to bet on it.''

''Uh, major, can I ask a question?''

Neel nodded.

''What if you hadn't been able to find the blood vessels in time to stop the bleeding?''

''Well, son,'' Neel said softly, ''our good captain here would have bled to death.'' He let that sink into Anders for a second. ''But, that's why a surgeon undergoes so much training - to prepare him to be able to handle almost all of these things and to prevent a death, if possible. It isn't always, but I'll say that we can do it successfully more often than not.''

''It must be a great feeling, major, to handle a surgery like this successfully.''

''Well, you should know, Anders, you've been just as much a part of it as we all have. So pat yourself on the back. After all you're the one who got him to us here alive, don't forget.''

Anders had begun to feel a special sense of pride in the knowledge that he had actually saved Captain Weatherby's life.

That was reinforced by Dr. Neel's reminders, and it was an indescribable feeling.

''All right, Anders, we can't rest on our laurels,'' Neel said. ''We've got to debride the devitalized tissue in the neck and face from these fragment wounds and get out any foreign bodies we can. I saw no other evidence of nerve involvement in the face, so it's probably going to be straightforward debridement.''

Neel set the younger man to the task of removing the dead skin from around the fragment entry wounds with small forceps and scissors, while he debrided the major wounds of the neck skin. After they had removed all the foreign bodies they could find, Neel irrigated the neck and entry wounds with an antibiotic solution.

''Tom,'' Neel said to the nurse anesthetist, ''we're going to change to a formal tracheotomy now, so be ready to switch to the new tube when we need to, okay?''

Burns nodded.

''Rose Ann, let me have a marking pen, and Sue, would you throw a number six silicone trach tube onto the field for us, please?'

Neel took the marking pen and drew a short curvilinear line on Weatherby's lower neck, just a few centimeters above the breastbone, and about the same distance below the current, but temporary, tracheotomy site.

''Scalpel, please,'' said Neel, who then passed it on to Anders by the handle. Anders just looked at the scalpel and then looked back up at Neel. ''Well, aren't you going to finish your job, Anders? You need to make a formal trach site into the upper trachea. We can't let the tube stay in the cricothyroid membrane, because it might lead to stenosis of the area below the vocal cords.''

''I . . I've never done that, major. I don't know how,'' Anders replied.

''That's what I'm here for, Anders, to show you. I remember my first tracheotomy as a senior medical student at Missouri. My professor was a man named Dr. Hugh Stephenson, a surgeon par excellence. He walked me through it and it really solidified my desire to become a surgeon. I owe that to him and now I'm passing it along to you.''

At first, Anders hesitated. Then he placed the scalpel on the skin and pressed down with the 'belly' of the scalpel blade, just as he had seen Neel do previously. Neel inserted some hook retractors and separated the tissues so Anders could use the cutting cautery to slice through the subcutaneous fat. The burning fat emitted an odor that reminded Anders of the time he had had a plantar wart burned off the bottom of his foot in the student health clinic at Madison. But, it wasn't an unpleasant odor and he put it out of his mind. He realized he was actually enjoying this, although he was more than a little bit nervous.

When he reached the vertical neck muscles over the thyroid, Neel showed Anders how to separate them in the middle, then he retracted them out of the way, exposing the isthmus of the gland. "Now here is where you can get some bleeding, Anders, if you poke a hole in that thyroid gland, so just be careful."

Anders handed the scissors to Neel. "Here, you do it. I don't want to cause a problem."

Gently, Neel pushed the scissors back. "No way, Jay, you're the surgeon on this trach, and I'm your assistant. It's your responsibility. Now, just free up that small portion of the isthmus and we'll put clamps around it, cut it and tie them."

Anders did as he was instructed, doing it well, and with no consequences. This time, Neel held up the hemostats so Anders could tie the small stumps of the mid portion of the thyroid gland. But Neel checked the strength of the ties himself before cutting, and was satisfied they were secure.

"Anders, you're looking at the anterior portion of the trachea right now. You're going to cut out a horseshoe-shaped flap to bring out to the skin that will serve as a safe conduit for the tube. If it got coughed out or accidentally dislodged, it would be very easy to replace by anyone." Neel drew the outline he wanted for the tracheal cartilage flap, based below, that Anders should follow.

"Now, use an 11 blade for the scalpel, as it will cut better into the tougher cartilage there. And, Tom, get ready to disconnect and hook up to the new trach tube after we have it in okay?"

Anders stuck the scalpel into the trachea with some trepidation, then gained more confidence as he cut in a sawing motion to outline the flap. Once it was free, Neel showed him how to tie it back with a 4-0 Prolene suture to secure it to the skin of the incision. "Did you check the balloon on the tube, Rose Ann?" Neel asked when she handed the tracheotomy tube to Anders.

"Yes, sir, it's fine."

"Now, Anders, just gently push it into the trachea while I remove the one up above. Good, that's it. Tom, you can hook up to ours now, and keep the captain asleep long enough for us to dress the wound."

The two men secured the tube to the neck with gauze ties and slipped a gauze sponge under it to cover the incision. "We don't suture the tracheal skin incision because air might get trapped in the tissues. That can cause a pneumothorax," Neel explained. "And, we'll need to get a postoperative chest x-ray in the recovery room to check for tube placement as well as to check for any complications of the surgery."

"Ladies, we'll need to pack the neck wound with gauze soaked in bacitracin solution and apply ointment to the facial wounds. Then, we'll wrap the neck loosely with Keflix. Tomorrow, we'll change the neck dressing and gradually pull out the packing in the neck. It's a rule of combat medicine, Anders, that you don't close most wounds, just leave them open to heal by themselves or close them in a delayed fashion. Less chance for infection that way."

The surgical team completed the dressing application and Captain Burns started to wake up the patient. "Tom, let's get another hematocrit in the recovery room, along with the chest x-ray. Anders and I will get a bite to eat and some coffee and see how he is in a few minutes."

Anders and Neel removed their caps, masks, gloves and gowns and went out to the small tent where the professional personnel slept. Neel sat on his cot and motioned Anders to the opposite cot. He reached into a duffel bag and pulled out two cans, giving one to Anders.

"Wow, a Diet Coke, I haven't seen one of these since I got here!" Anders grinned.

"Well, you deserve it, friend. I have been saving these for a special moment and I think we have both earned one. By the way, help yourself to an MRE over there."

Anders was suddenly famished. He wasn't sure when he had last eaten, but he thought it was sometime yesterday. He found his favorite entree, 'Chicken-ala-King', and opened it. Also inside were crackers, peanut butter and jelly. What a treasure!

The men eagerly attacked the food, happy to get some

sustenance into their systems. The Cokes were warm, but who cared?

Neel sat back on the cot and stretched out his legs. "So what are your plans for the future, Anders?"

Anders felt he could talk to this man, who although talented and respected, also made him feel at ease. "Well, sir, I'll finish up at U of Wisconsin as soon as I can get back. Then, well, I was supposed to apply to medical school, but I just haven't sent out the applications yet."

"Why not?" Neel asked.

"To tell you the truth, major, I didn't think I was competent enough to be a physician. I guess I just didn't have enough confidence in myself."

"And now?"

"Well, you helped me a lot today, sir. I really loved being in the operating room today, helping you - and, well, doing some surgery myself, too, I guess. Do you think I could really be a surgeon one day?"

Neel sat up and put his feet on the floor. "Anders, I've seen a lot of medical students. Taught a lot of them in and out of the operating room. You've got as much ability as any and more than most. If anyone can do it, you can. Don't ever sell yourself short. You've got a real talent with people and with doing things. I figure the Good Lord gave us these talents to use for others, and if we don't do it. then we're missing the whole point of why we're here at all."

Neel had never really verbalized those feelings, but he really did believe what he said and he knew it might help this young man become what he wanted to.

Anders stared at his Coke can for a few minutes. "I know you're right, major. Deep down, I know that. There's also a young woman I met over here. Becky Gold. I helped medevac her to a hospital when she had acute vertigo, and I think she's pretty special. She's a psychology student back in the states, and I think she might like me, too. Can you go through medical school and surgery training while you're, well, you know, while you're married?"

Neel thought about his own situation. He had been single during his training, except for the last of his fellowship and he had often been pretty lonely. "Sure, you can. In fact, it probably helps keep you sane and human if you have a significant other or a spouse to share it with and to relax with when you can.'' Changing the subject a little, Neel asked: ''If we got back this summer, could you still graduate next year?''

''Yes, sir, I could probably graduate in December. I've got the chance for a research job at Minnesota if it's still open when I get back, and I could probably work there or go to graduate school if I couldn't get into medical school right away.''

''How many hours do you need to graduate?''

''Only about six, if I can take my finals for the fall semester I got pulled out of to come here.''

''If you knocked them out at summer school, then you ought to be able to be placed on a waiting list for medical school, to start this fall, if someone drops out. But the whole thing rests on whether we get back in time for summer. I sure hope so myself.''

''It must be tough leaving your practice and family to come here, major.''

''Well, I figure the reason I was brought here was to do just what we did, Anders, to operate on wounded men and women. If I can save just one life, then it will have been worth it to me, and worth a whole lot more to that person and their family. But, yes, I do miss my wife. We're expecting a baby in May, so I'd really like to be back by then.''

''That's only two months away, sir. Anything can happen in that time. Maybe the war will end quickly and we'll all get out of here.''

''Yeah, maybe so, Anders, maybe so. Well, let's go see how our patients are doing.''

They arrived at the recovery room/ICU tent just as Captain Burns was coming out. ''How is he, Tom?''

''Doing just great. I started one unit of packed red cells because his hematocrit was down to thirty-five, but that may be the only one he'll need.''

Neel slapped Burns on the shoulder. ''Thanks, man, you're really good.''

Weatherby was awake, and was being suctioned by Major Oates. ''Captain Otto left for a few minutes of sleep, major, now that the captain is awake and stable. There's only a little bleeding on the dressing, but not much.''

"Thanks, Jocelyn. How's Sergeant Gonzales?''

"He's doing fine, too. His temperature is up slightly, so we're making him cough a lot. His urine output has increased and he has put out about two thousand ccs. in the last two hours."

Neel turned to Anders. "Burn patients begin to diuresis the fluid in their tissues once they've become stabilized, so that's a good sign. I also don't want him to get renal failure by having deposits of protein in the kidney block his urine output." They walked over to Captain Weatherby. His face was swollen and the neck dressing make him look rather grotesque, but his eyes were open.

"Hello, captain. Looks like you're back with us again," Neel grinned. "Remember, the trach tube will stay in for a few days and you won't be able to talk around it. If you want something, the people in here will give you a pen and paper to write it out. Now stick out your tongue for me and move it around. Okay, now purse your lips and then show me your teeth. Okay, looks fine. There were two blood vessels torn inside your neck from the fragments. We tied off one and fixed the other. Everything will sort itself out fine in your neck and you should do well. But, you'll have a major scar on your neck - your own 'red badge of courage'."

Neel noticed Weatherby wince at the reference, then he closed his eyes. *What did I say? Why did the reference to courage bother him?* He patted Weatherby on the shoulder and motioned for Anders to follow him to the next litter.

Sergeant Gonzales was looking better. He was drowsy and sluggish from the morphine and sedatives, but his lungs sounded clear when Neel listened to them. He looked over the graphic chart of Gonzales' vital signs and was pleased. Dr. Otto was doing a nice job of postoperative recovery and Neel had no additional suggestion. "Sarge, how are you feeling?"

Gonzales opened his eyes and blinked several times. He started to talk, but at first only a rasp came out. Then cleared his throat and tried again. "Hello, sir, how are you doing today?"

"Don't worry about me, you old dog, how are you? Do you have much pain?" Gonzales' eyes showed the answer, but he shook his head.

"This young man here, Trinidad, is the medic who picked you up in the desert and brought you to this expensive private hospital." He nodded at Anders.

Gonzales lifted his bandaged hand and laid it on Anders' forearm. "Thanks, man, thanks a lot," he rasped.

Anders blushed with embarrassment. "I'm really glad you're making it, Sarge," Anders finally managed - "I thought you were a goner until Dr. Neel got hold of you."

Cutting in quickly, Neel turned toward Captain Weatherby's litter. He told Gonzales: "We brought you a bed partner over next to you. An Apache pilot who shot down two Iraqi helicopters trying to plaster Anders here and the whole crew of a Blackhawk, not to mention a Navy flier and two SF guys. You two are about in the same shape, so help each other out, okay? He can't talk yet, because he's got a tube in his throat, but give him a word or two of encouragement, will you, Trinidad? He's been through a lot, just like you."

Gonzales nodded and craned his head over to the right so he could see the next litter. All he could make out was a man wrapped in gauze breathing noisily. *Sure, he'd help him out. He was just glad he was still alive and able to think about getting back home to see his family. Damn the pain and whatever, he was alive! He wondered if the man in the litter next to him had a family and where they were. Maybe they'd go back to Germany on the same air evac flight.* Gonzales was still thinking about that as he drifted into drugged sleep.

"Let's leave them, Anders, and let them rest." As they were leaving the tent, the two men turned and looked back at their patients lying next to each other in this special tent. *Who knows,* Neel thought, *they might even become friends.*

* * *

Neel and Anders had just entered the triage tent to check on the status of the Navy pilot, when the medic called Bobby hurried up. "Admin just called and said they received some sort of a call from a Huey coming back from an airborne assault. Seems they have two men on board they want to drop off, one wounded and one dead. Can we take them?"

Neel thought about that. "We don't have any facilities to hold a body, Bobby, but we can certainly put it in a body bag and clean it up for graves registration. Then, they can take it on with them to the 13th Evac down the line. But, we'll certainly be happy to take care of the casualty."

"Yes, sir, I'll tell admin." He ran off to the next tent to

relay the message.

Neel turned to Anders and looked him in the eye. ''Will you tend to the body, clean it up and package the personal belongings in a separate packet? Then place the body in the bag? We've got them packed away here somewhere. Bobby will help you. Then you might get a ride back to the 13th with them, if they'll go that way.''

Anders thought about his last experience with body bags, in the desert that night the helicopter was shot down by the Iraqi missile. He shivered slightly. *No, I don't want to do it,* he thought.

But he said, ''Yes, sir, I'll take care of it.''

They waited in the triage tent, drinking a cup of MRE coffee that had been brewed by the triage NCOIC. It wasn't very good, but with a lot of sugar, was almost palatable.

When, the sound of a helicopter, unmistakably a Huey, was heard, the litter team ran into the tent and picked up two litters, hurrying back out to landing pad. When they returned, they were carrying two victims, one clearly dead.

Neel first went to the dead man, checking for a heart beat and pupillary eye reaction. Finding none, he made the pronouncement. He'd have to sign paperwork later, but he'd leave that to Anders and Bobby. He turned his attention to the wounded soldier.

He was still alive, but barely. They must have been in a tremendous firefight up north - the man had multiple gunshot wounds over his trunk and extremities. But none were life-threatening. He had survived the initial shock and blood loss and was capable of being resuscitated. He appeared healthy and strong and that would serve him well.

Neel mobilized his triage team and called for Captain Collopy to help him with the extremity wounds. They would take the patient to the operating room and repair the holes and replace his blood and fluids. Hopefully, that would save him, along with a strong dose of divine intervention.

While Neel was taking the wounded soldier to the OR, Anders was removing the few personal effects he could find on the dead soldier. Not much to go by. Must have kept most of his valuables somewhere else. Just a watch and pocket knife and some jewelry. He cleaned up the man's skin and clothing as best he could. The eyes were still open, staring at unseen things. Anders gently pulled the eyelids down and closed the eyes. With Bobby's help, Anders placed the man in the rubber bag, zipping it up. Suddenly, he had a hard time thinking there was a body in the bag, it seemed so . . . final. Almost ashamed, he reached up and unzipped the top of the bag just a little, thinking the strange thought that this man's soul might need a little room to get out if it was going to leave. *The soul of anyone who dies in battle ought to go to heaven.*

Bobby suddenly startled him from his reverie: ''Okay to take him back to the aircraft, now? They're waiting for him, you know.'' Anders nodded and started to lift the body. Between them they struggled with it and made it to the aircraft. After they lifted it into the cabin and secured it, Anders asked the pilot, ''Okay if I tag along to the 13th with you, lieutenant?''

''Sure, Doc, come on it. We'll be there in thirty minutes. Got any gear?''

Anders shook his head. He looked back at the hospital, wanting to say goodbye to Major Neel, but knowing he was already in surgery. *Well,* he thought, *I'll figure out a way to see him again. You just don't share a part of someone's life and never see them again.* He climbed into the Huey and strapped himself in. As the helicopter lifted off and banked, Anders realized his life would never again be the same.

* * *

Two days had passed since the surgery on Sergeant Gonzales and Captain Weatherby. Both were improving as was the third casualty from the firefight at the Republican Guard base. Neel had changed Weatherby's neck dressings twice and was pleased with the healing. He had also debrided and applied new Silvadene to Sergeant Gonzales' burns every eight hours. The skin grafts looked good and were a nearly hundred percent take. The Navy flier had been evacuated the day before and all three remaining patients were scheduled to be picked up by a medevac chopper some time that day.

Neel had removed the trach tube from the captain's throat and he could talk if he pushed on the gauze dressing covering the holes. Weatherby looked over at Sergeant Gonzales and saw he was finally awake, having been asleep for several hours.

''Hey, Sarge,'' he rasped. ''How are you doing today?''

''Not bad, sir. I see you can talk now. That's great.''

''Yeah, it was a weird feeling with that thing in your throat, not being able to say anything or tell anyone what you needed." The captain's voice was still thick and hoarse, but understandable. "How'd you get burned anyway?" he asked.

"Well, we were in a firefight with a company of Iraqi tanks and all of a sudden, there was some kind of mistake, like the chopper pilots got us mixed up with the Iraqis and knocked out a couple of our own tanks. I just went over and pulled out the guys, and 'whoosh', the tank exploded. I guess I got burned from that." He looked over at the captain and saw a stricken look on his face.

Weatherby stared at the door for a minute, not being able to talk or even swallow. They he turned to look directly at the sergeant. There were tears in his eyes.

"My God, man, I'm so sorry. I did that to you, I guess, because I was in one of the choppers that fired on the tanks by mistake. I'm so sorry." His voice broke and he closed his eyes, letting his head go back on the pillow.

Gonzales could just barely see the chest of the aviator heaving with sobs. He didn't know what to think or say. Sure, he had felt anger and betrayal back then. But now, here was a man, a real person, the one who had done it. It was different when it was a 'helicopter' that shot at them. Now, it was a man, no better off than he, who obviously felt so guilty about it it was tearing him up inside.

Gonzales was silent for a moment. "Listen, captain, I don't blame you personally for this. We were in a crazy firefight and anything could have happened. You came to help us and it just backfired. I could have died in Vietnam and I didn't. I could have died here in Iraq and I didn't. And, you're alive here, too. Don't you think that the Good Lord didn't have something important in mind for us when he let us live? No one got killed by your helicopter, captain. We're all going home to our families, including you. I hold you no ill will. I'm a Christian and I know how to forgive. Learn how to forgive yourself."

Weatherby nodded and lay still. Then, Gonzales painfully reached out with his bandaged arm and extended it toward the captain. Weatherby looked at the arm and reached out his own, both men touching in the space between the litters, and holding that touch for a brief time.

Neel had been just inside the tent during this conversation and had seen and heard everything. He took a deep breath and left the tent quietly, walking out to the edge of the sand berm protecting the small hospital compound. It was just a few hours past dawn, and Neel facing the east, watching the sun rise over the desert. The latest news on the short wave radio indicated the Coalition was claiming victory against the Iraqis and that the enemy was being driven from Kuwait. The war would be over soon. He thought of the casualties he had seen and treated. Of the lives he had saved. He thought of the new future for all the survivors of this massive mobilization of American military personnel. He hoped he would be able to return soon to Kansas City, to mend the recent unpleasantries with his wife, and to witness the birth of his first child.

He looked out over this desert, this site of ancient Biblical history. So much had happened here over thousands of years. This episode of Desert Storm will be just a small part of that history.

He remembered when the ground war had started and they had begun the drive into southern Iraq, there had been a desert storm rising. Now, the storm had passed and the sun felt incredibly warm and comforting on his face.

CHAPTER 15

THE CEREMONY TOOK place on the south lawn of the White House. The fall leaves were beginning to drop and swirl around the ground in a mild autumn breeze. While the day was not chilly by Washington standards for that time of year, the women and children were dressed warmly. Most of the men wore military uniforms, except for a small group of civilian guests and reporters. The ceremony was closed to the public, but the reporters would spread the word through their respective print and broadcast reports.

Eagerly awaiting the President, the crowd was respectfully hushed. Finally, George Bush walked out the door from the Oval Office, to begin the event. With him were the Vice President, Speaker of the House, both senators from Texas, the Secretary of Defense and the Chairman of the Joint Chiefs of Staff. The President waved to those gathered for the ceremony, and nodded for the Secretary of Defense to begin. He passed the signal on to the White House chief of military protocol, who stepped to the podium on the lawn above South Executive Avenue. The President gazed out across the Ellipse and beyond, appreciating the soaring majesty of the Washington Monument. Each time he saw the mighty obelisk from his window in the White House, it symbolized to him the strength and character of the American people. Today's ceremony was particularly special to him.

At the podium the colonel began. "Ladies and gentlemen, welcome on behalf of the President of the United States to this military ceremony. We gather here to honor two men who served their country bravely during the Persian Gulf conflict, and, as much to honor their families."

The officer straightened his back and raised his voice. "Attention to Orders," he called, reading from the paper in front of him on the podium.

'For conspicuous gallantry in the face of enemy

> *hostilities during service to the Army of the United States of America. As the leader of the security detail at Khobar Towers, Dhahran, Saudi Arabia, Sergeant First Class Trinidad Gonzales did distinguish himself in exemplary fashion, above and beyond the call of duty by single-handedly repelling a hostile terrorist attack on American troop positions that would most certainly have resulted in the loss of many American lives and the causing of considerable casualties. Later, during the course of action in a tank battle against superior enemy tank forces in southern Iraq, as a member of the First Battalion of the First Brigade, 3rd Armored Division, Sergeant First Class Gonzales further distinguished himself in the field of battle by destroying three enemy tanks, and, at great risk of personal danger, singlehandedly rescued four fellow soldiers from a burning tank. After rescuing them and carrying them to safety, Sergeant First Class Gonzales was severely burned by the exploding tank. All of the rescued men survived, owing to the bravery and actions of Sergeant Gonzales. His exceptional courage, dedication, and devotion to duty reflect great credit upon himself, the 3rd Armored Division, and the United States Army. For these feats of extraordinary bravery above and beyond the call of duty, Sergeant First Class Trinidad Gonzales is awarded the Congressional Medal of Honor.''*

The Colonel looked down to the front row of the seats in front on him. ''Sergeant Gonzales,'' he said softly, ''will you now come to the front and stand by the President. Your family is welcome also.''

With some difficulty, Sergeant Gonzales stood up from his chair, wearing his Army dress blue uniform. With one hand holding his wife's and the other draped around his three daughters, he slowly and painfully made his way toward the line of American leaders. Once he reached the President, he dropped his right hand away from the children and gave the President a perfect salute. The

President returned the salute and stepped forward to take Gonzales's right hand in both of his. The President leaned down and spoke, first to the sergeant, then to his wife. Finally, he placed his hand on each of the girl's heads and patted them.

The Chairman of the Joint Chiefs and the Secretary of Defense stepped forward, standing to the right of Mrs. Gonzales. The President was handed an open case containing the nation's highest award for bravery in the line of duty, and gently lifted the medal from its satin resting place. Turning once again to Sergeant Gonzales, who was standing as rigidly as his contracted burn scars would allow, the President reached down and slipped the blue ribbon with its attached medal over Sergeant Gonzales' head. Then, in a moment of impulse, he embraced the smaller man and held him there for a moment. Releasing him, the President also gave Mrs. Gonzales a hug and turned them both around for the guests at the ceremony to see. There was a loud and sustained applause, and everyone rose to cheer this brave soldier from El Paso, Texas.

The President stepped to the podium. He carried no notes. He knew exactly what he wanted to say, because it came from the heart. "My fellow Americans, you have just witnessed an event that does not occur often in the life of a President, nor of the nation. To be able, as President of the United States, to award the Congressional Medal of Honor to a man who demonstrated such bravery, such total disregard for his own welfare in the interest of his comrades, is truly an honor." When the President's hair flew awry from a sudden gust, he reached up to brush it from his eyes.

"Occasionally in the course of the conflicts of our nation, we see feats of bravery such as were described to you here today. It makes us proud, as family, as Americans, to know that such acts are performed by people we have grown up with, talked with, loved. Ordinary Americans who summoned extraordinary reserves to respond to the face of death and risk and to give us all an example of what can be done, if the heart is pure. This man in front of you today, this family of his, those of you who are his friends, are all part of a human race that seeks to find peace, and only through the acts of courage like this can aggression in the world be stopped."

The President gestured toward Sergeant Gonzales and put his hand around his shoulder, drawing him nearer. "This man has lived with pain and suffering for six months now, healing from terrible burns he sustained in battle. Through the healing powers of great physicians and the hand of God Almighty, he will live on and continue to be a fine father, husband, citizen and soldier. Sergeant Trinidad Gonzales, you are a true hero and we salute you.''

The President applauded. The Vice-President applauded. So did the Speaker of the House, the Texas Senators, the Secretary of Defense, and the Chairman of the Joint Chiefs. Mrs. Gonzales was crying, and the Gonzales girls shyly clutched their father's pantslegs. Sergeant Gonzales stared straight ahead at the crowd and looked into the eyes of the people who had come to honor him. He saw them as if peering through a motion picture camera viewfinder.

There was the medic, Allen Jay Anders, who had picked him up on the battlefield. Anders was standing next to a striking brunette, who was holding his hand. *Probably the fiancee he had spoken of. Nice match, the two of them.*

Next he saw the man who had really saved his life, Major Thomas Mortimer Neel, now just plain Dr. Neel. He was grinning from ear to ear, holding his new baby son, with his wife, Marty, clinging to them as if she never wanted to let them go.

And there were Sergeant Smith and the other three men from Smitty's crew whom he had pulled out of the destroyed tank that fateful night in the desert. He was beginning to remember more about the events than before, and unfortunately, still suffered the occasional nightmare. When Smitty gave him the old 'thumbs up,' Trinidad smiled at him. These four men had brought their families and Gonzales had had a chance before the ceremonies to meet them all. It had warmed his heart.

Lieutenant Rick Hanes was there, too, as well as two members of Trinidad's own crew, Corporal Ron Jennings and Sergeant ''Bull'' Jones. They were whooping and whistling, like you might expect from a couple of tankers. He loved them anyway.

Gonzales moved slightly to the right so he could see the tall man standing with his wife and sons behind Dr. Neel. There he was, dressed in his resplendent military uniform, tall and erect. He was clapping his hands, but more than that, he was smiling. Tex Weatherby had forgiven himself, as Trinidad Gonzales had forgiven him, and they had become friends. Theirs was a kinship built from desperation and the love of life. Gonzales slowly raised his hand and gestured to Weatherby, who raised his in return.

The President and the other members of the White House party all shook hands again with Sergeant Gonzales and his wife. Then, the Chairman of the Joint Chiefs grasped Gonzales by the elbow, and escorted him back to his seat with his family. Before returning, the general whispered something in the sergeant's ear, and watched closely for the sergeant's response. When he had heard it, he smiled and nodded.

After the Chairman returned to the line, the President stepped back to the podium. ''We are also gathered here today, to pay honor to another of our men in uniform. Unfortunately, that hero fell in the course of battle, and returned to the city he so loved, to be buried in Arlington National Cemetery. Colonel Bland, please read the citation." Colonel Bland returned to the podium as the President stepped back. ''Attention to orders,'' he called out.

> *''For exceptional bravery in the field of battle, while a member of Charlie Company, First Battalion, 503rd Parachute Regiment of the 82nd Airborne Division, during an airborne assault on a fortified Republican Guard position in southwestern Iraq. During this engagement, Staff Sergeant Lucius Tatum did perform many acts of courage and leadership, which saved the lives of men in his squad and helped to turn back a counterattack by enemy soldiers. In addition, under direct enemy fire, and with total disregard for his own safety, Sergeant Tatum returned to the battlefield in search of a Special Forces team to help them evacuate. He found the only living member of the team, who himself was unconscious and severely wounded, and carried him to safety on his back. It was during the rescue of this officer that Sergeant Tatum was mortally wounded by enemy fire. Staff Sergeant Lucius Tatum's devotion to duty, his courage in the face of enemy fire, and his exemplary behavior will serve as a source of inspiration to the 82nd*

> *Airborne Division, the United States Army and to our country. For these acts of bravery, Sergeant Lucius Tatum is posthumously awarded the Distinguished Service Cross.*

The President stepped forward and received the medal in its case from the Colonel's aide. He and the White House leadership walked down the grass to where Mrs. Tatum and her three children were seated. The President presented the medal to her, as well as an American flag which had flown recently over Arlington National Cemetery. He spoke with the family privately for a few moments, then allowed the rest of the dignitaries to pay their respects.

After the dignitaries made their way back, the President stepped to the microphone again and leaned heavily on the podium. ''It gives me both sadness as well as a deep sense of gratitude to present this medal to the wife and children of this brave man. Sergeant Tatum gave his life for his country, but not until he had saved so many other lives of his fellow paratroopers, and of the young Special Forces officer, who would otherwise have died. Every human life is sacred to us, but to die for one's country sets an example of courage and dedication for all of us. Mrs. Tatum, Lucius Junior, Samantha, and Jessica, your husband and father was a man for each of us to be proud of. He was an American of legendary proportions, and we can only hope his brave passing can somehow serve as an example that will make this country better and more aware of our obligation to our fellowman. I think your husband and father would have liked that.''

The President moved his hand over the expanse of the Independence Mall in the distance. ''We stand before the monuments to this great country, but I say to you today, that there are no greater monuments anywhere, than those of these two great men we have honored today - Sergeant First Class Trinidad Gonzales and Staff Sergeant Lucius Tatum. They are truly outstanding Americans. Let us now bow our heads for a moment of silent prayer for the fallen brothers of this and other conflicts.'' The President bowed his head and stood silent. The audience followed his example, each lost in his or her own thoughts.

Jay Anders, saw a vivid combination of Sergeant Gonzales in the desert, burned and in pain. Seeing him here receiving the Congressional Medal of Honor from the President of the United States made Anders very proud indeed. His other thought was of the remains of Sergeant Tatum on the litter at the surgical hospital in southern Iraq. He remembered having to lower his eyelids before closing the body bag. He knew that this good man's soul had gone to Heaven, and he and his actions on earth would continue to serve as examples for all of them.

For Mary Tatum, her thoughts were of this fine man, her husband, who had just been honored by the President. He was a good husband and father, and they would miss him terribly. After the military funeral at Arlington Cemetery, the minister of the Baptist church they attended frequently when in Washington, D.C., had approached her and given her the letter her husband had written before the ground war. It was to be delivered by the pastor only in the event of her husband's death in battle.

She had cried for hours after reading it, but had been compelled to obey Lucius' wishes and share it with their children. They had cried too, and had clung to the letter as the last remnant of their father in this life. These were good kids, she knew, and they would grow up being proud of their father. She had found a strange crucifix in the personal belongings that the Army had sent to her after the burial. She knew it wasn't his, but had no idea where he might have gotten it. Until the answer would be made known to her, she had placed the Catholic cross next to his picture over the hearth in the government housing at Ft. Bragg. It served to show them that God was with Lucius until the very end. He wanted the children to be educated and somehow, with God's help, she would see that was done.

For Trinidad Gonzales, the relief that came to him was like a weight being lifted from his shoulders. He no longer carried the bitterness of Vietnam in his soul. His country had recognized that the profession of arms was noble and indispensable to the American way of life. It was a valued profession and he loved his work. He also felt so humble, so small and human, to be granted this highest award by the President of the United States himself. He thanked God above that He had allowed him to live through that horrible time in the desert and to come back to his beloved family. He also thanked the Lord for giving him the strength to save those men from the burning tank. *Surely this is a great and beautiful country to provide the opportunity for a poor boy from the border to be honored like this. God Bless America, and thank You for my family.*

For Tex Weatherby, he realized that the experiences in the desert had been a trial for him, a test of his true strength and personality. He finally realized his life had developed into something he was not proud of - he had become someone not even he could respect. And Tex understood how others could not respect him. He knew that somehow, after the gut-wrenching, soul-searching he had experienced after the friendly fire episode, he had become a better man, one he was happy with. Fortunately, the Army had exonerated him and Perez from any wrong-doing. It was simply a misfortune of war. Also, the second chance that he had been given to prove himself was an answer to his prayers, and he thanked the Lord for that. He looked at Sergeant Gonzales, seated in the front row and Tex realized this was a very special individual, and that he felt blessed by his friendship.

For Tom Neel, his thoughts were on his family. He had never felt so close to his wife as he did at that moment. Here, at this place, at this ceremony, holding his new son, with his wife's hand on his arm, he felt a sense of peace and fulfillment he never had felt in his professional life alone. He was proud to have been a part of Sergeant Gonzales' survival, and wished him the very best. Perhaps now Trinidad would be free of the devil that had plagued him since Vietnam. Neel's own future was bright and happy and he was thankful for all his blessings. He loved his country more than ever.

For newly promoted Captain Scott Porter, he wished he had known this hero, the black man who had saved his life, and who was honored today. He remembered nothing of the rescue, nor of the first several days in the hospital, but he had talked to everyone who could fill in the blanks. Sergeant Lucius Tatum must have been quite a man. But, the one thing that bothered him, was that he had heard Sergeant Tatum was somewhat intolerant of what he thought was the 'privileged white officer corps.' To be saved by a man who gave his life for a white officer, when he clearly didn't need to come back looking for the Special Forces team, told Scott something about the strength of the man's heart and values. He certainly did not feel that his life was worth more than Tatum's, and he would always have to live with that. He deeply regretted never knowing Lucius Tatum.

The President raised his head again and smiled. ''We have so much to be thankful for, living in this great country. Look around this audience today.'' He gestured with his hand. ''See the children, the sons and daughters of men and women who sacrificed and gave of themselves so our country may be free and great. Let us not forget that these children are the future of our country. And men like Sergeant First Class Trinidad Gonzales and Staff Sergeant Lucius Tatum will serve as a shining point of light for their children to follow. God bless all of you, and good luck.''

The President's aides hurried to get the Tatum and Gonzales families up to the back of the White House steps for photo opportunities with the President and the other dignitaries. The rest of the audience stood up, stretched, and either watched the photographic session or began to talk among themselves.

Tom and Marty Neel went up to Jay Anders and his friend, Becky. ''Well, Jay, how goes the first month of medical school?

''Dr. Neel,'' Jay said appreciatively, ''ever since you got the medical school at Missouri to consider my late application and they accepted me, I just don't know how to thank you enough. I was flabbergasted the way it all came about. I guess I didn't think someone as busy as you would bother to help a college kid like me.''

Neel looked him in the eye and frowned. ''Listen, Jay, you're a very special person. Don't forget that combat medical badge and the Air Medal with the V-device for valor they gave you. You think that's nothing? That means you're a brave and special person. I saw myself fifteen years ago in you, Jay, and I expect you to make great things of yourself. And, if you are lucky enough to marry this young lady, you'll be even better off.''

Jay put his arm around Becky. ''Well, sir, I can tell you that I just proposed to Becky before the ceremony and she said yes. I figured no better place for a proposal than the White House lawn, right?''

The Neels congratulated the two young people and delighted in their good news. ''That calls for a celebration. We'll get Marty's folks to watch Tom Junior here and let's go out to dinner in Alexandria. Our treat. Okay with you two?''

Anders looked at Becky and she nodded. They were staying

with relatives of Becky's in Georgetown and had one of the family cars for their use. They'd enjoy dinner with the Neels. They didn't need to leave for school back in Columbia again until Sunday afternoon, so they had a whole twenty-four hours to tour the D.C. area.

Just as Neel was beginning to say something, one of the President's aides came up to Neel and introduced himself. "Dr. Neel, I'm Jeff Tudor, special assistant to the President. We know that your father was a Congressional Medal of Honor winner in Vietnam, and that you yourself were awarded the Silver Star recently for your combat work in the Persian Gulf War. The President would be proud to have his picture taken with you and your family if you'd care to accompany me."

Neel looked at Marty. She had harbored some bad feelings about Neel's trying to emulate his father when he was mobilized and deployed to the Persian Gulf. They had not talked about it since then. "Marty?" he asked, "what do you think?"

Marty Schaefer Neel, recently awarded her Ph.D. in mathematics, looked at her husband and met his gaze. Then she smiled and said confidently, "Of course, Mr. Tudor, we'd be delighted. I'm very proud of the Neel heroes in our family and it would be right to honor them in this way." She hooked her arm around her husband's and they walked toward the President. She leaned close to Neel's ear and spoke softly: "Tom, I realized today that I acted so selfishly toward you when you left Kansas City to go to the Gulf War. I couldn't see it then, and maybe it was because of our new marriage and the pregnancy. But being here, seeing what you must feel about these men and what they did, I finally understand. You didn't want to leave us, but there must have been something in you, a deep and strong conviction, that made you feel responsible for helping those injured soldiers. I really am proud of you and I hope this little boy will carry that Neel love of America that you and his grandfather had."

Neel glanced back at Jay Anders and Becky. He then turned toward Marty and stopped. Smilng, he kissed her cheek and then the cheek of his small son, Samuel. "Honey, I love you two more than life itself. What you just said means more to me than you can ever imagine." Their eyes locked together for a long second. Then, holding hands, they made their way up the gentle grass slope to the White House veranda.

"He's a great man and a great physician, Becky. I hope I can be like him some day," Jay Anders told his fiancee.

"Jay," Becky replied, "I have no doubt that you will be. No doubt at all." And she gave him a hug.

Captain Tex Weatherby was still sitting down, trying to explain the ceremonies and their significance to his two young sons, Richard and Kyle. The boys, aged six and eight, had been awed by the President and the White House, but didn't understand why that black sergeant had to die. He had a family and now he was gone. What would those kids do without a father now?

"Boys, we have no guarantees in life that we are all going to live a long time and grow old. You know that what I do, flying helicopters, is very dangerous. But so are a lot of other jobs. We try to be careful, but sometimes the good Lord has a better job for us up in heaven. But, I can tell you, after He let me live over in the desert after being shot, I figure He's got a big job for me yet to do here on this earth. And I figure that this job has a lot to do with being a good father to you boys, and a good husband to your mother, here." He reached over and gave his wife a kiss. The boys both giggled, then groaned. Tex smiled and knew everything was all right.

He had been selected for promotion to lieutenant-colonel and should get his silver leaves sometime before Christmas. He had been assigned as deputy commander of the 6th Separate Air Cavalry Brigade at Fort Hood, Texas, and they would be moving there next month. He looked forward to a job with more regular hours and more time for the family. He could take the boys over to the Weatherby Ranch near Waco for many weekends of hunting and fishing, so they could get to know their grandfather better. Tex was settled with himself and happy with his life. He smiled at his wife, Nancy, who smiled back and winked at him.

After the President had finished the photo sessions and gone back inside the White House, Sergeant Gonzales found Weatherby and walked stiffly over to him, bringing his family with him. The two men shook hands, and Weatherby put his arm around the sergeant's shoulder. "Let me see that medal, Trinidad, I've never seen one up close." Tex peered at it closely and felt a great respect for this short, swarthy man. Weatherby himself had been awarded the Distinguished Flying Cross in ceremonies in Germany with the 2nd Armored Cav Regiment, but the Congressional Medal of

Honor was 'The Medal'. "You deserve it, Trinidad," he said softly.

Gonzales shook his head. "There were lots of guys out there, including yourself, who did as much or more than I did. I don't feel right accepting it. But how can you turn down the President?" They both smiled at that.

"By the way, what did the Chairman of the Joint Chiefs say to you at the end of the ceremony?" Tex asked.

"Well, he asked me if I had decided what assignment I wanted now. He said I had my choice of anything."

"Well, what did you say? A nice cushy job at the Pentagon? A tour at Fort Bliss in El Paso? What?" Tex asked.

"Well, I told him I thought they could use a good sergeant major at the headquarters of the 6th Separate Air Cav Brigade at Fort Hood. And I warned him that the new executive officer didn't know his head from a hole in the ground, and someone ought to be there to keep it on straight for him." Gonzales grinned, and looked over at his wife, who was also smiling. "So, I think you're stuck with me."

Weatherby shook his head and roared with laughter. "You crazy Mexican. I ought to call you a 'wetback,' but watching the way you walked over here, I think you're better called a 'stiff back.'"

The two men laughed at each other. The two wives smiled at each other, knowing their futures would be entwined from here on.

CHAPTER 16

IN SILENCE, CAPTAIN SCOTT PORTER walked to his car from the White House next to his father, still limping slightly from his leg wound. Major General Nathan Hale Porter had asked to accompany his son to the ceremony today, and Scott was a bit surprised at that. They had enjoyed some light conversation over lunch at the Washington Capitol Hotel before going to the White House, and had sat together during the ceremonies. When they reached Scott's car, he unlocked the door for his father. General Porter had raised an eyebrow when he found out Scott had sold his Porsche 928 and bought a used Jeep Cherokee. But, he didn't ask why, preferring to let Scott tell him if he chose to.

Scott pulled onto Constitution Avenue and headed west, entering the circle that took him onto the Arlington Memorial Bridge. They drove past Jefferson Davis Highway and pulled into the parking lot of Arlington National Cemetery. Scott parked and shut off the engine. Looking at his father he said, ''Dad, you're welcome to come with me, but you don't have to, if you don't want to. I won't be long.''

Holding his gaze with the same steel-grey Porter eyes, the general replied, ''Son, I'll go with you for sure.''

Scott got out of the driver's seat and went to the back of the Jeep, raising the back hatch to gain access to the storage area. He reached in and gently lifted out a large bouquet of roses. The roses were red, white and blue, with an American flag centering the arrangement. Scott shut the door and locked the car, motioning for his father to follow him.

The captain knew just where he was headed, having been there many times before in the past six months, ever since the burial ceremony. They walked past monuments from the Civil War, and past more recent ones from Vietnam and Grenada and Panama. Scott remembered his experiences in Panama and how some good men had died there.

They came to a new area of the cemetery with a number of fresh headstones. Looking at the first eight in a row, he slowly pulled out one rose from the bouquet, and placed it on the first headstone. "Master Sergeant Juan Lopez." He went on to the next and placed a rose there. "Chief Warrant Officer Two William C. Nichols." Then, "Staff Sergeant John Purcell." And so down the line of the eight members of his Special Forces team who were killed in the battle at the Republican Guard base in Iraq. Scott stood still for a moment, looking at their graves and remembering each man—his personality, his strengths, his weaknesses, his dedication, his bravery. He'd never forget them.

Moving down the line, he stopped before another grave, and knelt down beside it. The headstone simply read: 'Staff Sergeant Lucius Tatum, 82nd Airborne Division, killed 26 February, 1991, the Persian Gulf.' Porter knew there was more to the man than that simple epitaph. Much more. It would be carried in the hearts of the people who knew and loved him, and by Captain Winfield Scott Porter, who owed him his life. Scott placed the rest of the bouquet on the grave and bowed his head.

Sergeant Tatum, I'll look after your family. I started an education fund for your children, and put down the first $25,000 installment last week. By the time they're ready to go to college, they'll each have a free college education, plus a little extra for a professional school, if they are interested and qualified. That's the least I can do for you.

Porter looked at the flowers. *Red, white, and blue,* he thought. *Fitting for such a hero. I thought first about getting black and white roses, but I think these colors say more about the man. And, perhaps more about me, too.*

I've got my job cut out for me now. As the new commander of Company A, Third Battalion, 5th Special Forces Group, I'll be busy. But I won't forget your and your family, you can count on that. And whenever I'm here in Washington, I'll come visit you.

Porter felt his father's hand on his shoulder and, opening his eyes, looked over to find his father on his knees beside him. The general looked old and frail. "Scott, I want to thank this man, also, for bringing my son back alive to me. I'm so proud of the man you've become and I haven't ever taken the chance to tell you that. If you had been killed before I had the chance to say it, that would have killed me, too. I love you and I'm not ashamed to say it. You've made me proud. That's all I wanted to say." He put his arm around his son, and the two embraced.

Over the graves of fallen heroes, a father and a son had found each other.

About The Author

G. Richard Holt, M.D., is a Colonel and flight surgeon in the U.S. Army Reserve, having served over 22 years in both active duty and the reserve. He is airborne and air assault qualified and formerly was assigned to special operations with the Army. A decorated veteran of the Persian Gulf War, he has chosen to write about that conflict as his first fictional novel.

A native Missourian, Dr. Holt is a facial reconstructive and head and neck surgeon in private practice in San Antonio, Texas. He is married to Jean E. Holt, M.D., and has three children.